Praise for R.J. Ellory

'A mesmerizing tale whose intrigue will pull you from one page to the next without pause, casting you into the gloom of dread and the shadow of grief until you reach the climactic end. R.J. Ellory's remarkable talent for probing the unknown establishes him as the master of the mystery game. The perfect author to read late into the night'   Clive Cussler

'R.J. Ellory is a uniquely gifted, passionate, and powerful writer'   Alan Furst

'R.J. Ellory's *A Quiet Belief in Angels* is that rarity, a book that will haunt you for years, in all the best ways. It is a riveting mystery that is as compelling as it is moving. Joseph is destined to become one of those seminal characters of literature. Here is a book that restores not only a quiet belief in the redemptive power of literature but is a novel you put on the shelf to read over and over again'   Ken Bruen

'R.J. Ellory is a class act. If you like James Lee Burke or James Sallis, he's a writer who speaks your language'
Val McDermid

'*A Quiet Belief in Angels* is a rich, powerful, evocative novel of great psychological depth'   Jonathan Kellerman

'An awesome achievement . . . a thriller of such power, scope and accomplishment that fanfares should herald its arrival'
Guardian

'*A Quiet Belief in Angels* is a beautiful and haunting book. This is a tour de force from R.J. Ellory'   Michael Connelly

'Ellory is a powerful talent . . . *A Quiet Belief in Angels* . . . seems set to launch him into the stratosphere of crime writers'   *Independent on Sunday*

'This isn't your standard shock and bore serial killer novel. It's an impassioned story of a man's life told in Ellory's distinctive voice, and it confirms his place in the top flight of crime writing'   *Sunday Telegraph*

R.J. Ellory is the bestselling author of six previous novels including *A Quiet Belief in Angels*, which was a Richard & Judy Book Club selection and won the Inaugural Nouvel Observateur Crime Fiction Prize in 2008. *A Quiet Belief in Angels* was also shortlisted for the American Barry Award for Best British Crime Fiction, the 813 Trophy, the Quebec Booksellers' Prize, and the Prix du Polar Award in the same year.

His other novels have been translated into twenty-three languages and both *City of Lies* and *Candlemoth* were shortlisted for the prestigious Crime Writers' Association Ian Fleming Steel Dagger. Ellory is married with one son, and currently lives in England. Visit his website at www.rjellory.com.

By R.J. Ellory

Candlemoth
Ghostheart
A Quiet Vendetta
City Of Lies
A Quiet Belief in Angels
A Simple Act of Violence
The Anniversary Man

The Anniversary Man

R.J. ELLORY

An Orion paperback

First published in Great Britain in 2009
by Orion
This paperback edition published in 2010
by Orion Books Ltd,
Orion House, 5 Upper St Martin's Lane,
London WC2H 9EA

An Hachette UK company

1 3 5 7 9 10 8 6 4 2

A CIP catalogue record for this book
is available from the British Library.

ISBN 978-0-7528-8310-6

Typeset at The Spartan Press Ltd,
Lymington, Hants

Printed and bound in Great Britain by
Clays Ltd, St Ives plc

www.orionbooks.co.uk

ACKNOWLEDGEMENTS

Seems I spend a good deal of time thanking people, without whom my books would never arrive in bookstores. Invariably, these people are humble, and they tell me not to make a fuss of them, but that element of humility merely serves to exaggerate their greatness in my mind. So, once again, here we go:

Jon, my editor; Euan, my agent; all those at Orion – Jade, Natalie, Gen, Juliet, Lisa, Malcolm, Susan L. and Susan H., Krystyna, Hannah, Mark Streatfeild and Mark Stay, Anthony, Julia, Sarah, Sherif, Michael G., Pandora and Victoria, Emily, Suzy, Jessica and Kim, Lisa G., Kate, and Mark Rusher. You have all worked so very hard, and I have done my best to meet your standards.

Robyn Karney, a remarkable copy-editor and a remarkable woman.

Amanda Ross, for your continued friendship and endless support. I am indebted.

Kate Mosse, Bob Crais, Dennis Lehane, Mark Billingham, Simon Kernick, Stuart MacBride, Laura Wilson, Lee Child, Ali Karim, George Easter, Steve Warne, Ben Hunt, Mike Bursaw, the crew at Cactus TV, Mariella Frostrup and Judy Elliott at Sky, Chris Simmons, Sharon Canavar, Barry Forshaw, Judy Bobalik, Jon and Ruth Jordan, Paul Blezard, all the guys at WF Howes, Jonathan Davidson, Lorne Jackson, Matt Lewin and Sharone Neuhoff. Also to Lindsay Boyle, Ciara Redman, Paul Hutchins and Andrew Tomlinson at the BBC for the truly remarkable Washington trip.

A special mention to June Boyle, Fairfax County Homicide, and Brad Garrett of the Washington FBI, and Walter Pincus of *The Washington Post* who all gave me a glimpse of the truth.

To my brother Guy, my wife Vicky, my son Ryan.

You all rock.

'And if you gaze for long into an abyss, the abyss gazes also into you'

Dedicated to all those who looked into the abyss, and yet never lost their balance.

For a long time John Costello tried to forget what happened.

Perhaps pretended that it had not.

The Devil came in the form of a man, around him the smell of dogs.

He wore an expression as if a stranger had handed him a fifty-dollar bill on the street. Surprise. A sort of self-satisfied wonder.

John Costello remembered the panic of wings as pigeons rushed away from the scene.

As if they knew.

He remembered how darkness approached in a hurry, delayed somewhere and now anxious to meet its schedule.

It was as if the Devil possessed the face of an actor – an unremembered actor, his name forgotten yet his face dimly recognized.

'I know him . . . that's . . . that's . . . honey, this guy here? What the hell is his name?'

Many names.

All of them meant the same thing.

The Devil owned the world, but he remembered his roots. He remembered he was once an angel, cast down to Gehenna for treason and mutiny, and he withheld himself as best he could. But sometimes he could not.

It was ironic, like sex in cheap motels with unattractive hookers. Sharing something so intense, so close, and yet never speaking your given name. Believing yourself guilty of nothing significant, and thus innocent.

John Costello was nearly seventeen. His father owned a restaurant where everybody came to eat.

After it happened, John was never the same.

After it happened . . . hell, none of them were.

*

1

Jersey City, out near Grove Street Station, always the smell of the Hudson; place looked like a fistfight, even on a Sunday morning when most of the Irishers and Italians were dressed up for church.

John Costello's father, Erskine, standing out front of The Connemara diner – named after the mountains where his ancestors fished in Lough Mask and Lough Corrib, and hauled their catch home after dusklight, and lit fires, and told tales, and sang songs that sounded like history before the first verse was done.

Erskine was a quiet tree of a man – bold eyes, his hair black like soot; spend enough time with him and you'd wind up answering your own questions out of loneliness.

The Connemara sat beneath the shadow of the El train platform with its wrought-iron steps and gantries like walk-ways to some other world – a world beyond all of this, beyond this universe, beyond the dreams of sex and death and the denial of hope for all that this strange and shadowed quarter of the city had to offer.

John was an only child, and he was sixteen years old in January of '84.

It was an important year.

The year *she* came to stay.

Her name was Nadia, which was Russian for *hope*.

He met her on a Sunday at The Connemara. She came on an errand for her father. She came for soda bread.

Always there was music from the radios, the rumble of laughter, the slap of dominoes. The Connemara was a hub for the Irish, the Italians, the Jews, and the drunks – the ebullient, the aggressive, the angry – all of them silenced by the food Erskine Costello made.

Nadia was seventeen, five months older than John Costello, but she had a world in her eyes that belied her age.

'You work here?' she asked.

First question. First of many.

A great moment can never be taken away.

John Costello was a shy boy, a quiet boy. He'd lost his mother some years before. Anna Costello, née Bredaweg. John remembered his mother well. She forever wore an

2

expression of slight dismay, as if she'd entered a familiar room and found the furniture moved, perhaps a seated stranger when no visit had been scheduled. She started sentences but left them incomplete, perhaps because she knew she'd be understood. Anna Costello conveyed multitudes with a single look. She angled herself between the world and her son. Mom the buffer. Mom the shock absorber. She challenged the world, dared it to pull a trick, a fast one, some sleight of hand. Other mothers lost children. Anna Costello had only one, and this one she would never lose. She never thought to consider that he could lose her.

And she spoke with some kind of instinctive maternal wisdom.

'They call me names at school.'

'Kind of names?'

'Whatever . . . I don't know. Just names.'

'Names are just sounds, John.'

'Eh?'

'Think of them as sounds. Just make believe they're throwing sounds at you.'

'And what good would that do?'

Smiled, almost laughed. 'Why . . . in your mind you just catch them and throw them back.'

And John Costello wondered later – much later – if his mother would have seen the Devil coming and protected them both.

He smiled at the girl. 'I work here, yes.'

'You own the place?'

'My father does.'

She nodded understandingly. 'I came for soda bread. You have soda bread?'

'We have soda bread.'

'How much?'

'Dollar and a quarter.'

'Only have a dollar.' She held out the note as if to prove she wasn't lying.

John Costello wrapped a loaf of soda bread in paper. Brown-bagged it. Passed it over the counter. 'You can owe me.'

3

When he took the dollar their fingers touched. Like touching electric.

'What's your name?' she asked.

'John . . . John Costello.'

'My name is Nadia. That's Russian for hope.'

'Are you Russian?'

'Sometimes,' she said. And then she smiled like a sunset and walked away.

Everything changed afterwards, after the winter of '84.

John Costello realized he would become someone else, but he could not have predicted how.

Now he finds safety in routines. In counting. In making lists.

He does not wear latex gloves.

He is not afraid to drink milk from the carton.

He does not take plastic cutlery to restaurants.

He does not collect psychotic episodes to share with some shallow pervert mind-voyeur on a five thousand-dollar couch.

He is not afraid of the dark, for he carries all the darkness he needs inside him.

He does not collect clipped fingernails or locks of shorn hair for fear that hoodoo will be performed and he will die suddenly, unexpectedly, in Bloomingdale's, his heart bursting in the elevator, blood from his ears while people scream hysterically. As if screaming could serve some purpose.

He would not go gently into that sweet goodnight.

And sometimes, when New York was bleeding the heat of its summer from every brick and every stone, when the heat of a thousand earlier summers seemed collected in everything he touched, he had been known to buy bottled root beer from the chilled counter, and press the bottle against his face, even touch it to his lips, with no fear of what fatal disease or virulent germ might be there upon the glass.

See him in the street and he would look like a million others.

Talk to him and he would appear to be just like you.

But he was not. And never would be.

Because he saw the Devil in the winter of '84, and once you see the Devil you don't forget his face.

*

She came again the following day.

She brought the quarter, and paid her debt.

'How old are you, John Costello?' she asked.

She had on a skirt, a tee-shirt. Her breasts were small and perfect. Her teeth were matchless. She smelled like cigarettes and Juicy Fruit.

'Sixteen,' he said.

'When are you seventeen?'

'January.'

'You got a girlfriend?'

He shook his head.

'Okay,' she said, then turned and walked away.

He opened his mouth to speak but there was silence inside.

The door closed behind her. He watched her reach the corner, and then he watched her disappear.

The Connemara was never empty. It always held atmosphere, if nothing else. But the people who came were real people with real lives. They all carried stories. More than the stories themselves, it was the words they used to build them; no-one talked like that anymore. The detractions and minor anecdotes they employed to fill the gaps, like mortar between bricks. It was the way those words sounded – the timbre, the pitch, the cadence – as they followed one another out of their mouths and into the world. Words the world had waited for.

Old men who selected pieces of their varicolored lives for sharing – different hues for different days – and unfolded them carefully, as if they were delicate gifts, fashioned to survive just one telling, and then they were gone. Gossamer stories, perhaps cobwebs or shadows. They told stories to be heard, so their lives would not go unnoticed by the world when their work was done. Some of these men had known one another twenty, thirty years, but knew nothing of occupations. They spoke of externals – baseball, automobiles, sometimes girls, all things outside, all things definable with phrases from newspapers and TV, some of which they used with no real understanding. Often their conversations were not conversations in the real sense of the word. Ask a question and then they'd tell you what *you* thought about it. Everything was a matter of opinion: their own. But they didn't see it. They saw a discussion, a two-way thing, structured and balanced, a meeting of minds. But it was not.

These old men, the ones who haunted The Connemara, perhaps they also saw their end when the Devil came. Perhaps they looked back at the gaping yaw of the past and they saw a world that would never return. Their time had been and gone. Their time had run out.

They heard of what happened to Costello's boy, to the girl who was with him, and they closed their eyes.

A deep breath. A silent prayer. A wonder as to what had become of everything, and how it all would end.

And then said nothing to one another, for there was nothing more to say.

Erskine Costello told his son that Man was the Devil in human form.

'A man went for cigarettes and never came home,' he said. 'You will hear that. It has become a thing all its own. Means something other than the words used. Like most things. Italians. Irish sometimes. He went out for cigarettes, he went to buy a pack of Luckies. Sure he went out for cigarettes, but whatever cigarettes he bought they were his last, you know? He'll be in the bottom of the Sound without his fingers and toes.'

Later – dental recognition, other scientific advances – they used to break the teeth.

Axes, hawsers, machetes, butchers' knives, hammers – ball-peen and flathead.

Burned a man's face off with a blowtorch. Smelled bad. Smelled so bad they never did it again.

'These things happen,' Erskine said. 'You go looking for the Devil, you'll find all the Devil you could ever want right there in a man.' He smiled. 'You know what they say about the Irish and the Italians? First son to the church, second to the police, third to jail, fourth to the Devil.' He laughed like a smoky train in a dark tunnel. Ruffled John's hair.

And John Costello listened. He was a little kid without a mother. His father was everything to him, and he could never lie.

And later – afterwards – John realized that his father had not

lied. You could not lie about something you did not under-
stand. Ignorance influenced his understanding, gave him a slanted
view.

   John saw the Devil, and thus he knew whereof he spoke.

She came three times in the following week.

   Nadia. Russian for *hope.*

   'I am studying art,' she said.

   'Art.' A statement, not a question.

   'You know what art is.'

   John Costello smiled with certainty.

   'So I am studying art, and one day I'll go to New York, the Metropolitan perhaps, and I will—'

   Costello's mind drifted, away to the sidewalk, the street beyond. It was raining.

   'Do you have an umbrella?' he asked, a question out of left field with a curve in its tail.

   She stopped mid-sentence, looked at him as if the only acceptable response was a headlock. 'An umbrella?'

   He glanced toward the window. 'Rain,' he said matter-of-factly.

   She turned and looked. 'Rain,' she echoed. 'No, I don't have an umbrella.'

   'I do.'

   'Well that's good for you then, isn't it?'

   'I'll get it. You can bring it back whenever you like.'

   She smiled. Warmth. A real sense of something. 'Thank you,' she said, and for a moment looked embarrassed. 'That's very thoughtful of you, John.'

   'Thoughtful,' he said. 'Yes, I s'pose it is.'

   He crossed from the counter to the window after she'd left the diner. He watched her hopscotch between puddles toward the corner. A sudden gust caught the umbrella, her skirt, her hair. Looked as if she'd blow away.

   And then she was gone.

Now he lives in New York.

   He writes everything down. Prints in blocks. He used to write down sentences, but these days he abbreviates.

   He still keeps a diary, more a ledger, a journal if you like. He has

7

filled many of them. If he has no event to describe he conveys the feeling of the day in single words.

Exigent.

Palpable.

Manipulation.

Something he likes, he learns all about it. Often he learns things by heart.

Subway stations: Eastern, Franklin, Nostrand, Kingston, Utica, Sutter, Saratoga, Rockaway, Junius. The stations on the 7th Avenue Express, all the way through Gun Hill Road to Flatbush.

Why? No reason. He just finds comfort in it.

Mondays he eats Italian, Tuesdays French, Wednesdays he has hot dogs with ketchup and German mustard, Thursdays he leaves open to chance. Fridays he eats Persian – gheimeh and ghormeh and barg. A small restaurant on the corner near Penn Plaza in the Garment District where he lives. It is called Persepolis. Weekends he eats Chinese or Thai, and if inspired he makes tuna casserole.

Lunch he takes in the same place every day, a block and a half from the newspaper where he works.

Routines. Always routines.

And he counts things. Stop signs. Traffic lights. Stores with awnings. Stores without. Blue cars. Red cars. Station wagons. Disabled people.

Safety in numbers.

He invents names for people: Sugarface, PaleSocrates, Perfectsilentchild, Deepfearhopeless, Drugmadfrightened.

Made-up names. Names that suit them. Suit the way they appear to be.

He is not crazy. He knows this for a fact. He just has a way of dealing with things, that's all.

Doesn't harm anyone, and no-one would know.

Because, on the face of it, he looks just like everyone else.

Same as the Devil.

John Costello and Nadia McGowan ate lunch together for the first time on Saturday, October 6th, 1984.

They ate corned beef on rye with mustard, and green pickles, and they shared a tomato the size of a fist. Scarlet, a blood-red thing, sweet and juicy.

They ate together and she told him something that made him laugh.

The following day he took her to the movies. *Places In The Heart.* John Malkovich. Sally Field. Won two Oscars, best actress and screenplay. John Costello did not kiss Nadia McGowan, nor did he try, though he did hold her hand for the last half hour.

He was nearly seventeen, and wanted so much to see her perfect breasts, the way her hair would fall across her naked shoulders.

Later, after everything, he would remember that evening. He walked her home, to a house on the corner of Machin and Wintergreen. Her father waited for her on the doorstep, and he shook John Costello's hand and said, *I know your father. From the soda bread.* And he looked at John closely, as if to ascertain intentions from appearance alone.

Nadia McGowan watched John Costello from her bedroom window as she took off her sweater. *John Costello*, she thought, *is quiet and sensitive, but beneath that he is strong, intelligent, and he listens, and there is something about him that I can love.*

I hope he asks me out again.

He did. The following day. A date fixed for the subsequent Saturday. They saw the same movie, but this time they paid attention to one another and not to the screen.

She was the first girl he kissed. Proper kisses. Lips parted, the feeling of a tongue other than your own. Later, in the darkened hallway of her house, there behind the front door, her parents out for the evening, she removed her bra and let him touch her perfect breasts.

And then later: the second day of November.

'Tonight,' she said. They sat together on a narrow wooden bench at the end of Carlisle Street near the park.

He looked at her, his head to one side as if bearing a weight on his shoulder.

'Did you ever . . .' she said. 'You know . . . did you ever have sex before?'

'In my mind,' he whispered. 'With you. A thousand times. Yes.'

She laughed. 'Seriously. For real, John, for real.'

He shook his head. 'No. You?'

She reached out and touched his face. 'Tonight,' she whispered. 'The first time for both of us.'

They fell into a rhythm, as if this was somehow familiar territory. It was not, but it didn't matter, for discovery was as much a part of the journey as the destination. Perhaps more than half.

She stood ahead of him and she held out her arms to close around him, but he smiled and moved to the right, and he stood beside her so she could rest her head against his shoulder.

'You smell great,' he said, and she laughed, and said, 'Good. I wouldn't want to smell bad.'

'You are—'

Ssshhh, she mouthed, and pressed her finger to his lips, and she kissed him, and he could feel her hand on the flat of his stomach, and he pulled her in closer.

They made love for the first time.

She said it did not hurt, but the sound she made when he pushed himself inside her told him something different.

And then they found the rhythm, and though it seemed to last no time at all it didn't matter.

They did it again later, and it lasted so much longer, and then they slept while her parents stayed overnight in Long Island City and were none the wiser.

John Costello woke in the early hours of the morning. He woke Nadia McGowan just so they could talk. Just so they could appreciate the time they had together.

She told him she wanted to sleep, and he let her.

Had she known she would be dead before the month was out . . . if she had known, she perhaps would have stayed awake.

He remembers so many things, which – he is sure – is the only reason he keeps his job.

He is an index.

He is an encyclopedia.

He is a dictionary.

10

He is a map of the human heart and what can be done to punish it.

He was sixteen when she died. She was his first love. The only one he really, really loved. He convinced himself of that. It didn't take much effort.

He has been through everything a thousand times and he knows it was not his fault.

It happened on the same bench, the one at the end of Carlisle Street near the park.

He could go right back there now, in his mind or in person, and he could feel something, or he could feel nothing at all.

It changed him. Of course it did. It made him curious about the nature of things, about why things happened. Why people love and hate and kill and lie and hurt and bleed, and why they betray one another, and why they steal one another's husbands and wives and children.

The world had changed.

When he was a kid it was like this: A child's trike on the corner of the street. Mom must have called the kid for supper. A passer-by would pick it up, set it to the edge of the sidewalk for later collection, so as no-one would fall over it and hurt themselves. A simple, nostalgic smile. A memory of their own childhood perhaps. Never a second thought.

And now, the first thought would be abduction. The child snatched inside a single heartbeat, bundled wholesale into the back of a car. The trike was all that would remain of them. The child would be found in three weeks' time – beaten, abused, strangled.

The neighborhood had changed. The world had changed.

John Costello believed that they were the ones who'd changed it.

After the death of Nadia McGowan the community fell apart. Her death seemed to mark the end of all they held important. People no longer brought their children to The Connemara. They stayed home.

His father watched it come to pieces, and though he tried to reach John it didn't really work. Perhaps his mother would have found him, hiding within whatever world he had created for himself.

But she was gone.

Gone for good.

Like Nadia, which was Russian for hope.

11

It was not easy, finding enough time to be together. John Costello worked and Nadia McGowan studied, and there were parents to consider. She would run errands to The Connemara as often as she could, and sometimes Erskine Costello would be there, and John was nowhere to be seen, and Erskine saw something in her anticipation, the way she hung back at the door before leaving, something that told him that soda bread was not the only reason she came.

'She's a pretty girl that one,' he told his son.

John hesitated, didn't look up from his plate. 'Which one?'

'You know which one, lad. The redheaded one.'

'The McGowan girl?'

Erskine laughed. 'That's not what you call her to her face now is it?'

They did not make eye contact, and neither of them said another thing.

Saturday November 17th, the McGowans out to see Nadia's grandmother once more. Anniversary of her grandfather's death, Nadia staying back saying she had work to do. As soon as the parents' car pulled into the street she walked to The Connemara, found John, told him that her folks were away for the night, would be gone until the following evening.

John left his room a little before eleven. He crept downstairs, feet to the edges of the treads, for the treads were old and they strained and creaked with his weight.

Erskine was waiting for him at the back door. 'Away are you?' he said.

John didn't speak.

'To see the girl,' Erskine added matter-of-factly, his voice monotone, his expression saying nothing. Smell of good whiskey about him, a familiar ghost.

John couldn't lie to his father. Had never been able to, and would never learn.

'She's a sweet girl she is. A studious one, no doubt.'

John smiled.

'You and your books and your writing things down . . . wouldn't be right for you to get a wild one with no sense for reading and things.'

'Dad—'

'Away with you, boy, away with you. You'll only be doing what I wished I'd been doing at your age.'

John made to step by him.

'Remember your mother, eh?' Erskine added. 'And don't do anything you'd be ashamed to tell her.'

John looked up at his father. 'I won't.'

'I know that, boy. I trust you. That's why I'm letting you go.'

Erskine watched as his only child, now a man, went down the back steps and hurried across the street. He had more of his mother in him, and she'd have been proud, but he was not one to be staying in Jersey City, at least not for long. He was a reader, a literary one, forever thinking of smart ways to say things that didn't need to be said.

Erskine Costello closed the door of The Connemara and walked back to the kitchen. The smell of good whiskey followed him, the familiar ghost.

To see someone die, someone you love, and to see them die so terribly, so brutally, is something you cannot forget.

I am the Hammer of God, he said.

John remembers the voice, that more than anything, though he never saw the face, and for years later wished that he had. So he would know.

He saw photographs of the man, of course, but there is no substitute for seeing the person themselves. There is something about a human being that a picture can never capture, not even a film, and that is their personality, the feeling around them, their smell, their thoughts, all those things that can be sensed.

If he had only seen him . . .

By the time John Costello spoke she was already buried.

Erskine had believed his boy might never speak again.

For the first days – four, perhaps five – he came every day and sat beside John's bed. And then it seemed Erskine Costello could not face the silence, the waiting, the fear, so he went home, and he drank, and he stayed drunk until New Year.

John could not blame him. To see his only son, his only child, lying there in a hospital bed, his head bandaged, nothing visible but his eyes, and those eyes closed, and tubes and pipes and lines of glucose, and saline drips, and the sound of monitors beeping, the constant hum of a room filled with electricity . . .

John could not blame him.

John Costello woke on the sixth day, the 29th of November, and the first person he saw was a nurse called Geraldine Joyce.

'Like the writer,' she said. 'James Joyce. Mad bastard that he was.'

He asked her where he was, and when he heard his own voice it was like listening to someone else.

'You'll sound like yourself after a while,' Nurse Geraldine told him. 'Or maybe you'll just get used to it and start thinking that that's the way you've always sounded.'

She told him there was a police detective outside who wanted to talk to him.

By then John Costello knew that Nadia was dead.

She was waiting on the stoop. The front door was open and upstairs there was a light in the window of her room. The rest of the house was in darkness.

She held out her hand, and the last few yards he ran toward her, as if they were meeting at the train station. He'd been away to the war. His letters had never arrived. For a long while she thought he might have been killed, but had never dared to believe it.

'Come in,' she said quickly. 'Before someone sees you.' The Irish lilt in her voice, gentle yet distinct.

They'd made love twice before. Now they were professionals. Now they were no longer shy or embarrassed, and she left her clothes along the upstairs hallway as they hurried to her room.

Outside it started raining.

'Do you know what love is?' she asked him when light started to find a way between the drapes.

'If this is it, then yes,' he said. 'I know what love is.'

Later, they sat beside one another at the window, naked beneath a blanket, and they watched the world as it rained. Saw an old man in slow-motion, his angular gait distorted through the rivulets of water on the glass. Come daylight there would be a gaggle of children in slickers and galoshes, the excitement of puddles, hand-in-hand on the way to church.

'Do you need to get back?' she asked.

He shook his head. 'It's okay.'

'Your dad—'

'He knows where I am.'

A sudden intake of breath. 'He . . . oh my God, he'll tell my parents . . .'

John laughed. 'No he won't.'

'God, John, if they find out they'll kill me.'

'No they won't,' he said, meaning that they wouldn't find out, never thinking to mean that they wouldn't kill her.

Because they wouldn't.

That, it seemed, was to be someone else's job.

Most people who kill people look normal.

The man who said that to John Costello was a Jersey City homicide detective called Frank Gorman.

'My name is Frank,' he said. He held out his hand. He told John that the girl was dead. Nadia McGowan. The funeral had already taken place the day before. Apparently it was a small affair, primarily a family thing, but the wake was held in The Connemara and it filled the place to bursting, and out along Lupus and Delancey, all the way down Carlisle Street near the park, there were people crowding to make themselves known to the grieving parents. More friends in death than ever in life. Wasn't that always the way of things? And they left flowers near the bench where she'd died. So many flowers it wasn't long before the bench disappeared beneath them. Lilies. White roses. A wreath of something yellow.

So Frank shook John's hand, and asked if he was okay, if he wanted a drink of water or something. He was the first one to ask questions, and he would come the most times, and he would ask more questions than anyone else, and there was something in his face, in his eyes, that told John that he was persistent and determined and unforgiving of failure. He was also Irish, which helped when it came down to it.

'A serial,' he said. 'This guy . . . the one that attacked you.' He looked away toward the hospital room window as if something silent demanded attention.

'We know of four victims . . . two couples. Perhaps there's more, we don't know. You're the only one—' He smiled understandingly. 'You're the only one who's survived.'

'That you know of,' John said.

Frank Gorman took a notebook from his jacket pocket, a pen also, and he leafed through page after page to find some space in which to write.

'He attacks couples . . . we presume couples who are out together, you know . . . doing things that couples do when they're together . . .' His voice trailed away into silence.

'I feel like I can't remember anything.'

'I know, John, I know, but I'm here to help you try.'

'First loves are the most important,' Erskine Costello told his son.

Seated in the back kitchen, there across a table, a meal finished, a glass of beer on the side.

'Have to tell you, your mother was not my first love.'

'You sound like you're apologizing for something.'

'Wouldn't want you to be disappointed.'

'Disappointed? Why would I be disappointed?'

Erskine shrugged his broad shoulders. Raised his hand and ran it through coal-black hair.

'That Nadia McGowan . . . she's a beautiful girl.'

'She is.'

'Her parents know you're courting?'

'Courting?' John said. 'Who says *courting*? It's 1984. I think people stopped courting in 1945.'

'Okay, John, okay, so let's be blunt like a fist, eh? Do her good Catholic God-fearing parents know their daughter is having sex with a sixteen-year-old whose father is a drunk who hasn't stepped inside a church for thirty years or more? That blunt enough for you, lad?'

John nodded. 'It is. And no, they don't know.'

'And if they found out?'

'There'd be trouble I'm sure.' He looked up at his father, expected the Riot Act, but Erskine Costello, the sharp edges of his mind and tongue worn smooth by the gentle insistence of good Irish whiskey, merely said, 'So be careful you don't get caught, eh?'

'I'll be careful,' John Costello said, and knew that if his mother were alive there'd be a storm.

'How can I remember what I don't remember?'

Frank Gorman, Jersey City homicide detective, didn't answer the question. He merely smiled as if he knew something of which the world remained ignorant, and once again looked away toward the window.

'Can you go back through it for me?' he said.

John opened his mouth to speak, to tell him that he'd gone over this time and again in his mind, but whenever he looked there was nothing.

'I know you've gone through this for yourself,' Gorman said, 'but not with me . . . not with me here listening, and I need you to do this.'

John looked at him, at the way he smiled – like a child who'd made a mistake, and just wanted you to be patient with him, to be understanding, sympathetic.

'Please . . .' he said quietly. 'Just lean back, close your eyes, and walk me right through it from the beginning to the end. Start with the morning of that day, and tell me about the first thing you can remember . . .'

John Costello looked at Frank Gorman for a moment longer, and then he moved the pillow behind his neck and leaned back. He closed his eyes as Frank had asked, and he tried to recall how he'd felt that morning.

'It was cold,' he said . . .

And John Costello turned sideways and lay for a while beneath the covers of his bed. It was six days after the night he'd stayed over with Nadia.

He glanced at the clock beside his bed: four minutes to five. Any moment his father would hammer on the door and shout his name. Beneath the covers he was warm, but when he edged his foot out from beneath the blanket, he felt the chill of the room. He relished those few minutes before the day began, lying there aware that life had changed more than ever he could have imagined.

Three minutes past five and he rose and opened his

17

bedroom door a handful of inches to let his father know he was up.

Bread to make. Bacon to fry, sausage, pancakes, hash browns; and bucketfuls of coffee beans to grind.

Could hear the run of water from the bathroom. Erskine Costello still used a straight razor, gave it an edge on a leather strop, whipped that thing back and forth without a second thought and then shaved with cold water and a froth of coal tar. Old school. A regular guy.

The day ran as any other. Breakfast eased seamlessly into lunch, from there into mid-afternoon sandwiches, flasks of coffee and slices of apple pie to ferry over to the lumber crew in McKinnon's Yard. Darkness started somewhere around four, and it was less than an hour until it filled up the spaces between things and hung shadows around the lights.

He saw her as she crossed Delancey Street. It was something past seven. She had on a pair of jeans, a red flower embroidered on the hip, flat shoes, a suede windbreaker. Her hair was tied up on one side, and she wore a diamante barrette like a butterfly.

He opened the door and went out onto the sidewalk.

'Hey,' she said. Reached out her hand, touched his arm.

'Hey.' Wanted to kiss her but there were customers.

'Time you done?'

'Nine, maybe nine-thirty.'

'Meet me down on Carlisle at nine-thirty. Have something to tell you.'

'What?'

Nadia McGowan glanced at her watch. 'Two hours . . . you can wait two hours.'

'Tell me now.'

She shook her head, kind of laughed. 'Nine-thirty, the bench on the corner of Carlisle, okay?'

'You hungry?'

'No . . . why?'

'Got some cinnamon Danish . . . made it myself.'

'I'm good, Johnny, I'm good.'

She reached out, touched his cheek with the back of her hand, and then she turned and walked away, reached

18

the corner before she looked back over her shoulder once more.

He raised his hand and he saw her smile . . .

'And you saw no-one?'

John Costello shook his head without opening his eyes.

'And the people in the diner?'

'Were just the same people that were always in the diner. No-one different.'

'And in the street—'

'No-one in the street,' he interjected. 'Like I said before, there was no-one . . .'

'Okay,' Detective Frank Gorman said. 'Go on.'

'So I watched her cross the junction, and then she went around the corner . . .'

And then she was gone.

Used up two hours waiting. Dragged like a heavy thing, and John forever glancing at the clock by the mirror, the hands weighted, running slow.

Erskine was back and forth, saw the frustration in his son's face. 'Get away early why don't you?' he asked.

'Not meeting her 'til after nine,' John replied.

'So go out back and clean the enamels. Time'll fly if you're doing something.'

He did as his father asked, hosing down pots and pans, a box of salt on the side with which to scrub them.

Eight-thirty came and went in a heartbeat. John cleaned himself up, changed his shirt, combed his hair.

Carlisle Street was no more than a five-minute walk, but he left The Connemara at ten past nine.

'And you saw no-one then either . . . as you left?'

John shook his head. He opened his mouth to speak, but felt there was nothing to say.

Frank Gorman stared at him for a little while, possibly no more than seconds, but those seconds were well disguised as minutes, even hours. It felt that way in the confines of the room. Tense. A little claustrophobic.

Gorman's right eye was not centered. Gave him a curious look.

19

John wondered if such a physiological idiosyncrasy enabled him to
see angles that others could not.
  'And so you walked from the restaurant to Carlisle Street?'
  'Yes,' John said.
  'And you saw no-one on the way?'
  'No, I saw no-one.'
  'And when you reached the corner of Carlisle Street . . . ?'

He sat down on the bench, and pulled his windbreaker
around him. He looked out toward Machin, the direction
from which Nadia would come. Pools of sodium yellow
beneath the streetlights. The sound of a dog howling for
something only a dog would understand. The distant hum
of cars on Newark Avenue. Skywards there were the faraway
lights of planes heading out of Irvington and Springfield. It
was a cold night, but it was a good night.
  John Costello zipped up his jacket, dug his hands into his
pockets, and waited . . .

'For how long?'
  John could feel the tension of the bandages. 'Ten minutes,
fifteen maybe.' He looked directly at Gorman. It was hard to
catch him straight, one eye dead-center, the other five degrees
starboard and watching for storms.
  'And what happened then, John? Once you saw her coming?'
  'When I saw her coming, I stood up . . .'

And started walking toward her, and she raised her hand as if
to slow him down. She was smiling, and there was something
anticipatory about that moment, as if he knew something
was coming, and there was every possibility that it was
something good.
  'Hey,' he said as she reached the corner of Carlisle.
  'Hey back,' she replied, and she walked toward him, reaching out her hands.
  'What's up?' he asked.
  'Let's sit down,' she said. Looked at him, and then glanced
away, a sudden flash in her eyes that told him that maybe the
something wasn't so good.
  And had he known that she would never tell him, that he

would learn of it from a stranger in a hospital room, and had he understood why such a truth would be denied in that moment, he would have pressed his finger to her lips, stayed her words, taken her hand and hurried her away to safety.

But hindsight arrives after the fact, never before, and the irony was that after her death, after the terrible thing that happened, the foresight – the intuitive *shift* that he felt for such things – would have been so useful.

The shift would have told him to run back home, to take her with him, to let it be someone else's night to die.

But it wasn't.

Always the way of such things.

It was Nadia McGowan's time to die, and there was nothing that John Costello could have done about it.

'She was going to New York City to study,' Gorman said.

John was silent, absorbing this thing. Had she planned to leave him there? Would she have asked him to go with her?

He looked up at Gorman. 'She didn't have a chance to say anything.'

'And you heard nothing? I mean, until he was right there behind you?'

John Costello shook his head, once more felt the tension of bandages.

'And what did you see?'

John closed his eyes.

'John?'

'I'm looking.'

Gorman fell silent, and suddenly a sense of unease and disquiet came over him.

'I saw the pigeons . . . a sudden rush of pigeons . . .'

And Nadia was startled, a little afraid of the sound, and she sort of fell against John and he grabbed her arm and pulled her close, and she laughed at herself for being scared of something so silly.

'You all right?' John said.

She nodded, she smiled, she let go of his arm and walked toward the bench.

21

John followed her, sat beside her, and she leaned against him and he felt the weight and warmth of her body.

'What is it you wanted to tell me?' he said.

She turned and looked up at him. 'You love me?'

'Of course I love you.'

'How much do you love me?'

'I don't know. How much is it possible to love someone?'

She held her arms wide like a fisherman telling tales. 'This much,' she said.

'Five times that,' John replied. 'Ten even.'

She looked away, and John followed her line of sight, all the way down to the end of Carlisle and across toward Pearl Street and Harborside.

'Nadia?'

She turned back toward him . . .

'And it was then that he appeared?'

'I don't know that appeared is exactly the right word. I don't even know what word you would use.'

'How d'you mean?'

'Appeared. Yes, maybe it was like that. It was as if he suddenly materialized out of thin air. There was no-one, and then there was someone.'

'And there was the sound of the pigeons again?'

John nodded. 'Yes, she turned back toward me . . .'

And she took his hand, and she leaned her head against his shoulder.

'I've been thinking,' she said, and her voice was almost a whisper.

'About what?'

'About what we talked about before . . . what I said that time—'

The pigeons had returned. A crowd of them around the base of a tree no more than five yards from the bench. Old women sometimes came and sat; they brought breadcrumbs, had for years, and the pigeons congregated in anticipation for when they would return.

'What time?'

A breeze, back and to the left of John, and . . .

'I felt it against the side of my face – a breeze – and if I'd turned at that moment . . .'

'You can't do that John. It doesn't do any good.'

'Can't do what?'

'Keep asking yourself what would have happened if. Everyone does that, and it just prolongs the pain.'

John looked down at his hands, his wrist still in its cast, his fingernails black, the swelling on his right thumb that would be there for the rest of his life. 'But you can't help it,' he said. 'You can't help going back through it, can you?'

'I s'pose not.'

'Something this bad ever happen to you?' John asked.

Gorman looked back at him with his off-center gaze and said, 'No, nothing like that ever happened to me.'

'But you've seen it happen to others, right?'

'All the time. Well, not seen it happen as such, but seen the effects of it. That's what I do. I am a police detective. I look behind the barriers and the yellow tapes. The terrible things that human beings are capable of doing to one another.'

'And why do you think things like this happen?'

'I don't know, John.'

'Psychiatrists know, right? They know why people do these kinds of things?'

'No, I don't think so, John. Not in my experience. If they knew why people were crazy then they'd be able to do something to help them. In all the years I've been working, I've never seen one of those guys do anything to help anyone.'

'So why do you think it happens? Why do people hurt other people, Detective?'

'Seems to me that everybody does whatever they do for the same reason.'

'Which is?'

'So other people will know they're there.'

'Seems a hell of a way to let people know that you're there, doesn't it?'

'It does, John, it does . . . but then I don't profess to understand what this is all about. I just do everything I can to find the people who are responsible and insure they don't have a chance to do it again.'

23

'By killing them.'

'Sometimes, yes. Most times by taking them into custody, seeing that they get to trial, seeing them in prison for the rest of their lives.'

John was silent for some time. 'Do you believe in hell, Detective Gorman?'

'No son, I don't believe in Hell.'

'Neither do I,' John replied.

'But I can't say the same about the Devil,' Gorman said. 'If only from the viewpoint that—'

'That he can occupy a man's thoughts,' John interjected. 'Can make him do things . . . like the Devil isn't a person as we are, but more like—'

'A concept,' Gorman said. 'More like an idea that gets hold of people and makes them do things that they wouldn't otherwise do.'

'Exactly,' John said.

'Exactly,' Frank Gorman echoed.

Silence for a little while, and then Gorman looked up at John Costello.

'So you felt a breeze,' he said.

'Yes, and then . . .'

He squeezed Nadia's hand, and sort of tugged her toward him. There was something she needed to say, and she was having difficulty saying it. In that moment it did not worry him. He did not feel a sense of concern for what it might be. He did not suspect that she was leaving him, for such a thing had never happened, and he did not believe it could.

'Nadia?'

She looked back at John, and it was as she looked back that the pigeons rushed away for the second time.

She jumped again, started to laugh, and as she opened her mouth to laugh the shadow grew up behind her.

Dark. Black almost. And around the shadow was the smell of dogs, and the shadow obscured the streetlight, and it was as if someone had flipped a switch and suddenly there was midnight behind her.

She saw John's expression change, and she frowned. A momentary flash of anxiety in her eyes.

John looked away from her, looked up, and it was then

that he saw the vague impression of a face within the shadow. A man's face. A face punctuated by eyes that seemed distant, expressionless, absent of light. Eyes that gave the impression that there was no-one behind them.

John smiled – an involuntary reaction, the smile you would give a stranger, perhaps someone that interrupted you to ask for the time, to ask for directions, for that was all it was. Wasn't it? Someone late. Someone lost. Someone needing something.

And whoever it was just stood there for a moment, and didn't speak, didn't say a word, and John opened his mouth to ask what was up, and it was then that . . .

'He just raised his hand, and I could see there was something there . . .'

'But you didn't know what it was?'

'Not then, not until he swung his hand down and . . . and he said that thing . . .'

Gorman frowned. 'He said something?'

John nodded. 'Yes. He said, "I am the Hammer of God", and that was when I saw that he actually had a hammer in his hand.'

Gorman wrote in his book. 'And his face?'

John tried to shake his head, an involuntary response to the question, but found he could not do so without causing a sharp pain at the back of his neck. 'I didn't see his face, not really. There was just darkness, and then the sense of someone's face inside the darkness. It wasn't like really looking at anyone.'

'And he hit Nadia first?'

John wanted to cry but he could not. His eyes ached with emptiness. The pain, the bandages around his face – he could feel them so clearly, but he could not feel the emotion that he wanted to experience. He had drifted back and forth through unconsciousness, and much of the time it had possessed the awkward uncertainty of dreams. The images. The sounds. The sudden realization of what was happening. The fact that this man had brought the hammer down upon Nadia's head so swiftly, with such finality. Brought that hammer down upon her head in a single uninterrupted blow . . . a blow of such force that her head was split from hairline to jaw.

'She was dead before she even realized what had happened,'

25

Nurse Geraldine Joyce had told him earlier. 'Believe me, I know.'
Telling him this to reassure him, to make him understand that she
had felt no pain, that the man with the hammer had been
generous enough, big-hearted and compassionate enough to insure
that when he killed Nadia McGowan he'd made it swift, definitive,
precise and exact. Do it once. Do it right. That was his philosophy.
  I am the Hammer of God.
  'Yes,' John whispered. 'He hit Nadia first . . .'

And for a moment, a handful of seconds, John did not
understand what had happened.

There was no point of reference. There was no way for him
to explain what he was seeing.

The shadow rose up behind her. A man. A man with a face,
and eyes in that face which looked at him with such blank-
ness, with such absence of light, that there was no way of
determining what it was that the man wanted. He just stood
there, and there was a half-smile, an awkward little half-
smile, playing around the edges of his lips – the kind of
expression you'd expect from someone who was about to
tell you a joke, a humorous anecdote, and they knew the
punchline and they were just about to hit you with it.

But he didn't.

He stood there for a moment, and then his hand came up
to his side, and he raised his arm and brought it down with
such force, and the hammer connected with the top of her
head, right there behind her hairline, and for a moment she
seemed to feel nothing at all, and after a second, perhaps less
than a second, a thin line of blood, needle-fine, as thin as
thread, wound its way from the point of impact and started
down the side of her nose, and then the flow increased, as if
someone was slowly opening up a faucet, and the expression
on Nadia McGowan's face changed, and whatever light
might have existed there behind her eyes seemed to dim,
and John sat there trying to make sense of what he was
seeing, and then the blood was running down her cheek,
and then there was blood running over her eye, and Nadia,
panicked by the sensation, instinctively raised her hand to
brush it away.

And the back of her hand touched her cheek, and it was as

if the movement caused her to lose all sense of balance, and she leaned sideways just in time for the man to say that thing again: *I am the Hammer of God.*

The voice was calm and self-assured, and then he brought the hammer down one more time to connect with the side of her head, a point just above her ear, and the sound was like something dropped from a great height, the sound of something reaching the sidewalk after a seven-floor descent, the sound of something so powerful she would never come back from it . . .

And even as John Costello felt her hand slip from his, even as he rose from the bench and tried to stop her falling, he saw that arm raised up one more time, saw the momentary light of a yellow streetlamp reflected in the steel head of the ball-peen hammer, and heard him say for the third time . . .

'I am the Hammer of God.'

'And that's when he hit you?' Gorman asked.

For a little while John didn't speak, and then he looked at Gorman closely, looked at him as if trying to understand reason and rationale.

'Can we go back for a moment?' Gorman asked. 'After he hit her for the second time? I'm interested in anything else he might have said.'

'If he said anything else then I didn't hear it.'

Gorman wrote in his book again. 'And then?'

John tried to stand, tried to reach out toward her, to hold his hand up as some sort of defense against the blows that were raining down, but the Hammer of God turned and came at him like a flash of lightning, and he broke the force of the first blow with his hand, and his wrist was shattered, and then the second blow struck his shoulder, the third his arm, and by this time John Costello was bleeding and screaming, and he knew that he was going to die . . .

He fell sideways, his knee against the edge of the bench, and for a moment he was caught in indecision, in the conflict between self-preservation and his instinctive need to protect Nadia from further attack – even though he knew in that very moment that the blows must have killed her.

27

He tried to get up, to put his hand on the back of the bench, but the hammer came down and glanced off his ear, down the side of his neck, broke his collarbone, dropped him to the ground like deadweight.

It was then that he heard screaming.

Someone screamed.

It was not Nadia, it was not himself. The sound came from across the street . . .

And the fact that someone across the street had seen the attack, the fact that some woman across the street had seen what was happening and screamed, was the only reason that he survived.

The hammer came down one more time, was already on its way when the woman screamed, and it connected with the side of John Costello's face, and there was enough force brought to bear against the jaw beneath his ear that his nervous system shut down.

He saw nothing then. Nothing at all.

Everything went cold and lightless, and there was the smell of blood and there was the smell of dogs and there was the sound of running feet.

John Costello didn't wake up for a long time, and when he did the world had changed.

Gorman turned as the door opened.

Nurse Geraldine Joyce. 'Enough now,' she said quietly. 'He needs to rest.'

Gorman nodded, stood up. He leaned toward John Costello. 'We'll talk again,' he said, and then he thanked him for his time, and told him that he was sorry about the girl, and then he walked away from the edge of the bed and went through the door without looking back.

He came four or five times in the subsequent days, and they talked about the same handful of minutes over and over again.

It was Nurse Joyce who brought the paper on the following Wednesday.

She left it on the edge of the small table beside John Costello's bed, and he saw it when he woke.

JERSEY CITY TRIBUNE
Wednesday, 5 December 1984

City Arrest in Hammer Killings Case

A statement released by the Jersey City District Attorney's Office today confirmed earlier reports that an arrest has been made in the recent hammer murders case. Though the name of the suspect has not been released, Detective Frank Gorman of the Jersey City Police Department Homicide Task Force was quoted as saying 'We have reason to believe that the individual in custody can give us some important information regarding these recent murders.'

Jersey City has been terrorized by the deaths of five teenagers in the last four months, beginning with the brutal killings of Dominic Vallelly (19) and Janine Luckman (17) on Wednesday August 8th, subsequently the slaying of Gerry Wheland (18) and Samantha Merrett (19) on Thursday October 4th, and the fatal attack on Nadia McGowan (17) on the evening of Friday, November 23rd. All the killings are believed to have been carried out by the same person. The young man who was with Nadia McGowan at the time of the attack, John Costello (16), suffered serious head injuries but was reported as stable in Jersey City Hospital.

Frank Gorman came after lunch. Stood in the doorway – silently, patiently – and waited until John Costello spoke.
'You got him.'
Gorman nodded.
'He gave himself up?'
'No, not exactly.'
'What's his name?'
Gorman shook his head, stepped into the room and walked to the edge of John's bed. 'I can't tell you that just yet.'

29

'What happened?'

'We followed a lead . . . we found his house. We went there, knocked on the door, he opened it, and that's when he confessed.'

'What did he say?'

'He said the same thing. I am the Hammer of God.'

'And he confessed to the attacks.'

'He confessed to attacking a total of three couples. You were the last ones.'

'And what happens to him now?'

'He gets psych evaluation. He gets all the routine things. He goes to trial. He goes to Death Row. We execute him.'

'Unless he's declared insane.'

'Right.'

'Which he will be.'

'There's a good possibility, yes.'

John Costello was quiet for a little while, considering. Then, 'How do you feel about that?' he asked.

'About the fact that he might be declared insane and not be executed?'

'Yes.'

'I try not to feel anything about it. Why? How do you feel?'

John hesitated, and then he frowned, almost as if he was surprised at his own answer. 'I don't feel anything either, Detective Gorman . . . I don't feel anything at all.'

'Is there anything else that you can remember now? Anything else that you remember him saying?'

'Why does it matter now? He's confessed.'

'Because it might give us a better understanding of what was going through his mind.'

'Why would you want to know what was going through his mind?'

'Because we are trying to find everything we can that will convince the District Attorney and the judge that he knew what he was doing. That he had some sense of awareness of his actions. That he was really aware of what he was doing.'

'Why? So you can prove he was not insane?'

Gorman nodded. 'Yes. So we can say he was responsible for the consequences of his own actions.'

'So you can execute him.'

'Yes.'

John Costello closed his eyes. He tried to think, but there was nothing.

'No,' he said. 'I'm sorry, Detective . . . I don't think he said anything else.'

WARREN HENNESSY/FRANK GORMAN–ROBERT MELVIN CLARE INTERVIEWS. SECTION ONE (PAGES 86–88).

WH: So, Robert. Tell us again, tell us what the deal was with the hammer?

RMC: What do you want to know?

WH: Why they had to be killed with a hammer.

FG: Yes, Robert. Why the hammer? Why not just get a gun or a knife or something?

RMC: Part of the ritual.

FG: The ritual?

RMC: The cleansing ritual. They had to be cleansed.

WH: Cleansed of what, Robert?

RMC: Of what had been done to them.

WH: The things that you did to them?

RMC: No. I didn't do anything to them. They had to be cleansed of the sexual things that had been done to them. Can I get a drink? Can I get like a drink or something? Can I get a 7-Up here or what?

WH: We can get you a 7-Up in a minute, Robert.

RMC: I'm thirsty. Wanna 7-Up here. Too much to freakin' well ask for, is it? Can't talk much if your mouth is full of sand and sawdust, right? Need a 7-Up . . . need a 7-Up . . . need a 7-Up.

FG: I'll get you a 7-Up, Robert . . . you tell Detective Hennessy here what the deal was with the cleansing, okay?

RMC: Okay.

[Note: At this point Detective Frank Gorman left the interview room for approximately two minutes.]

WH: So let's get back to the cleansing, Robert.

RMC: Right, the cleansing.

WH: So what was the deal with that?

RMC: The deal? There was no deal, Detective Hennessy.

I didn't make any deal with anyone. It was just what had to be done.

WH: Okay, okay, okay, we're getting away from ourselves here, Robert. Let's just go back to what you were saying about how these kids had to be cleansed after what had been done to them.

RMC: After what had been done to them, yes.

WH: So tell me again.

RMC: They had to be cleansed.

[Note: At this point Detective Gorman returned and handed an opened can of 7-Up to the interview subject, Robert Melvin Clare.]

RMC: Thank you, Detective Gorman.

FG: You're very welcome, Robert. Sorry to interrupt you. You were telling Detective Hennessy about something?

RMC: I was telling him about the cleansing.

FG: Right, right . . . so carry on with what you were saying.

RMC: The things that were done were dirty things, you see? They were very dirty things . . . the kind of things that would blemish the mind and the soul forever. There is nothing that can be done to wash away that kind of dirt. You have to make them look different.

WH: The kids?

RMC: Right, the boys and the girls. You have to make them look different.

WH: Why, Robert? Why d'you have to make them look different?

[Subject is silent for approximately fifteen seconds]

WH: Why, Robert? Tell us why you had to make the girls and boys look different?

RMC: You don't know?

WH: No, Robert, we don't know. Tell us.

RMC: So God wouldn't recognize them. So he wouldn't recognize them as the ones who did those dirty, dirty things.

FG: And what would happen to them if God recognized them?

RMC: He wouldn't let them into Heaven, would he? He would cast them down into Hell. But I cleansed them, you see? I made them look different and God didn't recognize them.

32

WH: And so what happened to them, Robert?

[Subject is silent for approximately eighteen seconds.]

FG: Robert?

RMC: They became angels, Detective Gorman. Every single one of them. God didn't recognize them. They got in through the gates of Heaven. They got all the way into Heaven and became angels.

JERSEY CITY TRIBUNE
Friday, 7 December 1984

Hammer Killings Suspect Named and Charged

In an official statement from the Jersey City Police Department, Detective Frank Gorman, head of the Second Precinct Homicide Task Force, was quoted as follows: 'This morning we have charged Robert Melvin Clare, a resident of Jersey City, with the murders of Dominic Vallelly, Janine Luckman, Gerry Wheland, Samantha Merrett and Nadia McGowan. He has also been charged with attempted murder in the case of John Costello. At this time no formal request for representation has been made by Mr Clare, and a Public Defender will be assigned to afford him all necessary service as he prepares for trial.'

Robert Clare (32), a Jersey City native, currently residing in Van Vorst Street and employed as an auto mechanic at Auto-Medic Vehicle Repair and Recovery on Luis Muñoz Marin Boulevard, was reported by work colleagues to be 'kind of intense'. The owner of Auto-Medic, Don Farbolin, refused to comment beyond saying that 'just because I give someone a job doesn't make me responsible for what they do when they go home'.

FG: You truly believe that's what happened to them, Robert? That they became angels and got into Heaven?

RMC: Yes, that's what happened.

FG: All five of them?

[Subject is silent for approximately twenty-three seconds.]

WH: Robert?

RMC: There were six.

FG: Five, Robert. The last one, the boy . . . he's gonna make it.

RMC: Make it? That's exactly what he will not do, Detective.

WH: Apparently so. Doctors say he's gonna come through this.

RMC: Doctors? I'm not talking about doctors. I'm talking about making it . . . making it in the eyes of the Lord. Making it into the Heaven. The five will make it. The sixth, unfortunately for him, will not. He is now cursed. He carries the curse. Always will.

FG: So tell us how these kids were chosen, Robert. Tell us about how that was done.

RMC: They all looked the same, didn't they? They were all young and beautiful and innocent, and they were doing things that they shouldn't have been doing. Doing things out in the street, in public. All of them. All of them were doing those things, and their faces had to disappear. I had to make them disappear, you see? I had to make them go away, and that was the only way they could ever get into Heaven.

FG: Did you choose them beforehand, or did you just go out at night with your hammer?

RMC: It was not my hammer.

WH: Whose was it?

RMC: God's Hammer. It was *God*'s Hammer. Have you not listened to anything I've said?

34

FG: Tell us about the first couple, Robert . . . tell us about Dominic and Janine. Did you watch them for a while? Did you select them, or was it something random?

RMC: They were selected.

WH: And how was the selection process carried out, Robert?

RMC: They had to look a certain way, I think. I don't know how they are chosen.

WH: Do you choose them, or does someone choose them for you?

RMC: They are chosen for me.

WH: And who does the choosing for you, Robert?

RMC: I don't know.

FG: You don't know, or you don't remember?

RMC: I don't know. I know that someone is sent, and someone shows me who has been chosen.

FG: Someone is sent?

RMC: I am not saying anything more about that.

FG: Okay, okay. So tell us what you remember about the first two you attacked.

RMC: I remember how she screamed . . . like she thought if she made enough noise someone might hear and come and help her. I hit the boy first. That was a mistake. I learned that you have to hit the girl first because they always make the most noise, but you have to be fast and hit the girl hard enough to silence her. Then you have to hit the boy before he has a chance to react.

FG: And what did you do to her, Robert?

RMC: I cleaned her up real good, you know? I can call you Frank? Is it okay if I call you Frank, Detective Gorman?

FG: Sure you can, Robert.

RMC: Frank and Warren. Okay.

FG: You were saying?

RMC: Yes . . . she got fixed up real good, Frank. That's a good name. Frank. Frank is a good name . . . a good masculine name, simple, no mistaking Frank, eh, Frank?

FG: No, Robert, no mistaking Frank. Carry on telling us what happened to her.

RMC: She had on white socks, I think – and sneakers. Yes, white socks and sneakers. And there was blood all over her. A lot of blood, I think. But she had this expression like there was something hopeful inside of her, something that told her to make like she was enjoying herself, and she might walk away alive.

WH: But she didn't, right, Robert? She didn't walk away from it did she?

RMC: No she didn't, Warren . . . she didn't ever walk again.

FG: And then?

RMC: And then nothing. I hit the boy, I hit the girl, everything was finished. I went home. I was gonna stop for pizza on the way back but I wasn't really hungry.

JERSEY CITY TRIBUNE

Thursday, 20 December 1984

Editor's Viewpoint

The Death of Community

As the Editor of a major city newspaper I am constantly alerted to the fact that our society has dramatically changed. In my twenty-three year career as a journalist and newspaperman, I have seen the headlines week after week, year after year, and it seems that the job of reporting has now become less a matter of relaying the facts as a matter of stomaching the brutal truth of what human beings are capable of doing to one another.

It is a tragic comment on our community when a man has to apply to the District Attorney's Office to protect his home and business premises from people he refers to as 'murder freaks'. (See Page 1 of this edition: ' "Hammer of God" Boss Instigates Legal Action Against Trespassers'.) Don Farbolin has lived and worked in

36

Jersey City for nineteen years. His wife, Maureen, works alongside him at the company they own, a small but moderately successful car repair and renovation shop called 'Auto-Medic Vehicle Repair and Recovery' on Luis Muñoz Marin Boulevard. Mr Farbolin has stated that his business has collapsed since the arrest of Robert Clare, currently being held in the State Psychiatric Facility in Elizabeth awaiting evaluation for fitness for trial for five recent murders. This collapse is due to loss of custom, the majority of this loss down to the fact that both his home and his business premises have been overrun by people seeking some sort of 'memento' of Clare, a serial murderer. 'I don't understand it,' Mr Farbolin said. 'Who, in their right mind, would want to own something that belonged to a person like Robert Clare? The guy killed people. He was a bad person, it's as simple as that. I feel like I've been targeted by people simply because I had the decency to give someone a job. It's not right. This isn't the American Way.'

(Continued on Page 23)

WARREN HENNESSY/FRANK GORMAN–ROBERT MELVIN CLARE INTERVIEWS. SECTION FOUR (PAGE 95)

WH: What happened then, after you went home, Robert?
RMC: I don't know what happens right away . . . later, when everything . . .
WH: Everything what, Robert?
RMC: I don't remember.
FG: Tell us something you do remember.
RMC: The blood. I remember the blood. I remember the sound of the hammer when it hit the boy. Again when it hit the girl afterwards. That was the first time I did it, and for a little while it made me sick to my stomach, but I didn't have a choice. I remember watching the first girl . . . the way her expression changed, you know? The things that were done to her . . . the way she became a woman before she was even

37

old enough to understand what being a woman was all about. I saw those things. They made me crazy, Frank, really crazy. All that kissing and touching . . .

FG: And how did you feel later? You know, later, when you got home. How did you feel after the first one?

[Subject is silent for forty-nine seconds]

FG: Robert?

RMC: How did I feel? How would anyone feel after such a thing? I felt like the Hammer of God.

SECTION FIVE (PAGES 96–97)

FG: And what about the second one?

RMC: The second one?

FG: The one after Dominic Vallelly and Janine Luckman? You remember them Robert? The 4th of October. Gerry Wheland and Samantha Merrett.

RMC: I remember them.

WH: Tell us what happened between the first attack and the second. ·

RMC: Happened? Nothing happened.

FG: You waited nearly two months to attack again. How come so long?

RMC: Everything was out of my control, Frank. Everything was way beyond my control by that point.

FG: What d'you mean, way beyond your control?

RMC: Everything took on a life of its own. It was like something possessed me . . . something got inside of me and I couldn't stop it. There they were – they were right in front of me – and there was nothing I could do to stop any of it happening. If I hadn't done it then everything would have been so much worse. I can't expect *you* to understand what it was like . . . you haven't ever seen anything like the things I saw—

WH: What you saw? Saw where?

RMC: The night I went out again. The second night. In October. I thought it wouldn't happen again, thought maybe two were enough. But that night I got the message again . . . the message to go out to work again . . .

WH: Where did the message come from, Robert?

38

RMC: I don't know. Didn't I already tell you I don't know? I don't know where the message came from . . . it's all dark inside, dark all the time, like there are no windows, and I go down there and I can see them, and hear them crying and screaming like their souls are crying and screaming . . . like they know what they're doing is wrong and they need to be cleansed, but they're too afraid to do it for themselves so they need me to help them . . . and I could feel how afraid they were, and I knew the only thing that would stop them being so afraid is if they were wished all the way up into Heaven. The instruction comes, and you don't ignore it, right? It was like a light came on above them and I knew they were the ones . . . And it proves beyond all doubt the compassion of God, that He loves all men regardless of what they have done.

FG: How so, Robert?

RMC: Because even the bad ones, you know . . . even the bad ones are given a chance. They're given a chance, and they take it, and all I had to do was go there and fix it so they'd get their chance when it was right.

FG: So what happened after the second attack? What did you do?

RMC: I went home and took a shower.

FG: You took a shower?

RMC: Right.

FG: To wash off the blood?

RMC: No, because I always take a shower. Every night before I go to bed I take a shower and then I have a glass of milk, and then I go to bed. I can't sleep if I feel dirty.

WH: So you went home and took a shower and went to bed?

RMC: Right. Oh, wait. No, I took a shower and had some milk and I watched TV for a little while.

FG: What did you watch, Robert?

RMC: I watched *The Rockford Files*.

FG: And this happened the same way with the next couple?

RMC: What did?

FG: The sequence of events . . . you went out, you attacked them, and once you were done you went home and had a shower and watched TV?

RMC: The third time I didn't watch TV. I went to bed early and read a book.

FG: Which book?

RMC: I was reading Raymond Chandler. I like Raymond Chandler. Do you like Raymond Chandler, Frank?

FG: Haven't read any, Robert.

RMC: You should, Frank, you should . . . being a detective and everything. You should read Raymond Chandler.

JERSEY CITY TRIBUNE
Thursday, 27 December 1984

'Hammer of God' Killer Suicide at Elizabeth Facility

Robert Melvin Clare (32), arrested and charged with five counts of murder and one of attempted murder, was this morning found dead in his room at the Jersey State Psychiatric Facility in Elizabeth. Initial reports suggest Clare hung himself with a rope fashioned from strips of sheeting. Head of the Facility, Dr Mitchell Lansden, was unavailable for comment, but a spokesman for the Facility said that a full and complete inquiry would be instigated immediately to determine how such an event could have taken place. Clare had already been questioned by Detective Frank Gorman, head of the Jersey City Homicide Task Force, regarding the recent 'Hammer of God' murders and had been bound over to the care of the Jersey State Psychiatric Facility for evaluation regarding fitness for trial. When asked for comment, Detective Gorman was reported as having been disappointed that Clare would not be tried for these murders. He also allowed that he was certain of Clare's guilt, and that with his suicide the State would not have to bear the cost of a trial, and the families of the victims would not have to endure the heartbreak of seeing their sons' and daughters' names and pictures in the newspapers. No official statement has been made by the District Attorney's Office.

'You heard what happened?' Gorman asked.

'Heard he killed himself.'

'He hung himself . . . made a rope by tearing a sheet into strips, and then he wound them together like a rope.'

'Where did he hang himself from?'

'Lifted up his bed and leaned it vertically against the wall. Truth was that he didn't so much as hang himself as choke himself to death. He had to keep his feet up off the ground.'

John Costello was silent for a while. With difficulty he turned his head and looked toward the window. 'You think he was the one?'

'No doubt about it,' Gorman replied.

'He confessed?'

Gorman was quiet for a few moments. 'I'm not supposed to say anything about his interrogation but yes, he confessed.'

'He say why he did it?'

'He did, yes.'

John smiled weakly, turned his head and looked at Gorman.

'It was crazy stuff, John. There was no reason. Of course there wasn't any rational reason. You can't rationalize irrational behavior.'

'But he had a reason he believed in, didn't he?'

'He did.'

'You wanna tell me what it was?'

'No, of course I don't want to.'

'But you will, right?'

'You think it'll do any good?'

'To me?' John asked. 'No, I don't think so. Like you said, it's crazy stuff. I mean it would have to be crazy, wouldn't it? Sane people don't go out and smash peoples' heads in with a hammer.'

'He thought he was doing something good,' Gorman said. 'He thought that he was helping the people that he killed get into Heaven.'

John smiled sardonically. 'That's just crazy.'

'Sure it is.' He paused a few moments, then said, 'Anyway, we'll

41

talk some more later. Get some rest. You look like you're on the
mend.'
   'You look like you never sleep.'
   'I don't.'
   'Maybe now, eh? Now it's over.'
   'Sure, kid. Maybe now.'

JERSEY CITY TRIBUNE
Friday, January 4th, 1985

'Hammer of God' Cop Death

Detective Frank Gorman, head of the Jersey City Homicide Task Force, most recently engaged in the investigation of the Hammer of God murders, died yesterday evening in the restroom of a city restaurant from what was believed to be a heart attack. Gorman (51), a Police Department veteran of twenty-eight years, unmarried and without children, was understood to have been dining alone. Chief of Police Marcus Garrick this morning gave a statement to the effect that Gorman was a diligent and committed officer who will be sorely missed. His funeral will be held at First Communion Church of God on Wednesday, 9th January. Instead of flowers, Chief Garrick has asked that donations be made to the Jersey Police Department Widows and Orphans Beneficiary Fund, care of the Mayor's office.

John Costello became the sort of person who finds safety in
routines. In counting. In making lists.
   He is not afraid of the dark, for he carries all the darkness he
needs inside him.
   See him in the street and he looks like a million others.
   Talk to him and he appears to be just like you.
   But he is not.
   And never will be.

ONE

The Carnegie Deli and Restaurant at 854, Seventh Avenue, with its faded yellow sign, its red arched awning, and the fact that they had always cured and smoked and pickled their own, was a little slice of heaven. And once inside, the aromas of salt beef, pickled herring and chicken soup with kneidles, the pictures on the walls, the veteran waiters, their famous rudeness countered only by smiling waitresses, gave a feeling of welcome familiarity.

Ray Irving, Fourth Precinct Homicide Division, was not himself Jewish, but believed his stomach was a hot contender.

From the extensive kosher-style menu came his breakfast – bologna omelette, pancake-style, perhaps Virginia ham, thick-cut, with eggs. Other times called for kippered baked salmon with cream cheese, lettuce, Bermuda onion, a bagel on the side, Elberta peaches, chocolate, fruit and nut babka, pumpernickel toast and cranberry juice.

For lunch there were sandwiches, but these were no ordinary sandwiches. These were the renowned salt beef sandwiches big enough to feed a small family, the Gargantuan Combos with names like Fifty Ways To Love Your Liver, Ah, There's The Reuben, Beefamania and Hamalot. And for dinner there was Meatloaf and Baked Short Ribs, Vermont Turkey Platter, Roumanian Chicken Paprikash, pastrami served open-faced on homemade potato knishes with melted Swiss cheese. You wanted a salad, they'd make you a salad: Central Park, Julienne Child, George Shrimpton, Zorba the Greek, AM-FM Tuna, the Hudson Liver, and Ray Irving's all-time favorite – Salmon Chanted Evening.

Irving owned an apartment in a three-story brownstone on

the West Side at 40th Street and Tenth Avenue. He was not married. He had no children. He did not cook. The Fourth Precinct house was on Sixth at 57th, and thus his route from home to work and back again allowed him to take in Carnegie's: park behind the Arlen Building near the 57th Street subway station, a short walk, and he was there. They knew him by face and by name, and they didn't treat him like a cop. They treated him like family. They took his messages when he could not be reached at his home or the precinct house. He ran a tab and paid it monthly. They never asked, and he was never late. Had been this way for years, no reason to change. Amidst the horror that was his life, the things he saw, the part he played as witness to the brutality that human beings were effortlessly capable of perpetrating one against the other, he believed that some things should remain inviolate and unchanged. The Carnegie Deli & Restaurant was one of them.

Ray Irving slept well, he ate well, and until seven months earlier he had visited a woman called Deborah Wiltshire in her apartment on West 11th near St Vincent's. They'd talked of nothing consequential, they drank bourbon and played cards, they listened to Miles Davis and Dave Brubeck, they made out like teenagers. Deborah was thirty-nine, a divorcée, and Ray believed that she might once have been a hooker . . . or maybe a dancer. He had known her for nine years, met her on a routine house-to-house after a teenager was found murdered in back of her building. She'd had no information that helped him, but when he was done asking questions she'd looked at him with that light in her eyes and told him to come back if he needed anything else. He'd gone back the following day to ask if she was single, to invite her for a drink. They saw one another for some months, and then he'd started in on what the lawyers would call 'a request for further and better particulars'.

'You ever want to make this thing more—'

'More what?' she'd said. 'More serious?'

'Sure. You know, like—'

'Like you want me to move in with you or something?'

'I don't mean that, no. Not unless you wanted to, of course. I just meant—'

'Hell, Ray, why mess it up? We're good for each other. We're good company. Figure if we saw each other any more often we'd most likely discover all those little idiosyncrasies that end up being the reasons you leave someone. This is good. I've been through this enough times to know that this is better than any other arrangement I've had, and I like it this way. If I didn't I wouldn't do it.'

He hadn't asked again.

Little had changed for the better part of a decade, and then Deborah Wiltshire had died. Late November 2005, sudden, utterly unexpected, a hereditary weakness in her heart. Down and gone. Dropped like a stone.

Ray Irving took the news like a head-shot. He'd been useless for a month, and then had somehow clawed his way back to reality.

In the final analysis, the thing that heralded Irving's return to the real world was a child murder. The killing of children could never be explained or justified. Didn't matter who did it or what the circumstances, the supposed reason and rationale back of it, a dead child was a dead child. The case had been arduous, had lasted months, but Ray's diligence and commitment had resulted in the successful conviction of an irredeemable man.

In the subsequent six months Irving had used his job as an anchor and, with the stability it offered, he had pulled himself back from the brink of the abyss. He would never forget Deborah Wiltshire, would never wish to forget her, but he had begun to believe that the small world within which he existed still required his attendance. There was no easy way out of grief – that much he understood – and so he stopped looking.

Ray Irving's apartment looked the same as the day he'd moved in eleven years before. Eight trips in a station wagon from his previous place of residence, armfuls of belongings, no boxes, no packing crates. Those possessions had assumed their rightful positions, and had remained there for the duration. His mother did not visit because she had died of emphysema in early '84. His dad played dominoes and mumbled baseball scores in a nursing home other side of Bedford-Stuyvesant. There was no-one to tell him that he should live differently. This was how things were. This was how he believed they always would be.

Morning of Saturday, June 3rd, a little after nine, Ray Irving took a call-out. Rain had varnished the streets and sidewalks. Inadequate distance between earth and sky. It had been overcast all week and the atmosphere was close, brooding, impenetrable. The weather seemed raw and unfinished, perhaps served some purpose for farmers and horticulturalists, but to Irving it was simply trouble. Rain obscured evidence, turned earth to mud, washed things down, erased partials.

By the time he reached the edge of Bryant Park, back of the library and close enough to Fifth to smell the money, the uniforms had taped the scene. The grass was flat, the ground was oatmeal, and already the traipsing back and forth had chewed the perimeter ragged.

'Melville,' the first officer said, and then spelled his name.

'Like Herman, right?' Irving asked.

Melville smiled. They all wanted to be remembered. They all wanted the call from Homicide or Vice or Narco: You done good, boy, you gonna get the badge.

'What we got?'

'Girl,' Melville replied. 'Teenager I'd say. Head staved in. Body wrapped in black plastic and left under the trees down there.'

'Who found her?'

'Couple of fat kids from across the street. Twins. Fourteen years old. I have someone over there with the parents.'

'Did the kids know the vic?'

Melville shook his head. 'Not from her clothes. Head is too fucked-up for a facial ID.'

'Walk with me,' Irving said.

The ground sucked at his shoes. The rain had eased off some, become a fine mist that surreptitiously penetrated everything. Irving was unaware of how wet his hair was until he brushed the back of his head with his hand and felt droplets coursing down his neck.

Irving didn't know trees, but the ones beneath which the girl's body had been unceremoniously dumped were short, thick-trunked, the lower branches providing a dense canopy.

This was helpful. The ground beneath seemed relatively firm considering the rain. There were scuffs and marks in the dirt, areas of flattened grass, and two precise patches beside the body where it appeared that someone had knelt. The body itself was shrouded in black plastic sheeting. The girl was obscured from the upper torso to her feet. Her shoulders, her neckline, the little that remained of her face was all that was visible. Irving put on latex gloves, carefully lifted the sheeting at one side and looked at the girl's hands. They were apparently untouched. Perhaps she would be identified by prints, perhaps by dentals. He lowered the sheeting. Behind the trees was a wrought-iron fence, beyond that the 42nd Street sidewalk. The fence and the trees provided a more than ample screen. Irving wondered how many people, maybe even her parents, had walked right past the body and never realized a thing.

'Forensics on the way?' he asked as he peeled off his gloves and tucked them into his jacket pocket.

Melville nodded. 'May be a little while . . . half an hour perhaps.'

Irving rose to his feet. 'Get a couple of guys on this side, another couple on the road. I want to talk to the kids.'

Melville had been compassionate in his description. The twins were not fat. *Clinically obese* was the phrase that came to mind. Taut skin, cardiac stress already evident in their eyes. They looked pale, cold, upset, identical. The parents were the opposite, the mother painfully thin, the father of average height, less-than-average build.

Melville hung back at the front door to alleviate potential crowding.

A female officer rose from a chair at the kitchen table when Irving appeared. He knew her from the precinct. She was married to a narc undercover who had good arrest and conviction stats, but a too-generous record of one-eighty-ones for excessive force.

'Mr and Mrs Thomasian,' she said, and then she nodded at the boys. 'And this is Karl and Richard.'

Irving smiled.

Mr Thomasian rose, extended his hand, asked Irving to sit down.

Irving smiled, thanked him, said he wouldn't be staying. 'I won't keep you. I just wanted to make sure the boys were okay, see if you needed anything, someone to come down and talk to them perhaps.' He looked at each of the kids in turn. They stared back at him with expressions of vacant, sugar-shocked emptiness.

'We're okay,' Mrs Thomasian said. 'We're dealing with it. We're gonna be okay, aren't we, boys?'

One of them looked at his mother, the other just stared at Irving.

Mrs Thomasian smiled once again – forced, almost painful. 'We're gonna be okay now . . . we really are.'

Irving nodded, walked to the kitchen door, asked the officer to join him in the front hallway.

'Adopted,' she told him. 'Lost their birth parents four or five years ago. Some kind of accident. They're okay. They don't know who the girl was. They had extra tutorial this morning with one of the teachers from the school. Karl threw Richard's workbook over the fence. The pair of them walked round to retrieve it and they found her.'

'Have the parents witness the statement, both of them, and get the kids to sign it too. No questions without both parents there.'

'For sure . . . wouldn't consider it.'

Irving left, and he and Melville walked back to the crime scene. Forensics were unpacking field kits.

Lead CSA, a tall, narrow-set man called Jeff Turner, held up a baggie. In it were two or three items, amongst them a school ID card.

'If the card is hers then her name is Mia Grant, fifteen years old,' Turner said.

Irving turned to Melville. 'Call it in. See if she's a runaway.'

Melville walked back toward the black-and-white parked back of the subway station.

'So what we got?' Irving asked, his tone one of philosophical resignation.

'First report, that's all. COD is the blunt force trauma. No other obvious signs. No ligature marks, no GSW. Have to do a rape kit, but right now it doesn't look like she's been sexually assaulted, and she died somewhere else. This is just the dump location. At a guess I'd say twenty-four hours, maybe less. I'll do liver temp but I don't think that's gonna help us much with the weather as it is.'

'Out Friday night,' Irving said. 'Never came home.'

Melville called Irving from thirty yards away, waved him over.

'We got her on a Missing Persons,' he said. 'Parents called it in last night, just after eleven. Said she went out at seven-thirty, think it might have been after a job. Lives in Tudor. No official report because it's not been forty-eight hours, but there's a notation in the desk log.'

'We need a proper ID before we talk to the parents,' Irving said. 'I'm not going down there to question them about their daughter's murder only to find out it's not their daughter.'

'The chance it's someone else—'

'Is pretty much zero,' Irving interjected. 'I know that, but I have to be absolutely sure.'

Turner nodded. 'We'll need an hour here . . .' He glanced at his watch. 'Call me at eleven, we'll see what we have.'

Eleven-fifteen, Jeff Turner reached Irving in his office. 'We got her,' he said. 'She has her prints on the system. Her father's a lawyer. Anthony Grant, bigshot private defense attorney . . . put his daughter on that ID database thing when she was thirteen. I've got them coming down here now.'

'I'll meet you there.' Irving tugged his jacket from the back of his chair and signed out to the coroner's office.

TWO

Evelyn Grant was a wreck. Her husband, attorney-at-law, a man that Irving now vaguely recognized from some noisy murder trial a handful of years before, sat like a spartan – resolute, outwardly emotionless, but in his eyes that drawn and terrified smack of reality that would now never be forgotten.

'A job?' Irving asked.

Anthony Grant nodded. 'She was saving for a car. She wanted to have enough for a car by the time she went to college. I told her I would double anything she earned. I wanted her to understand—'

He paused as his wife gripped his hand. A strangled sob hitched in her throat and she buried her face in her handkerchief.

Grant shook his head. 'I wanted her to understand the importance of working for something.'

'And the job? '

'Just domestic stuff, cleaning or something. I don't know.' Grant looked at his wife. His wife looked away, as if she somehow held him responsible. 'She was an independent girl,' Grant went on. 'I let her do what she was capable of doing. She visited people she knew, she came back at the times we agreed. Sometimes she stayed over with friends. She was very adult about these things.'

'First thing I have to ask, of course, is about you, Mr Grant,' Irving said. 'Unhappy clients. Obviously if you were a prosecutor it would make more sense, but even as a defense attorney you're going to make enemies.'

'Of course.' He hesitated, then shook his head. 'Jesus, I don't know. I've fought hundreds of cases. I win more than I lose by a long way, but I do lose. Who the hell doesn't? There's a lot of people in prison who are pissed off at me.'

'And people who are now out who hold you responsible?'

'Could very well be.'

Grant looked at his wife again. Recrimination flashed in her eyes, and Irving sensed she was a cold woman. He figured that the husband did all the work to keep their relationship together.

'Look, I understand all of this is necessary, but must it be now? I really don't think this is something—'

Irving smiled understandingly. 'I just need to know if you have any idea of where she was going.'

Grant shook his head. 'All she said was that there was the possibility of a part-time job in Murray Hill. She was going to use the subway. I would have driven her but my wife and I had a prior engagement.'

'And the time Mia left the house?'

'Six, six-thirty maybe. We left about half an hour later, got back just after ten. Mia wasn't home, didn't answer her cellphone, and at eleven I called the police. They told me—'

'That they couldn't file a report for forty-eight hours,' Irving interjected.

'Yes, that's right.'

'And she didn't say anything else about where she was going or who she was going to meet?'

Grant was silent for some time, and then he slowly shook his head. 'No, nothing that I can remember.'

'Okay . . . so as far as reaching you?'

'I'm going to take my wife to my mother's in Rochester,' Grant said. 'I'll drive back in the morning to deal with everything.' He took a sheet of letterhead from his briefcase and gave it to Irving. 'My office and cell, and here—' He wrote two more numbers on the page. 'That's my house here in the city, and that's my mother's number if you really need to reach me tonight. Call my cell first, but there's very little signal where she is, and I'd prefer it if you didn't call. I'll come see you tomorrow. You're at the Fourth Precinct, right?'

'Yes, up on Sixth at 57th.'

Grant rose from his chair, helped his wife. Mentally, perhaps spiritually, she was no longer in the room. She had long since gone. She didn't see her husband, didn't see Irving, didn't see the uniformed officer who opened the door for them and showed them to the exit. She'd be like that for days. Grant would inevitably call a doctor and the doctor would give her something to postpone reality a little longer.

Irving took a left down the hallway and found Turner.

'No sexual assault,' Turner told him. 'Haven't unzipped her, but there are no outward signs of anything but the blunt force to the head. Looks like a hammer, something small, you know? From lividity and laking I'd say between nine-thirty and eleven last night. Wherever she was killed she didn't stay long. Moved almost immediately. The horizontal laking from where she lay in the park is primary, not secondary. That means you have another scene to find.'

'If there's anything else would you call me?'

'Sure.' Turner nodded. 'The parents?'

'Nothing of any great use as yet. Girl went out after a job. Six-thirty, thereabouts.'

'He didn't say anything when he saw her, you know,' Turner said. 'Even looking the way she did, it didn't seem to affect him.'

'It will,' Irving said. 'Tonight, tomorrow, next week. It will.'

'He's not a suspect?'

'They're all suspects until they're not. But Grant for the murder of his own daughter? I don't get that from first impressions. Could be a revenge killing, someone he didn't do such a good job defending. But hell, the truth is always stranger.'

Turner's pager buzzed. He had to leave. He and Irving shook hands. Turner assured Irving that if anything significant arose in the autopsy he would call him.

It did not.

Forensics drew a blank as well.

Reports came in from both departments on the morning of the fifth. Mia Emily Grant, fifteen years old, date of birth February 11th, 1991. Cause of death was blunt force trauma to the head, massive internal bleeding; there was no sexual assault. The edge of Bryant Park beneath a canopy of trees was confirmed as the dump site, not the primary. Extensive walk-about had turned up very little. The subway crews at

34th and Penn, 50th, 42nd, Times Square, Grand Central, 33rd – all those that might have seen Mia Grant as she made her way from her home near St Vartan's Park to Murray Hill, were shown her picture and questioned. Of course, Irving knew that there was no guarantee that she'd even taken the subway. He knew that she might never have made it further than a block from her house. He also knew that the part-time job might have been nothing but a ruse to misdirect the parents. Bright, pretty, fifteen-year-old girl . . . Enough said.

On Saturday, 10th of June, just a week after the discovery of her body, the case went cold. Every lead, every line, every potential scenario that Irving could extrapolate from the girl's death, had been explored, explored again, explored a third time. The parents' alibis were incontrovertible. There was nothing. Irving repeatedly put his hand into a paper bag and came back empty.

The file sat on the edge of his desk. It was very soon hidden beneath a copy of *The New York Times*, an envelope of photographs that seemed to have lost its case-ID tab, a coffee cup, an empty Coke can.

No more than half a dozen blocks south west, John Costello sat staring at a cork board across from his desk in the research office of the *New York City Herald*. Pinned at eye level was the small two-inch column detailing the discovery of Mia Grant's body, the few details regarding her age, her school, her father's occupation, and at the very bottom – now underlined in red – the fact that she had apparently been en route to a job inquiry in Murray Hill.

Beside the newspaper clipping was a half page torn from the locally circulated freep, and on it – circled in ink – was an ad from Thursday June 1st.

Girl wanted. Part-time domestic work. Negotiable rates of pay. Flexible hours.

The phone number given carried a Murray Hill prefix.

In John Costello's measured and precise hand he had written *June 3 Carignan Want Ad* and then, alongside the circled item *????*.

It seemed, from where he sat and the intense expression on his face, that he was transfixed by these items.

When the phone on his desk rang he started, snatched the receiver from the cradle.

He listened, half-smiled, and then said, 'Yes ma'am, be there in a moment.'

THREE

'The simple truth is that we're looking at something like eighteen thousand murders a year in the U.S. That's fifteen hundred a month, roughly four hundred a week, fifty-seven every day, one every twenty-five and a half minutes. Only two hundred a year are the work of serial killers . . .' John Costello smiled. 'As far as is known.'

New York City Herald Assistant Editor-in-Chief, Leland Winter, leaned back in his chair. He steepled his fingers and looked enquiringly at Karen Langley, Senior Crime Correspondent, the woman for whom John Costello worked as a researcher.

John Costello counted the bonsai trees on Winter's desk. There were eight. The second from the right was almost perfectly symmetrical.

'So what do you want from me?' Winter asked.

'Three pages, three consecutive Sundays,' Langley said. She glanced at Costello and smiled.

'Feature editorial on the serial killer victims that never make the headlines?'

'Right,' Karen Langley said.

Winter nodded slowly and then turned to Costello.

Costello looked at Winter. He tilted his head to one side. 'Can I ask you something, Mr Winter?'

'Sure,' Winter said.

'The trees . . . the ones on your desk—'

'John,' Karen Langley interjected. The sound of his name was a whispered syllable, a prompt, a reprimand.

Winter smiled, leaned forward. 'The trees . . . what about them?'

Costello nodded his head. 'I don't know that I've ever seen anything so beautiful, Mr Winter. They really are the most remarkable specimens.'

'You know bonsai?' Winter asked. 'And for God's sake, John, no-one calls me Mr Winter except the IRS and the police. Call me Leland.'

Costello shook his head. 'Do I know bonsai? No, not really, only enough to know when someone else knows what they're doing.'

'Why thank you, John. That's most appreciated. They really are a great passion of mine.'

'I can see that, Leland, I really can.'

Leland Winter and John Costello sat there for some moments. The room was silent. They looked at the bonsai trees from opposite sides of the desk. Karen Langley believed she might as well not have been there.

Eventually Winter turned and looked at her. 'So propose me something, Karen . . . put a few boards together, let me see how it looks, okay? I don't know about three full pages, but let's see what we've got, okay?'

Karen Langley smiled, rose from her chair. 'Thanks, Leland, that's great . . . we'll get something together by the middle of the week.'

John Costello stood up, took a step forward, extended his hand.

Leland Winter shook it, smiling. 'How long have you been here, John? At the paper, I mean.'

'Here?' Costello turned his mouth down at the corners. He turned and looked at Karen Langley.

'Eight and a half years,' Karen Langley said. 'John's worked for me for eight and a half years . . . started about six months after I arrived.'

'I'm surprised we've never met . . . I mean, I've only been here half that time, but even so—'

John Costello nodded his head. 'No-one told me you had bonsais, Leland, or I'd have been up here a long time ago.'

Leland Winter smiled some more, and showed them out of his office with a self-satisfied expression.

'You're unbelievable, John,' Karen Langley said. 'That was just the most outrageous thing I ever saw.'

'So maybe you get your pages, eh?'

'We'll see . . . you gotta help me put something together

now, okay? Gotta have something for the planning meeting, latest Wednesday.'

'I'll check my calendar,' Costello said.

Langley swung the leather portfolio she was carrying and connected with Costello's arm.

'Check your calendar . . . Jesus, you should do a half-hour stint at the Comedy Club on Saturday night, get it out of your system.'

They reached the elevator, she pushed for *down*.

'Question,' Costello said. 'Why did you tell him I'd only been here for eight and a half years?'

Karen smiled. 'I didn't say you'd been here for eight and half years, I told him that's how long you'd worked for me.'

Costello raised his eyebrows.

'John, seriously. I tell people that you've been here for nearly twenty years it bothers them that they don't know who you are. It – well – it makes them feel awkward.'

Costello opened his mouth to say something but seemed to change his mind. He shrugged his shoulders, then turned toward the stairwell.

'Oh right,' she said. 'No elevators.'

He smiled unassumingly, then made his way through the doorway and started down the stairwell. He counted the treads as he went, same as always.

FOUR

Morning of Monday, June 12th, Max Webster was caught in a jam on Franklin D. Roosevelt Drive. Had planned to take the Queens Midtown Tunnel, changed his mind when he saw the depth of gridlock at the end of East 42nd, figured that the Williamsburg Bridge might be a safer bet, and took it. Max was middle-aged, whatever the hell that meant. Salesman out of the lower east side, small but profitable chemical firm on Rivington Street that hawked its wares as far north as Waterbury, Conn., as far south as Atlantic City. Max was a regular guy; a guy that would never be known for anything but his decency and basic goodness. Part of that fraternity of simple people with simple lives, long beyond the point of frustration about what might have been, could have been, should have been, never would be. Not complicated, just limited.

Max had two client visits, and then back to the office to cold-call some prospects. His firm, Chem-Tech, didn't have to fight for the trade any more, and in some small way Max was aware that the challenge had slipped right out of the business. He wasn't hungry these days, not like ten years ago. Back then it was closing pitches, 'buy nows' and lead-times faster than the competition. Back then it was arguing with stock managers and delivery crews and warehousemen. Back then it was three Hail Marys as he climbed from his car and made his way toward the site office, pumping hands, grinning wide and foolish, making the prospect think he was calling the boss to see if they could shave a point off the dollar if the order exceeded three grand and change. Back then it seemed like something to get up for. Five years and he would call it quits, buy a boat and go fishing, and five years of routine and repetition he could stand. For Max Webster was a decent stand-up guy, a guy that would die and leave people remembering little of him at all except that he was okay.

Gridlock he could do also. He was on schedule for his appointment. But that morning he'd drunk a second cup of coffee, and seated in his car on Roosevelt he felt like someone cruel had tied a knot in his bladder and was squeezing the contents into the base of his gut. Max, for all his good points, was not so good at breakfast. Maybe he smoked too much. Whatever the reason, he seemed to wake with food as the last thing on his mind. Always been that way; wouldn't eat until ten or eleven, and this morning that second cup of coffee rolled around inside him.

Fifteen minutes later he'd crawled no more than a quarter mile forward. His knuckles were white as he gripped the wheel. A thin film of sweat had broken out along his hairline, and he felt that if he didn't go he would pee his pants right where he sat.

He glanced right toward the empty emergency lane, and then turned sharply, hit the accelerator, and burned down the last few hundred yards to the turn-off. He cut underneath the expressway and pulled up on the edge of the East River Park. A water-filled balloon was trying to push its way out the middle of his body. He hesitated for a second or two then, in a moment of unbridled spontaneity, he killed the engine, exited his car, and hurried down the embankment toward an outcrop of trees by the river.

Relief was overwhelming and immediate. He urinated with such force he could have broken a pane of glass. He urinated like the State champion. As was always the case in such moments, the quantity he produced was far, far greater than two cups of coffee, and he glanced nervously both left and right to insure he wasn't being seen. The trees were dense enough, their cover ample, and it was only when he glanced down that his sense of relief drew to a stuttering close.

At first he merely frowned, and then as realization quietly dawned, slipping into his mind like the sun into the Gulf of Mexico from Ponce De Leon Bay, he squinted at the ground, began focusing on what he was seeing there. Amidst the fallen leaves and bottle caps, amidst the damp shreds of discarded newspaper and a single rusted Coke can, amidst the things one would expect to find in a clump of trees at the side of the highway, lay a single human hand, palm upwards. The fingers were curled toward him, almost pointing, almost accusing, and though the wrist had disappeared under a damp heap of fallen leaves, it seemed that the fingers were growing from the earth like a bizarre and unnatural plant.

Max Webster, decent guy though he was, sprayed the front of his antique brogues. The last shot of urine soaked the right leg of his pants and, his pecker barely back inside, he was hot-footing his way out of the trees, turning suddenly and nearly falling, the blood drained from his face, his eyes wide and staring as he hurtled up toward his car. He snatched his cellphone from the dash compartment and called 911, and for the first time in as long as he could remember he said the F-word – like, *There's a fucking body, a goddamned fucking body down in the trees!* – and the operator on the end of the line kept her cool and made him explain where he was and what he had seen, and gave him strict instructions not to move.

And he didn't move. Didn't even want to look back down toward the trees. Thought for a moment what he would tell them, whether there was a law against urinating within a couple of hundred yards of Franklin D. Roosevelt Drive, but good guy that he was he decided that the truth was the truth. And he told that truth to the guys who came down in the black-and-white, a couple of youngsters who couldn't have been more than a year or so out of police academy, and one of them stayed with Max while the other went down to the trees to confirm that the hand Max had seen was in fact human, and not some dumbass trick-or-treat stage prop thrown in there by some kids.

The hand was real, the body beyond it equally real, and the police officer came out from the trees looking similarly shocked and pale. He called it in. Operator contacted the ME's Office, and the County Deputy Coroner was dispatched forthwith. His name was Hal Gerrard, mid-forties, knew that without an Act of God he would never be the coroner, and had philosophically resigned himself to the fact many years before. He took a CSA with him, a man called Lewis Ivens, and between the two of them they cleared the area around the body and found a second one. Two girls. Young, no more than sixteen or seventeen. Gerrard made initial notes, concurred with Ivens' TOD estimate of twenty-four hours. One girl had been shot in the back of the head, then in the chest; the other in the back of the head, the exit wound near her right eyebrow, and had taken a second bullet which had exited behind the left ear. Despite their young age, both girls were dressed for work, the first girl in denim cut-offs and pink halter-top, the second in fishnets and stilettos, a mini-skirt no wider than a belt.

'They're already working,' Ivens asked, 'at this age?'

Gerrard just shook his head resignedly. He said nothing. He'd seen it all and then some, and there really was nothing to say.

They searched the immediate area to verify there was nothing else of significance or interest. They found a purse, in it lipstick, breath spray, a can of mace and six condoms. There was a crumpled Marlboro pack nearby, three cigarettes left, a matchbook from the EndZone nightclub squashed down inside it. Gerrard and Ivens cordoned the crime scene with black and yellow tape, took a whole roll of shots from every conceivable angle, and then called for a second vehicle from the County Morgue.

The attending policemen, John Macafee and Paul Everhardt, took a brief statement from Max Webster as he sat in the back of their black-and-white. They took his business card, his cellphone number, told him they'd contact him if they needed any further information. Max walked back to his own car and called the office. He told his area manager what had happened, asked if he couldn't blow out the appointments and take the day off. The manager, a compassionate and understanding man, said he would take care of the appointments himself. Max Webster drove home. He would read about his discovery in the newspapers, see his own name in typeface, would tell the story a further twenty-three times at assorted get-togethers, barbecues, garden parties and sundry business appointments. He would speak to a Detective something-or-other Lucas only once, a relatively brief telephone conversation, but as far as dead teenage girls were concerned he had played his part, played it like a pro, and he was off the hook. Never again did he drink two cups of coffee in the morning, and never again did he pull over to urinate at the side of the highway.

Word got out to Karen Langley at the *City Herald* within the hour. One reporter was dispatched to find Max Webster, a second to survey the site of the discovery. The first hack was met with a frosty reception by Max's wife, Harriet. She told him in no uncertain terms that Max was not available for comment. The reporter was not blessed with the same defense-attorney-style charm as Karen Langley, and thus went away empty-handed. The other reporter stood at the top of the incline looking down toward the clump of trees, black and yellow-striped crime scene tape encircling the trunks and sectioning off the area, and he wondered what the hell he was supposed to do next. He took a couple of photographs, but there were uniforms down there and they wouldn't let him approach.

Karen Langley called the coroner's office, sweet-talked Gerrard and got the scoop on the dead girls.

She called John Costello. He was quiet for some time.

'John?' she prompted.

'The caliber. They were shot, right? I need to know what caliber.'

'God knows, I didn't ask. Why?'

Again, Costello was quiet for some time. Karen Langley could hear him breathing through the earpiece.

'Can you find out, Karen? The caliber of gun they were shot with? Can you find out if it was a .25?'

'I don't know, John . . . I'll call Gerrard back.'

'Yes, if you could do that. That would be good.'

Karen hung up, frowning. Costello was a strange and remarkable man, no doubt about it. Extraordinarily bright, an exceptional memory, an encyclopedia of facts, most of them dark and disturbing. She knew of his history, had read the 'Hammer of God' articles, and though she had asked him about it one time, he said little and made it obvious he didn't wish to discuss it further. Regardless, twenty-some years in the newspaper business and she'd never had a researcher like John Costello. She didn't want to lose him, so she hadn't pushed the point.

She called Hal Gerrard. He was unavailable but she got Ivens.

'I can't tell you that, Karen . . . confidential, you know?'

'I need to know if it was a .25, Lewis, that's all.'

Lewis Ivens was silent. He was thinking. And when he spoke there was something in his voice that Langley recognized. 'You want to know if they were shot with a .25 caliber?'

'Yes, a .25.'

Once again Ivens was silent for a few moments.

'If I guessed they were shot with a .25 would I be incorrect?' Langley asked.

Ivens inhaled, exhaled slowly. 'If you *guessed* that they were shot with a .25 I wouldn't have any problem with that,' he replied.

'I appreciate that, Lewis, I really do.'

'Nothing to appreciate,' he said. 'We didn't speak today. I don't know you. We've never met.'

'I'm sorry . . . I guess I got a wrong number,' Langley replied, and hung up.

She picked up the phone again, dialed Costello's extension.

'A .25,' she said matter-of-factly.

'And there were two of them? Teenage girls, right?'

'As far as I know, yes.'

'Okay, okay, okay . . . leave this with me. I might have something for you in a few days.'

'Like what? What we got here?'

'Something— Nothing. I don't know yet. Before I can be sure I have to find another one.'

'Another what, John? Find another what?'

'Leave it with me . . . I'll let you know if it comes to anything. If I tell you now you're just gonna get excited and be a pain in the ass.'

'Fuck you, John Costello—'

'Hey, that's just un-fucking necessary,' he said, and she could hear him laughing as he hung up.

FIVE

A little after one p.m., Monday, June 12th, 2006, the bodies of fifteen-year-old Ashley Nicole Burch and sixteen-year-old Lisa Madigan Briley were formally identified in the County Coroner's Office by Deputy Coroner Hal Gerrard. Lewis Ivens was present, as was Jeff Turner, lead Crime Scene Analyst from the Grant murder case. There was no similarity between the cases – Turner was not present for any reason other than that he knew Ivens personally. That afternoon they were scheduled to attend a seminar given by a Dr Philip Roper from the Scientific Investigations Division, Support Services Bureau, on *Undocumented Origin Bullet Recovery: Lands, Grooves, Riflings, Striations*. They left together at one-twenty, bought coffee at Starbucks, drove west in Ivens' car. Hal Gerrard called Detective Richard Lucas of the Ninth Precinct, he of the brief telephone conversation with Max Webster.

'Got your girls here,' Gerrard told him. 'Reports done, as much as you need right now. Two shots each, point blank, from a .25 caliber . . . Putting the bullets through the system, but you know how these things are, right?'

Lucas asked if someone had been to tell the parents.

'Not a clue . . . your territory, my friend, and you're welcome to it.'

Lucas asked about drugs.

'Alcohol, a good deal of it. They'd have been walking sideways I think, but no drugs.'

They said their farewells, and the call ended.

Lucas called up one of the female officers from the duty roster, sent her over to collect the reports and the victims' addresses, waited for her to return and then told her to accompany him. The addresses were on the same block of the Chelsea Houses off Ninth Avenue at Chelsea Park.

As was always the case with such daytime visits, the fathers were working and it was left to the mothers to receive the bad news and answer the questions. Ashley Burch had told her folks that she was staying over with Lisa Briley; Lisa Briley had informed her parents that she'd be sleeping at Ashley's. It was an old trick, but the old ones were the best ones. They had evidently dressed up like hookers, gone to EndZone, drank a skinful, and then . . . well, they'd collided with someone, and that someone proved to be the last person they'd ever see.

Lucas called for another female officer from the Ninth, had one stay with each of the respective mothers until the fathers were contacted and had returned home from work. He made his way over to EndZone, showed them pictures of the girls, went through the routine, leaned on the manager, made a noise about serving under-age girls. It went nowhere. The place had been heaving with people, hit capacity at sixteen hundred. It had been a good night.

Lucas left empty-handed.

Nothing happened for two days.

Eight p.m., evening of Wednesday June 14th, an anonymous caller asked to speak with the officer investigating the death of the two girls found on the previous Monday. Fortunately Lucas was at his desk. He took the call personally.

'I think my lover is a murderer,' the caller told him.

'Who is this?' he asked. 'Who am I speaking to?'

'Just listen,' she said, 'or I'll hang up.'

'I'm listening,' Lucas replied, and motioned for one of his colleagues to hit the *record* button on the control box.

'What I'm trying to do is to ascertain whether or not the individual I know, who happens to be my lover, did in fact do this. He said he did. My name is Betsy.'

'Betsy?' Lucas asked.

'Did I say Betsy? No, my name is Claudia.'

'This is very good of you,' Lucas said. 'We really appreciate your help. Can you tell us the name of your lover?'

'No, I can't do that.'

'Can you tell us anything at all, Claudia?'

'I can tell you he has curly brown hair and blue eyes. His Christian name is John, and he's forty-one years old. I've

65

found a duffel bag in his car full of bloody blankets and paper towels and his clothes.'

'Okay, okay, this is very good . . . can you tell us his name, Claudia?'

'He tells me he fired four shots,' the caller went on, seemingly oblivious to Lucas's question. 'He tells me he fired four shots. Two in one girl's head and virtually blew her head away. One shot in the head and one shot in the chest of the other girl. He used a .25 caliber pistol. Does that jibe with what you've got?'

'Yes, yes it does . . . this is definitely of great assistance to us, Claudia . . . but we really need to know this man's name. If you can give us his name I'm sure it will insure that no-one else is hurt—'

The line went dead.

An hour later Richard Lucas requested a print-out of every applicant for a .25 caliber gun in the last year. He ran a search on every known violent offender aged forty-one with curly brown hair and blue eyes who lived within the New York city limits.

Richard Lucas, with the very best intention in the world, instigated an operation that would consume the better part of three-hundred man hours over the subsequent three days.

All for nothing.

There were no leads that resulted in any forward progress.

The following day, standing by the water cooler on the ground floor of the *New York City Herald* building, John Costello glanced at *The New York Times* squib of June 13th regarding the Burch and Briley killings; the squib he had circled in red and underlined three times.

In his small office on the second floor he cut out the column and pinned it beside that of Mia Grant. He attached a Post-It beneath the column and wrote *June 12 Clark, Bundy, Murray – Sunset Slayer* and again added four question marks.

He stepped away, raised his hand to the back of his head and smoothed down his hair. He counted the words in each article, and then he counted them again.

He could feel the narrow scar beneath the hairline above his neck.

He could feel the quiet urgency of his own frightened heart.

SIX

Of Ashley Burch and Lisa Briley, Ray Irving knew nothing. They were Richard Lucas's case – different precinct, different MO. Irving was pragmatic, methodical, prone to momentary flashes of genius, but these – as he aged – grew fewer and farther between.

Ray Irving was a detective by nature, intensely curious, ever-questioning, but familiar enough with the reality of the world within which he lived to understand that some things would always and forever remain unanswered. Perhaps unanswerable.

Nietzsche said that whoever fought monsters should see to it that in the process he did not himself become a monster. He said that when one looked into the abyss, the abyss would look right back.

Irving had walked the edges of the abyss for some years. His footsteps had been measured, even predictable, and though he had worn a track around the perimeter he nevertheless sensed that the perimeter was growing smaller. He neared the center of something with each new case. He recognized more of the madness with each killing, each instance of unmitigated brutality perpetrated by one human being against another. Sometimes, despite all he had witnessed, he found himself still staggered by the sheer inventiveness applied to the demise and destruction of identity and individual. And he had learned that irrationality could not be rationalized. As with addiction, the power of necessity was greater than any loyalty or agreement. Those who killed in anger were one thing; those who committed murder in the throes of passion were a specific breed. Those motivated by a *desire* to kill did not in fact exist: it was not desire, but compulsion. Compulsion was greater than love, than family, than any promise or vow made to oneself or another. Here were individuals who killed because they *had* to kill. It was not desire, it was obligation.

So much of his life he bore witness to events that opposed the natural order of things. Parents buried their children. People confessed, held out their bloody hands, and then walked free to kill again. Truth did not set men free. Legal technicalities were the route to salvation these days. Such things should never have been, but they were.

Ray Irving believed that he might go to his grave understanding some small measure of what he had seen, but he would never understand all of it. Understanding all of it was just not possible.

A month had passed since the death of Mia Grant. He had never known her, therefore did not miss her. Deborah Wiltshire, however, he did miss, and missed her in a different way than before. She had been dead for seven months, and though there were small reminders of her presence, her personality, left in Irving's apartment – a ceramic hair straightener, a pair of flat-soled shoes with the right toe worn through – he perceived these things with a sense of balance and perspective that had come with time. At first he had been unable to move them because of what they represented; they had remained simply because they were all that was left of her. Now, with more than half a year gone, he saw these objects as constant reminders of the person she had been, the progress he himself had made, the quiet sense of closure they symbolized. Deborah Wiltshire, the unacknowledged love of his life, was gone. The only irony, strangely, was that she had not been murdered. Seemed to Irving – perhaps from some small and narrow strain of darkness he carried within himself, the shadow from the abyss that had gained entry even as he peered down into its depth – that the only fitting way for her to die would have been something such as that. He was a homicide detective, and if whoever or whatever was responsible for the karma of his life had been really thinking with the program, then they would have had the woman murdered. That would have been fitting. That would have been appropriate. But no – no such thing. Her life had been stolen away quietly, silently almost, a progressive deterioration of minutes, each one shorter than the next as she fought with something she couldn't even see. And then she was extinguished. She did not gutter. She blew out. She did not disappear by imperceptible degrees, a watercolor painting that faded with time. She simply vanished.

And Ray Irving was left with an emotion he could neither appreciate nor comprehend. It was neither loneliness nor self-pity. It was emptiness. Emptiness that could not be filled. He remembered something from Hemingway about losing things. If you lost things, whether good or bad, it left an emptiness. If it was a bad thing the emptiness filled up by itself; if it was a good thing you had to find something better or the emptiness would remain forever. Something like that. It made sense to Irving, though he could neither define nor imagine what might be better than Deborah Wiltshire.

The emptiness, if indeed that's what it was, would remain.

He went about his business, he ate at Carnegie's, he peered into the darkness and held a handkerchief to his face. He witnessed the way in which lives were randomly smashed. He asked many questions but received answers to only a few. He closed each day by standing at his apartment window and watching the world fall into silence.

Morning of July 29th the world came to find him. It came in colors, with cheerleaders and bandstands, with decorated floats and brass bands, with Sousa marches and baton twirlers. It came with the face of a clown. The Murray Hill end of East 39th and Third. Had it been east of Second, it would have fallen outside Irving's jurisdiction, but no, the world wanted him to visit with James Wolfe.

James was a good kid who became a troubled young man. Hailed from the lower east side, edge of Vladeck Park. Had aspirations for architecture, design, other such things, but his father was a tough guy, a blue-collar sweat-and-cold-beer kind of guy who had worked on Piers 34 through 42 beneath the shadow of the Manhattan Bridge, air from Wallabout Bay in his lungs for as long as he'd possessed the strength to haul and hammer. Dennis Wolfe was not an educated man, he had no certificates or qualifications. He once carried a man three quarters of a mile to a hospital and saved his life by stanching the blood that was rushing from a stomach wound with a handful of rags wrapped in a plastic bag. 'Figured I should do that,' he told the attending triage nurse. 'Stuff a bunch of rags in there and they're just gonna soak up the blood and let it keep on leaking, right? Wrap it in a plastic bag and it's gonna act like a sealant . . . least that's what I thought.' Dennis Wolfe had guessed right. Acted awkward, embarrassed even, when they held a party for him a week later. Pier chief came down and shook his hand, gave him a little brass plaque with his name on. Dennis had prevented an industrial accident becoming an unlawful death lawsuit. He wrapped that plaque in newspaper and stuck it in the crawl space in the roof above the stairs, same place he put all the odds and ends he didn't have a great deal of use for. Anyone in their right mind would've done the same was what he thought, and that's what he believed. Didn't mention it again.

Dennis Wolfe struggled with his son. Felt sure the kid wasn't a faggot, but he just didn't get the artistic thing. James's mother, Alice, was a good woman, perhaps a little simple, but pragmatic and methodical. There was nothing artistic there. James had taken her to the Whitney Museum of American Art a couple of years before. She'd commented on the tea they'd been served in the small cafeteria outside. The tea was all she noticed, pretty much all she remembered. James had two sisters, both married, both young mothers, both tied in with a world that Dennis understood as their husbands worked on the Piers. There was a future in predictability. There was substance in tradition, repetition, doing what was known, not new things untried, untested. Architecture? Interior design? Such things had a place, for sure, but not in the Wolfe family. The Wolfes were workers, not dreamers. The Wolfes broke a sweat while the uptowners graced coffee bars and talked shit.

Dennis Wolfe came out of his break early to take a call in the Pier foreman's office. Foreman had a mallet for a head, blunt features, blunter character. The call was brief and to the point. Dennis Wolfe showed no emotion, merely explained to the chief that there was a family matter he had to attend to. He'd make up the time – tomorrow, maybe the next day.

Three blocks from the car park Dennis Wolfe slowed for the lights, and then it kind of hit him: He wouldn't have to worry whether his son was a faggot anymore, because his son was dead.

By the time Ray Irving reached the back of Wang Hi Lee Carnival & Firework Emporium the scene had been taped and cordoned. Duty uniforms had erected sawhorses and strung black-and-yellow around the building, giving a twenty-five foot perimeter within which to work on all sides. Lead CSA from the Mia Grant killing, Jeff Turner, was already there, and the expression on his face when he saw Irving made the detective uncomfortable.

'Indications he was strangled first, more than likely with a rope,' Turner said. 'That's my initial on COD. Positive ID hasn't been done, but the kid had a wallet with a college pass inside. If it's genuine then his name is James Wolfe.'

'Strangled first?' Irving asked. 'And second?'

'Well, whoever did this pretty much broke his body in half.'

'Broke his body in half? What the hell does that mean?' Irving asked as they ducked beneath the crime scene tape and headed toward the rear of the building. Everywhere hung the smell of sulfur and paint.

'Forced his body into a square trap in the floor, some kind of drain outlet or something. Three by one and a half feet, give or take, and it looks like rigor had already set in. If it had—' Turner shook his head. 'If he was rigored then someone would have had to jump up and down on his stomach until the poor bastard folded in half. Otherwise there would have been no way to get him in there.'

Up ahead a uniform slid back the vast wooden warehouse door to permit entry.

'And he got his face painted,' Turner said.

Irving slowed up and stopped. 'What?'

'His face . . . the kid got his face painted and someone put a red wig on him . . .'

'You're kidding me.'

Turner took a deep breath and looked ahead. 'Come on. I'll show you.'

SEVEN

The picture of James Wolfe, his face painted like Pennywise the Clown, his body awkwardly crammed into a hole in the concrete floor of the Wang Hi Lee Carnival & Firework Emporium, appeared on the front page of the *New York Daily News*. All it had taken was a police officer with alimony, car payments, an ex-wife or two, and a camera phone.

Shapes in the background – grotesque carousel horses, a jack-in-the-box eighteen feet high, the head of a Chinese dragon – and red banner headlines were paraded on the newsstands and carried on the subway and talked about over water coolers and backyard fences. The Clown Killer. Give it a name; always had to give it a name, because a thing wasn't a thing until it had a name.

Morning of Monday, July 31st, Ray Irving stood quietly in the corridor opposite the door of his office. The corridor had a window overlooking the street; his office did not. Sufficient longevity to warrant a room to himself, insufficient to warrant daylight. He had pot plants – a fern of some description, a peace lily. He had a percolator, which filled the room with the bitter scent of dark Italian coffee when the mood took him. He had a desk, a phone, a filing cabinet, a chair with a sprung back to ease the tension he carried in his spine, and on the wall a cork board. Upon this were pinned mementoes of things; alongside crime scene pictures, scraps of paper upon which were scrawled barely legible phone numbers, was a recipe for almond muffins, a monochrome snapshot of himself and Deborah Wiltshire when he was younger and she was alive. His office was not dissimilar to his apartment. His office was inconspicuous, unadorned, impersonal. Had it been suggested to Irving that he get a life, perhaps he would have smiled and said *A life? This* is *my life.*

Mia Grant and James Wolfe were the unfortunates, among

so many unfortunates. The U.S. was home to eighteen thousand murders a year, and New York was among the front runners as to a locale of choice. In essence New York was a crime scene, perhaps better now than in the eighties, but nevertheless from his perspective it appeared that the quiet times – the times *between* the killings – were distant and seemingly disconnected. His life moved swiftly and smoothly from one primary to another.

The Mia Grant secondary was a small plot of earth beneath an overhang of trees back of a fence off a busy sidewalk; the primary was still unknown. The Wolfe primary was still being analyzed, but in a couple of days it would be nothing more than a hole in the floor in back of some warehouse owned by a Chinese firework company. That was all that was left. The body would be buried, cremated, whatever the family wished, and then the rest of the world would forget. The family would *try* to forget, feel guilty for attempting such a thing.

Irving sighed. He closed his eyes for a moment, and then turned when he heard the phone ringing in his office.

'Irving.'

'Ray? Got a reporter from the *City Herald*.'

Irving sat down. 'Go for it,' he said resignedly.

'Detective Irving?'

'Speaking.'

'Hi there . . . thanks for speaking to me. My name's Karen Langley, calling from the *New York City Herald*. Had a couple of questions I thought you might be able to answer.'

'Shoot.'

'Mia Grant.'

'What about her?'

'Wondered if there had been anything from the coroner on the weapon used.'

'We have chosen not to release that information,' Irving said.

'So you do know what weapon was used?'

'Of course we know what weapon was used, Ms Langley.'

'But you're not saying?'

'I just said that.'

Karen Langley paused. 'The teenage girls isn't your case, right?'

'Teenage girls?' Irving asked.

'The two girls found in the East River Park, fifteen and sixteen years old. Gunshot victims. I have their names here—'

'I don't have any teenage gunshot victims,' Irving interjected. 'Not in the last couple of weeks. When was this?'

'No, you're right,' Langley said, 'it's Detective Lucas at the Ninth.'

'So you'll have to speak to him about that.'

'Okay, one other thing . . . this clown killing thing—'

'I hate that you do this, you know?' Irving said.

'What?'

'Give these things a name, for God's sake.'

'Not guilty, Detective . . . think you'll find that that was someone else's unbridled creativity.'

'Yeah, okay, but it's bad enough having to deal with this stuff without the free press that these animals get. Jesus, the vic was nothing more than a kid. What was he? Nineteen years old?'

'I'm sorry, Detective Irving—'

Irving sighed audibly. 'Hell, I don't know what I'm complaining about . . . seen enough of this to last any number of lifetimes. What was your question, Ms Langley?'

'So the victim was found on Saturday, right?'

'Right, Saturday. Two days ago.'

'And can you tell me whether he painted his own face or it was painted by his killer?'

'What?'

'If he painted his own face . . . you know, like he was going to a party or something? Or if his killer painted his face. That's what I wanted to know.'

'I can't tell you that, Ms Langley, not because I don't want to, but because I don't know.'

'Was he dressed as a clown?'

Irving paused.

'Detective?'

'I heard you.'

'So . . . was he dressed as a clown? If he was dressed as a clown then it seems more likely that—'

'I know where you're going with this, Ms Langley.'

Karen Langley was silent. She waited patiently for Irving's response.

'Why?' Irving eventually asked.

'Why? Because I have an interest in whether or not—'

'An interest?' Irving echoed. 'You have something on this one?'

'Something? No, I don't have something on this one in particular—'

'You're asking specific questions about three unrelated cases, Ms Langley.'

Langley was silent.

'Right?' Irving prompted.

'My turn to say nothing,' Langley replied.

'You have them connected?' Irving asked.

'They could be,' Langley said.

'Blunt force trauma, gunshot victims, and a strangulation . . . unrelated victims, three different locations, two different precincts. The MOs—'

'We extrapolate, Detective Irving, just as you do.'

'Don't start something with this, Ms Langley.'

'Start something?'

'Something in the newspapers, something that gets people all worried that there's more going on here than there actually is.'

'Four teenage murders in seven weeks?'

Irving leaned back in his chair and closed his eyes. 'Ms Langley, seriously—'

'I just wanted an answer to a couple of questions, Detective, that was all. We make something out of it, or we don't. Maybe if you answered the questions it would dispel whatever ideas we—'

'That's bullshit, Ms Langley, and you know it. You can't honestly believe that I'm going to fall for that.'

'We do what we do, Detective, and we do it whichever way we can. Thank you for your time.'

'You're not going to give me any leeway on this, are you?' Irving asked.

'Leeway?'

'You're gonna cook up whatever story you can think of, and then run it without liaising with us.'

'When did the press ever liaise with the police department on such things?' Langley asked, a smile in her voice. 'More pertinently, when did the police department ever liaise with us?'

'Isn't that half the problem?' Irving asked.

'I'll take that as rhetoric. I asked, you answered, or didn't answer, and that's the end of it.'

'I s'pose it is.'

'You have a good day, Detective Irving.'

'You too, Ms Langley . . . oh, one moment.'

'Yes, Detective?'

'You were a trainee reporter from which paper?'

'Very funny, Officer Irving, very funny.'

The line went dead and Irving hung up.

He opened the Wolfe file on his desk and stared once more at the brutally garish painted face of the teenage clown, the startling red wig, his body jammed into a hole in the ground, his tongue swollen and protruding, the starkly defined ligature marks on his throat.

Kind of a life is this? he asked himself for the thousandth time, and then reminded himself that it had in fact been his choice.

EIGHT

As far as the attending crime scene analysts and the city coroner could determine, the three teenage victims discovered in the early hours of Monday, August 7th, had been dead for less than eight or ten hours. At first the killings seemed unrelated, for there were two crime scenes, but the simple matter of cellphones clarified the connection. Beneath an overhang of the Queensboro Bridge, the naked and battered body of a teenage girl was found. Nearby, still switched on and displaying a screensaver image of a young man, was her cellphone. The attendant CSA called up the last number dialed, pressed the little green phone symbol, and was surprised when it was answered by a voice he recognized. The CSA at the second crime scene – the discovery of two teenage boys shot and left in the trunk of a car – answered the cellphone found in one of the boys' jackets. They later learned that his screensaver was an image of the murdered girl. Perhaps the last thing each of them had seen was a digital image of the other. The primaries were thirty-seven blocks apart – two different jurisdictions, two different precincts – but the presence of identical tire tracks at both locations made them one murder case.

NYPD Homicide Detective Gary Lavelle, Fifth Precinct, was assigned to the dead girl. ID on her person identified her as seventeen-year-old Caroline Parselle. From cursory examination it appeared she had not been sexually assaulted, but she had been strangled with something.

'Not a rope,' the CSA told Lavelle. 'More like a bar, you know? Like whoever this was used a bar, a length of something, and forced her down against the ground with this across her throat until she choked.' He walked the detective over to where the girl's body still lay spread-eagled in the dirt. 'See,' he said, pointing to the fury of marks around her

78

feet, her hands, her elbows. 'She fought against it, tore at the ground . . . she put up a struggle but someone just leaned down on her throat with something. It was someone a hell of a lot stronger than her, and that was that.'

The other primary was a great deal more disturbing. Overseen by a detective from the Third Precinct, the dark grey Ford, its trunk unlocked, was cordoned off and a wide perimeter established. The car had been noticed earlier that morning, parked on the corner of East 23rd and Second, just across the Gramercy jurisdictional line. A curator for the New York Police Museum, an ex-sergeant from the Eleventh Precinct, had approached the car simply because it was parked in a no-park zone. The fact that the trunk was visibly ajar, and a bullet hole evidently punched out through the upper edge of the rear wing, gave him cause for suspicion.

Within an hour the boys had been identified and cause of death established. Seventeen-year-old Luke Bradford had died from two gunshots to the head. One of those bullets had first passed through his arm as if he'd raised it in self-defense. The second victim – Caroline Parselle's eighteen-year-old boyfriend, Stephen Vogel – had been shot four times in the head, one of those shots a cranium through-and-through, its exit path travelling out of rear wing of the car. In all, six shots had been fired. The boys had been murdered in the trunk of the car, and the car had been left unlocked and visible.

Simply stated, it was as if the killer had wished it to be found as soon as possible.

Ray Irving ate breakfast at Carnegie's that Monday morning. He ordered pancake-style bologna omelette, drank two cups of coffee. Traffic was heavier than usual, and by the time he arrived at the Fourth it was past nine-thirty. There was a message on his desk. *Go see Farraday soon as you arrive.*

Irving and Captain Bill Farraday maintained a dispassionate working relationship. Farraday had been at the Fourth Precinct for sixteen years, and the burden of those years followed him like a second shadow, forever clouding his eyes with an ever-present sense that something somewhere was going wrong.

'Ray,' he said matter-of-factly as Irving entered the room.

'Captain.'

Irving sat down. He scanned the month since they'd spoken, tried to count the number of incomplete and unresolved cases. There had to be fifteen, perhaps more.

'Tell me about Mia Grant,' Farraday said. He perched on the window ledge, his shoulders against the glass.

'Specifically?'

Farraday shrugged. 'Tell me anything you've got.'

Irving turned down the corners of his mouth. 'Very little. Teenager found by a couple of kids at the edge of Bryant Park back of the library. Head staved in and her body wrapped in black plastic. Father's a lawyer.'

'Apparently she was responding to a want-ad?'

'Apparently, yes. At least that's what she told her folks.'

Farraday nodded slowly. 'I didn't read the file, you know,' he said. His voice was measured and calm.

Irving frowned.

'Know how I know about the want-ad?'

Irving shook his head.

'I read an article that may or may not wind up in the *City Herald*.'

Irving opened his mouth to speak, but Farraday stayed him, said, 'You know a guy called Richard Lucas at the Ninth?'

After a moment's thought Irving shook his head. 'Can't say I do . . .' And then he paused. He thought of the call from the reporter. What was her name? Langdon? Langford?

'He got a case in the second week of June. Couple of teenage girls found about two hundred yards from Roosevelt Drive. Gunshot vics.'

Irving shifted uncomfortably in his chair. He too felt that something somewhere was going wrong.

'And you got something on Saturday, didn't you?' Farraday asked. 'Some kid in a warehouse. Had his face painted, right?'

Irving nodded.

'Do you read the *City Herald*?'

'No.'

'I do,' Farraday replied, 'and so does the Chief of Police. He and the editor are buddies it seems, and the Chief got a heads up on this thing . . .' He leaned forward, lifted some papers from his side of the desk and tossed them to Irving.

The heading shouted at him:

Washington Copycat Mimics Past Murders

The byline was Karen Langley.

Irving looked up at Farraday.

Farraday raised his eyebrow. 'You can read, right?'

Irving looked back at the pages. Before he even started he felt the hairs rise on the back of his neck.

'This is the rough draft of a proposed feature,' Farraday said. 'Right now the *Herald*'s editor is holding off on it, but he's only doing that because he owes the Chief a favor.'

Irving started to read:

On Tuesday, May 1st, 1973, a want-ad was placed in the Seattle Times regarding a job at a local gas station. The ad was replied to by a 15-year-old girl named Kathy Sue Miller. She was helping her boyfriend find work. The man who answered the phone when Kathy Sue called told her he was looking for girls, and Kathy Sue agreed to meet him after school. The man arranged to pick her up outside the Sears Building, then drive her over to the gas station to fill out the application forms. Kathy's mother insisted that her daughter not go to the meeting with the prospective employer. Kathy promised she would not. She later disobeyed her mother, and was never seen alive again.

On June 3rd, two 16-year-old boys found Kathy Sue Miller's body in Tulalip Reservation. The body was wrapped in black plastic and was so badly decomposed it was at first difficult to ascertain the gender of the victim. Identification was made with dental records, and the autopsy determined that she had died as a result of severe blunt force trauma to the head.

Many years later the killer, a man called Harvey Louis Carignan, ultimately responsible for as many as fifty homicides, was asked a simple question: If you could be any animal what would you be? His answer: A human being.

Thirty-three years later, again on June 3rd, two school-children found the plastic-wrapped body of a 15-year-old girl called Mia Grant amongst the trees at the edge of Bryant Park. She had died as a result of severe blunt force trauma to the head. There is a strong possibility that she was responding to a Murray Hill want-ad for part-time domestic work in the local free newspaper, colloquially referred to as the freep.

Irving looked up. 'This is true?'

Farraday shook his head. 'Who the fuck knows? I hope to hell not. Read the whole thing.'

On Thursday, June 12th, 1980, the naked bodies of two attractive teenagers were found on an incline off of the Ventura Freeway in Hollywood. Their names were Cynthia Chandler and Gina Marano. Cynthia had been shot twice with a .25 caliber weapon, the first bullet entering the back of her head and lodging in her brain, the second penetrating her lung and causing her heart to burst. Gina Marano had been shot twice also, one round entering her head behind her left ear and exiting near her right eye-brow, the second through the back of her head. Two days later a woman called the LAPD Northeast Division at Van Nuys. She told the detective who answered the phone that she thought her lover might be a murderer. 'What I'm trying to do,' she said, 'is to ascertain whether or not the individual I know, who happens to be my lover, did in fact do this. He said he did. My name is Betsy.' Before the call ended she changed her name to Claudia, and added, 'He has curly brown hair and blue eyes. His Christian name is John, and he's 41 years old. I've found a duffel bag in his car, full of bloody blankets, paper towels, and his clothes.'

To date the full details of the killing spree perpetrated by person or persons known as the Sunset Slayers are not fully clear. Three people were involved – Douglas Clark, Carol Bundy and John 'Jack' Murray. They killed Los Angeles prostitutes, at least five of them. Carol Bundy and Jack Murray were lovers. She loved him so much that on Sunday, August 3rd, 1980, she shot him twice in the back of the head, repeatedly stabbed him with a heavy boning knife, and then decapitated him. For a while she drove around with Jack Murray's head in the passenger seat of her car. Carol Bundy ultimately went to prison for life, Douglas Clark to Death Row at San Quentin.

And now, twenty-six years later, on Monday, June 12th, the bodies of 15-year-old Ashley Nicole Burch and 16-year-old Lisa Madigan Briley were discovered by a travelling sales representative called Max Webster.

Irving was shaking his head. 'This can't be right,' he said. 'If this is true then—'

'You've read the entire thing, right through to James Wolfe?'

Irving turned back to the paper, a sense of disorienting unease growing ever more profound and unsettling.

In the locale of the emergency exit off Franklin D. Roosevelt drive, in a bank of trees in the East River Park, the two bodies were found a little after nine in the morning. Both girls had been shot with a .25 caliber weapon, two bullets each. The pattern of wounds was precisely that of the June 1980 Chandler/Marano killings.

It has often been stated that once is circumstance, twice coincidence, and yet a third time indicates conspiracy.

Such must be considered in light of the most recent case.

John Wayne Gacy, one of America's more infamous serial killers, was responsible for the murder of a 17-year-old teenager called John Butkovich in Chicago. Butkovich maintained and raced his '68 Dodge, an expensive hobby which he supported by doing remodeling work for Gacy's firm, PDM Contractors. On Tuesday, July 29th, 1975, Butkovich, believing that Gacy had withheld some of his pay, went to Gacy's house. Employer and employee argued bitterly. The argument did not resolve, but later Gacy called Butkovich over to the house. Apparently, he apologized to Butkovich, agreed there had been a mis-understanding, and after offering the teenager a drink he killed him. Gacy wrapped the body in tarpaulin and dragged it into the garage. There it stayed until the smell became an inconvenience, so Gacy, unable to easily move the body to another location, dug a drainage hole approximately three feet by one and a half feet in his garage floor. Due to rigor mortis Gacy had to jump up and down on Butkovich's body numerous times. When Butkovich's body was finally recovered the coroner determined that he had been strangled to death with a rope.

On July 29th, just eight days ago, the body of 19-year-old James Wolfe was found in a three-by-one-a-half-foot hole in the concrete floor of the Wang Hi Lee Carnival & Firework Emporium on East 39th Street. He had been strangled to death with a rope.

The only additional, and perhaps most disturbing as-pect to this case, was the fact that James Wolfe had been dressed as a clown. His face had been painted, and on his head he wore a bright red wig. The attire in which he was found is significant. John Wayne Gacy was a dedi-cated public figure, apparently philanthropic, an organizer of the Polish Constitution Day Parade, an event where he was photographed shaking hands with Rosalynn Carter, then-First Lady. Gacy raised money for retirement homes; he was Secretary-Treasurer of the Norwood Park Town-ship Lighting District, and finally part of the 'Jolly Joker's Club' – that band of individuals, too old to be Jaycees themselves, yet still allied to the River Grove Moose

Lodge. It was in his capacity as a Jolly Joker that he dressed as 'Pogo the Clown' to entertain children at parties and in hospitals. It was Gacy, finally on Death Row, who was quoted as saying: *There ain't nothin' more scary than a clown after dark.*

Three individual murder cases, a total of four victims, each of them precise in manner of death, precise also as to date. Each of them almost identical in method and manner to earlier killings perpetrated by people who have since been executed, or are still held within the confines of the Federal penitentiary system. There are facts unknown at this time. In the case of Mia Grant, did her killer use a hammer to inflict the fatal wounds to her head as Harvey Carignan did in the original Kathy Sue Miller case? Only the County Coroner and those intimate with the specific details of that case would know such a thing. And after the gun killings of the two teenagers found by Max Webster off the East River, did an anonymous female call the police and leave a message identical to that left after the deaths of Cynthia Chandler and Gina Marano in June of 1980? If so, then who? And, more importantly, why?

These questions remain unanswered, as does the matter of the killer or killers' identity. Is this a case of the present echoing the past? Does New York have a serial killer that chooses to murder his teenage victims in a very particular and individual manner, or is this a rare and extraordinary case of remarkable coincidence? The latter, given the facts, seems most unlikely, and thus we are faced with the inevitable conclusion that one or more perpetrators are still at large.

Harvey Louis Carignan is now seventy-nine years old, secured within the confines of the Minnesota Correctional Facility in Stillwater, Minnesota. John Murray is dead, Carol Bundy is serving two life sentences, and Douglas Clark awaits his appointment with the executioner in San

Quentin. John Wayne Gacy made his appointment and was executed by lethal injection on the 10th of May, 1994 in Stateville Penitentiary, Crest Hill, Illinois.

The question thus remains: Is New York playing host to a serial killer who is mimicking past murders? Representatives of the Fourth, Ninth and Fifth Precincts remain unavailable for comment, as does the public relations department of the police, the Chief of Police and the Mayor's office.

Irving leaned forward and put the pages on the edge of Farraday's desk. His heart was running ahead of itself, his palms were sweating. This wasn't the rush that came with new evidence on a stale case; this wasn't the sense of urgency when a stake out was paying off. This was something altogether more disturbing. Ray Irving felt as if something had crawled beneath his skin and settled for the duration.

Farraday smiled knowingly. 'You wanna know something really fucking scary?'

'Scarier than this?'

Farraday pushed himself away from where he'd been perching on the window sill and sat at his desk. 'I called Detective Richard Lucas at the Ninth Precinct, and two days after those girls were discovered they got an anonymous call. Caller was a woman, and she said the exact same thing as this woman back in 1980. They have it on tape and I read them what was in the *Herald*. They compared it . . . it was the same, exactly the fucking same.'

'And they know who made the call?' Irving asked.

'God knows,' Farraday replied. 'An accomplice? Someone he paid to make the call for him? I have no idea.'

Irving looked up at Farraday. 'This reporter called me,' he said. 'This reporter. Karen Langley.'

'You're kidding!'

'She called me a week ago. Asked me about the warehouse kid, whether he was dressed as a clown or not.'

Farraday didn't speak.

'It wasn't any different from any other press call—'

Farraday raised his hand. 'Problem we have is that

86

someone else, a fucking reporter for God's sake, has found a connection between three apparently unrelated crime scenes, and if this is what she says it is—'

'Then we're in trouble.'

'Go see her, Ray. Find out what the fuck is going on, eh? Find out if she has a line into the PD that isn't healthy. Find out how the goddamn hell she knows shit that we don't.'

Irving rose from his chair.

Farraday leaned forward. 'So far this morning I've had nine calls. The Mayor's office, the Chief, three newspapers, someone from the FBI, the Chief again, some woman from the Committee for Mayoral Re-election, and someone from the CBS press office. And that's just as a result of word of mouth. God knows what the fuck would happen if that actually wound up in the paper.'

'What are we doing with it?' Irving asked.

'Undecided. First we put a cap on this newspaper thing. We put a stop to whatever incendiary bomb of speculation they're building over there. I got a meeting with the Chief in a couple of hours. Me, the other captains, this guy Lucas from the Ninth, a few others. They asked for you but I told them no.'

Irving raised his eyes questioningly.

'You have more years than most. They wanna put someone in the front-line on this then it's more than likely gonna be you. That's what I don't want. I can't have this place being the focus of some bullshit media circus right now.'

Farraday stood up, put his hands in his pockets. His eyes were resigned to the inevitability of bad news and, once it was delivered, the certainty that more would be on the way. 'Go speak to the hack. Tell her how this shit works. Tell her to calm the fuck down and let us do our job, okay?'

'On my way,' Irving said.

He closed the door silently behind him and made his way down the corridor to the stairs.

NINE

Irving took a right on Ninth past the Port Authority Terminal, found the offices of the *New York City Herald* on the corner of 31st and Ninth, across from the General Post Office. The sky was overcast, like tarnished silver. He was aware of the smell of the city, the air thick, as if breathing would take work. Parked his car back of the *Herald* building and walked around to the front desk. Showed his ID, waited patiently, was told that Karen Langley would be another hour. Irving was polite, said he'd go get a cup of coffee and return at eleven. The girl behind the desk smiled back. She was pretty, hair cut short in back, long at the sides. It framed her face like a picture. Made him think of Deborah Wiltshire, not the way she looked but the feeling of having someone there. Remembered the days after her death, those moments he'd paused in his kitchen, how he'd opened a cupboard and stopped dead in his tracks, or leaned forward and touched his forehead to the uppermost edge of the fridge. Felt the tight, breathless vibration of the motor through his skin, like a single exhalation with no respite. How it had clicked off suddenly, startled him; how he was aware of tears in his eyes. All because there was a jar of mustard on the shelf. He disliked mustard. He had bought it for her, the odd occasion she was over and made sandwiches. Something like that. A little thing which became a big thing.

He drank his extra shot half-and-half in a corner booth with a narrow view of a synagogue in the distance. He wondered if a man such as himself would find solace in religion. He wondered if the questions he carried would ever be answered, and if answered would he then let them go. Or had the weight of those questions become familiar, comfortable, necessary?

At four minutes past eleven he stood ahead of the pretty girl with the beautiful hair.

'She's back,' the girl said.

'You have beautiful hair,' Irving replied.

The girl smiled widely, seemed very pleased. 'Thank you. I wasn't sure if . . . well, if it wasn't a bit severe . . . you know?'

Irving shook his head. 'You look like a movie star.'

For a moment she seemed unable to speak, and then she lifted the receiver and called Karen Langley.

Words were shared, the receiver returned to its cradle, and the girl indicated the elevator. 'Go on up,' she said. 'Third floor. Karen will be there for you.'

Irving nodded, started walking.

'You take care now,' the girl called after him.

'You too,' he replied.

Karen Langley was an attractive woman, but when she opened her mouth she said, 'You've come to tell me to shut the fuck up, haven't you?' and there was an edge to her tone which made Irving uncomfortable.

He smiled, tried to laugh off the severity of her question, but there seemed to be little humor in the woman's eyes or her voice.

She showed him into an office to the right of the elevator. There was little personality on display. Nothing decorative, no family photos on the desk or the shelves.

Karen Langley walked around the desk and sat down. She didn't invite Irving to sit, but he did so regardless.

'I'm busy,' she said.

'Aren't we all?' he replied.

Karen Langley smiled – a little forced, but it gave away something of the person behind the emotional stab-jacket she was sporting. She was late thirties, maybe early forties. Color of her eye-whites said she drank a little too much. Skin was clear, didn't have the worn-out taint and crease of the heavy smoker. Fingernails were cut short but manicured. No polish. Plain dark skirt, white open-necked blouse, a single silver chain around her neck. No rings, no ear rings, hair shoulder length, mostly straight with a slight wave in the ends. She looked businesslike because she wanted to look that way. To Irving she seemed lonely, the sort of woman who filled up all the empty spaces with work that wasn't required.

'I'm Detective Ray Irving,' he said.

'I know who you are.'

'I was on the Mia Grant case—'

'Was?' Langley frowned. 'It's closed already. I thought you hadn't got anyone for that.'

Irving nodded. 'I *am* on the Mia Grant case.'

'And James Wolfe, right? And the Ninth has Richard Lucas on the Burch and Briley killings from June twelfth, and now we have Gary Lavelle from the Fifth and Patrick Hayes from the Third on the triple from yesterday.'

Irving said nothing.

Karen Langley smiled knowingly. 'I told you that to piss you off,' she said. 'You didn't know about the triple from yesterday, did you?'

Again he said nothing. He was being cornered and he didn't like it.

'Three kids. Two boys shot in the trunk of a car, girlfriend of one of them found naked and strangled a mile or two away.'

'And you know this because?'

'Because we have scanners. Because we have people we talk to. Because we have anonymous tip-offs, most of it bullshit, but sometimes there's gold in them thar hills.'

Irving smiled. 'Are you really as tough as you sound?'

Langley laughed. 'I'm putting on the kitten-soft front just for you, Detective. Normally I'm a bitch.'

'And the significance of the triple yesterday?'

'You ever hear of a guy called Kenneth McDuff?'

'Can't say I have.'

'Executed November 1998. Did a triple back in August '66—'

'The sixth, right?'

'Nail on the head. August sixth, triple homicide. Two kids found in the trunk of a car. A girl found about a mile away who'd been strangled with a broom handle. Had an accomplice, a halfwit called Roy Green. McDuff was an animal. No soul. Know what he told Green?'

Irving shook his head.

'Killing a woman's like killing a chicken. They both squawk.'

'Sounds like a real star.'

Langley reached over to the right of her desk and retrieved a manila file. She opened it, leafed through a few pages, and handed one of them to Irving.

'That's a copy of some of Green's statement after he was arrested.'

Irving glanced over it, looked up at Langley.

'Go ahead,' she said. 'Read the thing.'

```
Monday 8 August 1966
Statement from Roy Dale Green, accomplice to
Kenneth Allen McDuff, given to Detective Grady
Hight, Milam County Sheriff's Department,
Texas.


Murder of Robert Brand (18), Mark Dunman (16)
and Ellen Louise Sullivan (16) on Saturday
August 6th 1966.


We rode around the baseball park and wound up
on a gravel road. He [McDuff] saw a car parked
there, and we stopped about 150 yards in front
of it. He got his gun and told me to get out. I
thought it was all a joke. I just didn't
believe what he said was going to happen. I
went halfway to the car with him, and he went
on. He told the kids in the car to get out or he
would shoot them. I went on up there and he had
put them in the trunk of their car. He drove his
car back to their car, and he told me to get in
his car and follow him. I did, and we drove for
a while across the highway we had come in on,
and he pulled into a field. I followed, and he
said that the field wouldn't do, so we backed up
and went to another field. He got out and he told
```

91

the girl to get out. He told me to put her in the trunk of his car. I opened the trunk and she climbed in. It was then that he said we couldn't leave any witnesses, or something like that. He said 'I'm gonna have to knock 'em off,' or something like that.

I got really scared. I still thought he was joking, but I wasn't sure. They were on their knees, begging him not to shoot them. They said, 'We're not going to tell anybody.' I turned toward him and he stuck the gun into the trunk of where the boys were and started shooting. I saw the fire come out of the gun on the first shot, and I covered my ears and looked away. He shot six times. He shot one twice in the head, and he shot the other boy four times in the head. A bullet went through a boy's arm as he tried to stop the fire. He [McDuff] tried to close the trunk, but it wouldn't close. He then told me to back up his car. By that time I was almost dying of fright, and I did what he said. He got in the boy's car and backed it into a fence, and he got out and told me to help him wipe off the fingerprints. I wasn't going to argue with him. I was expecting to be next so I helped him.

We wiped out the tire tracks and got into his car and drove off another mile and turned off on another road and he stopped, and he got the girl out of the trunk, and put her in the back seat. He told me to get out of the car, and I waited until he told her to get undressed. He took off his clothes and then he screwed her. He asked me if I wanted to do it, and I told him no. He asked me why not, and I told him I just didn't want to. He leaned over, and I didn't see the gun but I thought he would shoot me if I didn't, so I pulled my pants and shirt off and got in the back seat and screwed the girl. She didn't struggle or anything, and if she ever said anything I didn't hear her. All the time I was on top of the girl I kept my eye on him. After that he screwed her again.

He told the girl to get out of the car. He made her sit down on the gravel road, and he took about a three-foot piece of broomstick from his car and forced her head back with it until it was on the ground. He started choking her with the piece of broomstick. He mashed down hard, and she started waving her arms and kicking her legs. He told me to grab her legs and I didn't want to, and he said 'It's gotta be done,' and I grabbed her legs, and held them for a second or so, and then let them go. He said 'Do it again,' and I did, and this time was when she stopped struggling. He had me grab her hands and he grabbed her feet and we heaved her over a fence. We crossed the fence ourselves, then he dragged her a short ways and then he choked her some more. We put her in some kind of bushes there.

Irving looked up from the page.

'Enough?' Langley asked.

He nodded.

'I can pretty much guarantee that the MO on yesterday's crime scene report is gonna read the same as that,' she said.

'Two boys, one girl you say?'

Langley nodded. 'Two boys found shot dead in the trunk of

a car, a naked girl found about a mile away who'd been choked to death with something.'

'So we have a copycat.'

'A copycat who does it on the anniversary of the original killing. And copying not just one killer, but several. Right now he's done Carignan, colloquially known as 'Harv the Hammer', Murray the Sunset Slayer, John Gacy, and now Kenneth McDuff. Seven victims, all teenagers, all within two months.'

'We're gonna ask you not to run your story.'

'I know you are,' Langley replied.

'You're gonna tell me that the public have a right to know, freedom of the press, all that shit.'

Langley shook her head and smiled.

She looked so much better when she smiled, Irving thought.

'No, I'm not gonna quote that stuff. It's irrelevant whether the public has a right to know, and as far as freedom of the press is concerned . . . well, you and I are both cynical and world-weary enough to know that freedom of the press only counts for so much. No, I'm gonna tell you that you're gonna have to get a court order to shut me up simply because I'm a troublemaker. I've spent far too much of my life doing what I'm told, and I've finally reached a point where I like my job, I want to keep it, and this kind of shit sells papers.'

'I'll get a court order,' Irving said.

'Knock yourself out, Detective.'

Irving liked the woman. Wanted to slap her, but he liked her regardless. He rose from his chair.

'So how long have I got?' she asked.

Irving glanced at the Roy Green statement on the desk. 'You gonna run a story on this triple homicide?'

Langley shrugged. 'You gonna ask me not to?'

'I'm not asking anything of you but simple common sense and an appreciation for what we're trying to do.'

Langley opened her mouth to speak, and then she paused. 'I'm gonna give you that one, Detective Irving.' She stood up, walked around the desk and stood facing him. 'Twenty-four hours,' she said. 'Back here within twenty-four hours with a court order on this and you win, I'll not run it. No court order, it goes in tomorrow evening's edition.'

Irving extended his hand. 'Deal,' he said.

They shook.

'Oh, one other thing,' Langley said. 'We have to give him a name, of course. No-one's anyone until they have a name. Copycat is so passé, don't you think? It's so eighties.'

'I'm not gonna even dignify that with a response,' Irving said.

'He replicates murders on the same day as the original,' Langley said. 'I like it. The Anniversary Murders.'

'You know something, Ms Langley, I really think that you . . .' He paused, shook his head.

'What?'

'Never mind,' Irving replied. He left the room, closed the door firmly behind him.

TEN

'She didn't say anything else about the want-ad?' Farraday asked.

'What else was there to say? They took a shot in the dark and hit something . . . I don't think they *know* that they hit something.'

Farraday leaned forward and picked up the draft article. *'There is a strong possibility that she was responding to a Murray Hill want-ad for part-time domestic work in the local free newspaper, colloquially referred to as the freep.* That's what Karen Langley wrote.' He tossed the newspaper onto the desk. 'And she took a stab at the phone call on the double gun killing, the two girls off the Expressway.'

'She's unreasonable,' Irving said. 'She's not as tough as she sounds, but she's hard enough to argue the case on this. If she knew about the Betsy phone call, she'd be a nightmare to deal with.'

'And now she has this statement she showed you on another triple killing, a killing that wasn't even included in their article . . .' Farraday's voice trailed away.

Silence, then, 'We won't get a court order,' he said matter-of-factly.

'I know,' Irving replied.

'Isn't even worth asking.'

'What about the Fifth and the Ninth?'

'What about them?'

'Well, they have Lucas heading up the investigation on the two girls, and then Lavelle and Hayes are on this triple homicide, the boys in the trunk and the girl that was strangled, right? Get them over here, let's collaborate on this thing. We've got a pattern of some sort. I know it's different MOs, different victims, different jurisdictions, but at least we have something—'

Farraday smiled sardonically. 'And what we have comes courtesy of the fucking *New York City Herald*. Thing I don't get is how they put these things together so damned fast. They take three murder cases, and within a space of days they have them connected to earlier murders going back forty years, and now they've got a couple more with this girl and the boys in the car.'

Irving shifted uncomfortably in his chair.

'Doesn't make sense,' Farraday said. He looked up at Irving as if Irving would say something contributive, but the detective was silent, expressionless.

'I'll speak to the Chief,' Farraday said after some moments. 'See how long his favor is gonna last with the *Herald*'s editor. I'll tell him what we've got, see what he says about you working with these other guys.'

'And now?'

'Go back and see this Langley again. Find out what they've got on the want-ad – where did this thing about the freep *come* from? How did they get that? She's gotta have someone with an inside line somewhere . . . want to see if there's a leak we need to plug.'

Irving nodded, rose from his chair, turned to the door.

'And Ray?'

Irving looked back at Farraday. 'If you get word that someone at this precinct is on their payroll, come tell me first, okay?'

'Now who the hell else would I go tell?' he replied.

An hour later Ray Irving was back in the lobby of the *City Herald*. The girl from the morning was not there, perhaps she'd taken an early lunch, and the guy who'd replaced her was brusque and unhelpful. He merely told Irving to wait until Karen Langley could be found.

By the time word came it was close to one. Langley would be back within a quarter hour. She knew Irving was waiting, was willing to speak with him but had very little time.

'I am very, very busy,' she announced as she flew through the lobby. Her arms were laden with files, back of her a second man with a camera, a shoulder bag, a tripod. Karen Langley stopped in front of Irving. Irving did not get up.

'Later, Karen,' the camera guy said.

'Put all the pictures on back-up,' she said. 'E-mail them down to me and I'll try and go through them later.'

The man nodded and disappeared through a door to the right of the stairwell.

'So what d'you want?' Langley asked.

'Fifteen minutes,' Irving replied.

'I don't have fifteen minutes.'

Ray Irving reached across the chair and picked up his overcoat. He stood slowly, faced her for a moment, and said, 'Another day then.'

He stepped by Karen Langley and started toward the door. Slowed up as he heard her laughing.

'You are so full of shit,' she said.

He turned.

'Come on,' she said. 'But seriously . . . only fifteen minutes, okay?'

Irving shrugged noncommittally.

'What the hell was that?' she asked.

'What?'

'That thing there . . . what you did just then, like it doesn't matter. Jesus, Detective, you've been waiting for me for more than an hour.'

'That's nothing,' Irving replied. 'I've been known to sit still for more than two hours on occasion.'

Langley smiled. A real smile. The second Irving had seen from her. It was the kind of smile that made it obvious she did in fact possess a heart.

He walked toward her. She unloaded the files she was carrying into his arms.

'Carry these, would you?' she said.

'Least I can do, Ms Langley.'

'Karen,' she said. 'We're gonna spend time bullshitting one another we might as well be on first name terms.'

'I'm Ray.'

'I know. You told me already.'

They sat at the same desk, same office. She offered him coffee; he declined.

'The connections,' Irving said. 'I'm intrigued how you

made the connections between now and then. These murders go back as much as forty years.'

She shook her head. 'I can't tell you that.'

'The want-ad,' Irving went on. 'How did you figure that into it? Without the want-ad it was nothing more than a dead girl.'

'She was wrapped in black plastic,' Langley said. 'That was the similarity. All it took then was looking at where she lived, where she was found, drawing a line and seeing which districts were on that route. We go through the freep, we find a want-ad—'

'No way,' Irving said. 'Couldn't be that simple. You found a want-ad?'

Langley nodded.

'To even know to look for a want-ad you would have had to be familiar with the original case back in – when was it?'

'Nineteen seventy-three. Girl called Kathy Sue Miller.'

'So you'd have had to have known something about that case to even go looking for a want-ad. I've seen a good number of bodies left wrapped in plastic trash bags.'

Langley didn't speak.

'You're not saying anything?'

'No, Detective, I'm not.'

'And the girls? Your article was very specific about the fact that they had been shot with a .25 caliber weapon, and that the pattern of wounds was the same as the earlier murders.'

'The Sunset Slayer. Cynthia Chandler and Gina Marano. June 1980.'

'You have someone inside the lines, right?'

Karen Langley laughed. It was neither condescending nor embarrassed, just the simple reaction of someone who wanted to do something other than look back directly at Ray Irving.

'I'll take that as a yes,' Irving said.

'I'm saying nothing.'

'You don't have to.'

'So we're going nowhere, Detective Irving—'

'Ray,' he interjected. 'We're on first name terms, seeing as how we're bullshitting each other, remember?'

'So we're going nowhere, *Ray*. I have a lot to do—'

'How about a trade,' Irving said.

Langley frowned.

'You ask me a question, I tell the truth. Then we turn it round.'

'If you go first,' she said.

'You don't trust me?'

'Hey, I don't even know you 'cept to bullshit with. Of course I don't trust you, you're a cop.'

'I can't believe you said that.'

Langley shrugged. 'Believe it. Deal with it.'

'So whaddya think?'

'One question.'

'One question, right.'

'And I'm asking first?' Langley said.

'Sure, what the hell . . . we all know that newspaper hacks are more honest and reliable than police officers.'

'The phone call,' Langley said. 'After the two teenagers got shot, did an anonymous woman call in and leave a message?'

Irving nodded in the affirmative.

'You're kidding me?' Langley said, genuinely surprised.

'Word-for-word. They have it on record at the Ninth.'

'Jesus,' she said. 'That is just fucking unreal.'

'Unfortunately it's very real,' Irving said. 'And now it's my turn.'

She looked at him.

'The connections. How did you really make the connections between these killings and the ones from the past?'

Langley smiled. 'I didn't,' she said.

Irving frowned.

'I didn't do the research on this, Ray, someone else did. I have a researcher.'

'And his name?'

Karen Langley rose from her chair. She smiled at Irving, extended her hand as if to show him the door. 'That's two questions,' she said.

Irving got up. 'You are a tough bitch, aren't you?'

'So – until tomorrow?' She smiled again.

Irving crossed the room. 'Or later today.'

At the end of the corridor Irving took note of a name on an office door at the top of the stairs. Gary Harmon. He then glanced over his shoulder. He caught Karen Langley disappearing back into her office as if she'd been watching him but hadn't wanted to be seen.

Down in the lobby the girl had returned.

'Back again?' she asked.

'Can't stay away,' Irving said. 'Tell me something . . . Karen Langley's researcher, that's Gary Harmon, right?'

The girl frowned. 'Gary? No, it's John. John Costello.'

Irving smiled, as if he'd been caught in a moment of absent-mindedness. 'Of course it is,' he said. 'Thank you very much.'

'You're welcome,' the girl replied, and Ray Irving looked at her pretty smile, her movie-star haircut, and thought, *Some other life. Perhaps in some other life . . .*

ELEVEN

Ray Irving trawled through back issues of the freep. Didn't take long to find a Murray Hill want-ad. The number given was a cell. He called it; it was out of service. Called the exchange, spoke to three people, finally resolved that the number had been provisionally issued for a non-contracted phone. Thirty dollars, a cheap disposable unit, use up the call-time and throw it away. Untraceable.

He phoned Police Archives, got a line in with someone who wanted to help him.

'Old cases,' Irving said. ' '66, '73, '75 and '80.'

'Here?'

'Different places. L.A., Seattle, Chicago and Texas.'

'You're not serious?'

'As I have ever been.'

'Then I don't know that I can help you . . . well, I *could* help you, but the hours that it'd take . . . Jesus, I'd have to call each Division that dealt with the original crime, get authorization to transfer records, have someone down there find them. This is not a couple of hours work, Detective Irving, and someone somewhere has to okay the time and the expenditure.'

'So what do I gotta get?'

'You have to get something called an Inter-State Archive Requisition Transfer Mandate. Has to be signed by a captain or above, nothing less. Then, and *only* then, can I help you.'

'And I get one of these from where?'

'Give me your e-mail address and I'll send one over. Print it hardcopy, fill it out, get it signed, then we'll talk.'

Irving thanked the man and hung up.

At his own computer station he looked up John Costello. Found three Johns, one Jonathan. All of them were New York residents, two of them DUIs, one aggravated assault, one involved in some white-collar invest on a tax evasion scam back in the early eighties. Of these, two had left the state, one was dead, the only extant New York resident was close to sixty and he lived in Steinway. Unless the guy had a compulsion to commute, Irving doubted he was the man. He then accessed the *City Herald* website, selected *About Us*, found pictures of Karen Langley, Leland Winter, and the paper's editor, a grave-looking man called Bryan Benedict. Costello wasn't listed. He did a search on *costello researcher*, came back with a list of unrelated articles containing the word, statements from university lecturers, nothing of significance. So, John Costello had no criminal record. John Costello worked for the *New York City Herald* and had somehow made the connection between a series of current murders and those going back forty years.

Irving took the phone number, called the *Herald*, and asked for Costello.

'He doesn't have an extension,' the receptionist told him.

'I was there earlier,' Irving said. 'Detective Irving.'

'Yes, of course. Hi there. How are you?'

'I'm fine, just fine, but I need to speak to John Costello.'

'Then I can send a message down and have him call you back, or I might see him when he finishes for the day.'

'When is that?' Irving glanced at his watch. It was quarter past two.

'Five maybe. Perhaps five-thirty.'

'You gonna be there then?'

'Sure I am. I'm on 'til six.'

Irving paused for a moment. 'I'm sorry, but I didn't get your name?'

'Emma,' the receptionist said. 'Emma Scott.'

'I wanna do something, Emma. I wanna come down there about quarter of five and wait for Mr Costello to come out, and when he does I want you to tell me who he is and then I can talk to him right away.'

'Is he . . . well, is he in some kind of trouble?'

'No, not at all, quite the opposite. I think he could save me a lot of trouble. He did some research on something and I need his advice.'

'And this is all legal, right? I'm not going to get—'

'It's completely fine, Emma. I just need you to point him out so I can speak with him.'

'Okay,' she said hesitantly. 'Okay . . . I s'pose that'd be fine, Detective Irving. You come down here about quarter of five then and I'll introduce you to John.'

'Appreciated, Emma . . . see you then.'

The Inter-State Archive Requisition Transfer Mandate was a nine-page document in close-type, single-space, font-size ten. He knew the names and dates of the previous victims, but only from Karen Langley's draft newspaper article. He didn't know divisions, departments, or names of detectives – more than likely long-since retired, or dead. He had seen the Roy Green transcript in Langley's office, the name of the interrogator at the top, but for the life of him he could not recall it. Tempted to call Langley and ask her, he resisted. He didn't want her help, he didn't want her to feel that she had contributed in any way to this case. The *City Herald* had shown up the police department. The *City Herald* intended to tell New York something that the police department did not know. How? Because of John Costello, whoever the hell he was.

Of course, Irving's first thought was for Costello as the perp. Anniversary killings. Only days after the fact, a proposed newspaper story makes the connection. Unlikely, even in the best of worlds. From what little Irving understood of serial killers, he knew many of them were in it for the publicity. *I have a tiny dick, I have no social life, I cannot get laid by any other means than threat with a deadly weapon, and when I'm done I will destroy the evidence of my wrongdoing. I was abused as a child. I am a sorry motherfucker for whom everyone should feel sympathy and compassion. I had to kill them all because they were all really my mother. I have important work to do, a business venture if you like . . . why not invest your daughter? I am a fucking nutcase.*

Enough already.

Irving smiled to himself, went back to the paperwork.

TWELVE

Ray Irving was rarely caught off-guard.

There were, in fact, very few people who could confound him, or so he believed.

John Costello did just that, and he did it in a way that Irving would never have expected.

'I cannot speak with you,' were the first words that Costello said as Irving approached him in the foyer of the *New York City Herald* offices on 31st and Ninth.

John Costello looked no different from a hundred thousand other men in their late thirties who worked the offices and banks and computer stations of New York. His haircut, his clothes – dark pants, a pale blue open-neck shirt, a sport jacket, the dark brown attaché case he carried; the way he held open the door to let a female colleague pass ahead of him; the way he nodded and smiled when she thanked him; his seemingly relaxed manner . . . All of these things made it easy for Irving to reach out and touch John Costello's arm, to say his name, to introduce himself: *Mr Costello, my name is Detective Ray Irving, Fourth Precinct. Wondered if you had a moment—*

And Costello cut him short with five words: *I cannot speak with you.*

Irving smiled. 'I understand you're in a hurry to get home—'

Costello shook his head, kind of half-smiled, and said, 'A man stands in the middle of the road. He's dressed in black from head to foot. Has on a black ski mask, wears sunglasses, black gloves. All the streetlights are broken, and yet a car traveling at eighty miles an hour with its headlights off manages to see him and swerve. How does this happen?'

'I'm sorry,' Irving replied. 'I don't understand—'

'It's a riddle,' Costello said. 'You know the answer?'

Irving shook his head. 'I wasn't really listening—'

'It's daylight,' Costello said. 'You assumed it was night when I mentioned the broken streetlights, but it's daytime. The driver of the car can see the man because it's day-time. There is an old saw about assumption, something to do with fuck-ups.' Costello tilted his head to one side and smiled.

'Yes . . . yes, of course,' Irving said, and took a sideways step toward the exit as if to pre-empt Costello.

'You have assumed I'm available, yet I'm not. I'm sure whatever you have to discuss with me is very important, Detective Irving, but I have an appointment. I cannot speak with you now, you understand.' Costello glanced at his watch. 'I must go.'

'Okay, yes . . . I understand, Mr Costello. Perhaps I could speak with you after your appointment. Perhaps I could come to your house?'

Costello smiled. 'No,' he said, and said it with such firm finality that Irving was left momentarily speechless.

'You want to speak with me about the draft article,' Costello said matter-of-factly.

Irving nodded. 'Yes,' he said. 'The article about—'

'We both know which article, Detective Irving, but not now.' He glanced at his watch again. 'Now I really *have* to go. I'm sorry.'

Before Irving had a chance to formulate a reply, Costello had stepped by him and disappeared through the door.

Irving glanced up at Emma Scott. She was engaged in conversation with a middle-aged woman. He looked toward the street, and in a moment of sheer impulsiveness decided to follow John Costello.

Costello, a fast walker, turned right, away from the build-ing and headed up Ninth toward St Michael's. Here he turned left along West 33rd, and Irving – hanging back as best he could without losing sight of the man – followed him to Eleventh, where Costello turned right toward the Javits Cen-ter, but before he reached it he turned right again onto 37th, paused for a moment to look into his attaché case, and then hurried up the steps of a building and through the door.

By the time Irving caught up, there was no sign of his

quarry. He looked at the building. A short flight of stone steps, an ornate miniature streetlamp on each side of the wide doorway, and painted in discreet letters on the glass fanlight above, the words Winterbourne Hotel.

Irving hesitated, wondered whether he should just turn around and head back to the precinct. He glanced at his watch: it was twenty past five. He crossed over to the other side of the street and looked up at the hotel's facade. There were lights in several windows – three floors in all, two windows to each floor. Assuming that there were also rooms to the back of the building, there would be twelve rooms in all. The Winterbourne Hotel. Irving had never heard of it, but then there was no reason why he should have.

It was close to six by the time he decided to go in there. In his mind he'd considered many scenarios. He had no idea where Costello lived. Always the assumption that people owned houses or rented apartments, but no, some people lived in hotels. People went to hotels for dinner, for sexual encounters, for private rendezvous that they felt could not be conducted at home. People visited other people who were staying in hotels . . .

Irving could not presume to know what Costello was doing in the hotel. He either went in there and asked, or he went away.

He chose the former.

The man behind the desk was elderly, late sixties, perhaps, or early seventies. He smiled warmly when Irving approached, his face creased like a paper bag.

'You're the detective,' the old man said.

Irving stopped suddenly, started laughing – an awkward, nervous reaction.

'Mr Costello left a message for you.'

'A message?'

The old man smiled again, produced a folded slip of paper.

Irving took it, opened it up, and saw printed in a fastidiously neat script, *Carnegie's Delicatessen, 7th Avenue at 55th Street. 8.00 pm.*

Irving's eyes widened. He experienced a strange sensation, as if something was crawling up his spine toward the back of his neck. He shuddered visibly, turned away from the desk, hesitated, turned back.

'Sir?' the old man said.

'Mr Costello left this for me?' Irving asked, still finding it hard to believe, let alone understand.

'Yes sir, Mr Costello.'

'Tell me, does he live here?'

'Oh no, sir, he doesn't *live* here, just comes here for the meetings. They all do. Second Monday of every month. Have for as long as I can remember.'

'Meetings?' Irving asked. 'What meetings?'

The old man shook his head. 'I'm sorry, sir, I'm not permitted to tell you.'

Irving shook his head, incredulous. He felt as if he'd walked into some funhouse reflection of real life. 'You're not allowed to tell me?'

'No, sir.'

'What . . . it's like Alcoholics Anonymous or something?'

'Or something. Yes, I s'pose you could say it was something.'

'I'm sorry, I don't understand. Mr Costello comes here for a meeting on the second Monday of every month, and you're not permitted to tell me what those meetings are.'

'That's right, sir.'

'And other people come too?'

'I cannot say.'

'But you said it was a meeting, right? You can't have a meeting by yourself, can you?'

'I suppose not, sir, no.'

'So other people must come to these meetings.'

'I can't say.'

'This is ludicrous,' Irving said. 'What's your name?'

'I'm Gerald, sir.'

'Gerald . . . Gerald what?'

'Gerald Ford.'

Irving nodded, and then he stopped. 'Gerald Ford. Like President Gerald Ford, right?'

The old man smiled with such sincerity Irving was taken aback. 'Exactly right, sir, like President Gerald Ford.'

'You're kidding me.'

'Not at all, sir. That's my name.'

'And you own this hotel?'

'No, sir, I don't own this hotel. I just work here.'

'And how long do these meetings go on for?'

Ford shook his head.

'You can't tell me, right?'

'That's right, sir.'

'This is crazy . . . this is just utterly crazy.'

Ford nodded, smiled again. 'I s'pose it is, sir.'

Irving looked back at the piece of paper, the address of the restaurant he frequented almost daily, and wondered if any aspect of what he was dealing with was a true coincidence, or . . .

'Okay,' he said. 'Okay . . . tell Mr Costello I got his message and I will meet him at eight.'

'Very good, sir.'

Irving took a step toward the front door, paused, looked back at the old man behind the desk, and then made his way out and down the steps to the street.

For a moment he was uncertain of what to do, and then he decided to walk back to his office through the Garment District. He could have taken the subway, but he wanted time to think. He didn't understand what had happened at the Winterbourne Hotel. He didn't understand the brief words he had shared with Costello in the foyer of the *City Herald*. He felt out of his depth, and did not understand why he should feel such a thing. Nothing made sense. Nothing at all.

Back at the precinct house, Irving learned that Farraday had left for the day. He was somewhat relieved; he didn't want to try and explain something that he did not understand himself. Instinct told him that, despite the fact that he had nothing but circumstantial suspicion, he should drag John Costello in for questioning – interrogate him, find out how he'd supposedly put two and two together on these murders, but the thought of Karen Langley stayed his hand. There was already one proposed newspaper article, and one was more than sufficient.

There were no messages on his desk, and he assumed there

had been no agreement reached on a collaborative investigation between the different precincts involved. Once again there was no proof, not even circumstantial evidence of any probative nature, that these recent murders were linked. There was no more than an article, written by Karen Langley and researched by John Costello.

Ray Irving sat at his desk with a cup of black coffee and trawled the internet, looking to understand more about the original murders that were apparently being replicated. He read some pieces about Harvey Carignan, the man whose 1973 murder of Kathy Sue Miller had been replicated in the death of Mia Grant. He found a quote about Carignan from a man called Russell Kruger, a Minneapolis PD investigator. 'The guy's the fuckin' Devil,' Kruger had said. 'They should have fried him years ago, period, an' they would have queued up to pull the switch. When he was dead they should have driven a stake through his heart and buried him, digging him up a week later to ram another stake in, just to make sure he was fuckin' dead.'

He also found a piece about the execution of Kenneth McDuff, the murderer whose 1966 triple killing had been re-created with the deaths of Luke Bradford, Stephen Vogel and Caroline Parselle. McDuff had been executed on November 17th, 1998 in Walls Prison, Huntsville, Texas. He was responsible for at least fifteen homicides and, according to reports from those present, not one anti-death penalty protester had shown up. His execution was overseen by the Assistant Warden-in-Charge of Executions, Neil Hodges.

Hodges was quoted as saying, 'People think this is all painless and stuff like that. It ain't. Basically, they suffer a lot. They are sort of paralyzed, but they can hear. They drown in their own fluid and suffocate to death really. Yeah, we get problems. Sometimes the guy doesn't want to get on the table. But we have the largest guard in Texas here. He gets them on that table, no problem. They are strapped down in seconds. No problem. They go on that mean old table and get the goodnight juice, whether they like it or not.'

Irving looked at the clock above the door. He felt a disquieting sense of unease in his lower gut. It was six-forty. Another hour before he left for Carnegie's. He drank his coffee. He craved a cigarette for the first time in as long as he could recall.

He took note of the fact that there seemed to be websites running for those who possessed a particularly unhealthy interest in the lives and deaths of serial killers. He considered himself someone who could not be easily surprised, but in some of the articles he found disturbing indications of idolatry and fixation. An obsessive and compelling desire to know what really went on in the minds of Jeffrey Dahmer and Henry Lee Lucas and their ilk as they butchered dozens of human beings did not seem such a healthy pastime.

Still – in some small way akin to slowing to look at a car crash – Irving found himself drawn back to Kenneth McDuff, the man's final hours, the report that had been posted about what had really happened at his execution.

This was the man responsible for the deaths of Robert Brand, Mark Dunman and Edna Louise Sullivan in August 1966, the killings that were described in the statement that Karen Langley had shown him. Irving recalled the complete lack of humanity displayed by this man as he repeatedly raped a sixteen-year-old girl and then choked her to death with a three-foot broom handle. It had taken thirty-two years to finally bring him to justice. McDuff had been given three death sentences in 1968, two years after the Brand/Dunman/Sullivan homicides. Those death sentences were later commuted to life, and McDuff had been freed on October 11th, 1989. Within days he murdered again. Two years later, on October 10th, 1991, he inflicted an excruciatingly torturous death on a prostitute. Five days after that he killed another woman, and four days after Christmas, he kidnapped a five-foot-three, 115-pound woman from a car wash. Her raped and murdered body wasn't found for seven years. On and on it went – a catalog of brutality and inhumanity that McDuff seemed incapable of stopping. And he didn't just kill his victims, he savaged them. He bludgeoned with sticks and clubs. He raped with a sadistic fury that gave veteran investigators nightmares. He blew off his victims' faces at point-blank range, he slashed and butchered them with knives.

Irving went back to the report of McDuff's execution, and

couldn't help but feel some sense of retributive satisfaction in reading it.

McDuff had been driven the fifteen miles from Ellis Unit to the Walls. He was given a cell, in it nothing more than a bunk, a small table and a chair. Beside it was a *strictly no contact* cell, the door covered with a fine steel mesh screen. McDuff ate his final meal – two T-bone steaks, five fried eggs, vegetables, french fries, coconut pie and Coca-Cola. At 5.44 p.m. he was given a pre-injection of 8cc two-percent sodium pentothal. Waiting silently, in an adjacent room, were the extraction team, all of them attired in protective clothing and armed with mace. At 5.58 p.m., McDuff learned that the Supreme Court had denied his final request for a stay of execution. Witnesses were already arriving, and were being escorted through the main prison gate and directed toward the Death House viewing room. At 6.08 p.m. McDuff was invited to leave his cell and walk to the chamber. He did not resist. He was laid on the gurney and left for an hour before the straps were tied. Paramedics inserted two 16-gauge needles and catheters into both of his arms, each of them connected by tubing to the executioner's position. A cardiac monitor and stethoscope were attached to McDuff's chest. The curtains that separated the chamber from the viewing room were drawn back and Warden Jim Willett asked McDuff if he had any final words.

McDuff simply said, 'I'm ready to be released. Release me.'

In the viewing room sat the seventy-four-year-old father of Robert Brand, the eighteen-year-old boy who'd been murdered alongside Mark Dunman and Edna Sullivan thirty-two years earlier.

Over the next ten seconds McDuff was injected with sodium thiopental, a fast-acting anaesthetic. After a further minute he was given 15cc of saline to ease the passage of 50mg/50cc Pancuronium bromide, a curare-derived muscle relaxant that paralyzes respiratory functions. McDuff would have felt an intense pressure in his chest, a suffocating feeling that made him instinctively gasp for air, and dizziness and hyperventilation, his heart beating faster and faster as his entire nervous system was barraged with poison. McDuff was then unable to move, but was still capable of hearing and seeing. His eyes dilated, every hair on his body erect, and then a further 15cc of saline opened his veins in readiness for a massive dose of potassium chloride. When injected intravenously potassium chloride burns and hurts. It immediately disrupts the chemical balance of the body. It causes extreme contraction in every muscle, and when it reaches the heart it causes it to stop beating. Unable to scream, McDuff would have felt nothing but an excruciating cramp enclosing his heart. After a further two minutes he was examined and pronounced dead. Another witness, Brenda Solomon, mother of one of McDuff's victims, was moved to say, 'He looked like the Devil. He's going where he needs to go. I feel happy . . . I feel wonderful.'

At the bottom of the article Irving noticed that the author had given the cost of the drugs used to kill McDuff. Eighty-six dollars and eight cents.

Irving sat back in his chair, closed his eyes and pondered. He had aspired to make detective, had left Narcotics and Vice to come to Homicide. He had studied and crammed and stayed up late to pass exams and gain qualifications. None of it had prepared him for the horrors he had witnessed, but Irving – cynical and bitter though he could sometimes be – still believed in the fundamental goodness of Man. He believed that those who killed, even in an explosion of jealousy and hatred, were in the minority. But such things as this, these sadistic murders, and the state executions that seemed nothing more than the most coldly precise and bureaucratic revenge, were a world apart from most peoples' lives. It was the eternal question: life imprisonment or execution? Was it really an eye for an eye?

And who were such people, Irving asked himself. And why were they this way? In one further article he read, another convicted serial killer stated simply, 'There was nothing they could have said or done. They were dead as soon as I saw them. I used them. I abused them, and then I killed them. I treated them like so much garbage. What more do you want me to fucking say?'

In the silence of his office, of the corridor beyond, the question was right there at the front of Ray Irving's mind: If Langley and Costello were right, *if* they were right, then there was someone out there deliberately carrying on where these people had left off . . .

He rose from his desk and stepped out of the room. There was no-one else around. The lights in the offices further along the corridor had been switched off.

He felt disturbed, uneasy. For the first time since his childhood he experienced that same sense of disquiet that crawled over you when you were alone in a dark house.

He went back for his jacket, his car keys, and then hurried out of the room and down the stairwell.

He was relieved to see familiar faces on the ground floor, to acknowledge the desk sergeant, and then he was out into the street, the hubbub of crowds and traffic, the noise and smell and sounds of the city.

He thought once more of John Costello, the approaching rendezvous at the Carnegie Deli – and the bizarre riddle about the speeding car. Assumption limits observation; an old saw given him at the Academy a thousand years ago.

Assumption limits observation, and observation is for the purpose of seeing what is really there, not what you expect to be there.

Irving buried his hands in his pockets and made his way down the ramp to the underground car park.

THIRTEEN

A tear-shaped mark on the detective's tie. Such a mark would come out with a clean cloth and some club soda.

John Costello counted the diamonds in the pattern on that tie. There were thirty-three, thirty-five if you took into consideration the two that were partly obscured at the edge of the knot.

The shadows around Irving's eyes told John Costello that Ray Irving was tired of being alone.

Alonefatigue.

Something such as this.

Irving was a difficult man to read. There were angles, and the angles gave the impression of depth, though Costello could not be sure the depth was there.

Costello was aware that someone had died. Someone important. People wore such a thing as if a second skin.

'Were you married?' he asked Ray Irving.

Irving smiled. 'No, I wasn't married. Why d'you ask, Mr Costello?'

Costello shook his head. Said nothing.

They had been seated for a good eight or ten minutes before Costello told him why he had chosen the restaurant.

'I looked you up back in June, after the Grant girl was killed. It wasn't difficult to find out which precinct you were from, and then someone I know saw you in here a couple of times. We figured you couldn't live too far from here if you frequented this place.' Costello smiled.

'We?'

'A friend of mine . . . an acquaintance really.'

Irving shook his head. 'I'm missing something here, Mr Costello . . . you say you looked me up in June?'

'Right.'

'And what would you look me up for?'

'Curiosity.'

'About what?'

'About who was going to run the Mia Grant case. We – I – was curious as to whether you would learn anything that wasn't already known.'

A waitress appeared to Irving's right.

'I'm okay,' Costello said. 'You want something, Detective Irving?'

Irving shook his head.

Costello smiled at the waitress. 'Some coffee . . . just some coffee for now, please.'

The waitress brought a cup, filled it, left a jug of half-and-half.

Irving leaned back and looked closely at John Costello. Apprehension? Suspicion? Simply ill-at-ease? There was something unreadable in Costello's expression.

'Tell me what you know about these killings,' Irving asked.

'Not a great deal more than you, Detective. Someone, perhaps more than one person, is replicating killings from earlier serials. That's the way it appears to be. The intriguing thing to me is that of the three detectives that are involved in these seemingly unrelated investigations, you are the only one who came down to talk to Karen Langley.'

'You're her researcher, right?'

Costello nodded.

'Well, Mr Costello—'

'John.'

'Well, John . . . you can imagine my first thought—'

'That I might be your man?'

Irving was caught off-guard once again. The meeting at the newspaper office, the message left at the hotel, the fact that they were now sitting together in Carnegie's. He felt pre-empted at every step. This was not the way it was supposed to be.

'Well, you can imagine my reaction to the article,' Irving said. 'You mentioned the fact that Mia Grant might have been responding to a want-ad for some work in Murray Hill.'

'I think we said there was a strong possibility.'

'So the question is—'

'How did I know that?'

'Right.'

'I looked at where she lived. I looked at where she was found. Figured that if she'd been en route somewhere then it more than likely would have been Murray Hill. Got a copy of the freep, scoured the ads, found the only one that a girl of her age might have been responding to—'

'I know that,' Irving interjected, 'I understand that. But the thing I don't understand is *why* you figured she might be on her way to a job interview.'

Costello frowned, seemed bemused by the question. 'Because of Kathy Sue Miller.'

'The original victim.'

'June third, 1973. The girl killed by Harvey Carignan.'

Irving could feel irritation and frustration rising in his chest. 'Yes, Mr Costello – John – yes I understand that,' he responded, with a touch of impatience. 'But even knowing who Kathy Sue Miller was, raises a question. You'd have to be familiar with a murder that happened nearly twenty-five years ago to even get the similarity between the two. You'd have to know that Kathy Sue Miller had been on her way to a job interview even to go looking in the freep. That's the question that needs to be asked. And then these later killings, these two girls—'

'Ashley Burch and Lisa Briley.'

'Right, yes . . . you're saying that these murders are related to similar incidents that occurred back in the early 1980s.'

'June 12th, 1980,' Costello said. 'Cynthia Chandler and Gina Marano, killed by the Sunset Slayers. That's as far as I can tell. I don't have access to the coroner's report, and I can only surmise that Burch and Briley were killed with a .25.'

'And then this teenage boy that was found in the warehouse.'

'That was stretching things a little.'

'Stretching things?'

'Yes . . . there was a little artistic license taken with James Wolfe. The killer was supposed to be replicating the murder of John Butkovich, but John Gacy never painted his victims' faces like a clown – he painted his own. Only thing I can think is that whoever is doing this is trying to make sure we get the connection . . . he's underestimating our ability to recognize similarities without—'

'Okay,' Irving said, raising his hands. 'Enough already. Something has to tie together here. You're telling me that you're able to take the details of a present murder and correlate it to a murder in the past, a murder that could be as much as forty years ago, and recognize similarities—'

'Sure. Of course.'

'And you can do this with any murder case?'

Costello shook his head. 'You're reading a lot more into this than you need to, Detective. This isn't some psychic thing we're talking about here, it's a technical study. This is the result of many, many years of trying to understand why people do these things. This is an attempt to understand and appreciate what it is that makes someone do something like this.'

'And this is part of your job at the paper?'

'In a way. It's an interest. I belong to a group that looks at such things and tries to draw conclusions from what little information we can gather—'

'A group?'

'Sure.'

'You mean there's a group of people who study murders—'

'Serial murders, Detective, only serial murders.'

'And . . . ?'

'And we meet on the second Monday of every month at the Winterbourne Hotel, and the rest of the time we're in touch through the internet or by phone . . . whatever.'

Irving – lost for words, quiet dismay filling his thoughts – leaned back in his chair.

'And we read the papers and watch the news,' Costello went on, 'and some of the group have police scanners and contacts within the department, and we put two and two together and try to make four.'

'And then?' Irving asked.

'And then what?'

'The information you've gathered. You come to conclusions about—'

'About nothing in particular, Detective, about nothing in particular.'

'So why do it? Surely you can't find this sort of thing fulfilling? Reading about people who do these things to other human beings?'

'Fulfilling?' Costello laughed. 'No, definitely not fulfilling . . . it's simply a matter of dealing with things. For some it's a sense of closure perhaps, for others a chance to actually meet people who have felt similar things . . . to try and make sense of what happened to them in the light of other people's experiences.'

'Experiences with what, John, experiences with what?'

'With being murdered . . . or, rather, almost being murdered.'

'Murdered?'

'That's the thing you see, Detective. That's what the group is all about. We all have one thing in common.'

Irving raised his eyebrows.

'We all survived. One way or another we all survived.'

'Survived what, John? What are you talking about?'

'Attempted murder, Detective. We were all intended murder victims . . . victims of serial killers, and for whatever reason, a reason most of us have stopped even looking for, we survived.'

Irving looked at John Costello in silence.

Costello smiled, the simplicity of his expression almost disarming.

'You survived a serial killer?' Irving asked.

Costello nodded. 'Most of me, Detective . . . most of me survived.'

FOURTEEN

Irving talked with Costello for a while longer, made it clear that he was now an integral part of the investigation, that he should not leave the city, nor should he talk to people about the questions Irving had asked or the answers he'd given. Costello seemed unconcerned. Irving asked Costello for his home address and phone number, but Costello was unwilling to give either, said that he could be contacted without any difficulty at the newspaper. Irving felt he could not force the man, and so the request was dropped.

'You understand that I am not altogether convinced—'

'Convinced of what?' Costello interjected. 'That someone could know about serial killers the way that other people know about baseball players or football teams? If I'd told you that I knew the result of every Giants game for the last twenty years, that I knew the names of players, their score averages—'

Irving stopped him with a gesture. 'Don't leave the city,' he said matter-of-factly.

'I have absolutely no intention of leaving the city, Detective Irving, believe me.'

Eventually there was nothing further to ask. Irving let Costello go, had no reason to detain him further, and watched as the man disappeared out of the door and headed left.

Irving walked to the corner at East 57th, took a south west route to Tenth. By the time he closed the front door of his apartment and kicked off his shoes it was nearly ten.

In the kitchen he poured an inch and a half of Four Roses into a glass, stood before the window that looked out toward De Witt Clinton Park. In the distance he could see the ghosts of piers on the Hudson, left as far as the Sea-Air-Space Museum, right as far as the Convention. Traffic snaked along the West Side Highway. The world went about its business. People opened and closed small chapters of their lives. People connected and disconnected, remembered then forgot. Within the same minute, somewhere in the world, everything was happening. Whoever had killed Mia Grant, slaughtered Ashley Burch and Lisa Briley; whoever had pummelled James Wolfe's body until it surrendered to the hole in a concrete floor; whoever had shot two boys in the trunk of a car, and then taken a broom handle and leaned with all their weight on some poor girl's neck . . . Person, or persons, unknown, they were somewhere. Thinking things, eating, sleeping, working things out, dealing with issues, feeling afraid – or not. Perhaps energized, perhaps uncaring and giving no second thought to what they had done.

And Ray Irving tried not to think about John Costello, because John Costello did not fit into any frame of reference Irving possessed.

John Costello, if what he said was true, was the survivor of an attempted murder by a serial killer. He belonged to a group of similar people. They met on the second Monday of every month and talked about their experiences. They talked about murders that had happened, *were* happening perhaps, and they drew assumptions and conclusions. And then did nothing. Except write a newspaper article. They did that, and that newspaper article was now, at least potentially, the source of unending trouble for the police department. There was nothing worse than a case delivered to the police department that the police department knew nothing about. It was an embarrassment, a political and diplomatic *faux-pas*. It served to raise questions, awkward moments at press conferences, discussions between the Chief of Police and the Mayor about revenue allocations, budget reconciliation, candidacy renewals. Such a thing fueled rumor, internally and externally, and gave rise to the possibility of public outcry, even panic . . .

New York had a serial killer, or killers, of which the police department was unaware.

It set precedents for the Press; they could print what they wished – supposition, scuttlebutt, hearsay, theories . . .

But Ray Irving knew this was not the case. Ray Irving knew

that John Costello had touched the edges of something that held more truth than perhaps even Costello realized. Because those girls *had* been shot with a .25 caliber, because an anonymous call from 'Betsy' *had* come in two days after the East River Park killings, because Irving knew in his heart of hearts that the anniversary killings were just that. He sensed that they were a recognition, a celebration even, a means by which someone somewhere was making a statement that no-one had yet received.

And he would keep on going until the message got through.

Wasn't that what they all wanted? To know the world was hearing what they had to say?

And that person, that single voice out there, could that be John Costello?

Irving hoped that it was not. If John Costello was the Anniversary Man then his audacity was perhaps more terrifying than the killings themselves.

Over the next two weeks, the traffic that came into the Fourth never slowed or stopped. Between the 7th of August and the 10th of September there were a further nine deaths – two leapers, one drowning, a hit and run, a liquor store clerk shot at point blank range with a Mossburgh Magnum 12-gauge, formally identified by a tattoo on his earlobe (said earlobe found in the street eleven yards from the rest of his body); two suicides and, finally, a suicide-homicide: Man and his wife arguing, he threatens her with a beating, she tells him she isn't gonna take any more of his shit, tries to leave . . . he chokes her, realizes what he's done, gets in the car, drives eighty miles an hour down the highway and merges seamlessly with a concrete bridge support. How did they know it was vehicular suicide? No skidmarks on the road.

Mia Grant and James Wolfe stayed on Irving's desk, but they garnered his attention only occasionally, and then only for minutes at a time between one human detonation and another.

Farraday did not speak of Lucas, Lavelle or Hayes again. There was no word from the Third, the Fifth or the Ninth. It appeared that one draft newspaper article wasn't sufficient a threat to the status quo to justify expensive collaborations and task forces.

Irving recognized his own cynicism, but recognition didn't change it.

Karen Langley didn't phone him, and he heard nothing from John Costello. He had investigated Costello, found that at least one thing he'd said was true.

John Costello and Nadia McGowan. Sixteen and seventeen years old respectively. November 23rd, 1984, a Saturday evening.

And before them there had been Gerry Wheland and Samantha Merrett, before them Dominic Vallelly and Janine Luckman.

The Hammer of God killings.

Irving had found very little detail about the case, but what he'd read had left him with a disquiet that did not diminish with time. There was something unnerving about the idea. John Costello was a serial-killer victim, a survivor, and he met with other survivors who should have been dead but weren't. And on the second Monday of every month they sat in an anonymous hotel room and talked about how someone they didn't know had wanted to kill them.

Irving tried not to think of those people, but they were there. He knew there was depth to this thing, and it was no longer a question of whether or not it would haunt him, but for how long.

It was as if it was all waiting for him, and it would wait as long as was necessary.

He knew that *it* – whatever *it* was – had all the time in the world.

FIFTEEN

Fifth anniversary of 9/11: that was the significance of this day. Monday, September 11th, 2006, and Carol-Anne Stowell, who had lost no-one back then but still possessed enough compassion and humanity to understand and appreciate the importance of this day, considered for a moment what would happen if she did not go to work.

Carol-Anne was twenty-seven years old. She supported a heroin addiction that cost her the better part of two hundred dollars a day. Her working name was Monique, and she no longer considered herself to be two different people. What she believed and what she convinced herself to believe were now the same thing. She'd stolen her own mother's car and sold it for three hundred and fifty dollars. She had been raped, beaten, mugged, stabbed; she'd been arrested thirty-one times, charged and bound over, arraigned, spent three months in Bayview Correctional, and all of it for the rush. She knew the rush. She knew it well, better than her own name. And the more she smoked the stuff the further the distance grew between herself and the rush. In its place came the nausea and vomiting, the bad teeth and inflamed gums, constipation, sweats, depression, inability to orgasm; the memory loss, insomnia and the sleepwalking, the thousand and one substitutes for the rush that were the trade-off for the thing itself. So she hooked. Had started when she was twenty-one. She trawled for traffic any place she could. Men were always looking. That's what men did. They looked, she smiled, she walked, she talked, she sold herself, she fucked them, they paid. It wasn't rocket science. Wasn't much of anything. Stopped *feeling* a long time ago. It was fifty dollars, sometimes sixty, or eighty if they wanted bareback or anal. It was a business. She possessed a commodity. Hell, everyone was a hooker. Someone was always screwing someone else for money.

A little after midnight, early hours of Monday the 11th, Carol-Anne put on scuffed stilettos, a skirt no longer than eight or ten inches, a skin-tight nylon short-sleeved blouse. She did her make-up, all of it exaggerated, over-emphasized, as if she needed to look like a clown to be seen as normal in the dark – always in the dark. Even she – desperate and deluded – understood that in daylight she looked like death. Night-time was different. Night-time she could look like whoever they wanted her to be. They made believe anyway; made believe she was the lost love, the little girl across the street, the cheerleader, the Prom Queen. She sold a dream, they paid in dollars – and those dollars paved the way to temporary freedom.

Sometime past midnight she blew some guy in the back of his station wagon. He called her Cassie. When he was done he couldn't get away fast enough, almost pushed her out of the car. He would drive home sick with guilt, worrying about disease despite the fact that he'd worn a rubber. He would wonder if HIV could be passed through the fingertips, through sweat, through a hooker's clothes. He would try to remember if, in the heat of the moment, he had touched her. Carol-Anne had seen the wedding ring. He'd feel sick about hugging his wife, his kids, terrified he was now the harbinger of some virus that would decimate his family . . . As far as Carol-Anne was concerned it was only a blowjob, it wasn't the end of the world. She had seen the end of the world, and a blowjob was not it.

Handful of minutes after one, a midnight blue sedan pulled up. Window came down a fraction. Carol-Anne did the walk, one hand on the roof, another on her hip. Smiled like there was paparazzi.

'How old are you?' the driver asked. The window wasn't down far enough for her to see him clearly.

'Twenty-two.'

'Bullshit,' the driver said. 'Tell the truth or walk.'

'Twenty-seven,' Carol-Anne said.

'Twenty-seven is good,' the driver said.

She heard the lock disengage. Leaned up, stepped back, pulled the handle and opened the door.

Once she was inside she could see the driver properly. Dark hair cut short in back, good eyes – not a druggie. Clean-shaven, straight teeth. Looked like a city guy.

'No weird shit,' he said matter-of-factly. 'Straight sex, blow me first for a while.'

'Sixty,' she said.

'Good enough.'

Carol-Anne smiled to herself. He was a newcomer. He was supposed to haggle with her, get her to take forty-five.

'What's your name?' she said.

The man shook his head. 'Doesn't matter.'

'Gotta call you somethin'.'

The man smiled. It was a good smile. 'Best guy you ever knew?' he asked.

'The best guy I ever knew . . . jeez, what a question. Best guy I ever knew was a teacher in high school. Real sweetheart.'

'What was his name?'

'Errol.'

'Then call me Errol,' the man said. 'Remind you of better times, eh?'

Errol reached out and closed his hand gently over Carol-Anne's left knee. His grip was gentle, his hand was warm, and for a moment she felt as if they might have been friends. Another life. In another life they might very well have been friends.

Errol changed gear, pulled away from the sidewalk, drove a block and a half and turned right into a sidestreet. He didn't talk, he didn't ask any questions. He seemed completely at ease, which struck Carol-Anne as unusual considering the lack of bartering. He acted like a man very familiar with such things, but he hadn't argued with the price. Did it matter? Did it, hell. Sixty bucks was sixty bucks. Couple of these and she'd be home and dry.

He turned off the engine and switched off the dashboard lights.

He turned to Carol-Anne and smiled again. 'Need you to do something for me,' he said.

126

Here we go, she thought.

The man reached over into the back seat and pulled up a paper bag.

'Need you to put these on,' he said.

'What is this?'

'Jeans, a tank-top, some flip-flops.'

'What?'

Errol smiled. 'This is what I want you to do,' he said. He spoke slowly, his voice kind, as if he really cared how she looked.

He smiled again – sincerely, almost sympathetically – and nodded at the bag.

Carol-Anne took out the contents. A pair of Calvin Klein denims, a white tank-top with red shoulder straps, a pair of blue flip-flops.

'Serious?' she said.

'I sure am,' Errol said. He took out his pocketbook, counted four twenties. 'Do this for me and you get another twenty.'

Carol-Anne smiled, was already kicking off her shoes.

'I need you to take everything off except your panties,' Errol said. 'Your stockings, blouse . . . everything. Just wear the jeans, the top, the flip-flops.'

'You want me to be someone?' Carol-Anne asked.

Errol nodded. 'You got me there.'

'High-school sweetheart?'

'Maybe.'

'What was her name?'

'Her name?'

'The girl in the jeans and the tank-top.'

'Her name . . . her name was Anne Marie.'

'*Was*?'

Errol turned and looked at Carol-Anne. Suddenly there was a coolness in his expression.

'I'm sorry,' Carol-Anne said. 'I didn't mean to—'

Errol reached out his hand and touched the side of her face. For a moment she could feel nothing but the sensation of his fingertips against her ear.

She inhaled, closed her eyes for a second. She wondered if she would ever remember what it felt like to have someone love you for who you were, not who they wanted you to be.

127

'It's okay,' Errol said. 'It's okay.'

'You want to call me Anne Marie?'

'Just put the clothes on, sweetheart.'

Carol-Anne struggled with the jeans in the confines of the car. She was better experienced at taking them off.

A handful of minutes and she sat back. Her own clothes were in the paper bag.

'Feel like I'm going to the beach,' she said. She scrunched her toes and made the flip-flops slap against the soles of her feet.

Errol put his arm on the headrest and turned himself toward her.

Carol-Anne reached out her hand and started massaging his groin. She pulled the zipper and snaked her fingers through the hole. With her other hand she unbuckled his belt, undid the buttons, leaned forward as she felt the response in his erection.

Her face was inches away from his thigh when she felt his hand on the back of her neck.

'Gently, gently,' she said, but Errol didn't seem to hear her. The grip on the back of her neck tightened.

Carol-Anne tried to lift her head away from Errol's crotch but the strength of his grip was far beyond her ability to fight back.

Her legs were in the well of the passenger seat, and when she kicked out her feet they collided with the door. Instinctively she jerked her knees up and felt excruciating pain as they connected with the underside of the dash.

'Hey!' she shouted, and that was all it took for Errol to jerk her head upwards, to grab her hair, to pull her right back until she felt the coldness of the window against her cheek, and then he had both hands around her neck, and the intense and unrelenting pressure of his thumbs as they were driven into her throat.

Had she even dared to scream she could not have done.

She felt her eyes swelling.

Waves of darkness momentarily clouded her vision. She could see the blood behind her eyes as it tried to escape through the sockets.

She gasped hysterically, but Errol maintained his grip, ever-tighter, until she felt as if his thumbs would meet his finger-tips in the middle of her throat.

She tried to raise her arms, but already her strength was diminishing. She managed to lift one hand, made her hand into a claw, fingernails ready to dig holes in Errol's face, but he saw the movement, jerked her head toward him, and then slammed her back against the window. Unconsciousness was swift, but momentary, a brief black-out – that was all, for she opened her eyes and realized she was still alive. Errol's face was inches from hers. He seemed unhurried, as if this was no more significant than buying coffee, and she could see he was smiling. Whatever thoughts he might have had were not evident on his face. He still looked kind, compassionate even, as if he believed he was doing something that was difficult, but nevertheless entirely necessary – as if someone *had* to do it, and it might as well be him.

Had Carol-Anne Stowell been any stronger, had her immune system been any less devastated, had her muscles not been ravaged and her respiratory system so weakened, she might have survived a few moments longer. Regardless, she was no match for her attacker. His strength was far in excess of her own, and the certainty of his actions made it all too clear that there was no possibility in the world she would ever walk away.

And so it was, on the fifth anniversary of 9/11. Twenty-seven years old. Not much of anything at all as far as a real life was concerned, and Carol-Anne Stowell gave up and stopped breathing. Maybe, in some small way, she might even have been relieved. Skag was nothing compared to dying. Dying had to be the biggest rush of all.

SIXTEEN

By the end of the late shift on Monday the New York Police Department, Seventh Precinct Homicide Division, ably represented by Detective Eric Vincent, had very little at all.

She was a hooker, no doubt about it, found just after six a.m. by a longshoreman down near Pier 67, a handful of yards from Twelfth Avenue. By seven-thirty they knew her name, had backtracked her movements to the edge of the theater district, and aside from a possible connection to a midnight blue sedan they had nothing at all. Eric Vincent questioned eight girls; five of them mentioned a guy in a car, slowing to ask them their age, nothing more. They had told him, he had questioned the veracity of their responses, they had answered truthfully, and he'd driven on. In their line of work it was not uncommon for a crawler to want a particular height, hair color, cup size. Age was a little different perhaps, but in this business even the strangest requests seemed normal after a while. A description? None of them had seen his face. The window had been lowered just enough for him to see them, ask the question, hear the answer.

Carol-Anne Stowell had been strangled to death. Her body had been thrown off the pier and was found on the gravel embankment at the edge of the Hudson. She was lying on her left side in a semi-fetal position. She had on a pair of Calvin Klein denims which had been pulled down around her ankles and turned inside out. A white tank-top with red shoulder straps had been wrapped around her right wrist, and a pair of blue flip-flops were found nearby. Aside from the bruising on her throat, an abrasion on her knee and a swelling on the side of her head, a hank of hair had been torn from her scalp and her eyes had been removed. CSA came down, took pictures, collected items from the area, but the body had to be moved. The water was rising and whatever crime scene they might have had would soon be lost.

Eric Vincent took what notes he could and informed the CSA that he would follow up on the autopsy. They parted company – Vincent and Carol-Anne Stowell – and he stood for a moment at the edge of Twelfth Avenue as the coroner's wagon pulled away. It was not the missing eyes that bothered Vincent, nor the clump of hair torn from her head. It was the flip-flops. No-one went to work in flip-flops, especially not New York hookers, and that meant that someone had dressed her – pre- or postmortem. And if someone had dressed her then they were not dealing with an opportunist, or a guilty trick who couldn't bear the thought of the girl telling someone what he had done to her. Nor were they dealing with her pimp, outraged at her decision to quit the business. No, they were dealing with premeditation and malice aforethought, with someone creative. And the creative ones were always and invariably the worst.

Irving was late. Some guy, couldn't have been more than twenty-five, had keeled over in Carnegie's in an epileptic fit. Irving had helped, laid him in recovery, held people back from their claustrophobia-inducing curiosity, and waited for the ambulance. Kid was fine by the time they arrived, but they took him anyway. He'd thanked Irving without understanding what he was thanking him for.

It was a little beyond ten when Irving checked in at the desk, and the desk sergeant – a man by the name of Sheridan – handed Irving a plain manila envelope.

Irving raised his eyebrows. 'What's this?'

'How the hell would I know? Some guy brought it in, handed it over. Asked him if he needed to see you and he said no. He went away. End of story.'

'Time was it?'

'Half an hour ago, forty minutes maybe.'

Irving smiled, thanked Sheridan, opened up the envelope as he walked to his office.

It took a couple of minutes for him to understand what he had there. Evidently the pages had been printed from some website. The link sequence was listed in the lower left-hand corner:

Somewhere within the depths of solitary confinement in Sullivan Correctional Facility, Fallsburg, New York, exists a man called Arthur John Shawcross. His name comes from the Old English *crede cruci*, literally 'belief in the cross' but nothing could have been further from the truth. Called 'The Monster of the Rivers' by the media, Shawcross is believed to have been responsible for at least 53 homicides, though only 13 have been conclusively attributed to him. A juvenile sadist, a burglar, rapist, pedophile, shoplifter, school drop out, he was first arrested as a teenager in December 1963 for breaking into a Sears Roebuck store. He was not jailed, but given 18 months' probation. By this time, little more than seventeen years old, he had developed certain idiosyncrasies and behavioral traits. He spoke in a high-pitched, childish voice. He employed a habit of walking 'cross-lots', moving at a fast pace, arms swinging by his side as if marching in the school band, his body erect, his arms rigid, walking over anything that was in his way. Secretly he enjoyed the company of much younger children. He played with kids' toys. He was accident-prone, knocked himself unconscious while pole-vaulting, was hit by a discus and suffered a hairline skull fracture, suffered electric shocks from faulty appliances, was hit by a sledgehammer, fell from a ladder, and was hospitalized after a truck collided with him in the street.

Irving scanned through half a dozen paragraphs, and then a highlighted section a few pages further on caught his attention:

Anne Marie Steffen, 27, was a heroin-addicted prostitute who started working to support her habit after her paralzyed sister died. By all accounts she was last seen alive on Lyell Street on Saturday, July 9th, 1988. From circumstantial evidence and Arthur Shawcross's later testimony, it has been determined that Shawcross met Steffen by the Princess Restaurant on Lake Avenue, and then walked with her to an area behind the Young Mens' Christian Association building. A little later he took her down to the Driving Park in his car, and during oral sex he strangled her. Once she was dead he pushed her body over the edge of the Genesee River Gorge. Anne Marie Steffen was found on her left-hand side in a fetal position, a pair of Calvin Klein jeans turned inside out and pulled down around her ankles. A white tank-top with red shoulder straps was tied around her wrist and a pair of blue flip-flops was located nearby, confirmed as having belonged to the victim. A large hank of hair had been torn from her scalp and her eyes were missing from their sockets.

Irving picked up the phone, called the desk.

'Any female homicides booked last night?' he asked Sheridan.

'Nothing so far . . . still haven't had reports in from all units, but nothing I'm aware of. Why?'

'I think there might have been,' Irving replied. 'I'll check the inter-precinct bulletins.'

Irving hung up, logged onto his computer.

He found two dead – one at the Eleventh, another at the Seventh. The Eleventh was a middle-aged woman, fatal GSW, still waiting on the coroner to confirm suicide or homicide. The report from the Seventh was vague, but still sufficient for him to call them.

When Irving spoke to the desk at the Seventh, he felt the hairs on the nape of his neck stand to attention.

'We got a hooker, I think. Eric Vincent was on it . . . he might still be here, hang on a minute.'

Irving waited, tension and a sense of unease in the base of his gut.

'Vincent.'

'Detective Vincent, this is Ray Irving from the Fourth.'

'What's up? I'm on my way home.'

'Won't take a minute. Just wanted some details on your homicide.'

'The hooker?'

'She was a hooker? You're sure?'

Irving could hear Vincent's sardonic smile. 'Hell, Ray, if she wasn't a hooker then she really had a problem with taking care of herself.'

'Where was she found?'

'Down off Pier 67 . . . why you asking?'

'Think I might have something on it, but wanted to check a few of the details.'

'Sure, sure . . . whaddya wanna know?'

'She was strangled?'

'Looked like it from the bruising on the throat. Either that or she was choked unconscious and then the drop from the pier broke her neck. Have to wait for the autopsy report.'

'And her clothes?'

'Her clothes?'

'Yes . . . how was she dressed?'

Vincent paused.

It was in that pause that Irving knew.

'Well, that's the odd thing. From what we can tell she was out working, but she had on jeans and flip-flops—'

Irving's heart missed a beat, then another.

'And a tank-top, but that was wrapped around her wrist for some reason.'

Irving swallowed. He took a deep breath. 'Twenty-seven years old, right? And her eyes were gone.'

Vincent didn't speak for a moment.

'Eric?'

'How the fuck do you know that?' Vincent asked.

'Because I think it might be a serial,' Irving replied.

'You have someone else with their eyes out?'

'No, but there's a connection with some earlier cases.'

'So what're you saying? You taking this one off me? Jeez, if you could do that I'd be real grateful.'

'I don't know yet,' Irving replied. 'I don't know what I'm

gonna do yet, I gotta speak to my captain, see if we can collaborate on this. You say you're off shift now?'

'I got my kid's birthday,' he said. 'This is a big deal. This is something I can't—'

'It's okay. I'll handle it,' Irving replied. 'My captain's gonna have to speak to the Chief. God knows how long this is gonna take, and whether or not anything will come of it . . . you know how these things are. You got a number where I can reach you?'

Vincent gave Irving his cell number.

'What was her name?' Irving asked.

'Carol-Anne Stowell.'

'And when was she found?'

' 'Bout six this morning.' Vincent inhaled audibly. 'This is freaky shit now, my friend. What the fuck is this?'

'I think whoever did this was looking for a particular type of girl of a very specific age.'

'Makes sense,' Vincent replied. 'We talked to some girls and five of them mentioned a trick in a midnight blue sedan, asked their ages, drove away until he found Carol-Anne.'

'None of them were twenty-seven, that's why,' Irving said. 'He needed a twenty-seven-year-old, and he took the clothes with him. Her own clothes could be somewhere, but more than likely he took them away after he'd killed her.'

'And this is a serial?' Vincent asked. 'How many have there been already?'

'So far, as best we know, your hooker would make it a total of eight.'

Vincent whistled through his teeth. 'What the hell is this? This guy trying for the record?'

Irving smiled. 'Not a prayer, my friend. Right now I'm reading about some charmer who was supposed to have done fifty-three.'

'Well, okay, better you than me. I'm gonna go do the birthday party if that's okay with you.'

The call ended.

Irving leaned back in his chair and closed his eyes. He breathed deeply, tried to stay focused on what was happening.

Mia Grant, the East River girls, James Wolfe, the two boys

in the trunk, the dead girl under the Queensboro Bridge, and now Carol-Anne Stowell.

He leaned forward and picked up the pages that had been delivered that morning. He scanned through them again, found the highlighted section.

Irving knew who had delivered the pages, and why. The thing that he could not understand was how rapidly the connection had been made. The girl was found at six, would have been on the radios about seven, seven-thirty, and by nine-thirty John Costello had identified the killing, found a website, printed off the relevant pages, and delivered them to the Fourth.

He reached for the telephone to call the *City Herald*, and then he stopped. He wondered whether the delivered documents could give him probable cause for a formal interrogation, for visiting the Winterbourne Hotel and talking to the rest of Costello's freak show. It was, after all, the second Monday of the month.

SEVENTEEN

It took a while, but they figured it out.

Editorial director of *The New York Times*, a veteran journalist called Frank Raphael, knew there was something awry when the letter came. It was the 9/11 anniversary, and the mailroom was on alert. *The New York Times* had always had its share of crazies and creeps, but on such a day it paid to hire extra staff, to put anything greater than letter-thickness through the metal detector, to employ two extra guys with an x-ray machine. It was a sorry state of affairs, but it was now the way of the world.

The letter came in with the regular post. It was opened by a girl called Marilyn Harmer, and when she saw the measured, almost perfect symbols, something triggered in the back of her mind. She set the letter down as carefully as she could, took one of the clip-top baggies provided, and slid the letter and its envelope inside. She called security, handed over the document, and waited.

It arrived on Frank Raphael's desk at six minutes past ten that morning, and by ten twenty-two he had three other editors, two columnists, a staff photographer and a political correspondent standing behind him and peering over his shoulder, all of them feeling that sense of awkward dismay that came with unidentified fear.

'Anyone know how many there were?' Raphael asked.

'In all, I think there were twenty-one.'

Raphael looked up at one of the assistant editors, mid-thirties, sharp as a blade. Name was David Ferrell.

'You know something about this?' Raphael asked, and then he seemed to become aware of how many people were behind him. 'For God's sake, will you people sit down or fuck off?'

They moved quickly. The staff photographer left the office,

the remainder took seats around the wide meeting-room table.

'Not a great deal,' Ferrell said. He took a seat to Raphael's right. 'I think there were twenty-one letters, started in mid-'69, ended in April of '78. Then there were about half a dozen other things called the Riverside Writings, and then there was a message left on the car door of one of the victims at Lake Berryessa.'

Raphael frowned. 'How the fuck do you know this shit? Jesus, man, you scare me sometimes.'

Ferrell smiled. 'Just interested, nothing more. I'm sure as hell not an authority.'

'Okay, so we have a copycat here. Maybe this is the same cipher, who the fuck knows, but from what I remember it sure as shit looks like it.'

'So who do we call?' Ferrell asked.

Raphael shrugged his shoulders. 'Hell, I don't know, call the Chief of Police maybe . . . what's the protocol on such things?'

'It's gotta be a fake,' Ferrell said. 'Consensus of opinion is that this guy is long since dead.'

'Whatever . . . so call the captain of the nearest precinct. Which is that?'

'The Second,' Ferrell replied.

'So call him and tell him we are the proud recipients of the first Zodiac letter in twenty-eight years.'

Second Precinct Captain Lewis Proctor knew Bill Farraday – professionally rather than socially – but well enough to recognize his name when a call had come through to the Chief of Police. Proctor had been in a mid-quarterly review meeting with Chief Ellmann when Farraday had called regarding some proposed collaboration between the Fourth and the Ninth.

'You know Farraday?' Ellmann had asked him when the call was over.

Proctor nodded. 'Some.'

'He's after a cross-precinct investigation, some whacko replicating previous serials.'

That was all that had been said, but when David Ferrell

called from *The New York Times* that Monday morning, an alarm bell rang in back of Proctor's head.

First call he made was to Bill Farraday, told him the news. Farraday was quiet for some time.

'You want to go down there?' Proctor asked him.

'You going?'

'Doesn't need two of us.'

'I'll take someone,' Farraday said. 'If it looks like anything I'll come back to you.'

'Appreciated, Bill.'

The call ended. Farraday paged Irving, found he was half a block away getting lunch.

Irving was in Farraday's office within fifteen minutes.

'We're taking a trip to *The New York Times* offices,' Farraday told him. 'They received a letter . . . looks like a Zodiac letter.'

Irving's eyes widened. 'You're fucking with me.'

'I'm not, but seems like someone is,' Farraday replied.

'This might not be related.'

'None of it might be related. We don't know, do we? We have to go take a look. Some guy at *The Times* called Proctor at the Second, Proctor called me, I called you. This is what's known as delegation. We go take a look. We find out if there's any connection.'

Irving thought to mention the documents that had arrived earlier that morning from John Costello about Arthur Shaw-cross and the Genesee River killings. He stayed his hand – just for now.

It was after midday by the time they reached *The Times* building. Editor Frank Raphael greeted them, was told why people had come from the Ninth and not the Second. He called David Ferrell through, who came with the letter and envelope in the baggie and a copy of Robert Graysmith's book *Zodiac*.

'I've deciphered the letter,' Ferrell said. 'The entire code is in this book, pretty much . . .'

He handed the original letter to Farraday, the translation to Irving.

Farraday, unfamiliar with the Zodiac letters, scanned the neatly printed symbols.

Irving took the deciphered copy and read it out loud.

'I have been asked, Did I kill? Yes, too many times for any one person to do. I have been a god unto myself. I've been the judge, the jury and the executioner. I, dear people, have murdered, butchered and totally destroyed fifty-three human beings in my lifetime. Why?'

Irving paused, looked up at Farraday, at Frank Raphael. The tension in the room was palpable.

'Go on,' Raphael said quietly.

Irving turned back to the letter:

'Picture in your mind: I was taught to sit for hours at a time and not move; I was taught to seek out and destroy the enemy as I perceived them to be.

'The prostitutes I am accused of killing were the enemy to me in their own fashion, because they can kill with social diseases and AIDS and get away with it. Do I regret it, I have been asked? My answer is, I very much regret it, to the point of wondering why I was chosen to carry out this assignment.

'The United States government taught me how to kill; what it did not teach me was the desire not to do so. I still get those feelings – but the pills I am now on dampen them to the point of calming me down. Why not before?

'Why am I like I am? Study it – seek the answer before too many people get killed. I am like a predator, able to hunt and wantonly destroy at any given time or moment. I have been pushed and threatened, but somehow the pills stop or slow down the desire to fight. I know that when I do fight there will be no control – I'll be the predator again.

'Most people tell me I will die in prison. (So what.) Do you have a choice of when and where you will die? Many people believe that when they die they will go to heaven. Not so. Your soul waits to be called: Read your Bible if that is what you believe in. As for me, I will live again and go on to the next transition. I am a spiritualist. Death is but a transition of life. The people I have killed are in their next transition. They will live again, but in a much better way than the one they left behind.

'Every man, woman or child from ten years of age and up is

able to kill knowingly. Many of you humans portray me as mad-crazy. This is your free will. What you think may not be so.

'Look to the heavens, I came from there. So did you but you won't admit it. My time is near in this transition. I will move on shortly, I feel what I feel. If every man, woman and child had the same as everyone else, then crime and war would be nonexistent.

'Remember: watch the heavens, we are coming to rescue you from you.

'I am, or am I?'

Irving looked up at Bill Farraday, at Frank Raphael and David Ferrell.

'Fuck,' Raphael said.

'So what do you know about this guy?' Farraday asked.

Ferrell leaned forward. 'I studied quite a bit about it for a research project I was doing a couple of years ago. I don't know a great deal, but from what I can see the letter has been written in the same style, cramped, blue felt-tip pen, some of the letters trailing down on the right-hand side. Whoever did this put double postage on the front of the envelope. That was another common trait. Zodiac used to put words on the outside of the envelope requesting that whoever delivered the letters did so in a hurry. Left-hand margins and the text are ruler-straight, as if he used a lined piece beneath as a guide. Zodiac wrote on a paper called Eaton bond. Have no idea if what you have there is the same, but it's seven and a half by ten which is the same size. He began every letter with the phrase "This is the Zodiac speaking", which our letter-writer has not done, but then there is an explanation for that—'

Ferrell paused.

'So?' Raphael prompted.

'There was something about it that reminded me of something. I checked out a few of the phrases in the letter on the net, and I found out whose letter it was.'

'Whose letter?' Farraday asked. 'What d'you mean?'

'Whoever sent this just transcribed an existing letter into Zodiac code and then sent it to us. It's not a Zodiac letter at all, it's a letter from another serial killer.'

'Name?' Farraday asked.

'Arthur John Shawcross—'

'Oh God,' Ray Irving exclaimed. 'The Genesee River killings.'

Farraday turned, surprised. 'Ray?'

'Shawcross,' Irving said. 'We got a Shawcross replica this morning . . . Eric Vincent at the Seventh.'

'This morning . . . how the hell do you know about it already?'

Irving reached into his inside jacket pocket and took out the folded pages. He spread them out on his knee, and then handed them to Farraday.

'What's this? Where did these come from?'

'Long story,' Irving replied.

Farraday nodded, rose to his feet. 'We're going to take this letter with us,' he told Raphael. 'This is part of something a lot bigger.'

'Understood,' Raphael said, 'but we need a story, Captain Farraday.'

Farraday smiled drily. 'Don't know that this is a story you want.'

'This is *The New York Times* . . . the story we don't want doesn't exist.'

'This is not a small matter,' Farraday replied. 'This is more than likely going to the Chief of Police. After that . . . well, after that I don't know what'll happen.'

'You can't just take the thing, it was sent to us.'

'You want me to get a storm going?' Farraday asked. 'I can do the DA phone call now, or we can have an agreement here, Mr Raphael.'

Raphael shook his head. 'Do what you have to,' he said resignedly, 'but we want whatever story comes out of it as an exclusive.'

'Police department doesn't give exclusives, you know that.'

'So first up on the press conference, however this thing comes out.'

'*If* it comes out.'

'So if it comes out we get first call on the conference, agreed?'

Farraday extended his hand and they shook.

The captain said nothing until he and Irving reached the lobby, and then he slowed up and stopped. 'Who was at the Ninth?' he asked.

'Lucas, Richard Lucas.'

'And this thing this morning?'

'Eric Vincent at the Seventh.'

'Anyone else?'

'Patrick Hayes at the Third and Gary Lavelle at the Fifth – a triple homicide in the first week of August.'

'Get them all together,' he said. 'Call them all, tell them to come to us. We have to talk about this.'

'Vincent I might not be able to get,' Irving said. 'He went off-shift this morning, has his kid's birthday.'

'Tell him there'll be other birthdays . . . we need everyone involved in this before the rest of the city finds out what the fuck is going on.'

EIGHTEEN

By the time everyone had been contacted it was close to three in the afternoon. Irving had stayed in Farraday's office, had told him what he knew about the sequence of killings, the dates, the anniversaries, about Karen Langley and John Costello. By one-thirty Chief of Police Anthony Ellmann realized something was going on. There was a brief call to Farraday, another to each of the captains at the relevant precincts. Each were given their instructions: there would be a meeting at the Fourth Precinct house at five that afternoon. No-one would be late. Deputy Coroner Hal Gerrard would be there, though Chief Ellmann himself would not attend; he had a meeting with the Mayor on an unrelated matter, but he wanted a full debrief in writing before close of business that day. Farraday had been assigned as co-ordinator until further notice. Once a specific course of action was decided upon, Chief Ellmann would review resources and reassign as he felt necessary. Their immediate task was to determine if indeed there was a pattern and connection to these killings and, if so, to pool their forensic and investigative results, establish a critical path analysis, propose a means and method by which the perpetrator or perpetrators would be arrested and secured for arraignment. All of this without creating any liability regarding the execution of their usual duties, the resolution of any other ongoing cases. Simple in theory; in reality – as was always the case – an entirely different matter.

Farraday cleared out the homicide department offices. He removed all partitions from the open-plan area, had three tables pushed together, sent for whiteboards and an overhead projector.

Close to half past four the Fourth Precinct became a confusion of activity as people were directed from the lobby. Uniforms had been assigned as ushers for the arriving detectives and CSAs, and files were ferried by the armful from the backs of vehicles and up the stairs to the third floor.

The attending CSA for each of the relevant cases arrived one by one, the assigned detectives also, and Ray Irving had already established a focal point for their discussion. At the head of the table he had stationed a large whiteboard, and on it had written the names of the current victims, alongside them the names of the original killers whose crimes appeared to have been replicated. Present – if not in body, but certainly in spirit – were some of the most extreme and sadistic serial killers that the U.S. had ever known. Beneath their names Irving had written their respective dates of birth and, where relevant, of execution; and in the case of those still within the federal penitentiary system, their last-known place of incarceration. Despite having access to the federal database, Irving had found it surprisingly difficult to determine the location of some of these people, but not Shawcross – ironic, considering he was the last man represented. Shawcross would not have been included had it not been for the discovery of Carol-Anne Stowell that morning and John Costello's subsequent delivery of documents to Irving. Arthur John Shawcross, Irving had learned, welcomed correspondence from anyone, and made his prisoner number and his address at Sullivan Correctional Facility in Fallsburg easily available on numerous websites. Even as the detectives gathered, Shawcross was languishing in a cell no more than eighty miles from where they sat.

Additionally, Irving had taken the initiative and copied the draft newspaper article, placing a copy ahead of each chair at the meeting. It was the first thing that the collective attendees read, and it was Karen Langley's article that established the foundation of their meeting.

Bill Farraday, unfamiliar with the protocol of such a meeting, nevertheless directed the proceedings. He fielded initial doubts regarding the article, dealt with the fusillade of questions that followed, and grounded the potentially heated debate that would otherwise have ensued by determining the parameters within which they were working.

Farraday rose from his chair and took steps toward the whiteboard.

'What we have here,' he said quietly, 'is a series of possibilities. That's all we have. If we consider that there is no link between these events . . .' He paused, smiled wryly. 'Then we have the most extraordinary case of coincidence that has ever been witnessed.' He looked at the gathered faces, each of them intent, focused. 'We *have* to assume, and I use the word assume reservedly . . . we have to *assume* that there is a connection.'

Lucas raised his hand. 'I don't think anyone is questioning the fact that these are related . . . I think we have to consider the possibility that we are very late in the game.'

'How so?'

'Who says that the Grant girl was the first?' Lucas asked rhetorically. 'This might have been going on for years. We have absolutely no idea.'

'I think I have an answer for that,' Irving said. 'I believe we have someone who wants us to know what he is doing.'

'That's a significant assumption,' Lucas interjected. 'Why do you think that?'

'Three reasons,' Irving replied. 'Firstly, the phone call after the double murder. Ashley Burch and Lisa Briley. For as I understand that call came through the Ninth's switchboard so we'll never trace it. He could have made the call himself with voice modulation software, he could have paid someone to do it. Who the hell knows. Secondly, in the case of James Wolfe, the perp went to the trouble of painting the boy's face like a clown. Gacy never did that. He never painted anyone's face but his own. Whoever did that did it because he wanted us to get the connection. And this morning, the fact that we found this girl's body and she was dressed the way she was dressed, that hair had been torn from her scalp, and her eyes had been removed . . . these things should have been enough to give us the connection to Shawcross and the Anne Marie Steffen case.' He paused. 'But no, he wanted to make really sure we got it, hence the letter to *The Times*. He uses the Zodiac code to give us the Shawcross letter.'

'Why the Zodiac code?'

'Theory again,' Irving said, 'but the thought I had was that he wants us to know that he's smarter than all of them . . .

146

Zodiac included. The previous perps were all caught, a couple of them executed, but not Zodiac—'

'So why not just do a Zodiac-style killing, why send a letter?'

'Perhaps he is only replicating killings of people who were caught,' Irving said.

'This is all supposition and assumption,' Gary Lavelle said. 'I saw the way that girl had been thrown under the Queensboro Bridge. Whoever did that battered the crap out of her. A mile away we get two boys shot to hell and put inside the trunk of a car. Whatever the hell we're dealing with, whoever this guy is trying to be, we're still faced with the very real fact that we have at least eight victims and no co-ordinated line of investigation. Already this has been going on since . . . well, since when?'

'First one, at least the first we know of, was Mia Grant back at the start of June,' Irving said.

'So more than two months this has been going on, and where the hell are we?'

'Where we are,' Farraday said, 'is exactly where we need to be, but the reason we're here is not actually because of what we have or haven't done, but because of this proposed newspaper article.'

'And what, may I ask, is the story with that?' Vincent asked.

'There is a group of citizens,' Irving said slowly. 'A group of people, how many I don't know, who meet in the Winterbourne Hotel on West 37th on the second Monday of every month. As far as I can understand they are all survivors of serial-killer attacks—'

'What?' Lavelle asked. 'You're not telling me that we've got a group of vigilantes?'

Irving shook his head. 'I don't know what we've got. One of the members is a guy called John Costello. He's Karen Langley's researcher at the *City Herald*, and he was the one who put two and two together on these killings.'

'He's a suspect?' Lucas asked.

'I don't know what he is. He's not a straightforward guy. He's a little left-of-center, but I don't think that Karen Langley is the brains behind the article. I think he is. I think he does the work, she writes the articles and takes the byline because he doesn't want the attention. Truth is, I don't know. I don't know what Costello's story is, and I don't know what the best course of action is as far as he's concerned. We may have something completely innocent here, just a smart guy who knows a great deal about serial killers. He's a crime journalist's researcher, for God's sake, he's *supposed* to know this shit. The mere fact that he put two and two together so quickly . . . well, that's another reason I suspect these killings don't go back further than Mia Grant. If they did I think we would have seen this article sooner.'

'Okay, so he wrote the article,' Lucas said. 'Anything else?'

Irving nodded. 'Within a couple of hours of this hooker being found this morning he delivered Arthur John Shawcross's biography to me here.'

'You're not serious?'

'As can be,' Irving replied.

'And who the fuck is this Shawcross anyway?' Lavelle asked.

Irving shook his head.

Hannah Doyle, Hayes' CSA from the Third, put her hand up at the far end of the table. 'I know a little about him, he was one of my research papers. He was called The Monster of the Rivers, also the Genesee River Killer. He claims to have killed fifty-three people, but they've officially only attributed thirteen to him. Usual history for serial killers . . . juvenile sadism, torturing animals, graduating to burglary and arson. The standard pattern, you know – unable to connect with people, difficulty managing relationships, accident-prone. He saw some military service, and did close on two years in Attica for attempted robbery and arson back in the early seventies. When he came out he got married – round April of '72, I think . . . Couple of weeks later he killed a ten-year-old boy, then three or four months after that he raped and strangled an eight-year old girl. They got him for that and he did nearly fifteen years, some in Attica, some in Greenhaven. He came out in early '87, killed again in '88, and then the next one was this Anne Marie Steffen in September of the same year. He was picked up again sometime around 1990, confessed to however many additional killings, and he's now doing two-fifty in Sullivan.'

'That's up in Fallsburg, right?' Vincent asked.

'Same place as Berkowitz.'

'Berkowitz?' Lucas asked.

'Son of Sam,' Hannah Doyle said.

'So this gets us where?' Farraday asked. 'We know something about these people, the killers who are being copied, but what does it tell us about the copycat?'

'None of these original killers are out on parole,' Deputy Coroner Gerrard said. 'Is that correct?'

'Far as I can gather,' Irving said, 'we have Carignan in Minnesota Correctional, Carol Bundy was given life but is eligible for parole. Douglas Clark is on Death Row in San Quentin, Jack Murray is dead. Gacy was executed in Stateville in 1994, and Kenneth McDuff in the Walls in Texas in November '98. And Shawcross, who's in Sullivan and won't be coming out.'

'And we are completely ruling out the possibility that the current perp could be any of these,' Gerrard said matter-of-factly.

Irving nodded. 'I consider that a relative certainty.'

'And Zodiac?' Vincent asked.

'Last suspected Zodiac killing was May 1981,' Jeff Turner said. He glanced at Hannah Doyle and smiled. 'I did Zodiac on my research paper, and there are certain characteristics about Zodiac victims that never changed. He killed on weekends in areas near water, always on a full or new moon. Apart from a taxi driver, he attacked couples, primarily young students. It was always at dusk or at night, and he used different weapons each time. Robbery was never a motive and he never sexually abused or molested victims, either before or after killing them. He was credited with killing forty-six people, but in actual fact there were only ever six that were conclusively attributed.'

Farraday leaned forward. 'We're not dealing with the Zodiac. I think we can safely rule out that possibility.'

There was a murmur of agreement from the gathering.

'So where now?' Vincent asked.

'Seems obvious that we get a warrant on this Winterbourne group,' Lavelle said.

'For what?' Farraday asked. 'For being too fucking smart for their own good?'

'For *our* own good,' Lucas interjected. 'Fucking whacko makes us look like a bunch of cunts.'

'Nice,' Hannah Doyle said sarcastically.

Lucas smiled awkwardly, raised his hand in a conciliatory fashion. 'Sorry. Forgot I was in company.'

'I'll go back there,' Irving said. 'They meet tonight—'

'You spoke to this guy, right?' Lucas asked.

Irving nodded.

'How'd he seem to you?'

Irving shrugged. 'Hell, I live in New York . . . everyone seems crazy to me.'

Murmurs of recognition from the others, then comments were shared and, for a moment, it seemed that Irving's wisecrack had eased the tension. Until that moment none of them had perceived it clearly, but it was there. Eight victims. They knew very little at all, and they were aware of how close that was to nothing.

'He's what . . . late thirties—' Irving began.

'He's a survivor, right?' Hannah Doyle asked. 'A survivor of what?'

Irving leaned back in his chair, folded his hands across his stomach. 'Anyone heard of the Hammer of God killings?'

Lavelle raised his hand. 'Early eighties, right. That was where? Jersey City?'

'Jersey City, yes. Guy called Robert Clare. Killed five, all teenagers, courting couples, you know? Beat their heads in with a hammer. Our guy, this John Costello, was the only one who survived. His girlfriend, Nadia McGowan, she didn't make it. He was sixteen, she was a year or so older. Costello was injured badly, spent some time in hospital, but he came through.'

'They got Clare, right?'

'They got him,' Irving said. 'December '84. He committed suicide before the trial. Hanged himself in a psych facility.'

'And your impression of this guy, this Costello character?'

'I only met him once. He figured out where I eat and asked to meet me there.'

'He did what?'

Irving smiled. 'He knew who I was. He knew I'd been assigned to the Mia Grant case. I went over to see Karen Langley at the *City Herald*, she gave away that he was the one who'd done the research on her article.'

'What the fuck is the deal with this Langley woman?' Lucas asked. 'She gets a rush doing this shit?'

'Don't break a sweat,' Vincent said, 'she's a newspaper hack. They're all the freakin' same.'

'Anyway,' Irving went on, 'far as I understand, this article is not going to be appearing in the *Herald* or *The New York Times*, and I'm not aware of any TV crews turning up at police precincts, or news bulletins or anything going out.'

'Give it time,' Lucas said. 'Just give it a little time. Once they get an idea we're collaborating on something they'll be all over us.'

'We're getting off track here,' Vincent said. 'The question is whether or not this Costello guy is in the frame for this.'

'He's as good as anyone right now,' Irving said. 'Gut feeling tells me no, but I've been wrong before. If he is our guy then he's seriously good at giving nothing away.'

'So a plan of action,' Farraday said. 'I propose that due to the fact the Fourth has two separate incidents, whereas the Ninth, Fifth, Seventh and Third have only one each, the temporary co-ordination point be established here. Any disagreements?'

There were none.

'Okay, as far as forensics and crime scene analysis is concerned, who out of you lot has the most years on this?'

Turner raised his hand. He was visibly the oldest of the group.

'Right, any objections to Jeff Turner as acting controller for the forensic and crime scene analysis issues?'

Once again, there were no disagreements with Farraday's proposal.

'Okay, so we have what we have. Irving and Turner pool their resources. I send a briefing to Chief Ellmann tonight. We get a silencer on this Karen Langley at the *City Herald*, and we establish an agreement with *The Times* that they do nothing on this Zodiac letter while there's an ongoing investigation. Any press queries, requests for statements or conferences come directly to me . . . and don't even be smart and say "No comment" to anyone. If you say "no comment" they know we're into something. Anyone asks what this was about it was a meeting regarding security for the Mayor's re-election walkabouts. The key to this is to keep it quiet, keep it discreet. We've worked to keep this thing under wraps so far and I want it to stay that way. Newspaper headlines I can do without, you understand?'

'And John Costello?' Lavelle asked.

'I'll follow up on Costello and this Winterbourne group,' Irving said.

Farraday rose from his chair. 'I suggest our line of investigation works through all known serial killers for the last fifty years. We get a database organized and establish the dates of all past serial killings that occurred between now and Christmas. I know that it'll be a nightmare. I understand that there is no way of predicting whose killing he might replicate next, but if we know that there was no killing that fell between, for example, now and next Tuesday, then we at least have some breathing space.'

He paused for a moment, looked at each individual present. 'Any questions?'

There were none, and almost immediately people stood up, moved around to talk to each other. The hubbub of discussion grew to such an extent that Ray Irving could barely hear Farraday when he said, 'Make this thing go away, for God's sake . . . can you do that for me?'

Farraday didn't wait for an answer. He merely straightened his jacket, circumnavigated the crowd of detectives and CSAs, and left the room.

Irving stood there for some time, trying to remember what his life had been like prior to June 3rd.

NINETEEN

'You got the envelope?' John Costello asked.

He stood on the sidewalk outside the Winterbourne Hotel on 37th Street. He smiled at Ray Irving as if this was the unexpected reunion of old and important friends.

'I did.'

'Shawcross, right?'

'Right.'

'Expect that rattled some cages.'

Irving nodded. He stood there for a moment and looked at John Costello as if he was seeing him for the first time.

Costello was of average height, perhaps five nine or ten. He dressed well – had on a smart pair of pants, a sport jacket, a clean, pressed white shirt. His hair was professionally cut, he was clean-shaven, his shoes were shined. He looked like an architect, a writer, perhaps an advertising executive who'd made his name with successful campaigns and now devoted his energies to consultations.

He did not look like a serial killer who spent his time replicating earlier murders and then wrote newspaper stories about them.

But then, Irving thought, who did?

'Are you making progress?' Costello asked.

'What do you want me to tell you, Mr Costello?'

Costello glanced back down the street and as if there was something he expected to see. 'I don't know, Detective . . . I suppose I'm still hopeful that you people will always be one step ahead of the other people.'

'The *other* people?'

'The Shawcrosses and McDuffs and Gacys of this world. Is it not frustrating always to be in a position where you are chasing those who have done terrible things, as opposed to getting to them before they do it again?'

'Maybe you have to look at it from the viewpoint that those we apprehend have been prevented from doing further terrible things. We can't undo what's happened, but we can save future lives.'

Costello closed his eyes for a moment, and then smiled resignedly. 'If you hoped to see who else was attending our meeting I had them leave by the back way. I'm not in good favor at the moment.'

'Because?'

'Because I have broken a cardinal rule of the group.'

'Which is?'

'That everything stays inside the group.'

'That doesn't seem to be a very responsible attitude.'

'Depends on your perspective,' Costello replied. 'I am the only member of the group whose attacker did not attack again. The man who attacked me—'

'Committed suicide, right? Robert Clare.'

'Yes, Robert Clare. The others all survived an attack by someone who then went on to kill again.'

'So there is no love lost between your group members and the police,' Irving said matter-of-factly.

'I think it would be safe to say that.'

'How many are there?'

'Aside from me, there are six. Four women, two men. Seven of us in all.'

'And who heads the group, who founded it?'

'A man called Edward Cavanaugh.' Costello smiled. 'Strictly speaking, what he started and what it became were not the same. Cavanaugh was not a victim, his wife was. He saw it as a means by which he could get some support and assistance from people he thought might understand how he felt. His wife was murdered some years ago, and he started this as a sort of bereavement group, for support, for fraternity if you like. The people who responded to his advertisement were people who had themselves survived attacks, not their loved ones or relatives.'

'And Cavanaugh is one of the male members you mentioned?'

'No. He committed suicide some time ago.'

'And how did you find out about it?'

154

'I was in touch with someone on the internet, back in 2000. She and I maintained a relationship, just e-mails, a few phone calls, you know? There was nothing between us except a degree of friendship. She found out about the group, wanted to go, but didn't want to go alone. She asked me to accompany her and I did.'

'And she's still part of the group?'

Costello shook his head. 'No, she actually met someone and got married, moved to Boston. I don't speak to her anymore. She was one of the lucky ones.'

'How so?'

'She got through it. She dealt with whatever she had to and she was able to start another life. I think she even had children, you know?'

'Let's go inside,' Costello suggested. 'Let's go get a cup of coffee or something. I can imagine that this is one of those unofficially official conversations, and if I tell you I have to go home then you're not going to be happy.'

'I do need to speak to you, Mr Costello,' Irving said. 'I think what you're doing is important, and I want to know everything that you've learned.'

Costello smiled. 'I'm flattered, Detective Irving, but I think you might be disappointed with what I know.'

They walked a block, found a diner on 38th and Tenth. Costello wanted black, no sugar. Irving asked for decaf.

'I don't sleep so good as it is,' he told Costello. 'Coffee makes it worse.'

They sat for a while in silence, and then Costello asked Irving what he felt would happen with his case.

'It might not be my case tomorrow,' Irving said.

'How so?'

'Because you have five different precincts involved, and each precinct has a captain, and each captain has a work-load and a number of resources, and the Chief of Police will assign as he sees fit. The whole thing may be turned over to someone else entirely.'

'But for now?' Costello asked.

'For now? Well, to tell you the truth, everyone involved in this is very interested in who you are, Mr Costello . . . and who your group is, and what they might have to do with this thing.'

'Which is understandable,' Costello replied, 'but I can assure you that no-one in the group has any direct connection with any of these murders, and their interest is purely academic.'

Irving smiled. 'You know that, Mr Costello, and I might be prepared to accept that, but—'

Costello raised his hand and Irving fell silent.

'There are a great many reasons for doing what we do,' Costello said. 'The common denominator has something to do with our willingness to face what frightens us. It's not complicated, and it certainly isn't a new idea. We talk about dying, and we talk about people who are capable of killing other people, and sometimes people talk about their nightmares, you know? That's what they do, and when they get over their initial anger and fear they start to look outwards a little . . . to consider the possibility that there might be a life beyond what they've experienced. Like people who are released from prison or who have been tortured, or been through war . . . something like that. After something like that it feels for a while as if that's all there is to your life, and when you speak to other people who've gone through the same things, well, then you start to think that maybe there *is* something beyond it.' He smiled wistfully. 'You're basically talking about a group of people, each of whom believe that they should be dead, but they're not . . . and that's a hard thing to deal with.'

'I get all that,' Irving said, 'but where does the amateur detective stuff come into it? Where does that figure into the equation?'

'Don't make something out of nothing,' Costello replied. 'That's a job for the newspapers, not the police.' He smiled at his own sarcasm. 'This area of analysis is my interest, predominantly at least, but there's someone else there, someone who has—' He paused, picked up his coffee cup, drank some, set it back on the saucer. 'An acquaintance of mine. He has a head for dates and times and places, you know? He remembers things.'

'He's the one who made the connections between—'

Costello nodded.

'And where does he think this thing will go now?' Irving asked.

'Where does he think it will go? Jesus, we're talking about people who have an interest in serial murders, not a spiritualist group.'

Irving smiled, and neither spoke for some moments.

'So tell me something, Detective Irving,' Costello said. 'Do you have anything on this guy at all? Do you have any idea of where this thing is going?'

Irving shook his head. 'I can't answer that. I can't talk about an ongoing investigation.'

'But you already are.'

'But I'm not telling you anything you don't already know—'

'So we make a deal, Detective.'

Irving raised his eyebrows.

'You tell me something I don't already know, and I'll tell you something in return.'

Irving thought of his discussion with Karen Langley. He leaned back in his chair, looked out the window, noticed a man across the street struggling with an inside-out umbrella and realized that it was raining. Cars passed, a taxicab, a bus, and all of it like a scene from a movie. The world was out there, and they knew nothing of what was happening.

'That's a potentially compromising situation,' Irving said, almost to himself.

'Trust is everything, Detective,' Costello replied.

'You work for a newspaper.'

'And you work for the New York Police Department.'

Irving smiled. 'Are you saying that the police are untrustworthy?'

'Not all, no.'

'But some.'

'Of course . . .' Costello's comment was left hanging.

'So what do you want to know?' Irving asked.

'Something that's not in the newspaper reports, that I wouldn't know from listening to police scanners. A detail. An aspect of personality. A fact that – to you – seems important to this case.'

'And in return?'

'I'll tell *you* something that you don't already know.'

'That has some bearing on this case?'

Costello nodded.

'And this is a firm agreement, not some bullshit game?'

'We're talking about people's lives—'

'There are no witnesses to this conversation,' Irving said. He reached forward suddenly, unexpectedly, and grabbed Costello's hand. Costello pulled back instinctively, but Irving's grip was firm and unrelenting. Within a moment Irving had run his hand over both of Costello's shoulders, down his chest, beneath each arm, and then he released him.

'What?' Costello asked. 'You think I might be recording this conversation?'

'I am a New York police detective,' Irving said. 'I've been in the police department for twenty years. I became a detective in 1997, Mr Costello, and I've worked in Vice, in Narcotics, in Homicide. I have seen more dead bodies than you could possibly imagine, and I'm not talking about websites and newspaper pictures. I'm not talking about some escapist pastime that makes people feel like they understand what being a police officer is all about . . . I'm talking about actual first-hand, up-close-and-personal material witness to the worst that people can do to one another. You understand me?'

Costello opened his mouth to speak.

'I'm not done yet, Mr Costello. You wrote an article. Okay, it didn't wind up in the paper, but it could have done. You put two and two together on some murders that happened in the last few weeks. You pieced it all together. You made the New York Police Department look like a bunch of dumb motherfuckers who struggle to tie their own shoelaces. I go to my office and you have been so kind as to deliver some pages about a case that even I didn't know of, and now we're playing games here. Now we're drinking coffee together and we're playing games about what I might know and what you might be able to tell me. This is real life, Mr Costello, this is very, very real, and right now I don't have a great deal of patience—'

'Enough,' Costello interjected. 'That's enough, Detective.

I am not the guilty party here. I'm a concerned citizen, and nothing more. I'm a crime researcher for a newspaper and I know things – I'm *supposed* to know things. It's what I do. I keep my eyes and ears open, I make calls, look at the net. I verify facts and write them in such a way as to insure that the newspaper does not incur libel and slander judgements. Whatever you think is happening here is not happening. I am *not* your suspect, okay? I am trying to help you, not make your life more difficult. I'm not a stupid man, Detective, and if I was somehow involved in these murders I certainly would not be sending you material that would assist you to catch me—'

'You'd be surprised, Mr Costello, believe me. You would be surprised what some of these whackos will do to get attention.'

'So what did this particular whacko do, Detective? What did he do that no-one except you people know about?'

Irving hesitated, looked at the street once more. The rain appeared to have stopped, but the sidewalk and the street were varnished. Reflections from the streetlights and store signs, people alone and in couples, the sound of music filtering through from a bar someplace nearby . . . it all gave the impression that here was a regular city, a safe place to live, a place where people could get on with their lives, unconcerned for their own safety. Not so. Never had been, not as long as Irving had been alive, and the way things were going he believed it never would be.

'Detective?'

Irving looked back at John Costello. He dared not trust the man. No-one could be trusted. Not completely.

'You know something that will help us?' Irving asked.

'I know of an avenue that you could take that might result in some progress,' Costello replied.

'That doesn't sound very positive.'

'Nothing is positive, Detective, you know that as well as I.'

'And what do you want from me?'

'Something, anything,' Costello said. 'A single fact . . . something I don't already know.'

'And if I tell you something, what's to prevent you telling me that you knew it already?'

Costello laughed. 'How is it to live your life with no trust, Detective?'

Irving looked right at him, and Costello did not look away. In that moment, for whatever reason, Irving allowed himself to believe that Costello was telling the truth.

'He sent a letter,' Irving said. 'This morning . . . a letter to *The New York Times*.'

'What did it say?' Costello asked.

'It wasn't so much what he said, not the words. It was a letter that Arthur Shawcross wrote, but our friend wrote it in the Zodiac cipher.'

Costello's intake of breath was audible. His eyes widened. He leaned back in his chair and shook his head. 'Like James Wolfe,' he said quietly.

'How so?'

'He really wants us to get the connection. He's performing for us, and he doesn't want us to miss any of it. He kills someone like a previous victim, but he's worried that we won't put two and two together.'

'So now I've told you something,' Irving said.

Costello was nodding, still thinking. 'You wonder if it's a message?' he asked.

'What?'

'The fact that he sent the letter in the Zodiac cipher?'

'About his next victim?'

'Right,' Costello said. 'That his next victim will be in the style of the Zodiac.'

'Who the fuck knows,' Irving said. 'Right now I have to work through every known serial killer for the last fifty years and tabulate every victim's date of death between now and Christmas.'

'You know that the Zodiac had only six confirmed victims?'

'So I've been told.'

'And you'd have to look at those that occurred only on specific dates, right?'

'Right.'

Costello took a notebook and pen from his inside jacket pocket. 'So who do we have?' he asked himself. 'September 27th, 1969 we had Bryan Hartnell and Cecelia Shepard, both of them stabbed at Lake Berryessa. He survived. She did not. October 11th '69 we had Paul Stine shot in San Francisco. 26th September 1970 we had Donna Lass in Nevada, except they never found her . . . September 29th, 1974, Donna Braun strangled in Monterey. Lastly we have Susan Dye strangled in Santa Rosa on October 16th, 1975. Of those only Hartnell, Shepard and Stine were actually verified as Zodiac victims. Hartnell survived—'

'You should write him,' Irving said. 'Ask him to come join your group.'

Costello didn't acknowledge Irving's sarcasm.

'So if he does a Zodiac killing you're looking for a murder that will happen on the 26th, 27th or 29th of this month, or he could wait until the 11th or 16th of October.'

'That's if he does the Zodiac.'

'Right,' Costello said. 'That's if he does the Zodiac, and that's if he chooses to replicate the unconfirmed killings. If he goes for the only known Zodiac victim then it's Hartnell and Shepherd on the 27th.'

'And if he doesn't?'

'Then you have to keep your eyes and ears open, because you start to factor in about two hundred serial murders a year spanning fifty years, then every day is going to be the anniversary of someone's death.'

'Reassuring.'

Costello closed his notebook, put it back in his pocket.

'And now you,' Irving said. 'Now you tell me something I don't already know?'

'There is a subculture, a group of people who collect artifacts,' Costello said. 'Artifacts from serial murders.'

'I know about this shit,' Irving said.

'No you don't,' Costello said. 'Not these collectors. These aren't your crazies, the ones who sell crime scene pictures and tee-shirts with bloodstains on. I'm talking about serious people, people with a great deal of money. The sort that will find you a snuff movie and it's the real thing.'

'And what have these people got to do with what's going on?'

'You should talk to them,' Costello said. 'There's a chance – at least I think there's a chance – that your man is one of

161

these people, or has come into contact with these people in an effort to better understand a particular murder.'

'This is supposition,' Irving said. 'We made an agreement here . . . we made an agreement that you would tell me something I don't already know—'

'I have a name for you,' Costello said. 'Leonard Beck.'

'And who the hell is he?'

'Someone I think might be able to help you more than you realize.'

'And where would I find this Leonard Beck?'

'In the phone book, Detective . . . right there in the phone book. Far as I know he now lives in Manhattan, and he'll be the only one listed.'

'That's it?'

'That's it, Detective.'

'And now I have two questions for you, Mr Costello.'

Costello raised his eyebrows.

'Was Mia Grant the first one?'

'I think she was, yes.'

'Why? How can you be so sure that this hasn't been going on for years?'

'I can't. Hell, how can any of us be sure about anything. I have . . .' Costello paused for a moment. 'This has been an area of interest for some time.'

'Serial murders.'

'Murderers. It's not what they do, but why they do it. It's the situational dynamics. The way things come together to bring someone to the point where they believe that killing another human being, someone they don't even know, appears to be a rational act, a solution to something.'

'Not to a problem that you or I would consider a problem.'

'No, of course not. You can't rationalize an irrationality. We're not talking about people who follow the accepted lines of thought and action, are we? We're talking about people who have long since left behind whatever passes for normality.'

'And what problem does this solve for you, Mr Costello?'

'Problem?' Costello shook his head. 'I consider myself an academic, Detective Irving, that's all. If you think I'm trying to exorcise some demon from the past then you're wrong. I was attacked by someone who had no reason to attack me. He tried to kill us both, but he only killed the girl I was with at the time. She was seventeen years old, and after I recovered from the physical injury I had to deal with the mental and emotional effect of what happened.'

'And you dealt with that how?'

'I've read a lot of books, Detective. Books about psychology, psychiatry, psychoanalysis, all manner of things, and none of them explain the way a human being works. Not with any real certainty, and not with any real appreciation of the degree to which an individual can understand himself. I feel I've reached a level of understanding about myself that makes it possible to go on living life without dragging the weight of the past along with me. I have my moments . . .' Costello smiled privately. 'I have my idiosyncrasies. I'm not in a relationship with anyone, and to tell you the truth I don't know that I ever will be.' He paused a moment. 'I count things—'

Irving looked at him, quizzical.

'What's your habit, Detective? What is it that you do that no-one really knows about? Do you avoid cracks in the sidewalk, or check the back door is locked three times before you leave the house?'

Irving laughed. 'I read the newspaper backwards . . . I don't mean actually reading stuff backwards, but I start at the back of the paper and work toward the front page.'

'Why? That makes no sense at all.'

Irving shrugged. 'God, I don't know, it was something my father did. Maybe I figured that's what he was doing, you know? Like he'd read the sports page, then the funnies and the horoscopes, then whatever news items he was interested in. I always had the idea that he was reading the paper backwards.'

'You were close?'

'Not particularly no . . . I think I was a general disappointment to him.'

'No brothers and sisters?'

'No, just me.'

'And were you a disappointment?'

'I hope not.'

'So maybe people have these little quirks and idiosyncrasies that they pick up from other people because it makes them feel safe . . . gives them an anchor to something, you know?'

'What is this?' Irving asked. 'All of a sudden I'm in therapy?'

'No,' Costello said. 'I was just making a point. We all do things that make no real sense at all, and most of the time we don't even know why we're doing them. The people that do these things to other people . . . the crazies, the psychos, the serial killers, well they're just the same, Detective Irving. Surely they, in their own twisted way, are just doing the things that they do with no real appreciation or comprehension of why they're doing them . . . the truth is that it doesn't matter, it actually doesn't matter why they're doing it, they just know that it has to be done, and it has to be done now, and there's no getting away from the fact that this is the way that life is. Whatever any of them do, to them it makes complete sense.'

'It's a very simplistic view, Mr Costello.'

'Who says it needs to be complicated?'

'The other question,' Irving said.

'Shoot.'

'This acquaintance of yours . . . the one who remembers names and dates, the one who put these connections together?'

Costello nodded.

'There is no acquaintance is there?'

Costello smiled.

'The names and dates of the Zodiac killings . . . the confirmed ones and the others. You remembered those dates, right?'

'I did, yes.'

'You remember all forty-six of them?'

'What is this, a pop quiz?'

'No, Mr Costello, it's not. I just believe that if you want to help me with this thing then everything, from this point forward has to be completely straight.'

'Are you asking for my help, Detective?'

'Are you prepared to give it?'

'If you think I can help you, yes.'

'Then I might come back and see you after I've spoken with Leonard Beck. You say there's only one in the Manhattan directory?'

'Only one that will be obvious. He's a doctor.'

Irving rose from the chair, extended his hand and Costello took it. He believed his sense of despair was somehow mirrored in Costello's expression. It was not an uncommon feeling, the knowledge that there were lives somehow held in limbo, that – dependent on decisions made now, dependent on actions taken – people would go on living, oblivious to the fact that some unknown person had wished them dead, even planned their death in intricate detail. And if Irving missed a clue, missed an answer, a life would be brought to a close with brutal and unequivocal certainty. Such things carried weight, and the burden grew more unforgiving with the years.

'So, we are done,' Costello said quietly.

'For now, Mr Costello, for now.'

TWENTY

Late, a little after ten, Ray Irving located Edward Cavanaugh on the internet, and found the details of his wife's murder. Sarah Cavanaugh, née Russell, the fourth victim of six. Kidnapped from outside her workplace, evening of Thursday, May 13th, 1999. Husband reported her missing that evening, again the following afternoon. An official bulletin was not issued until the evening of Friday the 14th. By that time the Manhattan PD Task Force – overseeing a recent spate of kidnapping-murders – realized that the MO of their perp was the same. She was found in a dumpster back of a seedy downtown hotel in the early hours of Saturday the 15th. She had been blindfolded with duct tape, her head had been shaved, her fingertips and toes had been removed with pruning shears. Cause of death had been a single puncture to the front of the throat, and she'd bled out from the jugular. As with the previous three victims, there was no indication of any sexual assault, though, on Sarah Cavanaugh's stomach – as with the other victims – the word *slut* had been carved with a boxcutter. The perp, a disarmingly handsome man by the name of Frederick Lewis Cope, had gone on to kill another two, one in June and one in August. All six victims had been professional women between the ages of thirty-five and forty-one, and had worked in offices and banks in the Manhattan financial district. They drove to work in the mornings from the suburbs where they all lived, drove home again in the evenings. All were childless, all were married to stockbrokers. Why Frederick Lewis Cope felt compelled to remove the fingers and toes of Manhattan stockbrokers' wives and leave them to bleed out in city dumpsters was never known. Cope, his work done, it seemed, cut his own throat on September 4th, 1999 with the same boxcutter he had used to embellish his victims.

Edward Cavanaugh had been a junior partner at Machin, Freed and Langham, a modest investment firm with offices in New York, Boston and Manchester, New Hampshire. After his wife's death he was given three months' paid leave, but never returned to work. From assorted articles and blogs he posted on the web, it seemed that Cavanaugh collapsed into himself and ceased to be the man he once was. Cope, colloquially referred to as The Slut Killer, appeared to have established himself as some sort of icon and role model for a rock band. The Slut Killers, self-styled 'anti-establishment cultural revolutionaries', maintained a cult following across the east coast between 2000 and late 2002. Their fans wore tee-shirts carrying Frederick Cope's image, and in some cases the images of his victims. Cavanaugh attempted to prosecute The Slut Killers, but the case was never heard. The legal stand was that the band was not responsible for the actions of their fans and, since the term 'slut killer' was neither a trademark nor a registered brand, there were no grounds for action. Cavanaugh posted his own website.

It was this website that instigated the meeting of several surviving serial-killer victims, the handful of people that ultimately became the Winterbourne group. Irving read numerous pages, and within them found himself face to face with the ever-diminishing spirit of a broken and desperate man. Where Cavanaugh had first spoken of hope and future, where he had initially maintained some semblance of desire to work with others who might have experienced similar things, the website ultimately became nothing more than a shrine to his dead wife. Cavanaugh spoke of their life together, the fact that they had begun trying for a child only a week or so before her death. They had planned a future, and within a heartbeat that future was extinguished.

In the days before Edward Cavanaugh's suicide he spoke of his dismay, his lack of faith in any sense of universal justice. He spoke of his upbringing, his churchgoing parents, how any belief he might once have possessed in God had long since disappeared. He spoke of chance, luck, fate, karma, of reincarnation; of the view that people were held to account for what they might have done in a former life. Many such things filled the pages, some of them passages of reasoned

167

and sequential thoughts, others rambling dissertations and monologues. And with each entry, he seemed to slip further and further away from the world he'd once inhabited and believed in. His last post, registered an hour before his suicide on Wednesday, May 15th, 2002, precisely three years after the discovery of his wife's body, read simply: *Fuck it.*

Edward Cavanaugh took forty-seven Seconal tablets and cut his wrists in the bath.

Irving leaned back in his chair and massaged his temples. He was exhausted but knew he wouldn't sleep. He wanted company, the kind of company that Deborah Wiltshire had so effortlessly provided. He wanted meaning and purpose, he wanted space and reason, and some simple understanding of the life he was living. He wanted to know what he was doing, and why. Certain that such things were currently beyond his reach, he turned instead to the Manhattan telephone directory and found Leonard Beck, M.D. His listing was bold, as obvious as John Costello said it would be, and when he looked up Beck on the internet he found his offices in the city no more than four or five blocks from the Fourth Precinct. Beck was a heart specialist, a man with more letters after his name than in it. He would visit Leonard Beck tomorrow.

Eleven-forty p.m., and Irving shut everything down.

He sat at the kitchen table, listened to the traffic on Tenth, and thought about John Costello, a man who chose to remember the dates and locations of murders as if such things would provide him with stability and reason. Or perhaps not. Perhaps there was no reason to it at all. Perhaps – as seemed to be the case with Harvey Carignan and Kenneth McDuff, with John Gacy, Arthur Shawcross and Frederick Cope – it was just something that had to be done.

TWENTY-ONE

The building was impressive. East 37th and Madison, near the Pierpont Morgan Library. Endless stories and a lobby like the Grand Ole Opry. Beck ran three floors all by himself. Big doctor. Big money. Big handshake when he came out to meet Irving.

'Detective Irving,' he said, and he smiled wide and friendly, but there was something inside of that smile that indicated a cautious man.

Beck's office was furnished out of a magazine, all planters and marble ornaments, his desk wider than Irving's kitchen. Despite the number of executive gadgets across it they all looked lonely.

He showed Irving to a deep armchair, asked if he wanted coffee, some fruit juice, perhaps a glass of water? Irving declined.

Leonard Beck was in his mid to late forties, Irving guessed. He had the measured approach of one who was certain about his place in life. He knew it, others knew it too, and there was little beyond that that needed to make sense. There was enough money here to make any awkward aspects disappear. It had not, however, been difficult to get an appointment to see the man. One call, the fact that Irving needed some help with a case, and he was instructed to attend immediately.

'I appreciate your willingness to see me,' Irving said.

'You're fortunate I'm here,' Beck said. He sat down facing Irving. 'I've been in the country for a few days, and tomorrow morning I'm leaving for Atlanta.'

'This is not an official inquiry, not as such,' Irving said, 'but I got your name from someone who felt you might be able to help me.'

'A medical matter?' Beck asked.

169

'No, not as a doctor . . .' Irving paused, felt awkward. 'It's somewhat of a strange—'

'My hobby?' Beck asked.

Irving's surprise was evident.

'In my line of work, Detective, I have no time to play games, much as you don't, I'm sure. I am a cardiologist primarily, and you don't soften blows when it comes to the heart. I have what some would call a morbid fascination with a particular area of the human condition. In all honesty I couldn't tell you why.' Beck smiled, crossed his legs, seemed nothing less than completely at ease. 'There is nothing in my past that would suggest a reason to pursue this line of interest, but when you train as a medical doctor you touch on certain elements of human psychology, psychosomatic ills, such things as this. It was something that seemed to warrant further study so I read a great deal, and in reading further I walked around the edges of psychiatry and psycho-analysis, and from there it was a few short steps to criminal psychology.'

Beck paused, and indicated the books to the left of his desk. 'Second shelf down, you'll see I keep a few volumes to hand.'

Irving followed Beck's line of sight, and there on the shelf he saw Geberth, *Practical Homicide Investigation: Tactics, Procedures and Forensic Techniques*; Ressler and Shachtmann, *Whoever Fights Monsters*; Turvey, *Criminal Profiling: An Introduction to Behavioral Evidence Analysis*; Ressler, Burgess and Douglas, *Sexual Homicides: Patterns and Motives* and Egger's *The Killers Amongst Us: An Examination of Serial Murder and its Investigation*.

'A relatively harmless interest, fascinating nonetheless, but not the subject you want to discuss with me.'

Irving shook his head. 'I don't know exactly what it is that I should be asking you, but I had the idea it might be less theoretical and more—'

'Hands on?' Beck interjected. 'You're talking about my collection.'

'Collection?'

Beck nodded. 'Could I ask you who gave you my name, Detective?'

'Sure, of course . . . a man called John Costello.'

'Hammer of God,' Beck replied.

'You know him?'

'John Costello. No, I don't know him. I know *of* him, but only because of the attack he suffered. He was the only survivor of that series.'

'So I believe,' Irving said, and was struck by confusion, a sudden feeling that he was at the edge of an abyss, as if here were defined the parameters between the world with which he was familiar, and something far darker.

'You believe correctly,' Beck said. 'November 23rd, 1984, he and his girlfriend, Nadia McGowan, were attacked by Robert Melvin Clare. She was killed, he survived. He's part of that group, isn't he? The one that was started by Edward Cavanaugh.'

'Yes, he is. People who have survived serial-killer attacks. They meet every month . . .'

'You look a little dismayed, Detective.'

'Perhaps,' Irving replied. 'It appears there is a small world beneath the surface—'

'There is always something beneath everything,' Beck replied. 'The Cavanaugh group, what I do . . . these things are nothing compared to what actually goes on. There are some people who are utterly obsessed and consumed by the subject. They spend their lives, every waking moment and every dollar they can find, tracking down artifacts.' Beck glanced at his watch, seemed to make a mental note of something. 'You've heard of Truman Capote?'

Irving nodded.

'His book, *In Cold Blood*, about the killing of the Clutter family in Kansas. They were shotgunned to death, but the father also had his throat cut. I know a man who spent eleven years and over eighty thousand dollars tracking down the knife that was used.'

Irving frowned.

'You wonder why?'

'Yes,' Irving replied.

'Same reason I became a doctor, same reason you became a detective. Why would someone want to bury their hands in someone's chest cavity, take out their heart, replace it? Why would someone such as yourself want to spend his days poring over the details of horrific murders?'

'I think what we're doing is a little different from pursuing a morbid interest in the lives and artifacts of serial killers,' Irving said.

'Perhaps it is, Detective – to us – but to those who do it, no. You will never successfully rationalize what you consider irrational.'

'That's not the first time I've heard that.'

'For an example,' Beck said. 'Can you imagine how someone like John Costello must feel? Can you imagine the kind of self-inspection he must have gone through in the months after the attack? He's sixteen years old, he's out with his girlfriend, probably the first real girlfriend he ever had, and he's attacked by someone with a hammer. They beat his head in. They kill her, but he survives. He wonders why it happened, he wonders why he survived and she didn't. He wonders about fate, about God, about divine retribution. He wonders if some mistake hasn't been made and he was the one who should have been killed. People ask questions, Detective Irving, and they answer them the best way they can. They have to make do with the answers they figure out, because there isn't anyone else out there who's an authority on such things.'

'So why do you collect things . . .' Irving paused, smiled. 'And what is it that you *do* collect?'

'Letters primarily,' Beck said. 'I have the foremost collection of letters and documents from known serial killers in the country, perhaps the world. I have documents that were signed by people. I have love letters, letters of complaint, letters of appeal and apology, letters to mothers and fathers, letters from surviving victims to their attackers, and letters from the attackers back to the victims. I have over thirteen thousand pages of words and drawings. I even have a drawing that was done by Perry Smith, one of the Kansas killers that Capote wrote about.'

'And to obtain these things?'

Beck smiled. 'This is why your friend Mr Costello suggested you come and speak with me, isn't it?'

'Is it?' Irving parried.

'In answer to your question, Detective . . . how do I obtain such things? I obtain such things by dealing with certain individuals I would most definitely not select as dinner guests.'

'Other collectors?'

'In a way, yes. There are two very different types of individual in this business. The collectors and the sellers. The sellers are the ones who go out looking for this stuff, and sometimes I don't want to know how they obtain these things. They find them, they let me know, I make some calls, I view the items, negotiate a price and buy what I wish. These days I buy a lot less than I used to. There's a huge market in spurious material nowadays – staged photographs, forged documents, the most intricate elements of corroboration created to give the apparency that something is genuine. The vast bulk of what I look at these days is either worthless or counterfeit.'

'Okay . . . so if I wished to replicate a crime scene. If I wanted to obtain photographs of a crime scene so I could accurately copy it . . . the position of the body, the clothes of the victim, that kind of thing?'

'Then you would need to start looking a lot further beneath the surface than you are looking now.'

'Which means?'

'The underground. The sub-subculture of this business. You would need to start visiting some of the places where such material can be bought.'

'And how would I get into these places? How would I even find out where they were?'

'Well, they sure as hell don't advertise in *The New York Times*.' Beck was quiet for a moment, and then he rose from the chair and went to his desk. 'The genuine material that is sold at such places has more often than not been stolen by someone within the federal or judicial system. Clerks, people in archives, stenographers, staff in evidence lock-ups . . . that's where most of the genuine stuff comes from. It's their equivalent of stealing staplers and Post-It notes from the office. An old case, files that are falling apart, a hand-written confession from some killer that no-one will ever look for because the guy was executed in 1973 . . . you get the picture. It disappears into someone's pocket, they sell it to someone for five hundred dollars, and I end up buying it three years later for twelve grand. The second type of material, and significantly more prevalent, is counterfeit. Either which way, these are both illegal activities. One is the theft and subsequent sale of stolen government documents, the other is forgery. The last person in the world that such people would want at their swap-meets is a police detective.'

'I wouldn't wear my uniform,' Irving said.

Beck hesitated. 'I believe there may be a meeting on Friday the fifteenth.'

'Where?'

'I am not so sure that—'

'We're talking real people here, Dr Beck,' Irving interjected.

Beck raised his hand. 'I can tell you where, Detective, but I cannot get you in. That is something you're going to have to do yourself.'

Irving didn't respond.

'Although I'm kept informed of these meetings, I haven't been to them for years. The people I work with have private viewings—'

'Where is this meeting going to happen, Dr Beck?'

'I cannot have you—'

'I appreciate the fact that you've been honest with me,' Irving said. 'I also understand that nothing would be gained by trying to influence you with threats. You know as well as I do that any attempt to investigate how you came about obtaining your documents and letters would come to nothing. I'm asking you to help me simply because—'

'The Village,' Beck said. 'West 11th and Greenwich, there's a hotel called the Bedford Park. It sounds fine, but it's not. It's a cockroach pit. There's a meeting there on Friday evening.'

'And I get in how?'

'Personal recommendation,' Beck replied. 'No other way.'

'And that's something I cannot ask you to do?'

'That is something I would be very pleased if you did not ask me to do, Detective Irving.'

Irving was quiet for a little while, and then he stood up, straightened his jacket, and said, 'Today is Tuesday. If I have nothing by Thursday morning I might come back and see you again.'

'Like I said, Detective, tomorrow morning I leave for Atlanta. I'm not returning until next Monday.'

'Is there some way I could reach you?'

Beck handed his card to Irving. 'My cellphone and my pager number are on there.'

Irving looked at the card, not to read what was written but to give himself a few moments to gather his thoughts.

Those thoughts, whatever they might have been, were interrupted by Beck. 'The reason for this?' he asked. 'Someone is killing people?'

Irving looked up. 'Someone is always killing people, Dr Beck. Seems to be the way of the world.'

TWENTY-TWO

Captain Farraday was not happy. Chief Ellmann had appeared that morning and asked to speak with Irving personally. Farraday dealt with it, said that Irving was pursuing a vital lead. Ellmann wanted specifics, Farraday bullshitted, Ellmann saw through it, told Farraday to straighten up and fly right on this thing. Those were his exact words. Irving found it difficult to believe that anyone actually said that. Then Ellmann told Farraday that the Fourth Precinct was home for this nightmare, that Irving was to head it up, that it was their case. They would get an overtime allowance for uniforms to work on the files, additional research, such things as this, but as far as pulling detectives from the Ninth, the Seventh, the Third and the Fifth it was not going to happen.

'How many homicides this year?' Ellmann asked Farraday.

Farraday shook his head. 'This precinct . . . God . . . two-forty? Maybe two-fifty, give or take.'

'How many detectives here?'

'Six.'

'That's forty or fifty each,' Ellmann replied. He fired statements at Farraday like shooting practice. 'Irving gets all eight. This is his baby. He's a good detective. He got cited. He's not been under IAD investigation. He can handle it. And keep it out of the papers for Christ's sake.'

'But—'

Ellmann shook his head. 'This is eight homicides. I have a campaign for Chief, the Mayor has his own re-election. Closed cases is what we need, Captain. I can't have four or five precincts collapsing all their manpower into what is essentially one investigation. Irving's a grown-up, he can deal with it. I got you a shutdown on the *Herald*, and we spoke with *The Times* about this letter they got. We have an

176

element of co-operation right now, and if they get wind of the fact that we're tying up all our available resources into this thing, you can just imagine how excited they're gonna get. Irving is the man. Tell him we need it done hard and fast.'

The message was relayed when Irving arrived.

It didn't surprise him. He had half-expected it.

'I've given you the back half of the big office,' Farraday said. 'All the files are up there. Everything has been brought over from the other precincts. It's a mess, but you can have a couple of uniforms to help you sort it out. I'm here for about three hours, and then I'm gone until Thursday morning. Anything you need immediately?'

'I need to check a hotel booking, then I need to put a watch on whoever turns up on that.'

'I'll sign what you need, have someone bring it to me.'

'How do I reach you if I need something else?'

Farraday shook his head. 'Officially you don't. If it's life or death, call my cell, leave a message. I'll come back to you as fast as I can.'

'Can I keep one of the uniforms?' Irving asked.

'No, I can't spare them. Right through to the middle of next month I can't have anyone out on their own. I have an even number of people today. I'm giving you two because I give you two or nothing. You get them until lunchtime and then they're out. Right now it's all about visibility on the streets—'

'The elections,' Irving said matter-of-factly.

'Our jobs,' Farraday said. 'Think about it that way and it doesn't feel so cheap.'

Irving visited his own office briefly and then made his way up one more flight of stairs to the third. The room they had used the previous day had been divided down the center by partitions. On the left were the regular homicide detectives' stations, their desks pushed together to create the necessary room, and on the right a pair of desks end-to-end, the white-boards and files and stacks of documents that had been brought over from the other precincts heaped on the floor.

Within minutes the two uniforms arrived.

'Take that wall,' Irving said. 'Push the desks against it

longways. Divide the case files into five sections, one for each murder, and then up on the wall I need photographs of the victims and crime scene images. Far right I need the Shawcross documents, the letter that went to *The Times*—'

The younger of the two present, Michael Kayleigh, interrupted Irving. 'Sir, I know for a fact that the letter has gone over to Forensics. I think Mr Turner took it yesterday.'

Irving nodded. 'Good. Saves one of you a trip.'

'I know what to do,' the second officer said. His name was Whittaker, a recent transfer from the Eleventh. 'I've done this kind of thing before.'

'Okay, so I'll leave you to it. Go through everything, find the holes in the paperwork, make me a list. Anything you're not sure of put it to one side and I'll deal with it when I get back.'

'You know we can only stay until lunchtime, right?' Kayleigh said.

Irving glanced at his watch. It was quarter of eleven. 'Better work fast then,' he said.

TWENTY-THREE

The name of the individual who'd booked the Bedford Park conference suite for Friday evening cost Irving forty dollars. The receptionist was wary, unconvinced at twenty, and thus Irving doubled it.

The Bedford Park was everything Irving had suspected it would be. Early fifties perhaps, built in the mad rush of expansion and prosperity that New York evidenced after the war. It had seen better days, and around it was an aura of lonely desperation that spoke of illicit trysts, drug deals, book-by-the-hour hookers and cockroaches. Within the building hung the smell of sweat, the memory of the unwashed and unwanted making their slow-motion way from one temporary job to the next. It was depressing, and Irving felt some considerable relief as he left.

George Dietz. That was all Irving had, all that his forty dollars had given him.

Back at the Fourth he ran a search and came back empty. He called archives, spoke to one of the girls about pseudonyms, records of aliases and AKAs.

'All computerized,' she said, 'but you need access from here, not from your own station.'

'Can you check it?'

'Give me the name.'

Irving spelled it.

'I'll call you back.'

Irving sat for a while watching Whittaker and Kayleigh decorate the wall with the recent murders. Eight faces looked back at him – Mia Grant, Ashley Burch and Lisa Briley, James Wolfe – the hideous rigor of his clown-face staring back accusingly, as if asking *Why weren't you there? Why wasn't anyone there to help me?* Next came the three from the Third and Fifth – Luke Bradford, Stephen Vogel and Caroline

Parselle. Last was the hooker, the Shawcross replica, Carol-Anne Stowell.

The phone rang.

'George Dietz, right?' said the girl from archives.

'Anything?'

'It's a known alias for one George Thomas Delaney, and if you punch his name in your station you'll find out what a charming and beautiful human being he really is.'

Irving thanked her, hung up, typed in Delaney, and watched the man's record unfold.

Delaney was forty-six years old, born in Scranton, Pennsylvania. Arrested seven times, starting at the age of nineteen. Lewd and lascivious conduct, exposure, attempted rape (charges never filed for lack of evidence), suspicion of pandering minors, burglary (a pornographic-film importer's warehouse), soliciting prostitution, attempting to bribe a police officer and aggravated assault. He had never done time. He had missed the bus by the skin of his teeth. Delaney possessed the narrow-eyed, blemished-complexion, greasy-haired demeanor that seemed requisite to his trade. He had booked the Bedford Park. There was nothing illegal in booking a conference suite, regardless of how degraded the use of that suite might be. Delaney was not the way in. Delaney would be too well-known.

Irving took Delaney's address, a condo no more than two or three blocks from the Bedford Park on Bleecker. He printed off a copy of the man's picture, tucked it into his jacket pocket, shared a few words with Kayleigh and Whittaker, thanked them for their time, and left.

He drove back the way he'd come only half an hour or so before, a straight run down Sixth, right into West 14th, Eighth to Abingdon Square and Bleecker.

George Delaney's condo was suitably exhausted for a man of his reputation and social standing. The paint peeled back in numerous places, a patchwork of rust stains discolored the walls beneath the guttering, and there was garbage of all kinds strewn along the walkway above the street – a broken chair, its stuffing creeping out along a swollen seam, a child's tricycle, once brightly colored but now discarded and forgotten, a stack of decaying newspapers tied with

180

string. Irving found it difficult to understand why people were willing to live in such a fashion. Had it been his condo he would have rallied the neighbors together, cracked some beers, cleared the walkway, painted the facade, made-believe that what they had was worth maintaining . . . But people here led desperate, solitary lives – unemployed, hunched in chairs as they smoked weed, drank warm beer, ate cold pizza, sweated through endless hedonistic images on the internet.

Irving parked across the street with a clear view of the building. There were cars parked out front, three of them, and he noted their license plates. The clock on the dash read ten to twelve. He took the picture of Delaney from his jacket pocket, unfolded it, propped it against the steering wheel. He looked at the man's face and wondered what dark and unforgiving universe lay an inch behind his eyes.

Irving, cursing himself for not bringing a sandwich or somesuch, eased back in the driver's seat and set himself to wait.

After forty-five minutes a beat-to-shit Buick Regal pulled up on the other side of the street. The man who exited the car could have been one of a hundred thousand. Faded jeans, leather jacket, hair slicked back, unshaven, a cigarette parked in the corner of his mouth. He locked the vehicle, hurried across the sidewalk, took the stairwell at a run and headed straight for Delaney's door. Irving took the license plate, called Dispatch and asked them to ID it.

The words that were shared didn't matter; that Delaney never appeared mattered less. The only fact of interest to Irving was the name being relayed back to him, that Delaney's visitor, one Timothy Walter Leycross, was precisely the kind of individual that Irving needed. Leycross was thirty-one, three outstanding traffic violations, did seven months in juvy, another two and a half years in Attica for attempted rape of a minor, and was currently awaiting word from the DA's office as to whether a computer in their possession was giving up its secrets. Leycross had been arrested in a city-wide crackdown on internet child pornographers, his computer had been seized, and the best computer hacks in the DA's employ were trying to untangle the maze of circuitous avenues and invisible boxes such people employed to obfuscate and hide the evidence of their proclivities. Irving was familiar with the case – Operation Secure – and though it hadn't crossed his desk, he had spent sufficient time in Vice to know how difficult it was to make charges stick. Police actions slowed down the efforts of these people, but they would never be stopped. And if they were successfully arraigned, charged, tried, convicted and imprisoned, the leniency of the system now permitted people like this to return to the world within months, whereupon they went back to their business with a vengeance. There was money in their line of business, plenty of it, though Irving believed they were far less interested in the financial returns than they were addicted to the subject matter. Delaney and Leycross were representative of a particular type of human being, and the world within which they existed was extraordinarily dark.

The conversation at Delaney's door lasted less than a minute. Something changed hands, and when Leycross turned toward the stairwell Irving saw him bury something inside his jacket.

Leycross drove away in a hurry, didn't look back, didn't appear to notice as Irving cruised up behind him. Irving followed the Buick for half a dozen blocks, fired the light on the dash as they crossed Gansevoort, and then pulled Leycross over beyond the corner of West 13th and Hudson.

Irving was unarmed, and left his handgun in the trunk of the car. He knew a thousand Leycrosses, and merely waited while this one hustled whatever he'd taken from Delaney beneath the passenger seat.

As Irving approached the rear fender of the vehicle, the driver's door started to open.

'Stay inside the car, Timothy,' he called out.

It was a standard ruse: get out of the car, approach the officer, engage him in conversation, keep him out of the vehicle, attention always away from the vehicle.

Timothy Leycross sat back and pulled the door shut.

The expression on his face when Irving looked down at him was all too familiar. *Fuck*, it said. *Fuck, fuck, fuck.*

'How are things, Timothy?' Irving asked.

'Okay . . . sure. They're fine, yes. I'm fine.'

'Good to hear you're fine. License and registration is where exactly?'

'In the glove box.'

'Go slowly, my friend. Open up and let me look before you take anything out, okay?'

Leycross seemed all-too-familiar with the routine. He co-operated. He didn't resist or protest or bitch or complain. He didn't ask why he'd been pulled over. He knew precisely why, knew also that he was going nowhere.

Irving – merely to prolong the anxiety that Leycross was experiencing – pored over the documents as if there was something important to be gleaned from them.

When he handed them back there was a moment, just a moment, something in Leycross's expression, that questioned whether that was it.

'You have three outstanding traffic violations,' Irving said.

Leycross's face fell apart.

'I meant to pay them—'

Irving raised his hand. 'You have a computer with the DA's office, Tim. They have your computer . . . going through it to see if they can find all the kiddie porn, right?'

Leycross feigned indignation, opened his mouth to vent something or other.

'I don't want to know,' Irving said. 'That's between you and the DA.' Irving leaned down, put his hand on the roof of the car, and smiled warmly. 'However, what I do want to know is what it is that you just bought from George Delaney.'

'Delaney? I don't know—'

'Anyone called Delaney,' Irving interjected. 'You don't know anyone called Delaney, or Dietz, and if it's gonna get you booked for something then I'm sure you don't know your own mother either.'

Leycross was agitated, annoyance creeping toward anger, but beneath that the unwanted certainty that this was not going to go his way.

Words went back and forth for no more than three or four minutes. Leycross challenged Irving's right to pull him over, said there was no probable cause for searching the car. Irving said that the very first thing that Leycross did as he'd stopped the car was reach forward and put something beneath the passenger seat. A gun? A consignment of drugs perhaps? Of course there was probable cause. He recognized the momentary flash of anger in Leycross's eyes, but just as soon as that anger was visible he seemed to fold up in defeat. Irving wanted something, there was no question in Leycross's mind that this was the case. Was it better to play tough and get booked, or throw in his hand and hope to hell whatever he had to trade wasn't that bad?

'Have to look at it like this,' Irving told him. 'Co-operate, and we'll get through this. Be an asshole and I don't doubt that someone will find whatever they want in your computer, and then you're back to Attica with a child-rape tag on your name.'

'I didn't rape nobody,' Leycross said.

'You've been there, Tim. You know how things are. They don't give a fuck whether you did it or looked at it, or sold pictures of it. There are some things that even the worst human beings in the world won't tolerate. Gotta remember that most of them have kids, and while they're inside worrying about their kids they see you out here going after them with your movie camera.' Irving reached into his jacket pocket and took out an empty clip-top baggie. He opened it, held it toward Leycross.

Leycross hesitated, and in that moment everything that he wanted to say was left unspoken. He gave up the package from beneath the passenger seat.

Eight DVDs, home-made, burned on a computer. No label, no nothing. He dropped them into the baggie and Irving slid the top closed.

'How old?' Irving asked.

Leycross frowned.

'The kids on these movies?'

Leycross shook his head.

'Any of them older than twelve, Tim?'

Leycross looked away, out through the windshield to the other side of the street.

'Tell you the truth, Tim, I don't even wanna know.'

Leycross looked back at Irving, his expression defiant.

'The party Friday night,' Irving said. 'You going?'

'What fucking party?'

'Careful about your choice of expletive there, Tim.'

'I don't know what you're talking about.'

'Party that your friend George is throwing over at the Bedford Park.'

Leycross's expression changed. A split-second's panic crossed his eyes. Had he not been looking directly at Irving, Irving might have missed it.

'Big night Friday night, my friend,' Irving said. His tone was throwaway, nonchalant. He spoke as if this was something that was old news for the entire NYPD.

'I don't know about any party,' Leycross said. 'I don't know what the fuck you're talking about.'

'Well, you either start knowing *exactly* what the fuck I'm talking about, or we're taking a drive down to the precinct house and I'm gonna book you on your traffic tickets, and then we're gonna go put these DVDs on the TV in the commissary and half a dozen or so weatherworn and cynical Vice detectives, all of whom have kids by the way, are gonna check out your pirate copies of *Jurassic Park* and *Star Wars* . . . because that's what I assume we have here, Tim. Am I right?'

Leycross lowered his head. He sighed deeply, and when he turned back to Irving there was something so resigned and pathetic in his eyes it was hard for Irving not to laugh.

'What is it that you want?' Leycross asked.

'I want you to take me along.'

'What?'

'To the Bedford Park Hotel, Friday night. I want you to take me as your guest.'

'You're outta your fuckin' mind, man!'

Irving leaned closer. He could smell Leycross's body odor through the open window. 'Either that, or we go down to the Fourth and talk about your long-overdue return to Attica.'

'Aah Jesus, man, what the fuck is this? You have any idea what'll happen to me if I take you down there and you start busting people—'

'I'm not gonna to bust anyone, Timothy. I'm a visitor, a

185

potential buyer of whatever the hell your friends are selling down there—'

'They're not my friends.'

'All the better then. Better that they don't know you. Means they won't question you about who I am.'

'You know so much about it, you know where it is, go there yourself.'

'I know how this shit works, Tim, believe me. These are places you don't go without an invite or a personal reference. Friday night, my friend, I am gonna be your date. Dress nice, okay?'

'Fucking bullshit—'

Irving slammed his hand on the roof of the car. Leycross jumped suddenly.

'Enough already,' Irving said. He held out the baggie. 'You take me to the Bedford or I take you to the Fourth.'

'Okay, okay, okay . . . Jesus Christ, man, this is just fucking bullshit scare tactics. This is fucking harassment! '

'And this?' Irving said, jabbing Leycross in the shoulder with the bag of DVDs. 'This is a little harmless home entertainment? You're a fucking animal, my friend, a fucking animal. Don't even talk to me about harassment, okay?'

Leycross raised his hands in a placatory fashion. 'Seven,' he said. 'You know St Vincent's?'

'The hospital?'

'Meet me in the parking lot there Friday . . . seven o'clock.'

'Do I need to tell you about speaking to anyone?'

Leycross shook his head. He glanced at the DVDs in Irving's hand.

'Oh no, my friend, I'm keeping these. These are my collateral. You don't show, or I go there and the meeting's been cancelled – I get even the slightest idea that they know who I am – then we're gonna be sharing your viewing choices with the rest of the fucking world, okay?'

Leycross didn't speak.

'Okay, Tim?'

'Okay, okay,' he snapped exasperatedly.

'Good. St Vincent's parking lot at seven.'

As Irving watched Leycross drive away, he wondered

what kind of God could create such people, and then he smiled to himself: He'd stopped believing in any kind of God so many years before.

TWENTY-FOUR

There were holes. Too many to count. Incident reports with
names omitted, counter-signatures on circumstantial eyewitness statements. Irving knew for a fact that the parents of
the fourteen-year-old twins who had found the body of Mia
Grant had signed a minors' statement disclosure agreement,
yet neither Kayleigh nor Whittaker had been able to find it.
Irving paged the female police officer who'd been at the
house, got a call back from a colleague to say she was away
for the rest of the week. Irving went through each of the
folders himself and came back with more omissions. Crime
scene photographs had been incorrectly dated. A sheet of
names – all those who had been questioned in the vicinity of
the Burch/Briley murders – was reported on the file summary,
but again had taken a walk. A statement from the man who'd
found the girls – Max Webster, a salesman – had his business
card logged, on it his cell and landline numbers, but Irving
couldn't find it. No doubt it had fallen from one of the files
in transit. Right now it could be anywhere, on a stairwell, the
back of someone's car, under a desk someplace. The guy
could be found easily enough, but that was not the point.
The fact that anything at all was missing suggested that other
things might be missing. And if he didn't know what they
were, he wouldn't know to look for them.

Irving locked Leycross's bag of DVDs in the lower drawer of
his desk. Once Leycross had gotten him into the Bedford Park
Hotel meeting, those DVDs would find their way into the
hands of Vice. As far as individuals such as Leycross were
concerned, Irving had no compunction whatsoever about
breaking his word. The scumbag would go back to Attica, no
doubt about it.

Irving noted on the whiteboard those things that needed
to be found. Beneath this he wrote *Winterbourne Group*,

beneath that *John Costello.* To the left of the board he wrote *Bedford Park Hotel, Friday 9/15/06 Timothy Walter Leycross*, beneath Leycross's name that of *George Delaney, aka Dietz.*

A meeting of serial-killer victims in one hotel on the second Monday of each month, members unknown. Another meeting of child pornographers, pedophiles and assorted lowlifes in another hotel. Did they connect? Were there dots that joined these people together, and was there something that would direct him toward the perpetrator he was now assigned to identify and locate?

Irving spent an hour typing up his initial report, forwarded a copy to Bill Farraday, and then searched the internet for the names and dates of the confirmed and suspected Zodiac victims dated between Tuesday, September 12th and Christmas. Thoughts of Christmas brought thoughts of Deborah Wiltshire, the fact that this would be the second one since her death. He directed his attention back to the Zodiac names before him, noted them on another whiteboard – five attacks, five victims, one survivor. Thought of Costello, how he'd survived the Hammer of God, realized that Robert Clare had done the same degree of damage in three attacks. Once again, just like the Zodiac, it had been five dead, one survivor.

He wrote down their names, the dates of their murders – September 26th, 27th and 29th, October 11th and 16th. Five dates, the closest now two weeks away. Could he find the Anniversary Man in fourteen days?

Irving had to face facts. Irrespective of the number of dead teenagers, if this case was not generating headlines and press conferences then, in essence, it was no different from any other case.

The Times and the *City Herald* had been advised that the NYPD and the Mayor's office wanted a moratorium on coverage until further notice. Such a request would only hold out so long. True, the greater the lapse of time between the last murder and today's news, the less the press would be interested. If it happened today, yesterday, then okay, they could work with it. Last week's news was good for lining bird cages and wrapping fish. The best indication of current support and resources was the two hours he'd been allocated from Kayleigh and Whittaker. What did that tell him? That Farraday was on his side, of course. But even Farraday's hands were tied with keeping uniforms on the streets, demonstrating a good police presence in light of the Mayor's office statements that crime figures were down because the police were visible. And then there was Chief Ellmann, establishing his own camp for the election battle. A new mayor could mean a new chief of police. Ellmann wanted the current administration to maintain its position. Ellmann was a good chief, one of the best Irving had seen, but he sure wouldn't be willing to sacrifice his job because of one case. Assigning twenty-five uniforms and four detectives to one case was just not going to happen. And that left what? Irving smiled grimly to himself. It left John Costello – crazy though he was and himself a suspect for want of anyone better – now helping Irving in small ways that Irving didn't really understand. This was the short straw, the hand with no pair, no three-of-a-kind. It was now Tuesday, three days before the Bedford Park meeting, and even that might give him nothing. It was a long shot at best. He needed more leads, more lines to follow. He had to go back through everything, rearrange, reorganize. He had to sift through every detail and find the loose threads. And he wanted to know who Costello really was and why he seemed so eager to involve himself in something that did not concern him . . . *apparently* did not concern him.

Ray Irving sat back and closed his eyes for just a moment. What he was facing came at him like a slow-motion nightmare. The better part of everything was right there in front of him – every image, every report, every eyewitness statement that they possessed – and somewhere there was a single fact, a narrow line, and if he found it he knew it could be followed. At the end of it was the man who was doing this. It was simply a matter of finding that one thread.

Irving opened his eyes, lifted the first stack of files from the floor and started reading.

TWENTY-FIVE

Wednesday morning, September 13th. Irving had slept for no time at all, had spent many hours wading through every page of every case to date, had not found the thread. He had looked, and grown fatigued with looking. After a while the bad handwriting and endless typographical errors had merely served to irritate him. No-one had called while he'd been there, not even Farraday. During those early hours, the world outside the incident room had been quiet, quieter than normal, almost as if there was a vacuum within which only Irving could make a sound. The world was waiting for what he had to say.

I have it . . . I've got who this guy is . . . I know where he lives . . . Black-and-whites are on the way . . .

Irving had left at two-thirty a.m., perhaps a little later, crawled home and lain on the bed until four. He then showered, went back to bed, tossed and turned restlessly until six. He tried to watch some TV, but couldn't focus.

Quarter past eight he drove to Carnegie's. He ordered Virginia ham, ate a couple of mouthfuls, drank a cup and a half of coffee, forgot to leave a tip. He wanted to smoke cigarettes, a carton, maybe two. He was stressed, recognized the all-too-familiar route he would now travel if he failed to maintain his objectivity. In this line of work it was always life or death. Not his own, but someone else's.

There were seven messages at the desk – three from Jeff Turner, one from Farraday acknowledging the report he'd filed, one from the dry cleaners, one from the phone company, and the last from Karen Langley at the *City Herald*. He called Turner first, learned that it was merely to say a photograph from the Mia Grant autopsy had been left behind and Turner was sending it over with a courier.

At nine-twenty Irving called Karen Langley, waited on hold

for a minute or two, and then she came on the line and started in with a question out of left field.

'How you holding up, Detective?'

Irving was caught blindside. 'Sorry?'

'You. How are you holding up now that this thing is your baby, you know? Now that your people have pulled my story.'

'You heard that?'

'I have big ears,' she replied, and he could hear the edge of bitterness in her voice.

'Hope you don't have a mouth to match,' Irving replied.

'Meaning?'

'Don't act stupid, Ms Langley, you're a newspaper reporter. You people are a breed all your own.'

'As are police detectives.'

'Yanking my chain is not, I'm sure, the reason you took my call, Ms Langley.'

Langley hesitated, and when she spoke the bluff tone had vanished from her voice. 'You know we got silenced, right?'

'That's a little melodramatic, don't you think?'

'Whatever you want to call it,' she replied. 'The fact remains that the story got pulled.'

'You appreciate why, of course.'

'I appreciate why someone *thinks* it should be pulled, but what I don't understand is why they feel it is necessary to do such a thing.'

'Because we're not in the business of satisfying some psychopath's ego by telling the world what a smart son-of-a-bitch he is—'

'You hold to that view?'

'What view?'

'That the people who do this kind of thing are looking for nothing more than attention?'

'I don't know, Ms Langley, I really don't, and to tell you the truth I'm always a lot less interested in why someone does something rather than how and when.'

For a moment she didn't speak, and then she changed direction unexpectedly. 'John . . . he was a help to you?'

'Mr Costello?' Irving asked. He leaned forward and rested his elbows on the desk, one hand on his forehead, the other holding the receiver. A frown creased his brow. 'Mr Costello is . . . he's—'

'An enigma?' Langley ventured.

'To say the least. I have had a couple of conversations with Mr Costello—'

'And the thought has crossed your mind that he could very well be the man you're looking for?'

'Until ruled out, everyone is a suspect—'

'But you're wondering if he's for real?'

'Is this just a bad habit of yours, Ms Langley?'

'What?'

'Finishing every sentence for someone?'

She laughed. 'I'm sorry, Detective Irving, I've just got—'

'No manners?' Irving interjected.

'Touché.'

'So I have a question for you, Ms Langley.'

'Karen.'

Irving smiled wryly. 'Ms Langley,' he repeated. 'We have a purely professional, and might I say very limited working relationship here . . . we're not on first name terms, and I actually don't think we should be.'

'You are a tough guy, Detective Irving.'

'Tougher than I look.'

'So what's your question?'

'About John Costello . . . I've done some background, but not deep. What is your relationship with him?'

'He's my researcher. Worked for my predecessor, came with the job. Been here about twenty years.'

'And would you say he was a friend?'

'Yes . . . he *is* a friend, but you don't have a friendship with John Costello that's anything like a friendship you'd have with someone else.'

'How so?'

'I don't know, Detective. You're asking me to be objective about something that's very subjective. I know without any hesitation that he's not your man. I know he wants to help you, but he finds dealing with people somewhat difficult.'

'You know about the group he belongs to, right?'

'The survivors?'

'Is that what they call themselves?'

193

'No, I don't think they have a name as such. They're just a bunch of people who meet each month and talk about things that only they could understand.'

'At the Winterbourne Hotel.'

'I don't know where they meet. John goes to his meeting on the second Monday of every month. Nothing gets in the way, nothing takes priority. Even if we have to work late we don't. Know what I mean?'

'Sure, yes. So what's your take on him? Honestly.'

'Jesus, I wouldn't know where to start. He's smart . . . uncomfortably so if you know what I mean.'

'That's an odd expression to use . . . uncomfortably.'

'You ever meet someone, and within five minutes you just know that they are so far beyond you in intellect that you think it might be better to just say nothing?'

Irving thought for a moment. He recalled a childhood neighbor. 'Yes,' he said.

'John's like that. He has the most remarkable memory, can recall a conversation we had five years ago . . . remembers names, dates, places, phone numbers . . . remembers things that there doesn't seem to be any reason or purpose to remember, and then you need it and you ask him and he's answered the question before you're even through asking.'

'With anything? He can remember anything?'

'Seems that way, you know? Like, I thought he might be autistic or something . . . one of those people who are just ridiculously smart, but when it comes to actually dealing with real life – speaking to people, or keeping things together – they're just fucking useless, can't make a piece of toast kind of thing, but he's not like that . . . But he does have his moments.'

'Moments?'

'Stuff he won't do. Quirks, idiosyncrasies. We all have them, right? Perhaps John has a few more than most.'

'Such as?'

Langley paused for a moment. 'I actually don't even know why I'm telling you this. This is personal stuff. This is about someone who is a good friend of mine—'

'Who has chosen to get himself involved in a multiple homicide investigation, and who is likely to be under intense scrutiny unless I can explain and justify why he's doing what he's doing. This is where we're at right now, Ms Langley . . . talking about him as a potential suspect, and though he seems like a real nice guy, idiosyncrasies or not, he's put himself in the firing line as far as likely candidates are concerned. I've even toyed with the idea of dragging him in for some pictures and a line-up—'

'He's not your guy,' Langley cut in emphatically.

'So if he's not my guy I need to know who he is and, more importantly, I need to know why he seems so eager to get involved in something that really doesn't concern him.'

'I can't say any more right now,' Langley replied. There was a sudden tension in her voice.

'Okay . . . then I'm going to have to pursue my own line of investigation into our friend—'

'No,' she said, 'listen to me . . . I can't say any more *right now*.'

Irving understood. 'He's there, right?'

'Yes.'

'Okay. So what—'

'You want to go out somewhere?'

'Sure. Go get a cup of coffee or something.'

'Yes, a cup of coffee, unless of course it wouldn't be proper for you to go out with me.'

'Proper? What d'you mean?' Irving asked.

'I'm asking you out, you know? You understand what that means?'

'Like *that* kind of out?'

'Don't sound so surprised. Jesus, anyone'd think I'd offered to shoot your mother.'

'Er . . . yes, sure . . . of course . . .'

'Don't be so defensive, for God's sake,' Langley said. 'You have the look of someone who does their own ironing, so I get the idea you're not involved with someone right now.'

'The look of someone who does their own ironing . . . what the fuck is that supposed to mean?'

'What I said, nothing more. You look like Columbo's understudy.'

'Jesus, you really are a very charming person.'

'So whaddya say? You wanna go out or what? We can have something to eat and we can finish our conversation.'

Irving hesitated, but only for a moment. 'Yes,' he said, realizing that this was something he actually wanted to do. 'God, why the hell not?'

'That's great,' Langley said. 'Makes me sound like the last resort for a desperate man.'

'I didn't mean that—'

'Hey, it's okay, Detective Irving . . . relax. I'm done about six, six-thirty, and I'm not taking you anywhere fancy so you don't need to dress up.'

'You're not taking *me* anywhere fancy?'

'The 1950s was a golden age, Detective Irving, but they're over. It's perfectly acceptable to be taken out by a woman.'

'Okay, yes . . . sure. Okay then. Six or six-thirty . . . I'll come meet you there if that's all right?'

'You don't want your colleagues to see me. I understand.'

Irving frowned. 'That's not what I meant—'

'Jesus,' Langley interjected. 'It's so easy to yank your chain. Loosen up, for God's sake, I'm just teasing you. Meet me here just before seven, okay?'

'Okay, Ms Langley.'

'Ms Langley?' She laughed. 'See you later, *Detective* Irving.'

The line went dead. Irving sat there for a moment with the receiver burring in his ear. And then he leaned forward and replaced it in the cradle, and with a strange half-smile on his face he rose from his chair and walked to the window.

He'd just been asked out. By a woman. Asked out by Karen Langley from the *New York City Herald*. He'd called her back set for a fight, but he didn't get one. He got propositioned, and he accepted the proposition, and in – he glanced at his watch – in about eight and a half hours he was going out on a date for the first time in a long, long while. Losing Deborah Wiltshire had broken his heart, and he'd been left stranded. Had he even thought about the possibility of starting all over again?

Ray Irving smiled to himself. He was ahead of himself by a mile. The woman had asked him out. They had a conversation to finish. As of this moment it was business, nothing more nor less. It would be better to keep it that way, but Irving knew what loneliness was and he found himself unable to concentrate on the task at hand.

It was this, above all else, that told him he was already in trouble.

TWENTY-SIX

Ray Irving owned one good suit.

Wool and cashmere, a deep rose-brown with a fine chalk stripe. He'd bought it for a wedding he'd attended with Deborah. A friend of hers, a good friend, and Deborah had told him that if he didn't make an effort she wouldn't take him. He'd wanted to go. It had been important to her, and he didn't want to let her down, so he bought the suit. Went to an exclusive outfitters on West 34th near the synagogue, and spent six hundred dollars. Had worn it once for the wedding, and then put it away.

Afternoon of Wednesday, September 13th, he drove home at five. He showered and shaved, ironed a shirt, found a tie. He took the suit from where it had hung in the cupboard for the better part of five years, hoped it would still fit him. It did, in all but the waist. He'd lost weight, just an inch or so around his middle, but it reminded him that his quality of life had been better with Deborah. She had insisted he eat well. She had made him stop smoking. She had taught him something about music and literature, made him listen to hours of jazz standards, Shostakovich and Mahler, got him to read Paul Auster, William Styron, John Irving. For Deborah he had made an effort. Deborah was the kind of woman who made him want to be a better man.

So he dressed in the freshly ironed shirt, the color-coordinated tie, the one good suit, and then stood for a moment by the front door of his apartment on West 40th and 10th and asked himself whether he could do this.

Go out with a woman.

A woman other than Deborah Wiltshire.

And if he could, would it be a new beginning, a change of heart, a different direction – or would it be a betrayal?

Before he left he went back into his bedroom, picked up a

198

small silver-framed snapshot that he'd kept. The only picture of Deborah he owned. Everything else he'd asked her sister to take away, and her sister had smiled, had understood, had accepted his doorkey and come over with her husband while Irving was at work. She'd taken almost everything, and only weeks later did he find the hair straightener, the pair of flat-soled shoes with the right toe worn through, the things he now perceived with a sense of balance and perspective. But his perspective had been that of a man alone, a man without someone. Now he was looking outside of himself, looking beyond the accepted parameters of what their relationship had represented. Unity. A simple agreement. We have one another. There is no-one else. Had this tacit understanding ever extended to *there will never be anyone else*?

Irving touched the smooth glass surface of the picture. Deborah Wiltshire looked back at him. She was half-smiling, an expression which said that everything of importance about this moment was already known. *I am here*, it said. *I am me. I will never be anything more or less than who I am now. Take it or leave it.*

Irving returned the picture to its rightful place on the surface of the dresser. He walked away without looking back. Her expression in the picture was neither judgmental nor censorious. She understood Ray Irving, had understood him better than anyone, and she would appreciate his situation now. Would she want him faithful to their memory, ignoring all others, ignoring his own emotional and physical needs, or would she want him to have a life? He considered that she would wish the latter, and so he didn't feel guilty as he let himself out of the apartment, and walked to the car, his shoes clean, his shirt pressed, his only good suit seeing daylight for the first time in half a decade.

Evening had begun without him. The sky was overcast and it looked like rain was on the way.

Irving arrived at the offices of the *New York City Herald* at six twenty-five. He didn't go inside, didn't want to be seen by anyone who might recognize him. Most of all he did not want to be seen by John Costello. Come what may, he had to maintain a measured viewpoint. He had to be realistic. Karen

Langley was a journalist. Costello was her researcher and, as of this moment, a man who knew perhaps more than anyone else about the significance of these recent murders.

In this light – waiting patiently for Karen Langley to emerge from the *City Herald* building on 31st and Ninth – he wondered if he hadn't already made a very serious mistake.

TWENTY-SEVEN

Perhaps Karen Langley felt the same sense of concern about who might see her, for she hurried around the back of Irving's car without waiting for him to open the passenger door. She was out of breath, a little flustered, and when Irving was settled in the driver's side she seemed eager to leave. Or perhaps not. Perhaps it was Irving's imagination feeding his uncertainties.

'East 72nd,' she said. 'Up near St James and the Whitney Museum . . . there's a place I like.'

Irving started the car, but before he pulled away he hesitated.

'What?' Langley asked.

He turned and looked at her. 'This is not something I usually do,' he said.

'What . . . driving?'

Irving smiled. She was trying to make him feel at ease.

Karen Langley reached out and touched Irving's arm. 'It's not something that any of us usually do, Detective—'

'I think we're gonna have to drop the formality now, don't you?'

Karen Langley shook her head and frowned. 'I'm sorry . . . what *is* your first name?'

'Oh fuck off,' Irving said, and he started laughing, and she was laughing with him. He started the engine and pulled away from the sidewalk. Whatever was going to be said didn't need to be said any more.

It was a good restaurant. It felt right, sufficiently quiet that they didn't have to fight to be heard over the hubbub of people. In the background was music Irving recognized – Teddy Wilson, Stan Getz. He felt overdressed with his good suit and his silk tie; she didn't comment on it, and for this he was grateful.

'You asked me about John,' she said, after they'd studied the menu.

Irving shook his head. 'We have to have a line, you know?'

She frowned.

'I'm heading up a multiple homicide case. You're a journalist. Whichever way you cut it, it's not a good combination for dinner discussion.'

'I am a human being, you know?'

'I didn't say you weren't—'

'That's not what I mean. I meant that there is a point where the job ends.'

Irving smiled resignedly. 'Maybe that's my problem . . . maybe there isn't a point where the job ends.'

'You're different,' she said.

'Different?'

'Your job means a great deal more to these people than mine does. Your job is to make sure that people stay alive, I just have to tell 'em about it after the fact.'

'So we have a line?'

She touched his hand again. 'We have a line, Ray, don't worry. There are no tape recorders.'

'And you don't have a memory like John Costello?'

'Jesus no, the guy is an encyclopedia.'

'What *is* the deal with that?' Irving asked.

Karen Langley unfolded her napkin and rested it on her lap. 'The deal? I don't know that there is a deal. From what little he's told me, it seems that the injury he suffered when he was attacked as a kid resulted in certain faculties being extended.'

'Extended?'

'That's the word he uses, calls them extended faculties. He says that he can just remember stuff. I mean, for what it's worth, you couldn't hope to have someone better as a researcher. The guy's like the internet, except you don't have to wade through three hundred pages of bullshit to find what you want. At first, for a few weeks or so, I would wait until he'd left the office and then go through everything and insure that all the dates and times and places were correct, and then after a while I stopped doing it.'

'Because it wasn't necessary.'

'Everything I checked came back accurate. It was unreal. Quite unreal.'

'So what do you think about him?'

'Honestly? He's a good guy. I don't know what to tell you. He does things a certain way. He eats the same thing each day of the week pretty much.'

Irving's expression said everything.

Karen laughed. 'Mondays is Italian, Tuesdays he eats French, Wednesdays he has hot dogs with ketchup and German mustard, Thursdays he leaves to fate, Fridays he goes to this Persian restaurant in the Garment District near where he lives. Weekends I think he has Chinese take-out or something. He has lunch in the same diner every day, a block or so from the office. I don't think he has a girlfriend, and if he does he's never mentioned her to me, not in nearly ten years. His parents are dead. He has no brothers or sisters.'

'Lonely,' Irving said.

'Alone yes, but I don't really see him as lonely,' Karen said. 'He does what he does, and the routine seems to be enough. Oh, and he counts things, and he also makes up names for people . . .' She smiled.

'What?'

'He has a name for you.'

Irving raised his eyebrows. 'A name for me?'

'Sure. He puts words together, makes up names for people that describe them. He has one for me, one for the other guys in the office, and now he has one for you.'

'Which is?'

'Detective Hardangle.'

' Hardangle? What the fuck is that supposed to mean?'

'John has a theory about people. He thinks that people are not just one character, one personality. He believes they have many different facets and, depending on their environment and things like upbringing, education, family relationships – you know, all the usual stuff – certain facets of the person become more prevalent than others.'

'Situational dynamics,' Irving commented.

203

'Right. So, depending on what's going on around some-one, there are certain aspects of their personality that come to the fore.'

'And this says what about me?'

'You really want to know?'

'Sure,' Irving said, smiling.

'He says that you're not as tough as you look, and that your job makes you wear this hard face, you know? He says that you actually do have a heart, and that there was some-thing that happened in your life that closed you down emotionally—'

'Okay,' Irving said. 'Enough of the armchair psycho-analysis.'

'Don't take it too seriously,' Karen Langley said. 'You wanna hear what he calls me.'

'And what does he call you?'

'He calls me the quiet tornado.'

'Meaning?'

'That he believes I have the capacity to strip away anyone's defenses without them even knowing it.'

'Well, all right then,' Irving said. 'So the weather's on its way out, don't you think? Seems that winter is definitely here. You ready to order? Would you like a starter or shall we go right for the main course?'

Karen Langley balled up her napkin and threw it at him. She smiled pretty. Very pretty. She had depth and color, and there was something about her that was a great deal more than he'd anticipated, and for a moment he felt a prick of guilt at the thought that what he was doing could be con-strued as a betrayal. Deborah had been dead for . . . He paused. She had been dead since November, the better part of ten months. Perhaps he'd been dead too . . .

Karen broke into his thoughts. 'You're a funny guy,' she said. 'You do actually have a sense of humor.'

'It's a rumor,' Irving replied. 'We think we've got a lead on who started it and we're closing in on them.'

'So,' she said, 'I want a cocktail. I want a Long Beach iced tea.'

'A what?'

'Long Beach iced tea . . . gin, rum, vodka, triple sec, sweet and sour and cranberry. You never had one?'

'Thankfully no, I never had one.'

'You will now,' she said, and signaled for the waiter.

She asked about his parents. He told her of his mother's emphysema, her death in the early part of 1984. Of his father – playing dominoes, mumbling baseball scores from 1973, reciting the names of B-movie actors, always able to find the dime-width frequency on the radio dial where some out-of-nowhere independent jazz station played Wynton Marsalis and Dizzy Gillespie at three in the morning. It was the last thing they held in common. After forty-some years it seemed that 'One by One' and 'Slew Foot' was all they had left.

'My mother's here in New York,' Karen said. 'She's doing okay. I see her once, maybe twice a week. She's too independent really. She fights me trying to help her.'

Irving knew the deal. It was not an unfamiliar situation.

And then she asked, 'So how come you're single? No Mrs Irving at home?' and Irving paused and looked at her, and wondered whether she was on the up-and-up, or if he was being prepped for an inside line on the anniversary killings.

He shrugged.

'Never been married?'

'No, I've never married. You?'

'Sure,' she replied. 'Was married for eleven years.'

'Who was he?'

Her face was deadpan. 'He was my husband.'

Irving rolled his eyes.

Karen smiled, raised her glass and sipped her cocktail. 'He was a reporter, like me,' she said. 'We met early on. He was my boss for a while, and then he moved to *The Times*, and now he's out in Baltimore as far as I know.'

'No kids?'

'No, career was everything for both of us. It was a mistake but, hey, what the hell. No use crying.'

'And is career still everything?'

'How old are you?' she asked, ignoring his question, hers sudden, unexpected.

'How old am I? I'm forty-four. Why?'

'You ever think you screwed it up good?'

'Screwed what up?'

'Your life. Where you're going, you know? You ever think that if you could have the time again you'd make one different decision and go in a completely different direction?'

'Sure,' he said. 'Don't we all?'

'But I mean for real . . . like you get to forty, and you start thinking that if you're gonna do anything different then you better do it right now, 'cause if you leave it any longer it's gonna be too late.'

'No, not now,' Irving replied. 'I'm the kind of person that actually believes they're doing something useful. Maybe I'm not, but I've worked on convincing myself I am for so long that I really believe it now.' He paused, seemed thoughtful. 'I kinda think that I wouldn't really be much good for anything else.'

Karen didn't reply. She picked up the menu, seemed to be reading it again. Irving saw where she was, and for a little while she was not with him. She was elsewhere, most definitely, and he sat patiently until she returned.

'Enough already,' she said after a few minutes. 'I guess we're getting a little deep for a first date.'

'This is a date?' Irving asked. 'I'm waiting for the interrogation to begin.'

'Interrogation?'

'Stuff for the next article about this guy. I know you're just waiting breathlessly for something else to happen on this thing.'

'Not true,' Karen replied.

'Is.'

'Whatever, Ray. Think what you like. I'm here to have dinner and talk bullshit with you. I had a real date but he had to go away on business.'

'The hell he did.'

'Think whatever you like,' she said. 'I'm ordering.'

She asked him to drive her back to the *Herald* building where her own car was parked. It was past eleven by the time she pulled away. She turned back on herself and drove past him as he stood there on the sidewalk. She raised her hand, and through the window he caught the flash of a smile. He walked a block, went into a diner and drank a cup of coffee until he felt grounded enough to drive home. He was DUI for sure. If he got pulled over he'd show his badge and that would be the end of that, but he didn't care. He felt good. Well, perhaps *good* was a little strong, but he felt like a human being, at least a little, and he believed that what had happened that evening was a watershed, an emotional turning point. They hadn't exchanged numbers. They didn't need to. He was at the Fourth Precinct, she was at the *City Herald*. Parting company he told her that he'd had a good time.

'Me too,' she replied.

'You wanna do this again sometime?'

She'd hesitated, looked thoughtful, and then shaken her head. 'No,' she said. 'It wasn't *that* good.'

'You are such a bullshitter,' he replied.

She leaned forward, touched his arm, and kissed his cheek. Then she held her hand to the side of his face and used the ball of her thumb to wipe away the smear of lipstick.

Her hair smelled good – citrus, something like that – and the feel of her hand on his arm, her lips brushing his ear . . . these things reminded him of something he'd forgotten.

Something important. Something that gave life some significance.

So he said, 'I want to do this again, Karen.'

And she said, 'So do I.'

'I'll call you.'

'I'll answer the phone.'

'Drive safely.'

She smiled, he opened her car door for her, watched her climb inside and pull the belt across. He closed the door, and within a second the window came down a half dozen inches or so.

'Goodnight, Detective Irving.'

'Goodnight, Ms Langley.'

And then she was gone.

Later, alone, he felt something. The shadow of guilt again, perhaps? At first he attributed it to the fact that he had spent

207

time with a reporter, and then he looked once more at the monochrome snapshot of Deborah Wiltshire and wondered what she would have thought. *You are who you are, Ray Irving,* she would have said. *That's something only you can learn to live with.*

TWENTY-EIGHT

Friday evening delivered a thunderstorm. The sky – overcast all day – finally broke around six, and when Irving hurried from the back exit of the precinct house to his car he was thrashed by rain that came vertically and sideways simultaneously.

He hadn't shaved that morning; had pulled on black jeans, a dark sweatshirt, a burgundy windbreaker, clothes for doing chores outside the house – emptying garbage, clearing the front yard of leaves. He looked rough around the edges. He didn't look like a homicide detective, did not *want* to look like a homicide detective. It was the better part of forty-eight hours since his date with Karen Langley, and he'd filled the time with reading back through everything. He hadn't called her, had received no word that she had tried to call him. He'd located the minors' statement disclosure agreement from the Mia Grant case, and a few other loose ends of paperwork that had gone astray. It had given him administrative closure, but no greater understanding of what he was facing. He couldn't find the thread, couldn't see the one thing that would reveal the truth. Four days since the last victim and he was none the wiser.

Farraday had not requested his presence. Irving had written his reports and filed them on time, but there had been no response. In a way he was grateful. He had been left to his own devices, and this was an operating basis he always preferred. New York was a city of millions. Eight people murdered – even if they were the work of one dedicated man – was a relatively insignificant percentage.

Tim Leycross was in the parking lot back of St Vincent's when Irving arrived.

'This is bullshit,' was his opening gambit.

'Don't you think I know that?' Irving said. He walked

209

around the front of Leycross's car and put his hand on the passenger side handle.

'My car?'

'My plate is registered to the precinct,' Irving said.

Leycross laughed, shook his head. 'Who the hell d'you think these people are? The NSA? They don't have any way of checking your license plate. Jesus, you act like they're gonna do retina scans and DNA fingerprinting.'

'We're going in your car, Timothy, end of story.'

Little more than a block, perhaps two, and Leycross pulled up near the Bedford Park Hotel. They could have walked, but Irving wanted them to be seen arriving together in Leycross's car. True, these people were not the NSA. They were little of anything at all. But often the slightest lack of attention was sufficient to undo the most rigorous of plans. One time a Narc undercover forgot to remove his wedding ring. His wife and kids got a triangular flag and a pension.

The meet-and-greet guy looked like a bare-knuckle prizefighter on his last legs. He was top heavy, would have gone over with a swift kick to the knees, but he served his purpose. He looked perpetually annoyed rather than menacing, but he had a foot of height over Irving. There were no membership cards for this party, just an entrance fee of twenty-five dollars. It paid for the room hire, that was all. There were no cocktails, no *hors d'oeuvres*. Guys like this drank generic brand beer and Gatorade.

It could have been a trade show for a fan club. Minor celebrities should have been present – cameo actors and walk-ons available to sign posters for the original *Battlestar Galactica* TV series. A dozen guys, all of them heavy set, mostly bespectacled, in thick sweatshirts or V-necks. They stood behind tables, and on those tables were collections of photographs and DVDs. Crash victims, suicides, burns, dismemberments, decapitations, amputees, leapers and hangers. Images that had evidently come from murder case files – stabbings, fatal gunshot wounds, people with their throats cut, their eyes missing, their tongues removed. Which of them were genuine, and which were the work of extraordinarily good make-up artists Irving would never have been able to tell, but as with any pursuit or interest there

210

were those that considered it their business to differentiate fact from fiction. In any field of interest, there were always experts, and the common denominator with experts was the fact that they always wanted to talk about how much they knew. They lived for such opportunities.

Irving browsed. Had he not been experienced, inured by repetition, he would have been sickened by what he saw. Despite his years in Vice and Narcotics, despite the recent tenure in Homicide, despite frequent visits to the morgue, standing patiently while some dead girl was unzipped from throat to navel, he was not completely without feelings. The image of a child rape victim said everything that needed to be said about the subculture of persons that purveyed such material. They were not very the lowest form of human life, but they were well on their way to getting there.

He spent an hour. He bought some crime scene pictures with the Third Precinct stamp on the back. They showed a woman who'd been strangled with her own lace stockings. He paid thirty dollars, didn't get a receipt. He got talking to the seller, a bearded man in his late forties called Chaz. Chaz wore bottle-bottom lenses which made his eyes seem a lot larger than they were. Chaz peered myopically at the world, and the world must have seemed awful strange.

'Good pictures,' Irving told him.

'Genuine, that's why,' Chaz replied. He leaned forward, his hand to the side of his mouth. 'Most of the stuff here is shit,' he whispered conspiratorially.

Irving shrugged. 'I'm kinda new to this,' he said. 'I've seen stuff on the net—'

Chaz nodded, smiling. 'The net is ninety percent bullshit, ten percent more bullshit.'

'You gotta study this stuff to know what you're getting.'

'You gotta make it your business. You gotta do it professionally or not at all. I have a reputation to uphold,' Chaz said. There was a sense of pride in his voice, as if he was providing a valid and honorable community service. This wasn't so different from girl scout cookies after all. People had needs, needs required fulfilling. Better that he worked to cater for that need than people went out killing to get their

own photographic subjects. There was always a rationaliza-
tion. There was always a way to justify something.

'These are the real thing no doubt,' Irving said. He turned
over one of the pictures. He indicated the stamp on the back.

'Can get you anything you like out of PD archives,' Chaz
said. 'Within reason, of course.'

'Anything?'

'Give me a name, a date, a police precinct, whatever the
hell you like . . . I can get you pictures. Got a contact. An
inside man, you know?' Chaz winked, half-smiled. He was
the big man on campus. He could sell you the world for
almost nothing at all.

'That's really something,' Irving said. 'I'm interested—'

Chaz raised his hand. 'Price is everything of course. The
harder the material the higher the cost.'

Irving nodded. 'You get what you pay for.'

'How right you are,' Chaz replied. 'Something you were
interested in specifically?'

'Perhaps.'

'How perhaps? Big perhaps or little perhaps?'

Irving turned his mouth down at the corners. 'I have a
thing . . . a thing for—'

'We all have our own particular tastes,' Chaz said. 'Girls,
boys—'

'Not kids,' Irving replied. 'I don't do kids.'

'So what can I find for you Mr—? '

'Name's Gary,' Irving said.

Chaz extended his hand. They shook. Chaz smiled. He was
doing the sales pitch. He had hooked a new boy. He was
reeling him in and he knew it.

'So, Gary . . . you tell me the kind of thing you like, and
then you let me see what I can do for you.'

'So we could have a private meeting?'

Chaz laughed. 'Sure. This is just the bring-and-buy sale.
This is the village fair. This is nothing. This is just a way for
people to network, make new contacts, know what I mean? I
run a business downtown. I gotta library of material to die for
– been doing this for fifteen years—'

'So when do you wanna meet?' Irving asked.

Chaz glanced at his watch. 'This'll run 'til eight-thirty,

maybe nine. There's no time like the present. I'm free tonight if you wanna have a sit-down talk.'

Irving tried to look naïve. 'You're not like – like a cop or anything are you?'

Chaz reached out and gripped Irving's shoulder. 'Yes, of course I am,' he said. 'I'm the New York chief of fucking police, don't you know? I'm the chief of police and you're all busted.'

There was a smattering of laughter from around the room. Chaz was the comedian. He was a funny guy.

'I'm sorry,' Irving said. 'It's just that . . . well, you know—'

'Gary,' Chaz interjected. 'Take a fucking chill pill okay? This is as good as it gets, my friend. We're gonna hang out here a little while. You can help me pack up shop, and then we'll go get a beer or something and talk about what I can do for you.'

'Sounds good,' Irving said. 'Thank you . . . I really appreciate this.'

'You're welcome, buddy. Gotta look after each other, eh? Gotta take care of our own.'

TWENTY-NINE

Leycross disappeared. One moment he was there, and then he was gone. He had gotten Irving into the meeting, evidently considered his job was done, and he'd left.

Quarter past nine and Irving was helping Chaz load his files of pictures into cardboard boxes. Chaz was talking about a Knicks game. Irving half-listened, ever alert for names that were being spoken in the room, making mental notes of faces – who seemed significant, who didn't. Chaz had a dark blue station wagon parked in back of the hotel. They loaded the boxes and took a walk down the block to a bar called Freddie's.

Irving knew this was a thread, nothing more nor less than that. He was not so naïve as to consider that Chaz was the man who had provided their Anniversary Man with crime scene photos. He couldn't even assume that their killer had actually worked from crime scene photos. The replicas were close but not necessarily perfect. They were an accurate replication of the original crime scenes. None of the killings had remained completely unknown. Information – cause of death, victims' manner of dress, body position, degree of decomposition – was all available in books, true crime magazines, on websites. This was a shot – long or short it didn't matter – but it was a shot. If there really was a contact, someone within the PD or a coroner's office, someone who had access to pictures and was stealing originals or making copies for sale, then that was a case all its own. If this came to nothing more than closing down such an operation, then so be it; Irving would have to be grateful for what he could get.

'So tell me, Gary,' Chaz said. 'Your particular predilection is what?'

'Multiples,' Irving replied. 'Two, three, more even. Multiple homicides.'

Gary smiled. 'Jeez man, that's easy. I figured you were gonna give me something really difficult.'

Irving frowned.

'You wanna get some of the things I'm asked for? Hell, man, you have no idea. The true originals are the most difficult. The headline cases. We call them historicals. They've earned a place in history. They stand out as significant.'

'Such as?'

'Oh, I don't know . . . original prints of confirmed kills . . . people like Ted Bundy, Zodiac, Aileen Wuornos, especially since that movie with Charlize Theron. And then you had the Capote thing—'

'Truman Capote?'

'Sure, the movie they made. The dude won an Oscar. Those killings in the fifties. Had a request to get original snaps of that family, the parents, the boy and the girl. You seen the movie?'

Irving shook his head.

'Good movie,' Chaz said. 'Tough call on the pictures though.'

'Did you get them?'

'Copies, not originals. Copies were good, but nowhere near as lucrative. Copies went for two and a half. Originals would have gone for ten times that, maybe more.'

'Twenty-five thousand dollars?' Irving asked.

'Sure, twenty-five thousand. That's nothing compared to some stuff I hear about.'

'Like?'

'Like what's the most expensive?'

'Sure,' Irving said.

'Most expensive I ever heard of was not a crime scene picture. Was a picture of Gacy.'

'John Wayne Gacy?'

'The man himself. Signed, and with a very Gacy-type message scrawled across it.'

Irving raised his eyebrows.

'Seems someone smuggled a picture of Gacy into prison, gave him five hundred dollars cash to sign it, write some-thing personal you know? Know what he wrote over his name? *Fuck you to death. Much love, John*. And then three kisses underneath.'

'You're kidding me?'

'No word of a lie. Fuck you to death. Much love, John. Three kisses underneath.'

'And it sold for how much?'

'Three hundred and forty grand.'

'No fucking way,' Irving exclaimed.

'Yes fucking way, believe me. Three hundred and forty grand to some Russian guy who had signed pictures from all sorts . . . Dahmer, Bundy, even the cannibal guy who ate all them folks, the Russian one, don't remember his name.'

'This is a hell of a business,' Irving said.

'Supply and demand, my friend, supply and demand.'

'And you have someone . . . where? In the police department?'

Chaz smiled knowingly. 'I have someone, and that's enough for you to know.'

Irving nodded. 'I'm sorry, I wasn't meaning to pry, I'm just fascinated by the whole thing.'

'It's a fascinating business. Anyway, you want another beer?'

'Sure,' Irving said. 'Let me get them.'

'Good man,' Chaz said. 'I'll have a Schlitz.'

They talked around things for an hour. Close to ten-thirty Chaz said he had to go. He put Irving on the spot. What did he want? What was he looking for specifically?

'Multiples,' Irving said. 'More than twenty years old, preferably showing clear details – you know, clothes, body position – stuff like that . . . not just faces, you know? The whole thing.'

'Just that? Just multiple homicides, right?'

'Anything with two or more, yes. Two victims, three, four. Or anything out of the ordinary, like the victim was dressed up, made to wear something that was significant to the killer.'

Chaz took a beer mat and scribbled his cellphone number. 'Call me lunchtime tomorrow, one, one-thirty, you know?' he said. 'I'll have word for you.'

Irving smiled, seemed surprised. 'So fast.'

'Gonna do something, do it professionally, that's what I say. I can either get you what you want or I can't. It's not complicated and I'm not gonna bullshit you. Call me tomorrow and I'll let you know if I can help you.'

They parted company in the parking lot back of the bar. Chaz had drunk four beers at least, should not have gotten behind the wheel of the station wagon, and Irving prayed that he wouldn't be stopped. A night in the tank would not bode well for tomorrow's phone call.

Irving walked back to St Vincent's, picked up his car and headed back to the office. It was nearly midnight by the time he arrived.

From the beer mat he took Chaz's cellphone number and the license number of his station wagon, and ran a search on both.

Charles Wyngard Morrison, 116 Eldridge in the Bowery. Irving found his landline number, his Social Security number, the fact that he worked as a computer software technician for a small firm in Bedford-Stuyvesant. Chaz Morrison had no record, though he had been given a warning for obstructing a police officer at a crime scene. He was a murder junkie. Probably went down there to take pictures.

Irving spent an hour filling out the required paperwork for a phone tap on both the landline and cell. He was thorough and careful. He missed nothing out. He stressed the point that he was scheduled to call Morrison by one p.m. on Saturday, and thus the tap needed to be on his phones as early as possible. Irving hoped that Morrison would leave his calls until late the following morning and not make them tonight.

The pictures he'd bought he locked in the drawer with Leycross's DVDs. He was becoming quite the collector.

He left close to one-thirty, drove home slowly. He was tired but he knew he wouldn't sleep. He would find that dime-width escape route on the radio dial, and there – as if they'd been waiting for him – would be Dave Brubeck and Charlie Mingus.

Made him think of his father, the fact that he had not visited since May. Reminded him that the living required as much attention as the dead.

217

THIRTY

Thinking not of Deborah Wiltshire but of Karen Langley, Irving woke with the underlying headache attendant to insufficient rest. It was six forty-five. He lay still until seven, tried not to think, tried not to be anywhere at all, and then he rose and showered. It was Saturday. It should have been late breakfasts and weekend newspapers, perhaps plans to see a ball game, a movie, the theater. But there was no room for such things in Irving's life these days – at least not yet.

He called Farraday from the Fourth, drove to his house and had him countersign the phone tap request. He took it directly to Judge Schaeffer, tough bastard, head like a mallet, known for his willingness to work with the police as opposed to against them. The tap was up and running by eleven, two uniforms briefed and stationed to listen in on every call that was made, incoming and outgoing, and Charles Morrison's sordid little world was on record. If he now organized the purchase that Irving had requested by phone, they would know who his contact was.

With little else to do but wait, Irving turned his attention to the Winterbourne group. If Costello himself was a potential suspect, then any member might be the one. He didn't know who they were, and the likelihood of obtaining a warrant to enforce the release of such information from the hotel proprietor was very unlikely. Costello had been nothing but co-operative, yet his willingness to involve himself in the investigation, formally or otherwise, was the very thing that raised Irving's suspicion. He knew little of serial murderers, their whys and wherefores, but he did know that it was not uncommon for a perpetrator to engage with the police, even to assist in the investigative procedure. A child abductor, for example, organizing locals to search an area for a child they themselves had kidnapped, raped, dismembered

218

and buried; or a killer of young women presenting themselves as a volunteer, ready to walk the streets and show pictures of the missing victim. What prompted such actions? Self-denial, an effort to disassociate themselves from the crime by becoming their own apparent nemesis? Some belief that, by doing this, they could determine how much information the police possessed and take measures to insure no further progress was made in their identification? A desire to prove themselves better, smarter . . .

Irving stopped for a moment.

He walked to the window of the incident room and looked down into the street. He could see the edge of Bryant Park, and across to the 42nd Street subway station. Pedestrians were still sparse at this time of a Saturday morning, traffic still relatively light.

A desire to prove himself better . . .

He was reminded of something Costello had said – had it been Costello? – that the anniversary killings were replicas of killings perpetrated by people who had all been caught. Some of them were buried forever within the federal penitentiary system, others had been executed, one had died of natural causes as far as Irving could recall. And then there was the Zodiac letter. For sure, it had been a word-for-word transcription of a Shawcross letter, but it had been in the Zodiac's code, the code broken by a history teacher and his wife after failed attempts by the FBI and the Office of Naval Intelligence. The Zodiac, by all accounts, had never been identified, and certainly had not been knowingly caught. Perhaps the Zodiac was even now languishing in a cell within some state prison, caught, tried and convicted for some unrelated crime, and no-one was any the wiser. Perhaps he would die someplace and leave evidence of who he was, what he had done . . . perhaps an explanation of why he did it. But currently he remained unknown. In serial-killer terms, Zodiac was a success. He did what he did. He got away with it. He remained an enigma.

Irving searched through the stack of pages on his desk for notes he had previously made until he found what he was looking for – the complete list of all Zodiac killings, confirmed and unconfirmed.

Michael Mageau and Darlene Ferrin, both incontrovertible Zodiac victims, had been shot on July 5th, 1969. Mageau survived, Ferrin did not. Further victims who were attacked or killed on dates preceding September 16th numbered twenty-seven. Irrespective of the year, for there were murders attributed to the Zodiac from October 1966 all the way to May 1981, there were five carried out in February, nine in March, one in April, two in May, three in June, five in July, one in August and, prior to today's date, the 16th, there was one that took place in September. The anniversary killer could have replicated any one of them, and even if he had adhered solely to those confirmed, it would have been a Zodiac anniversary on July 5th. As far as Irving knew no double murder had been reported on July 5th anywhere in the state of New York, and had there been, then Costello surely would have known about it.

Irving accessed the system and checked. He was right. There was no case county-wide that in any way bore similarities to the Vallejo shooting of Michael Mageau and Darlene Ferrin on July 5th, 1969. Which meant what? That the killer replicated only those killings perpetrated by identified and convicted individuals? Then why employ the Zodiac code to relay the Shawcross letter? Was he simply insuring that they got the connection between what he was doing and these past murders, or was there some other reason?

At twenty-five past twelve Ray Irving called the *New York City Herald*. He didn't find John Costello, but Karen Langley took the call.

'Hey there.'

'Karen.'

'You're after John?'

'I am, yes.'

A moment's hesitation, and then Irving said, 'I was going to call you—'

'You don't have to,' Karen replied.

'I know I don't have to, I want to. But I'm up against it, you know? You understand this shit. You get deadlines, right?'

'Sure I do.'

'I had a good time, Karen.'

'I know,' she replied.

'You are such a wiseass.'

'So, John's not here, he's home today. Well, I presume he's home. Tell you the truth, I have absolutely no idea what John does with his time.'

'You have his number?'

'I can't give it to you.'

'You *can't* give it to me or you won't?'

'I won't. I wouldn't do that to him.'

Irving was silent, a little puzzled.

'Oh come on, Ray, you've met him. You know how he is. He doesn't deal with people very well. He doesn't like a change in his routine.'

'So how the hell do I get to talk to him?'

'I'll call him. I'll tell him that you want to speak to him. I don't know whether he'll call you . . .' Her statement was left incomplete and Irving had to prompt her.

'He has an issue,' Karen said.

'An issue?'

'An issue with you.'

'What are you talking about?'

'The fact that we went out. John has a concern about you.'

'Me? Jesus, what the hell is that about?'

'Well, I'm his friend. We've worked together for years. He considers me his responsibility in some way. There's never been anything between us but a professional and platonic relationship, but he still considers that what happens to me is his business.'

'Okay,' Irving said. 'I can appreciate that, but what did you tell him? Did you tell him I was an asshole or something?'

'No, of course I didn't.'

'So what's the deal now? If I want to ask you out again I have to ask him to chaperone?'

'Don't be sarcastic, Ray. Deal with it. So do you want me to call him or not?'

'Please. That would be good. Tell him I need his help with this thing.'

'You need his help?'

'Sure. What's so odd about that? He's the fucking Rainman, isn't he? He's the one who can remember three hundred-thousand murder cases.'

'Enough already—'

Irving took a deep breath. 'I'm sorry, Karen, but—'

'But nothing. You treat him like anyone else, okay? Don't patronize him. If I hear that you've upset him—'

'I won't. I'm sorry, I really am very sorry, okay? I didn't mean that to sound the way it sounded.'

'Well it did, and I don't like it. He's a good person, and a very close friend of mine. You upset him and not only will you *not* see me again, but I'll run whatever fucking stories I like and you and the Chief of Police and the Mayor can go to Hell, okay?'

'Karen, seriously—'

'Okay, Ray, that's all I need. I need a simple acknowledgement here.'

'Yes. Okay. I understand.'

'Good, so I'll call John. You talk to him nice. You piss him off and I'll come down there and slap you. Then, when you get a moment, you can call me and talk nicely as well and I might go out with you again. And you can send me some flowers or something as an apology for being an asshole, all right?'

'You are un-fucking-real—'

'I'm hanging up now, Detective Irving—'

And she did.

The receiver burred in his ear accusingly.

It took him ten minutes to find the number for a city florist. As he reached for the phone it rang. Startled, he snatched it from the cradle.

'Detective Irving.'

'Mr Costello?'

'You wanted to speak to me.'

'I did, yes. Thank you for calling me.'

'You're gonna have to be fast. There's a TV program I need to watch.'

'Yes, of course. Jesus, you've caught me on the hop. It was just—'

'Something about the case?'

'Yes, something about the case . . . about our perp. The killings he replicates and the letter he sent.'

222

Costello laughed – a brief and unexpected reaction. 'You and I have been thinking the same thing it seems,' he said matter-of-factly.

Irving frowned. 'How so?'

'The question I have is why does he only replicate killings carried out by people who were caught, and yet he used the Zodiac code to send the Shawcross letter. Is that what you were wondering?'

Irving sat open-mouthed for some seconds.

'Detective? Are you there?'

'Yes . . . yes, I'm here . . . yes, of course. Jesus. This is a little unexpected. Sorry, you've caught me unprepared. I . . . I was—'

'Thinking the exact same thing?'

'Yes I was. That's quite remarkable.'

'No, not really. When you look at this thing objectively you can see that this doesn't make sense. That's the first thing you have to do with anything like this. Look for the one thing that doesn't make sense.'

'And I went through the dates of all the confirmed and unconfirmed Zodiac killings and found that—'

'He could have replicated any one of them in any month except January. There were reported killings in every month of the year except January.'

'Right . . . and the one that took place in September before today's date was—'

'On September fourth,' Costello interjected. 'Alexandra Clery. Beaten to death on September fourth, 1972. A Monday. Unconfirmed.'

'So he is not replicating the Zodiac.'

'Not yet, no,' Costello said. 'Though there were three other attacks that took place in September, but later than the sixteenth.'

'So where does that take you?' Irving asked.

'Homage,' Costello said quietly.

'Sorry?'

'The letter, I believe, was a homage to the Zodiac.'

'A homage?'

'Sure. He kills like other killers. What is he saying? He's saying that he can do what they do. He can do it better. He

223

can do it without being caught. He sends the Shawcross letter in the Zodiac code to serve two purposes. First, he knows that the police are not as smart as he is, so he has to make sure that they get the connection between the hooker found down near the pier and the Steffen girl that Shawcross killed in '88. Secondly, and I think more importantly, he wants to tell us where he's going—'

'Where he's going?'

'Into the textbooks, you know? Onto the True Crime channel. He wants to be a star of stage and screen.'

'He wants to be as famous as the Zodiac.'

'He wants to be Ted Bundy, John Wayne Gacy, probably even wants to be the real Hannibal Lecter, you know? But he wants to remain forever unknown like the Zodiac, and maybe he even wants to break the record.'

'Jesus, but Carignan killed over fifty people—'

'Unconfirmed. Confirmed kills were somewhere between twelve and twenty. That's always the difficulty. These people habitually lie about what they've done. They admit to killings they didn't do, and they refuse to acknowledge murders that were so evidently their work. It's always an estimate, you know? But from the commonly accepted information, we can gather the Sunset Slayers killed seven, Gacy thirty-three, Kenneth McDuff about fifteen as far as evidence tells us, and Shawcross says he murdered fifty-three, but again the realistic figure is somewhere between fifteen and twenty-five.'

'And the worst?' Irving asked.

'Hard to tell,' Costello replied. 'Worst ever isn't American. Colombian called Pedro Lopez murdered over three hundred. Next you have an American pair called Henry Lee Lucas and Ottis Toole who apparently killed over two hundred. Confessed to thirty or so after something called the Interstate Murder Spree. The de Gonzales sisters, Mexican brothel owners, ninety-one bodies found in their bordello in the early 1960s. Then you've got Bruno Ludke, German, maybe eighty or eighty-five. Next we have the infamous Chikatilo, Russian, a cannibal, and he killed somewhere over fifty. Onoprienko, another Russian, apparently wanted to hold the world record for serial killings but he was arrested after fifty-two murders.

Then we have another American, Gerald Stano, in prison at twenty-nine years old for killing forty-one women, mostly prostitutes and teenage runaways in Florida and New Jersey. He went to the electric chair back in March of '98. Gary Ridgway, the Green River Killer, anywhere between thirty-five and fifty victims, Seattle and Tacoma mainly. Gacy is next with thirty-three, then Dean Corll and Wayne Williams both with twenty-seven. Straight answer to your question is that our friend would have to do well in excess of fifty to get into the record books, and that's only as far as American serial killers are concerned. If he wants the world record he's gonna have to get very busy indeed.'

Irving was silent for a long time. He was having a conversation about something that he found almost impossible to comprehend.

'And so far we have eight,' he eventually said.

'That we know of,' Costello said. 'There's always the possibility that he could have come from another city. He could even have taken a break for a period of time, and we're not looking back far enough to catch the earlier part of the cycle.'

Irving felt the hairs on the back of his neck rise. *The earlier part of the cycle.* Such a thing made it sound so utterly clinical.

'The truth of the matter is that there is no way to predict who he will decide to be next,' Costello said.

'Unless, of course, there is some aspect of the preceding murders that give a clue, and we've missed it.'

'You think he's showing you what he's doing?' Costello asked.

'Who knows what he's showing us,' Irving said. 'Who knows what he's showing the world.'

'For what it's worth,' Costello said, 'I think he wants to show the world that he's the best.'

THIRTY-ONE

A few minutes after twelve-thirty, less than an hour before he was scheduled to call Chaz Morrison, word came from downstairs. Morrison had made a call on his landline at twelve-seventeen. He had explained his requirements to someone – multiple homicides, preferably more than twenty years ago; three, four victims, unusual body positions, articles of clothing left at the scene – anything a little out of the ordinary. Morrison and his contact made a joke about pedestrian tastes. The contact said he'd get what Morrison needed, that he should call back on Monday evening. The call ended. Within fifteen minutes Irving had had the number traced to an address in Greenwich Village near the 14th Street station. He ran the address on the city employee database and got a name. Dale Haynes, twenty-five, no priors, currently employed by the police department's Archival Restoration Unit.

Irving had the seller. They had him for theft, violation of the confidentiality clauses of his government contract, sale of stolen City property. What he was doing was not of major importance: what mattered was whether this man Haynes had provided crime-scene photographs for their Anniversary Man. When, thought Irving, did anyone ever use the term *short shot*? It was all long shots. That was the nature of the beast.

By one-thirty he had a search warrant and a surveillance unit on Haynes's apartment. This took precedence over the scheduled call to Chaz Morrison, and Irving decided to let that go. Farraday had asked Irving for a blow-by-blow account of what he was doing, had approved everything he'd asked for. He seemed satisfied with Irving's actions, told him to take a unit of six from the Fourth and deploy them as he saw fit. Haynes was not to run under any circumstances – as of this moment he was not a suspect in the killings, but he was a potential lead and had to be handled by the book. Irving had no authority to make a deal with Haynes without strict and specific authority from Farraday, and Farraday himself would liaise with the DA. The case was far too important to fuck it up with procedural errors.

At three minutes past two, afternoon of Saturday, September 16th, Detective Ray Irving stood to the side of Dale Haynes's apartment door and knocked loudly. He identified himself clearly, made no further attempt to alert the suspect as to his presence beyond waiting thirty seconds and then knocking again.

At four and a half minutes past they went through the door with a ram.

Confusion broke out as Irving and three uniforms ran through the apartment, clearing each room in turn. One door was closed, and before Irving had a chance to kick it open a voice from within shouted, 'Hold on a minute . . . hold *on* a minute!'

'Dale Steven Haynes?' Irving shouted.

'Yes . . . I'm here . . . what's happening?'

'Step out of the room. Hands over your head. This is the police.'

'What the—'

'Step out of the room, Mr Haynes. I'm counting to three. If I don't see the door opening we're coming through—'

'Okay, okay . . . Jesus Christ, what the fuck *is* this?'

Irving nodded at the uniforms, who stepped to each side of the door and flattened themselves against the wall. The door handle turned. Irving stepped behind a chair and crouched down. He had a clean line of fire to the doorway.

The uniforms pulled Haynes out into the room and had him cuffed, down on his knees, before he knew what was happening. He was wearing nothing but his tee-shirt and shorts, his eyes wide, his face white, his expression one of sheer terror.

'Dale Steven Haynes, you are under arrest for suspicion of theft of city property, for suspicion of the illegal sale of city property. You have the right to remain silent, but anything you say can and will be used against you in a court of law.

You have the right to an attorney. If you cannot afford an attorney one will be appointed you by the court—'

By now Haynes was crying.

'Detective?' one of the uniforms called from inside the bedroom.

'Keep an eye on him,' Irving told the second uniform, stepping past the kneeling man and walking through the doorway.

There must have been eight or ten boxes. Bank boxes, standard size, and inside each box were manila files, and within each file dozens of pictures. Everything imaginable, some of it truly horrific, and all of it taken from case files that were being repaired and moved for the NYPD archival project. All of them were closed cases, the pictures representing New York's criminal history. Here were its ghosts, its specters, here were the lives of endless thousands of people destroyed by killers known or unknown. Dale Haynes ran a sideline selling the darkest of New York's memories.

For a while Haynes couldn't speak, and when he finally gathered himself together all he could say was, 'I never meant it to get this bad . . . I'm sorry . . . I know what you want . . . I'm so sorry. Jesus, I am so fucking sorry . . .'

THIRTY-TWO

Haynes gave it up without any formal interrogation. He didn't request an attorney, though once Irving had made the call to Farraday, Farraday understood that there was some substance to the lead and insisted that a state-appointed attorney be found and brought to the precinct house. Farraday called Chief Ellmann, Ellmann called the DA, and the DA sent one of his assistants to sit in as an independent observer. Any information that Haynes might give regarding the possible purchaser of material relating to earlier murders had to be iron-clad. No coercion, no dubious interrogation techniques, no undue pressure.

By the time the circus had gathered it was near to three. Haynes was subdued but incessantly apologetic. He looked at everyone who appeared with the same expression of abject self-pity. He wanted the world to feel sorry for him. He wanted people to know that he was basically a good guy who'd gone astray, that he was just trying to make a living and it got out of hand . . .

While he sat in one of the interrogation cells, his apartment was searched. Nine bank boxes of stolen photographs were brought out. Haynes was certainly organized. He had arranged his pictures by gender, approximate age, and manner of death. Boys, girls, teenagers male and female, women over twenty, men over twenty, and then a category for the over forty-year-old victims. He had done his best to file them under suicides, gunshot victims, strangling, suffocation, poisoning, rape and subsequent murder, drowning, blunt force trauma, decapitations and stabbings. And then a category of miscellaneous one-offs, including a man who'd been tied to a chair, had his hands removed at the wrist and was left to bleed out. There were in excess of seven thousand pictures at first estimate and Haynes – ever the administrator

– had kept an accurate record of coded names, dates, numbers of photographs purchased, how much he'd been paid, and whether or not the client had collected them personally or requested they be mailed.

It was those records that Irving was most interested in, and it was from those records that he located listings for a client referred to as *1457 Post*. Whoever he might have been, 1457 Post had made three purchases in May of that year. Those purchases included photographs from the murder scene of Anne Marie Steffen, Arthur Shawcross's 1988 strangulation victim.

Present in the interrogation room at ten of four were Irving himself, two uniforms, ADA Harry Whittaker and the court-appointed attorney, a middle-aged woman called Fay Garrison. It was not a long interview, for Haynes answered Irving's questions without hesitation.

'According to your own records,' Irving said, 'which, I gotta say, are really helpful, you have made in excess of eleven thousand dollars from your enterprising little sideline. I think the IRS will be interested to know about this as well, don't you think?'

Haynes hung his head for a moment. He looked up, opened his mouth to speak, and when he once again started into how utterly, unbelievably sorry he was, Irving raised his hand and silenced him.

'You have a client,' Irving said. 'He bought three different sets of pictures from you in May this year. One of those pictures was of a prostitute murdered in the late 1980s called Anne Marie Steffen. You refer to your client as 1457 Post. What does that mean?'

Haynes tried to wipe his nose with his sleeve. It was awkward with his hands still cuffed. 'It's where I sent them,' he said.

'You never met the client?'

Haynes shook his head. 'Never met him. Only spoke to him on the phone. He called, told me what he wanted. Gave me the address.'

'And how did he pay you?'

'He posted the cash. Just the cash, nothing else. Gave me a post office box to send them to.'

'PO Box 1457?'

Haynes nodded. 'That's right. PO Box 1457, New York, that was all. I sent them there.'

Irving signalled a look to one of the uniforms. He nodded, and left the room quietly. He would immediately attend to the documentation required to request the box-holder's identity from the post office.

'Okay.' Irving leaned back in the chair. 'So this was quite some operation, hey, Dale? Quite some operation. We're gonna need a statement from you on everything. Dates, times, when – and how – this thing started . . . your whole life story as far as this little adventure is concerned. And then we're gonna charge you, set an arraignment, and you can look forward to your picture being in a file, ready for the new archive unit.'

Once again the abject expression. 'You think . . . you think that—'

'That you'll do time? Is that what you were going to ask?'

Haynes nodded, couldn't hold Irving's gaze.

'Who knows?' he replied. 'We have a lot of things to sort out before we get that far, Mr Haynes, so right now the very best you can do for yourself is write us a statement, as complete and honest as you possibly can, and make sure you don't miss out any important details.'

'Yes,' Haynes mumbled. 'Yes, of course.'

Irving got up. He left Dale Haynes in the care of the second uniformed officer and left the room, along with ADA Whittaker and Fay Garrison.

'He'll not do any time,' Whittaker said. 'He'll get a slap on the wrist, maybe a fine, some community service. Guy like that is small fish.'

'I know,' Irving said, 'but right now we have him quiet and co-operative and I'd like to keep it that way.'

Irving shook hands with both of them. 'Thank you for your assistance,' he said, 'but I have to move on this thing immediately.'

Whittaker and Garrison understood. They knew this was merely the edge of something one hell of a lot bigger.

THIRTY-THREE

Judge Schaeffer signed Irving's warrant at four forty-eight. Irving called the central inquiries number for the New York Post Office, identified himself, gave the warrant number, Schaeffer's name, and arranged an appointment to see the Deputy Security Controller at quarter past five. He put a light on the car and made it there by ten past.

DSC Lawrence Buchanan was as New York Irish-American as they came. No more than five-foot-five or six, maybe one-seventy, one-eighty pounds, he walked in squeaky crepe-soled shoes as if he was about to break into a run. He smiled warmly, he shook hands enthusiastically, seemed like a man who loved life with a vengeance. Irving told him that there was a very significant degree of urgency in what they were doing, that it related to a series of homicides. Irving need not have worried, for DSC Buchanan grinned from ear to ear and walked even faster.

'Then I, sir,' he said, 'will not be the one who slows you up.'

Five thirty-four and Ray Irving walked from the front entrance of the New York Post Office Central Inquiries Department with a piece of paper in his inside jacket pocket. On it was a downtown address: Apt. 14B, 1212 Montgomery Street. The name of the man who had rented PO Box 1457 was given as A. J. Shawcross.

Irving called ahead to the Fourth, spoke directly to Farraday, explained the significance of the given name. With this as sufficient cause, Farraday called Judge Schaeffer, organized the warrant himself, and assigned a SWAT team to the apartment search. A man who had killed eight deserved no less than the best.

Irving reached the Fourth shortly after six. Farraday met him in the incident room, acknowledged the speed and efficiency with which he had worked, told him that a great deal hung on this case, and that its swift resolution would earn them both a significant commendation. Like Irving, the captain felt the rush and punch of the chase. It was a nervous time, a time for predicting the worst-case scenario while anticipating the best; for preparing contingency plans but trying not to run at it too hard or too fast. Handled well, they could have their anniversary killer. One false step, one small fuck-up, and they were back at square one. Worse than that – evidence compromised, a violation of protocol – and the guy could walk on technicalities alone.

The operation commenced at quarter of seven. Three unmarked cars, a SWAT van, a back-up communications vehicle. The traffic was as expected, they took a straight route down Sixth and didn't turn until West Houston, and by twenty past seven they were crossing Delancey, the Williamsburg Bridge to their left, the lower east side area between Delancey, Franklin D Roosevelt Drive and the Manhattan Bridge forming a cul-de-sac of six or eight blocks. Beyond FDR Drive was Corlears Hook and Wallabout Bay; a clear day and you could see over the East River to the Brooklyn Navy Yard. The houses on Montgomery were walk-ups and tenements, fire escapes in back. Three men went in through the front of the building, three to the rear and up the wrought iron gantry. The SWAT team leader gave instructions as if his task was no more challenging than organizing entertainment at a kid's birthday party. Do this, do that, then do this, without needing to think but merely to act. Irving watched from the street, his heart clenched like a fist, and found himself praying for the first time in many months. It was no more than an instinctive reaction, for the last time he had prayed it had been for Deborah Wiltshire, and his words had gone unheeded.

On the second floor of the Montgomery Street house the SWAT advance man came along the hallway toward apartment 14B, his back pressed to the wall; six feet from the door, anyone inside would not have seen him through the peephole as the angle was insufficiently wide.

Advance man's name was Mike Radley, team mates nicknamed him Boo, and however many times he did this,

233

however many times he had yet to do it, it would never feel different.

Tension like a knot of hot wire in the base of his gut. Sense of balance, yes, but delicate. He watched movies – *Jarhead*, *Black Hawk Down* – and he believed he had some understanding of what such people experienced. Go to war. That should have been their motto. Wake up, brush your teeth, get dressed, go to war. The Lower East Side wasn't Beirut or Baghdad, it wasn't Bosnia or Stalingrad, but regardless of the terrain, a bulletproof jacket didn't protect your neck, your face, your shoulders. It didn't protect the huge artery that ran down your inside leg. A handgun was a handgun, whether the person aiming it was a terrorist, a junkie, a drug dealer, a whore, a pimp, a Bellevue escapee, or a man who'd taken it upon himself to clean the New York streets of lowlifes. Bullets were bullets. Dead was dead. Today, tomorrow, next week Tuesday – it was all the same. Your time came when your time came. It was simply a matter of delaying it.

So Boo Radley stood with his back against the wall, a foot or so from the front door of 14B. He stood there for some considerable time as he listened to the unit chief doing the *steady on, breathe deep, move slow, think fast* routine.

He motioned the code to his colleagues. He got word that the rear team were placed and on standby.

He knocked on the door.

He listened intently, every sense attuned for words, movement, some indication that the apartment was occupied.

There was nothing.

He knocked again, announced his presence, identified himself as police.

Radley waited, seemed like an age, and then he turned and indicated forward. His second and third came up with the ram. Radley spoke quickly and succinctly to the unit chief. They were going in – back and front simultaneous – and they would clear the apartment.

Later – once the door was through, once the shouting had started, once the rear team had accessed the apartment through the fire escape route and the kitchen window . . .

Later – when Irving was informed that there was no living person in the apartment, when he started the walk up the

234

internal stairwell, could already smell what was waiting for him and feel the sense of loss that came with having something such as this play out in some other way than he'd intended . . .

Later – when they found the dead girl on the floor, naked and beaten, her hands tied with white clothesline and pulled taut around her neck, the stench of decomposition almost beyond human tolerance, and scrawled on the floor beside her in her own blood a series of cryptic runes that Irving recognized immediately . . .

After all these things . . . Hal Gerrard on the way, Jeff Turner following him, cherry-blue flashing sirens rushing through evening traffic . . . emotions high and dizzy with panic. Irving in the hallway outside, a handkerchief to his face, feeling something akin to horror and delirium, feeling everything and nothing and trying to make some small and desperate sense of any part of this nightmare, cold sweats and nausea – not from the smell, not from the state of the poor girl beaten to hell and left in a disused apartment on Montgomery Street, a message on the floor that suggested something so much darker than any of them could imagine – but from the inevitability of disillusionment . . .

It was never simple. Never as simple as it needed to be.

It was then – after all these things – that Ray Irving truly appreciated the depth of the abyss.

The only thing preventing him from falling was a tenuous hold on reality, a promise of something better, the belief that somehow, some way, he would navigate a path through this and see the other side . . .

Worst thing of all, it seemed, was his desire to let go.

THIRTY-FOUR

By ten they knew her name.

And they broke the code, the symbols written on the floor in the girl's blood.

She was twenty-four years old, she worked in a record store downtown. No missing persons report had been filed. The people in the store would later give statements. *We just figured she didn't like the job . . . She'd only been here a couple of weeks.*

New York – a city big enough to lose people without effort. You were someone on the sidewalk, forgotten by the time you crossed at the corner.

Laura Margaret Cassidy.

On the floor it said *Oakland 9472 Bob Hall Starr was a pussy.*

Whoever had written the message had used a combination of ciphers taken from the Zodiac letters – those to the *Vallejo Times-Herald*, the *San Francisco Examiner* and the *Chronicle*. On the 4th of September 1972 in Oakland, California, a twenty-four-year-old girl called Alexandra Clery was found naked and bound, having been beaten to death. Clery was one of nine possible Zodiac victims from that time period – Betty Cloer, Linda Ohlig, Susan McLaughlin, Yvonne Quilantang, Cathy Fechtel, Michael Shane, Donna Marie Braun and Susan Dye. The majority of the victims had been murdered around the Summer, Winter and Fall Solstices, Linda Ohlig six days after the Vernal Equinox. Irving, having recognized the style of cipher left on the apartment floor, took no time at all to determine the connection between what they had and what had occurred thirty-four years before. He also found a reference, along with one other name, to Bob Hall Starr.

Hal Gerrard and Jeff Turner both confirmed that the Montgomery Street victim's date of death – ascertained from preliminary examination, the state of decomposition – could very well have been twelve days earlier. The 4th of September. The Anniversary Man had given them a Zodiac killing, but they hadn't known.

Laura Cassidy was taken to the coroner's department for autopsy. Jeff Turner and his crew of CSAs started in on the apartment.

Irving, meeting with Farraday back at the Fourth, made his thoughts known.

'I don't think the apartment will give us anything.'

'I think you're probably right,' Farraday said. 'One hope is that she was killed there . . . possibility that he may have left something. If she was dumped there post mortem, then we may get nothing without the primary.' He rose from his chair and walked to the window. He stood with his back to Irving. 'And Bob Hall Starr?' he asked.

'Was a name, a pseudonym really, for the San Francisco PD's favorite candidate.'

'For the Zodiac,' Farraday said matter-of-factly.

'Yes,' Irving replied.

'And we're assuming that there is no possibility that the Zodiac is still alive.' Farraday turned back, sat on the edge of the sill with his hands in his pockets.

'Assuming, yes.'

'So what do you conclude now?'

'That he might be trying to prove he's better than all of them. Just my opinion . . . but that's the conclusion we've come to—'

'We?' Farraday said. 'Who is *we* exactly?'

Irving realized the slip, cursed himself. He looked away, toward the wall where Farraday's citations, commendations, certificates of service and framed photos hung. He didn't look at them directly, but into the vague middle ground between. For a moment Irving was gone. He was tired and confused, disillusioned, disappointed, disheartened, angry, frustrated. He was also determined not to be made the scapegoat for whatever shit-storm of questions Farraday might find himself unable to answer. This was not the way it was supposed to be. This was not the way he had intended his life to go—

'Ray?'

Irving snapped to. He looked back at Farraday. 'I had some external assistance with a couple of aspects of this . . . well, not so much assistance really, more like some input.'

'Input?'

'The guy that researched the *City Herald* article . . . the one that put the connections together.'

Farraday didn't speak for a moment. He walked back to his desk and sat down. He seemed pensive, but there was something in his expression that suggested a difficulty in defining his own reaction.

'This is not good,' he said eventually. 'This is not the sort of external input that will read well . . .'

Irving leaned forward. 'Captain? Can we look at this in another light for just a moment?'

Farraday raised his eyebrows.

Irving took his career in his hands. 'Away from the Mayor and the Chief. Let's forget about the election, forget about who might or might not get a job next year. Can we just look at this from the simple perspective of an ongoing homicide investigation?'

'I trust that *is* the way you have been looking at it, Ray—'

'*I* have yes, but I don't know that anyone else has . . . at least not completely.'

'Explain.'

'Pulling back on resources first of all. I get two uniforms for only a couple of hours to help sort out the paperwork on more than half a dozen murder investigations. I get half an office to work in, no assistant investigator, and I get word that I can't have anyone because everyone is needed out on the street to make things look good for the Mayor and the Chief of Police—'

Farraday raised his hand. 'Enough already, Ray. I've got nine detectives, two of whom are on leave. That leaves me seven in all. You're on this, the other six are handling everything else that comes through the precinct, and that doesn't take into consideration the fact that two of our people are bolstering up the lines at the Eighth. We've got Captain Hughes getting the shit kicked out of him dealing with the homeland security people. We have the transit authority, airport security and the cab drivers' strike, as well as this bullshit with events co-ordination for Thanksgiving—'

'So let *me* get some help,' Irving interjected.

'Whaddya mean, let *you* get some help.'

'Let me get this guy over here—'

'What guy? The researcher guy? Jesus, Ray, are you out of your fucking mind? The Chief gets word that you've got a newspaper reporter working on an ongoing police—'

'He's not a newspaper reporter, he's a researcher, and as far as I can tell he knows more about this serial killer shit than anyone I've ever met, and he's not a psych, and he's not some narrow-minded bureaucratic fuck from the FBI. Okay, so he might have his quirks and idiosyncrasies—'

'What the fuck is that supposed to mean?'

Irving knew he was on thin ice, but he didn't care. Right now he didn't see how it could get much worse than it already was.

'We have someone here with a brain the size of a fucking planet who seems to have dedicated the last twenty years of his life to figuring out all the connections between God only knows how many serial killings, and he's offered his help. He *wants* to help. We know that because he calls up and tells me who these killings are replicas of. He finds stuff on the internet and he sends it over here to me—'

'And he could be your number one fucking suspect by the sound of it.'

'All the more reason to have him close, have him right where we want him, and in the meantime we use whatever information and input he can give us to work this thing. This is one almighty fucking nightmare, Captain, and I don't know that anyone could do this thing alone. I need some help. He wouldn't need paying, and if he had expenses I'll cover them myself, and—'

Farraday was shaking his head. 'If this is done then it gets done by the book. He gets hired as a researcher. He gets a name, he gets a security clearance – to a point of course. He acts with us, not on our behalf. He does not represent the police department, he is employed in a consultational capacity by the police department, and he gets paid an agreed-upon hourly rate. There is no way in the fucking world that I am having some newspaper reporter write a story telling the world how this department is so understaffed and under-funded that it has to hire outside unqualified help, and that their expenses have to be paid out of the pocket of one of the precinct's homicide detectives.' Farraday paused for a moment. 'You understand what I'm saying?'

'I do, yes . . . makes sense.'

Farraday stood up, went back to the window. He was quiet for some time. Every once in a while he shook his head. He seemed to be having a silent conversation with someone, explaining himself perhaps, justifying his actions. 'Okay, so speak to the guy,' he eventually said. 'Find out what he thinks he can do to help you. If it's worth it, then fine, get him in here and we'll put him on the system. If he's not, drop him and come see me, and we'll talk about maybe getting someone to handle your phone and admin traffic and a uniform to do some legwork, okay?'

Irving rose from his seat.

'Okay?' Farraday repeated. 'We understand one another, right, Ray?'

'Right, Captain,' Irving replied. 'We understand one another.'

THIRTY-FIVE

'I have no idea,' Karen Langley said.

Irving shifted the phone from one ear to the other. 'You have no idea?'

'No, Ray, I have no idea.'

'But you've worked with the guy for what? Eight, nine years?'

'How many people do you work with that you know where they live, hey? He lives in New York somewhere, Ray, I don't need to know precisely where. I'm sure his address is in the phone book. It's certainly going to be with personnel or payroll.'

Irving was struggling with what she was saying. 'I don't know, Karen . . . just seems strange that you've worked with a guy for all this time and you don't know where he lives.'

'You gotta take into consideration the fact that he doesn't want me to know where he lives.'

'Jesus,' Irving said to himself. It was Sunday morning. He'd called Karen Langley on her cellphone. She was home, alone he assumed, and she had seemed pleased to hear his voice. Until he told her what he wanted, of course. And then she seemed businesslike, a little distant and matter-of-fact. What he'd suggested to Farraday – that Costello be employed to assist him – had seemed to make so much sense the night before. Emotions had been high, he had been afraid – a sense of disconnection, as if no-one in the world could ever hope to understand what he'd been feeling. Another victim. A Zodiac replica from the Anniversary Man. And a message. *Bob Hall Starr was a pussy*. It was a challenge. *I am better than all of them. I am as good as it gets. I am so far ahead of you people you wouldn't even see dust . . . even better than that because I don't leave any dust for you to follow.* Irving had recognized that in the message – the unspoken defiance, the invitation.

Go for it, he was saying. *Try your hand.* It made sense to Irving, and in that moment he'd believed that John Costello, of all people, would perhaps be the only person who would appreciate what it meant.

Alongside this was another insidious suspicion. Costello had given him Leonard Beck, Beck had given him Chaz Morrison, Morrison had given him Haynes, and Haynes had been a direct link to the dead girl in the apartment. Without these connections she would not yet have yet been found.

Irving wanted to believe that this result had come from his own persistence and hard work, but – yet again – these events seemed all too coincidental.

A fractured and restless night's sleep behind him, viewing this thing in the cold light of day, it seemed to make no sense at all.

And Karen Langley . . . explaining to him that she had worked with Costello for so many years and didn't know where he lived . . .

'What's the problem, Ray? What is it that you're trying to handle here?'

Irving realized he'd been silent for some moments. He'd closed his eyes, pretending perhaps that if he couldn't see what was in front of him he could make-believe he was elsewhere.

'I need to go visit him.'

She hesitated for a second or two.

'What?' Irving asked.

'That's not going to happen.'

'What d'you mean, not going to happen?'

'You visiting John Costello. It's not going to happen. So you find out where he lives, look him up in the police computer or whatever? You have any idea how freaked out he's gonna be if you just show up at his apartment?'

Irving didn't let on that he had failed to find Costello's address on any system. 'No, I don't, but I'm beginning to wonder who the hell it is that you have working for you now.'

She did it again then – smiled as she spoke. 'What? You're concerned about me?'

'Sure I am, sure I'm concerned.'

'Why? Why would that matter?'

'Because I like you. Because you're a good person—'

'You didn't call me,' she said abruptly, and all of a sudden the conversation had changed direction without warning.

How was it that women always managed to do that . . .

'You what?'

'You didn't call me. We went out last Wednesday, four days ago . . . you said you were gonna call me, and you didn't.'

Irving was ready to hang up the phone. 'I'm sorry— Jesus, Karen, all of a sudden we're talking about the fact that I didn't call you?'

'Yes we are. You call me this morning, you say "Hi, how you doing?" That's it. Nothing else. Then you wanna know if I can get you into John Costello's apartment.'

'Are you pissed at me?' Irving asked.

'Of course I'm pissed at you. For God's sake, Ray, are you that fucking ignorant?'

'Okay, okay, Jesus, I'm sorry. I've been a bit preoccupied, okay? I've been a bit preoccupied with this thing. I have another dead girl on my hands, found late last night, and I'm trying to see some daylight through the fucking trees, and I spoke to my captain and told him that maybe there's a guy that can help us—'

'You what?'

'I spoke to my captain . . . spoke to him about John. Said that I figured he might be able to help us on this.'

For a while she didn't speak, and there was something about the way that she didn't speak that made Irving relax. Why, he didn't know, but the awkwardness between them seemed to dissolve without any further words.

'I'll call him,' she said. 'I have his number. I can't give it to you because he asked me never to give it to anyone. But I will call him—'

'You have to understand, Karen—'

'That none of this is for publication, right?'

'Right.'

'So I'll call him and call you back.'

'Thank you,' Irving replied. 'And about not calling you? I *am* sorry, okay? I'd like to tell you that I thought about it a

243

lot, but I didn't. I thought about you, but I've been so damned busy with this thing—'

'It's okay,' she said, and there was an element of empathy in her voice. 'I understand. Now hang up and I'll call him.'

'Thank you, Karen.'

The line went dead.

THIRTY-SIX

Irving went early to the Deli, took a table in back away from the Sunday lunch traffic.

Karen Langley had come back to him within minutes. Costello would speak with Irving, but he wanted Langley there, and not at his own apartment.

'Somewhere public he said,' Langley told Irving.

'Jesus, Karen—'

'Ray?'

Irving fell silent.

'Don't question it, okay? He says he'll talk to you. Take what you're given and be grateful.'

They arranged to meet at one. Irving made an effort to dress appropriately. A pair of black pants, still in the cleaner's bag from months before, and a dark blue sport jacket. He ironed a white shirt, decided to forego a tie, and cleaned his dress-uniform shoes. He needed a haircut. He needed another suit. He needed a lot of things.

When he stood in front of the mirror in the hallway – the mirror Deborah insisted he put there so she could give herself a final once-over as she left the apartment – he wondered if he was making the effort in order to look like the professional he was supposed to be, or if he was doing it for Karen Langley. It was something of both, he decided. This case, perhaps more than any of his career, was demanding of his most accurate attention. It was Sunday, a little past noon, and already he'd made calls for the Laura Cassidy autopsy report. This thing wasn't going anywhere without him. It was never going to quietly disappear or evaporate. He would not be reassigned to something of greater priority. Until it was over. Well, until it was over, it was his life.

Irving had arrived at Carnegie's with thirty-five minutes to spare. He ordered coffee, said it would be a little while before he was joined by two guests. He told the waitress that the discussion was of a somewhat confidential nature, and once they had ordered food – *if* they ordered food – then it would be better if they were left alone.

'You know me, sweetheart,' she said. 'Never one to interfere where I'm not needed.'

Irving put a folded ten-dollar bill in her hand, thanked her, took his seat.

Irving could have been wrong, but he believed that Karen Langley had made an effort too. She had on a pants-suit, a cream-colored blouse with a scarf tied loosely at the neck. She looked relaxed but effortlessly classy. She seemed to possess numerous facets, and Irving had yet to find one that he did not like.

John Costello, however, looked as inconspicuous and low-key as ever. Perhaps he chose to be singularly unremarkable. Perhaps it was his mission in life never to be noticed again – not by a serial killer, not by anyone.

'Karen. John.' Irving rose from the table and extended his hand to each of them.

Karen smiled. 'So formal,' she said. 'Sit down, for God's sake.'

Irving did as he was told.

Costello smiled at Karen Langley. He was the interested spectator, an observer in this small moment of theater.

'Thank you for coming, John,' Irving said. 'First things first – are we going to eat?'

'Sure we are,' Costello said. 'Sunday is an open day. How's the food here?'

'It's good. Great actually. I really like it.'

'What do they have?'

Irving shook his head. 'God, I don't know, everything. Lots of kosher, of course. I'll get us a menu—'

'You suggest,' Costello said. 'Okay with you, Karen?'

'Sure, of course. But no chicken liver. I don't like chicken liver.'

Irving caught the waitress's eye and waved her over. 'Can we have the pastrami, open-face on knish three times?' He looked at Costello, at Karen. 'You guys eat cheese, right?'

Costello nodded. 'Cheese is good.'

246

'Cheese on all three,' he said, 'and a Central Park salad to share.'

'Coffee?' the waitress asked.

'You have tea?' Costello asked.

'Sure we have tea. What kind of tea would you like? We got Darjeeling, English breakfast, Earl Grey—'

'English breakfast.'

'Coffee for me,' Karen said.

The waitress disappeared, returned moments later with their drinks, and refilled Irving's cup. 'Ten, fifteen minutes for your lunch, okay?'

Irving thanked her.

'I understand you found another one,' Costello said before Irving had a chance to speak.

'He did the Zodiac,' Irving replied.

'Which one?'

'Girl called Alexandra Clery . . . the one you mentioned before.'

'So you found her when?'

'Last night.'

'And she'd been dead since September fourth?'

Irving's eyes widened. 'You remember the date? You gotta tell me how the hell you do that.'

Costello shook his head. 'I read things. They stay with me. Not everything, of course, just things that seem to have some relevance or importance, I suppose. Don't ask me why or how. It just is.'

Irving believed that perhaps he didn't want to know.

'So?' Costello prompted. 'My question?'

'Dead since the fourth? Yes, more than likely. I don't have the autopsy report yet.'

'And she was beaten to death and left naked like the Oakland girl from '72?'

'Appears that way,' Irving said, and then held himself in check. 'Hang fire here,' he said. 'We're ahead of ourselves already.'

'Ahead of ourselves? What d'you mean?'

'This thing . . . here . . . what we're talking about. I haven't even told you what I wanted to discuss with you.'

247

'I know what you want to discuss with me, Detective Irving.'

Irving opened his mouth to speak.

'Karen told me. You want me to be an independent and external . . .' Costello paused, shook his head. 'An independent and external what?'

'Consultant?' Irving ventured.

'Sure, that'll do. A consultant.'

No-one spoke for a handful of seconds.

'Right,' Costello said. 'That's what you want?'

'Yes. Whatever you want to call it. Ordinarily I'd deal with criminal profiling, get the FBI involved, but there's no actual evidence of kidnapping and—'

'And they have a spectacularly narrow view of such things.'

'Who the hell knows?' Irving said. 'I have very little dealings with them.'

'Believe me,' Costello said. 'They have their routines and regulations. They want to be so orderly and organized, and to a large extent I'm sure they succeed. But when it comes to thinking like a serial killer . . .' He shook his head. 'There are no rules and regulations to what these people do aside from the rules and regulations they themselves create.'

'So this is something you are willing to consider?' Irving asked.

'Consider? Of course, Detective. I've already decided to help you.'

Irving tried to look neither surprised nor pleased. 'It will be official, of course. You will be formally employed by the NYPD as an external consultant, a researcher for want of a better word. You'll get paid an agreed rate—'

'Details are unimportant,' Costello said, interrupting quietly. 'I'm interested, that's all. This has interested me greatly from day one, and to have access to all the crime scene information—'

'Within certain parameters,' Irving interjected.

Costello sat back in his chair and put his teacup down. 'There cannot be any parameters,' he said. 'Not on information directly relating to the cases themselves. How the hell do you expect me to find your thread if I can't see everything?'

'We'll handle it,' Irving said. 'You have to understand that this has come about because of me. This is not something that has been requested from above. My captain took some convincing, and God knows what the Chief of Police would have to say if he knew what was going on. Fact of the matter is that this is very unorthodox. A private citizen with no formal qualifications in criminal profiling, no real familiarity with police work—'

'But twenty years' experience as a crime researcher,' Karen said.

'Sure, of course, yes,' Irving replied.

'And,' Costello added, 'the very best qualification of all, don't forget – something that no-one in the police department or the FBI can claim to have.'

Irving looked at him.

Costello smiled. 'I've been there, Detective Irving. I know what it's like to see someone like this up close and personal.'

THIRTY-SEVEN

They ate without further mention of the anniversary killings. Karen Langley had concluded their discussion neatly. She would speak with the paper's assistant editor-in-chief, Leland Winter, with Bryan Benedict if necessary, and she would help secure some sort of agreement for John Costello to consult for the PD without completely abdicating his responsibilities to the *City Herald*.

'John is my right hand,' she said.

Costello ignored her compliment. He ate intently, a man with a purpose, and seemed oblivious to the details they discussed.

At quarter of two he got up from his chair, folded his napkin neatly and placed it beside his plate. He thanked Irving for lunch, bade farewell to Karen Langley and then, without another word, he turned from the table and left the restaurant.

For a few moments Irving was speechless.

Karen had watched Costello go, and when she turned back to Irving she laughed at the expression on his face.

'You look like someone smacked you,' she said. 'That's John. Pay no mind to it. You'll get used to his quirks.'

'Will I?' Irving asked, more a question of himself.

'Sure you will,' she said. 'You don't have a choice do you?'

They stayed for another hour.

'This has now become our unofficial second date,' she said.

'Not the kind of thing I had in mind,' Irving replied.

Karen leaned back and looked at him quizzically. 'Were you always this serious?'

'You don't think I should be serious about this?'

'There's a difference between being serious and being serious *about* something. Sure, this is serious. This is a homicide

250

investigation. That's something to be serious *about*. I'm not speaking specifically, I'm speaking generally.'

'You think I'm too serious?'

'I think everyone's too serious, Ray. I think how seriously people take themselves is the cause of half their problems.'

'So what d'you want me to do? What d'you want from me?'

'What do I want? I don't want anything,' she replied. 'I think maybe you're the one who wants something . . . something a little more than just a homicide investigation—'

'I'm finding it pretty difficult to think about anything else at the moment.'

'Evidently.'

Irving tilted his head to one side and looked at her suspiciously. 'Meaning?'

'Meaning nothing more than you're taking what I'm saying too literally. I'm not going to tell you to lighten up because it wouldn't do any good, but I think you should—'

'Lighten up?'

'Hell, try it, Ray, you might like it.'

'I will,' he said resignedly. He knew what she meant. He believed that she didn't need to tell him, but being told was precisely what he *did* need. Why was there always an edge to what should have been the simplest thing of all? Talking to someone. Finding out about someone. Spending time with someone. There always had to be something else going on to confuse the issue.

'I have to ask you something,' Irving said.

'Shoot.'

'It's about confidentiality . . . about the fact that I have to maintain the integrity of this investigation now that—'

'Now that John will be involved?' Karen shook her head. 'You think I have conflicting interests here, don't you?'

'It would be hard for you not to,' Irving replied. 'You have a headline-worthy case, a researcher who is going to be directly involved, access to information that no other newspaper could ever hope to get, and you're going to get the usual internal demands from editors and assistant editors to deliver the goods.'

'If you think that, then you don't know John, and you certainly don't know me,' Karen replied. 'If John says he won't talk about something, then he won't talk about it. If he signs a confidentiality agreement then he'll stick to it.'

'I find it hard to understand how you can say that about him. That sort of thing implies a significant degree of certainty about someone's character—'

'When I don't even know where he lives?'

Irving smiled. 'Well, come on, Karen, it seems a little unusual.'

'I don't know how to tell you any better than I already have. John is the way he is . . . maybe he was always that way, maybe he became that way as a result of what happened to him. All I know is that he's invaluable to me. In this business I couldn't hope for anyone better but, like anyone, he has things you have to deal with in order to get along with him. Perhaps with him they're a little more obvious, a little more pronounced, but he's harmless—'

'You're sure about that?'

Karen looked surprised, a sudden change of expression. 'You still have some doubt about him?'

'I've only just met the guy, Karen. I don't know a god-damned thing about him.'

'Hell of a way to choose the help then, don't you think?'

'So tell me what else you can,' Irving said.

She smiled and shook her head. 'You're gonna have to find out for yourself, Ray. You got yourself into this, you're gonna have to get yourself out.'

'Oh come on, that's not fair—'

Karen slid sideways and gathered up her jacket. 'I'm going now,' she said.

'What?' Irving asked, surprise evident in his tone.

Karen Langley raised her hand and silenced him before he had a chance to speak further. 'I'm going,' she repeated. 'I'll speak to Leland, whoever else. I'll sort out this thing with John.' She rose to her feet. Irving started to get up too.

She smiled, reached out her hand and touched the side of his face. 'Don't get up,' she said. 'This isn't the right time for what we're thinking about.'

'But—'

She shook her head. 'Deal with this. When you're done dealing with it call me. We could start over perhaps.'

'Karen,' Irving started. 'I didn't mean to—'

'It's okay,' she said quietly. She leaned down and kissed Irving's cheek. 'You have my number, and when you don't want something from me you should call me, okay?'

Irving just looked back at her without speaking.

'Just nod, Ray. Just nod so I know you heard me.'

Irving nodded.

Karen Langley smiled, almost as if this was what she expected, as if she had long since prepared herself for this kind of thing and knew exactly how to act, and then she turned her back on him and walked to the door.

Ray Irving half-rose from his seat; the front of his jacket caught the handle of his coffee cup, and over it went. In the confusion of snatching napkins from the chrome dispenser he didn't see her go, and when he looked up she was gone.

Perhaps she'd looked back, a glance, a half-smile – something to reaffirm her position. He didn't know, and now he would never know.

He sat down again. The waitress came and asked if he wanted fresh coffee. He said no, and then changed his mind.

He stayed for a while – twenty minutes, half an hour perhaps. He watched the world through the window – Seventh Avenue on a Sunday afternoon – and believed, with certainty, that this had been the worst second date of his life.

THIRTY-EIGHT

Close to three, and there was little point in returning home. Irving went to his office, made some phone calls, tried to find whatever additional information he could about John Costello. The man had no criminal record, had never been arrested let alone charged, and thus his prints were not on the system. He finally located Costello's Social Security number, which gave him an address – an apartment in a building at West 39th and Ninth where Costello had been registered in January of 1989. If it was still valid – and Irving had no reason to consider otherwise – then Costello had lived in the same place for almost eighteen years. Irving could walk there right now. Fifteen, twenty minutes, and he'd be standing outside John Costello's front door, could get inside, take a good look at the world that John Costello had created for himself. How these people lived was always the very best indicator of their state of mind.

Irving stopped right there. *These people?* What was he thinking? What did he mean by *these people*? Was he now classifying Costello as somehow similar to the man he was looking for?

Irving quietly derailed that train of thought and focused on the computer.

The original records from the Hammer of God killings had been scanned and forwarded to him from Jersey. They'd been archived in late 2002. Irving knew of the project – a vast undertaking designed to give some sense of order and permanence to the enormous weight of files that existed in county archives; an effort to reduce storage space, to preserve the integrity of documents, to make cross-referencing by hand and eye a thing of the past. Of course, as with all such projects, either funding had finally run out or been withdrawn, or someone had taken advantage of the opportunity

254

and overcharged the taxpayer by using expensive consultants and data-input staff. Eventually someone would exhume the project, pick it up from where it was left off, and second, third, and even fourth attempts would be made to complete it. Irving was fortunate in that New Jersey had made it to early '86. The last of the Hammer of God attacks – that on John Costello and Nadia McGowan – had taken place in November of '84. Irving pulled the lot and hard-copied it. *Treeware*, he thought, and smiled, remembering the term computer geeks used for paper documentation. In the basement of the Fourth he accessed the newspaper microfiche system, pulled the original December '84 *Jersey City Tribune* articles: Wednesday, 5th – *City Arrest In Hammer Killings Case*; Friday, 7th – *Hammer Killings Suspect Named and Charged*; Wednesday, 12th – *Hammer Killer Arraigned*; an article from Thursday the 20th about Robert Clare's boss attempting to take legal action against serial-murder groupies coming around to Clare's place of work to gloat and collect mementoes. Finally, on December 27th, a report covering the bare facts of Clare's suicide. Continuing his search for any related Hammer of God articles, Irving found one that struck all too close to home. It was perhaps the saddest thing of all. It was dated Friday, January 4th, 1985, and the header ran *'Hammer of God' Cop Death*.

The article went on to say that Detective Frank Gorman, head of the Jersey City Homicide Task Force, had died of a heart attack in a restaurant bathroom. Gorman was a fifty-one year-old bachelor who, to compound the sense of tragedy, had been dining alone when he died. A twenty-eight-year veteran, he warranted only a two and a half inch squib in the *Tribune*.

Irving sat back in his chair, lost in reflection. He wondered how many people had attended Gorman's funeral on Wednesday, 9th January, 1985 at the First Communion Church of God . . . how many people that weren't cops.

Those simple paragraphs said it all. History was repeating itself. Gorman had been no different from himself. No family, no, kids, no legacy. No flowers required. They would only fade and be thrown away.

He closed down the microfiche and went back to the

incident room. He pored over the interviews that Gorman and Hennessy had conducted, found a note scrawled along the corner of the initial McGowan/Costello incident report. It was in Hennessy's handwriting, that much Irving could tell, and said, simply, *Copycat??*

Evidently, Frank Gorman and Warren Hennessy had considered some of the same questions as Irving. Costello had been the only one to survive. Had his own injuries been self-inflicted? Had he killed the earlier couples and then, to divert attention from himself, killed his own girlfriend and injured himself? If that was the case, then who was Robert Melvin Clare, and why would he have confessed? Compared to the current level of forensic and crime scene analysis, much of the technology had been in its infancy in 1984. Perhaps there was a simpler explanation – perhaps there were two such killers. Was there any possibility in the world that John Costello, a mere sixteen years old at the time, could have replicated a Hammer of God serial killing back then?

Irving shuddered at the thought. He was taking huge leaps of assumption. He had met John Costello a number of times now. Was it really possible that he could be the Anniversary Man? Had John Wayne Gacy or Kenneth McDuff, Arthur Shawcross or Harvey Carignan seemed to be who they really were? Or was the most powerful deception the most fundamental in such cases? *I am not who you think I am. I am not even who I believe myself to be.*

Irving searched for Detective Gorman's colleague Warren Hennessy in the internal database. Followed him as far as July of 1994. Twelve years had passed. Would Hennessy still be alive? Where the hell would he be? Was there any real point in spending the time and the resources necessary to track him down? What, if anything, would Hennessy be able to tell him about John Costello? That he too had considered the possibility that Costello replicated the Hammer of God killer's signature? That he had briefly suspected Costello of being the worst deceiver of all?

Irving let go of it. He didn't believe it. He was filling empty spaces with whatever he could find, and what he was using just didn't fit.

John Costello was a surviving victim. That was all. He was a man with an extraordinary ability to connect the dots, and that ability could prove useful in making some sense of what had happened. There was nothing more to it than that. The man was an enigma – granted – but Irving wanted so much to believe that he was not a serial killer.

By five p.m., fatigued from reading endless pages of close-typed documentation, he spent an hour rearranging files and photographs, putting things in chronological sequence. He underlined certain points on certain pages from original incident reports. He made notes of things he did not wish to forget when Costello came.

Before he left he called the coroner's office, asked for the autopsy report on Laura Cassidy. Hal Gerrard was not there, but one of his assistants said that Irving could drive over and pick it up.

Irving did so, went on home from there. A little after seven he sat in the kitchen of his apartment and read through the brief notes regarding the death of a twenty-four-year-old record store employee that New York had already forgotten. Laura Margaret Cassidy, murdered in the same fashion as Alexandra Clery, unconfirmed Zodiac victim.

Once again, it was all assumption. The connection was tenuous at best. What was it that could prove this spate of killings had been carried out by the same man? Nothing but the dates, that was all. Nothing but the fact that these people had been killed in certain ways on certain dates.

Was that enough?

Irving tossed the pages aside and leaned back in his chair. He closed his eyes, felt the onset of a headache somewhere back of his forehead.

It would have to be enough – that was the truth – because it was all they had.

THIRTY-NINE

'Do I get a badge?' Costello asked. His expression was dead-pan, no trace of humor.

'A what?'

'A badge. Like I've been deputized or something, you know?'

Irving frowned. 'You can't be serious.'

Costello shrugged. He rose from the desk in Irving's make-shift incident room and walked to the window, where he stood for a moment counting cars – white cars. It was twenty past ten, morning of Monday, September 18th. Karen Langley had spoken with Leland Winter, Winter had spoken with Bryan Benedict. Benedict and Captain Farraday had spent no more than fifteen minutes on the telephone, and Costello had been dispatched from the *New York City Herald* offices on West 31st and Ninth to the Fourth Precinct station house on 57th and Sixth. There were no concessions. There were no exclusives agreed if the case should break. There were no special favors granted. The *City Herald* was lending the NYPD a crime researcher, a man with twenty years' experience in the subject, a man who could perhaps think outside the orthodox framework within which these matters usually resided. John Costello – it was considered – would not think like a homicide detective. Somehow he would think differently, and this change of perspective, this shift of viewpoint, was what Irving believed they needed.

Costello turned from the window, hands in his pockets. 'Simply stated we have nine murder victims,' he said. 'Earliest one was June third, latest one, Laura Cassidy, we think was September fourth, even though she was discovered on Saturday eleventh.' Costello smiled at Irving. 'I wonder how he felt when she was left undiscovered.'

'I thought the same thing,' Irving said. 'Why send us the

Shawcross letter to make sure we got the Anne Marie Steffen connection, why paint the Wolfe kid's face, and then leave his Zodiac girl like that?'

'He must have been crawling out of his skin with frustration.'

'It could simply be a matter of limiting the clues. He wants us to get enough, but not too much.'

'Mystique,' Costello said.

'Mystique?'

'That's what it's all about really, isn't it? FBI profiler called John Douglas said that the motivation for all of these people is simply the effort to define and perpetuate their own mythology. They all want to be someone but they're not, so they have to make themselves someone in order to be heard.'

'The abused and neglected child cliché,' Irving said.

'Clichés are only clichés because they possess enough truth to be repeated.'

Irving walked to the boards at the end of the room. Within a moment Costello was beside him, each of them scanning the faces of the victims, their respective names, the dates and times of death, the pins and flags indicating crime scene locations on the city map.

'It doesn't have to make sense, does it?' Irving asked.

'Make sense?' Costello echoed. 'No, it doesn't actually have to make any sense at all.'

'Except to him.'

'To him it makes perfect sense, otherwise there would be no reason to do it.'

'Makes you realize how utterly fucking crazy some people are.'

'The feeling is mutual,' Costello said. 'This man feels the same way about us as we do about him.'

'You honestly believe that?'

'Yes, I do.'

Neither spoke for a while, and then Costello turned and walked back to the desk. 'Crime scene photographs,' he said. 'I think we should look at every picture that was taken, and if we can't find what we're looking for then we should go to the crime scenes themselves.'

'Look for the signature,' Irving said. 'I can get the pictures. Access to crime scenes I'm not so sure.'

'I appreciate the necessity for confidentiality, but if there are parameters—'

'Let's take a look at the pictures,' Irving said. 'If we need to go to the crime scenes we'll worry about that as and when.'

They started work, emptying the respective files of all pictures. In all there proved to be over two hundred images.

Costello and Irving moved the desks back against the wall facing the window. They laid the pictures out on the floor, side-by-side, case by case, until there was not an inch of carpet remaining visible.

Costello stood on the desk, hands on his hips, and surveyed the jigsaw of images beneath him. Irving stood by the window.

'Come up here,' Costello said. 'It will give you a different perspective.'

'Give me a different perspective? You are so—'

'Seriously,' Costello interjected. 'Come and take a look at this.'

Irving tip-toed his way between the lines of pictures and reached the other side of the room. He climbed up on the desk and stood beside Costello, the pair of them looking down at the myriad color photographs.

'The girl found in the apartment,' Costello said. 'Whoever took the PO Box had to provide ID?'

'You can take a box with a driver's license, something like that,' Irving said. 'Whoever it was used some false ID with the name Shawcross, and simply gave the Montgomery Street apartment as his address.'

Costello was silent for a moment, and then said, 'You see any similarity?'

'I've been through these things a dozen times. I've looked at them back to front, upside down, every which way . . . see if there was anything that stood out, and I can't see a goddamned thing.'

'There is no signature,' Costello said. 'He's a chameleon. He just assumes someone else's color.'

'Very poetic,' Irving replied, an edge of sarcasm in his tone.

'It takes a particular kind of person to sacrifice that much of themselves, don't you think?'

'Sacrifice?'

'Maybe not a good choice of word, but you know what I mean. Whoever this is, well he must be compelled to do this, right? This is a compulsion. These aren't crimes of circumstance. This takes planning, very methodical, very precise as to victim, manner of death, location of the body, the position in which it's left, all these things. He's a perfectionist, and yet he seems able to leave nothing of himself behind. He doesn't want us to know who he is on two levels. First, because he doesn't want to get caught, and secondly because he believes he is superior – not only to all these previous killers – but also to us.'

'Now you're beginning to sound like a profiler,' Irving said. 'We don't need you to tell us what he's like. We need you to put your knowledge to use in determining who he will replicate next.'

Costello came down off of the desk and stepped carefully between the pictures. He picked up an image of one of the girls found by the East River Park. He looked at it for a moment, and then set it down. Next was a picture of Mia Grant, the girl found by the Thomasian twins, the Murray Hill want-ad killing.

'Harv the Hammer,' Costello said. 'That was Harvey Carignan's nickname. Then you have the two girls at the park killed by the Sunset Slayers. John Wayne Gacy . . . far as I know he was never given a name, nor was Kenneth McDuff. Shawcross was called the Monster of the Rivers, and lastly we have the apartment girl, Cassidy, where we're given the most famous of them all, the Zodiac.'

'What are you looking for?' Irving asked.

'Whatever there is,' Costello replied. 'He chooses them for a reason, perhaps the original killers' names, the victims' names, the dates—' Costello paused, looked up at Irving.

'What?'

'I want to make a list of the dates, the original dates and the new ones.'

Costello and Irving did so, factoring in the discovery of Laura Cassidy on the assumption that she was murdered on the 4th of September. Costello noted the dates in sequence all the way back to Mia Grant on June 3rd, and then he calculated the number of days between them.

'Mia Grant to the two girls, Ashley Burch and Lisa Briley, is nine days. From there to the kid in the firework warehouse is forty-seven days. From there to the girl and her two friends in the trunk of the car is eight days. Then we have a twenty-nine day gap to the fourth of September and Laura Cassidy. Finally, even though she was found before the Cassidy girl, we have a seven day break to the killing of Carol-Anne Stowell. That's nine, forty-seven, eight, twenty-nine, and then seven—'

'Nine, eight, seven are the intervening numbers,' Irving said. 'If we drop out the forty-seven and twenty-nine-day gaps, we have a sequence.'

'Which would mean that if there's an *intended* sequence in it, he kills on some undefined date, and then kills again six days later.' Costello shook his head. 'I don't think there's anything in the dates. They're not prime numbers, they're not all odd or all even. The numbers that are half way between the differences don't follow a sequence.'

Irving sat on the window sill, hands in his pockets. 'He's just taken certain killers, or certain types of murders. I don't think it's any more complicated than what we first suspected.'

'He simply wants to share his brilliance with the world.'

'Whatever you want to call it,' Irving said.

'So if it's not the victims, and if he isn't limiting himself to killers who have been caught – which he isn't – then it will be something else . . .' He paused, then said, 'So we go to the crime scenes.'

'I'll do what I can,' Irving replied.

'And I'll wait for you to call me,' Costello replied. He rose from the desk and put on his jacket. 'Leave a message with Karen and I'll call you back.'

'A question.'

Costello smiled, as if he'd known it was coming.

'You live where?'

'You know where I live, Detective Irving.'

Irving couldn't deny it, didn't try. 'I find it hard to understand how you can live such an insular life—'

'Insular?' Costello asked. 'How is my life insular?'

'You go to work. The person you work for has never been to your apartment. You don't seem to have any particular social habits. I presume you are not in a relationship currently—'

'And you feel this is a problem?'

'Well, I don't know that it's necessarily a problem as such, but I just figure you must be kind of lonely—'

Costello buried his hands in his pockets and looked down at the floor for a moment. When he looked up he had a calm and unperturbed expression on his face.

'Seems we're two of a kind then, doesn't it, Detective?'

Ray Irving watched him leave and didn't say a word.

FORTY

The thought kept going: *A desire to define and perpetuate their own mythology.*

It kept Irving awake, and the more he considered it the more it made sense.

Somewhere after two in the morning he got out of bed and went to look up the word in a dictionary. *Myth*. It spoke of superhuman beings, demigods, deities. It spoke of *created* identities, those identities employed to explain the inexplicable.

It wasn't possible to rationalize what this man was doing. It wasn't even necessary to rationalize it. It was merely necessary to attempt to understand him, and with understanding would come the ability to predict. What would he do next? *Who* would he be? And when?

Irving fell asleep close to three, woke at seven-thirty, was out of the apartment by quarter past eight.

He decided to pass on breakfast at Carnegie's, picked up some coffee, and set out straight for the Fourth. Then he sat in gridlock on Tenth until he managed to take a detour on 42nd, which took him past the north corner of Bryant Park. Mia Grant. Fifteen years old. Dead in her tracks, Harv the Hammer-style.

Farraday was due in at nine, no word at the desk to suggest otherwise, and Irving waited in the corridor outside the captain's office until he appeared at the top of the stairwell.

'Good, bad or indifferent?' Farraday asked.

'I need to take Costello to the crime scenes.'

Farraday stopped, fingers holding the key. Put the key in the lock. Inhaled slowly, and closed his eyes for a moment.

'He's not our man,' Irving said.

'I have been thinking about this,' Farraday replied. He turned the key, opened the door, stepped inside his office.

Irving followed him, did not sit. He didn't intend staying long.

'Polygraph,' Farraday said matter-of-factly.

'On Costello?' Irving shook his head. 'Come on . . . that really is not going to fly. Those things are bullshit anyway—'

'Hear me out, Ray, hear me out.' Farraday sat down behind the desk, steepled his fingers and looked at Irving soberly. 'Sit down,' he said.

Irving did so.

'Okay, so he's employed temporarily. He's a crime researcher, he's serving some function here. So far so good, but let's go a different route. Let's say this fucks up. Let's say that it's someone from this hotel group of his. I don't know, I'm just throwing ideas out here, you know? I want to make sure that there is nothing that can come back at us for making this decision.'

'I am not going to polygraph this guy, Captain, seriously. Firstly, it isn't even admissible, and if something went wrong it wouldn't hold up as any kind of defense, and secondly . . . shit, the guy is nervous enough as it is. He's not doing this just because he wants to, he's doing it because he feels he has to.'

'But why?' Farraday asked.

'Who the fuck knows. His own history? Basic human nature, maybe.'

Farraday smiled cynically.

'Let me take him round the crime scenes. It's not a big deal. Who the hell is even gonna know? Let me take him round for a couple of hours, and that'll be the end of that. Hell, he might even find something that we've missed.'

'You really believe that's possible?'

'Well, he picked up on a couple of small points we missed before, right?'

'Sarcasm I can't use,' Farraday said. 'So go, do it, whatever.' He waved his hand dismissively. 'I don't want to hear about this from anyone but you.'

'You have my word.'

An hour and a half later John Costello stepped from a cab outside the Fourth Precinct and crossed the forecourt to where Irving was waiting for him. The day was dry and clear, refreshingly chill, and once again Irving was reminded of how soon Christmas would arrive, the inherent sense of loneliness it seemed to promise. He would never advise having a partner die in November.

'You okay?' Irving asked.

Costello nodded in the affirmative. 'Where first?' he said.

'Mia Grant,' Irving replied, and walked Costello to the car out back of the building.

Bryant Park, the low overhang of trees beneath which the Thomasian twins had discovered the girl's plastic-wrapped body. On from there to the expressway off Roosevelt Drive, adjacent to the East River Park, the two of them standing silently by the bank of trees where Ashley Burch and Lisa Briley had been found by Max Webster. Then, maintaining the crime scenes in sequential order, Irving took Costello to East 39th, to the Wang Hi Lee Carnival & Firework Emporium, the small hole in the concrete floor from where James Wolfe's grotesque clown-painted face had stared back up at them. On they went, to the site of Caroline Parselle's battered body, there beneath the Queensboro Bridge, and then the locale of the dark grey Ford on East 23rd and Second where the two boys had been found, at which point Costello asked about the car, where it was, what had happened to it.

'It's in lock-up,' Irving said. 'It had been wiped clean. Reported stolen nearly two months before, but nothing in it that gave us any direction.'

Costello nodded, asked no further questions.

Lastly they drove from East 23rd and 2nd to Pier 67 via Twelfth Avenue. Here Costello leaned over the parapet and looked down to where Carol-Anne Stowell's body had been dumped. The water that lapped in from the Hudson was grey and cold and unforgiving. Any trace that might have been left there had long since been washed away. All memories of Carol-Anne Stowell now resided in the depths of the river, and the river would never give them up.

Irving and Costello sat in the car in silence. It was three-twenty, the sky was overcast, looked like rain was en route again.

'What do you eat on Tuesdays?' Irving asked.

'Karen told you about that?'

Irving didn't reply.

'On Tuesdays I eat French food.'

'Kind of French food?'

'Whatever. Bourgignon. Crepes.'

'Is Cajun food French enough for you?'

Costello laughed. 'Why d'you ask?'

'I know a great Cajun restaurant . . . we should go eat there.'

Costello didn't speak for some moments, and then he smiled, almost to himself. He didn't turn and look at Irving, but he nodded his head slowly and said, 'Okay, stretching it somewhat, but I figure Cajun is French enough for a Tuesday.'

They didn't speak about the crime scenes. Seemed there was little to say. The effect had been sobering if nothing else. Costello said it had *grounded* him, but offered no further explanation. Irving had the urge to ask Costello about the attack he had suffered, about Robert Clare, about Frank Gorman – what the man was like, whether they had ever spoken of things beyond the immediate investigation – but he said nothing. Costello didn't offer up any words, and when they were done eating Irving drove him back to the *Herald* offices and thanked him for his time.

'Can't see that I was of any use to you,' Costello said.

'I needed to do that,' Irving said, 'and it was better not to do it alone.'

'So now what?'

'I re-interview the parents, the friends, the people who last saw the victims alive. I go see the people who found the bodies. I go through the whole thing again from the start.'

'You need me, you call me,' Costello said. 'I'll keep my eyes and ears open.'

'Appreciated.'

'It's a waiting game, isn't it?' Costello said rhetorically.

Irving nodded. 'We watch. We wait. We hope that we've seen the end of it.'

Costello didn't reply, but the expression on his face was eloquent enough.

Both of them knew full well that they had not seen the end of it.

Both of them knew that the Anniversary Man had only just begun.

They waited twenty-eight days.

Irving and Costello spoke on eleven occasions during that time, but it was merely a courtesy, a necessary reminder that they were still in touch, that John Costello was still looking and listening, that Irving acknowledged Costello's presence in the loop. Irving didn't contact Karen Langley on anything but a professional basis. Sometimes she would be the one with whom a message for Costello was left, and on one or two of those occasions they shared pleasantries, asked one another how things were, but the real questions were never asked. They both knew that for Irving there would be no breathing space until this thing was done.

There were meetings with Farraday, but those meetings tended to skirt around the issues. Farraday wanted to believe that the killings had stopped. Though he couldn't prevent Irving's continuing efforts to speak to every witness and relative, every known contact of each respective victim, though he couldn't dissuade him from visiting with Hayes, Lucas, Lavelle and Vincent, even the on-site CSAs from the five murder scenes, there were nevertheless rumors of reassignment, of Irving taking on additional cases that could be worked alongside his primary responsibilities. Irving didn't ask if such rumors were true. He didn't solicit discussions with Farraday. He stayed in the incident room or went out on the road. He worked himself into solitude and quiet obsession.

FORTY-ONE

Wednesday, October 18th. As if driven by nothing more than the perverse desire to show the world what he was capable of, the killer of Lynette Berry left her body equidistant between the statues of Alice in Wonderland and Hans Christian Andersen in Central Park, near the Loeb Boathouse, there at the edge of the Conservatory Pond. She was tall, she was black, and she was left naked on the grass. Laid on her stomach in a crucifix position but with the right hand crooked over, her legs apart, she had been strangled with what appeared, from initial observations, to be a piece of cloth. She was identified by Eleventh Precinct Vice officers. They knew her name, also knew her as 'Christy', as 'Domino', finally as 'Blue', as in Blue Berry, the name she used when she danced at the Showcase Revue Bar over by University Hospital.

At six minutes past ten Irving received a call from John Costello.

'They have another one in Central Park,' he said matter-of-factly. 'Black girl. Strangled. Don't know her name yet, but—'

Irving exhaled.

Costello stopped speaking.

Irving felt his heart drop into the base of his gut. He experienced an awkward conflict of emotions: unwilling confirmation that the killings had not ceased in September with Carol-Anne Stowell and Laura Cassidy, yet a flare of hope that this might now give them something, that a clue might have been left behind.

'Irving?'

'Yes, I'm here.'

'Like I said, I don't know the victim's name, but from what I can gather this is a replica of the killing of Yolanda Washington.'

'Spelled?'

'Y-O-L-A-N-D-A, and Washington I figure you're okay with,' Costello said. 'Original killing was October 18th, 1977, courtesy of Kenneth Alessio Bianchi, B-I-A-N-C-H-I.'

'Where'd you pick this up?'

'Scanner this morning.'

'Fuck,' Irving said.

'Bit more public than the others, isn't it?'

'Where are you?' Irving asked.

'At the office.'

'I have to make some calls. Stay there. I'm gonna need to go over there and you're coming with me.'

'I'll be here.'

Irving spoke with Farraday, Farraday spoke with Captain Glynn at the Eleventh. Glynn gave it to Farraday without a fight. Farraday told Irving he should take Jeff Turner with him to co-ordinate his actions with the CSAs already present. He hesitated when Irving told him Costello would be going.

'Remember our discussion,' Farraday said. 'This goes bad then . . .' He left the statement incomplete.

Irving called Costello back, told him to be ready in front of the *Herald* office, that he would pick him up. They were going to Central Park.

The fog hung low despite the time of day. It was quarter past eleven when Ray Irving, Jeff Turner and John Costello walked down to the taped area by Conservatory Pond. TV crews were there, at least four, and the scene had an aura unlike any of the earlier locales. Here was a circus of media and police activity. This was Central Park, late morning; it was not some dumpster behind a derelict hotel, not waste ground under a bridge.

'He's gone public,' Irving said, echoing Costello's earlier observation. Turner seemed not to hear, and went on down to speak with the CSA assigned. The coroner had been called, had not yet arrived, and Irving took his time establishing the perimeter, speaking with the homicide people from the Eleventh Precinct, insuring that foot traffic was kept to a minimum. This was the one. This *had* to be the one – a simple, single clue to give them the thread. Lynette Berry had to give them something . . .

Costello walked the edges of the perimeter. He made himself as inconspicuous as possible. Twice he was questioned by uniformed officers, twice he directed those questions to Irving. He stayed away from the TV cameras. He didn't like them, didn't want the world to witness his presence. The atmosphere was disturbing. The air seemed thick with an unidentifiable smell – neither blood, nor damp, nor anything he could define. He wondered if it was possible to smell fear, and shuddered at the thought.

Irving came back to him within an hour. 'This isn't the primary,' he said. 'She was killed elsewhere and moved.'

Costello nodded. 'That would fit with the Bianchi killing.'

'What was the deal with that? What was that about?'

'Hillside Stranglers,' Costello said. 'That's what they were known as. Kenneth Bianchi and his cousin, Angelo Buono. Los Angeles in the seventies. Killed fifteen or so between them. Young girls, hookers, co-eds, whoever they took a liking to. Buono died in 2002 in Calapatria State. Bianchi, as far as I know, is still in the special housing unit in Washington State Pen.'

Irving vaguely recalled the Hillside Strangler tag, but had never read up the cases.

Costello looked back toward the location of the girl's body. 'She give you anything?'

'Jeff is down there. He'll find anything that's here.'

'Can I go down and take a look?'

Irving seemed surprised by Costello's request. 'You really want to?'

A dry smile broke on Costello's face. '*Want* to?' He shook his head. 'Course I don't want to. Think I need to.'

'Walk with me,' Irving said. 'Stay close. Don't touch anything.'

Costello responded with the expression employed when the obvious has been unnecessarily stated.

Five yards from the body John Costello felt anxiety rising from his lower gut. There was a tension in his nerves, his breathing became shallow, and he felt sweat on the palms of his hands.

'You okay?' Irving asked. 'You look like you're gonna pass out.'

'I'm okay,' Costello said, his voice almost a whisper.

They moved closer, side-by-side, then Costello was looking down at the discarded body of Lynette Berry, at the human being that once was. Her tongue, black and swollen, protruded from a rictus grin. Her fingers were locked in awkward claws, her hair was matted with dirt and leaves, her skin stiff and cold, and her eyes stared back at them with an expression that was all too horribly familiar to Irving. *Where were you? Why was no-one there to help me? Why did this have to happen to me?*

'How old?' Costello asked.

'Late teens, early twenties,' Irving replied.

'Yolanda Washington was nineteen.' Costello looked up. 'You know, he used to trawl for victims in the same area as Shawcross – up in Rochester – long before he went out to L.A. to live with his cousin. They were known as the Double Initial Murders. Victims' first names and surnames both began with the same letter. Carmen Colon, Wanda Walkowitz, Michelle Maenza. First one was ten years old, second two were both eleven. November '71 to November '73. Rumor had it that the man who'd raped and strangled them had posed as a police officer, same thing that happened in L.A.'

'You're thinking that whoever dumped this one out here might have had on a uniform?'

Costello shrugged. 'Hell, I don't know. Police uniform is the one thing that no-one ever really pays any attention to, unless they're a criminal.' He looked once more at the spread-eagled girl on the grass and turned away. 'Enough,' he said quietly, and started walking back the way they'd come.

Thirty minutes later they sat in the car.

'You think she's going to give you anything?' Costello asked.

'See what Jeff finds,' Irving replied. 'He'll get the crime scene info, and then we'll have the autopsy report.'

'Did you actually think he might have stopped?'

'Because there's been nothing for a month?' Irving shook

his head. 'I hoped. Hope is a pretty useless commodity I know, but I didn't feel there was any harm in trying. Hell, I don't know what I thought. I've spent the past weeks talking to everyone again, upsetting people by going back over things they thought they were done with . . .' His voice trailed away, and he turned to look out the window toward the crime scene.

'Hillside Strangler case had eighty-four officers assigned to it,' Costello said. 'Ten thousand leads, a reward of a hundred and forty thousand dollars posted, and like I said, the word went out that the perpetrators were posing as police officers. People wouldn't stop for the police, they just kept on driving, so they implemented a policy that if a police car was trying to pull you over you could drive to the nearest station or precinct and stop only once you were outside the building.'

'You're giving me a great sense of reassurance,' Irving said.

'They got them though. They did finally get them.'

'But how many dead? That's the point, isn't it? How many people have to die before I actually stop him?'

Costello didn't reply. He followed Irving's line of sight; he counted trees, counted uniforms, counted cars as they passed.

Eventually he looked back at Irving and in his eyes was a question.

'What?' Irving asked.

'You ever get used to this?'

'The dead people?'

'What people do to each other,' Costello said.

Irving shook his head. 'Seems that just as I get used to what people do, they go and do something worse.'

FORTY-TWO

The phone rang incessantly; had it not he perhaps would have slept until noon.

Irving's body seemed to fight against him, to pull him back with some deep gravitational force. *Stay down*, it said. *Keep on going and this kind of thing will kill you.*

But the phone did not stop, and it roused him, walked him from his bed to the table beneath the window, and when he picked it up and slurred his name he was met with Farraday's voice barking at him angrily.

'You . . . you what?' he stuttered, and Farraday repeated himself, and Irving stood there stunned and speechless.

He was dressed and out of the apartment within fifteen minutes, hit the early morning traffic on Ninth, again on 42nd as he tried to cut across midtown. He missed his coffee, he did not stop at Carnegie's; by the time he reached the Fourth it was still only seven-fifteen, and his head hurt like hell.

Farraday was there, as was someone called Garrett Langdon from the NYPD's public relations liaison section, and they stood silently for a moment before Farraday held out the newspaper, and then tossed it onto the desk for Irving to pick up.

Page three of *The New York Times,* a good half page all told. A clear and unmistakable photograph of Detective Ray Irving, NYPD Fourth Precinct, alongside him John Costello, *New York City Herald* crime researcher, survivor of the Hammer of God killings made famous in Jersey in the early 1980s. They stood side-by-side near the statue of Alice in Wonderland in Central Park, in the background the crime scene tapes, the uniforms, the vaguely visible image of a black woman left strangled and naked on the grass.

'This,' Farraday said, long before Irving had a chance to

gather his thoughts, to estimate the import of this thing, to even begin to appreciate how devastated he felt, 'is exactly, and I mean *exactly*, the kind of thing I wanted to avoid.'

Irving opened his mouth to speak.

'There isn't anything you can tell me, Ray,' Farraday interjected. 'I wanted to keep this low-key, under the radar, but oh no, it's never that simple with you, is it? I ask you to be discreet, and God Almighty if I don't find a picture of both of you on page three of *The New York Times*! And that doesn't even take into consideration the news coverage on this girl in the park.'

'Captain—' Irving started.

Farraday stopped him. 'It doesn't matter why, Ray, it really doesn't. The fact of the matter is that it has happened. There's no going backwards on this thing. I am so fucking angry . . .' He shook his head slowly. 'Jesus God, that has to be the understatement of the fucking century.' He sat down heavily.

Irving sat down too. Whatever he had planned to say was long since forgotten.

Langdon stepped forward. 'Damage control,' he said. 'What we have to do now is establish a line that we use, and not digress from that line. The worst thing we can do is deny Costello's involvement. We employed him on an official basis, but it was only temporary and only in his capacity as a crime researcher, nothing else. There is no significance to his surviving a serial attack himself, and no, there is absolutely no connection between the murder that occurred in Central Park and the Hammer of God killings—'

'For God's sake, I'm not worried about what the goddamned newspapers say,' Irving replied. 'My concern is for Costello—'

'Well *my* concern, Ray, is very much for what the newspapers say,' Farraday interjected. 'This is page three of the goddamned *New York Times*. You have any idea the storm of shit that's gonna come down about this? Jesus, man, I can't believe you said that.'

'I have nine dead, Captain—'

'I am all too aware of how many dead there are, Ray,

believe me. That makes it all the more imperative to avoid any publicity about this thing.'

'Well, perhaps we're going precisely the wrong way. Maybe it's time to make this thing public. *He* certainly seems ready to start showing the world what he's doing.'

Farraday looked at Langdon. Langdon shook his head, carried the expression of someone at the tail end of their patience. They were faced with someone who just didn't understand the way the world worked.

'You go explain yourself to Chief Ellmann,' Farraday said, and then shook his head. 'Jesus, what the fuck am I thinking? You are the very last person to go and explain this to Chief Ellmann. That dead girl has been on the TV, Ray. How much longer before someone puts two and two together on these things? You tell me that this is another copycat from God only knows when, but what seems to be very evidently absent from your report is any kind of recommendation for dealing with it.'

'I'm doing all I can,' Irving said. 'Seriously, with the resources I've got I am doing everything I can.'

Farraday raised his hand. He did not want to hear another request for assistance. He looked at Langdon, held up *The Times*. 'And this?' he asked.

'We can deal with it,' Langdon said. 'We can deal with it if we stay focused on what we're trying to accomplish here. We need to minimize the relay effect. We need to speak to *The Times*, find out where the picture came from, who took it, insure it's not on syndicate. We can't have this turning up in every newspaper between Rochester and Atlantic City. The issue here is to play the whole thing down, deny nothing, give no official statement that will draw any more attention to it, and we can walk away from it without too much damage done.'

'You feel that that's the issue here? To walk away from this without attracting attention?' Irving asked.

'Absolutely, Detective Irving, absolutely that's the issue,' Langdon replied.

'Well, fuck almighty, I thought the issue was trying to stop a serial killer collecting any more victims.'

'Hey!' Farraday snapped. 'We can do without the fucking sarcasm, Ray.'

Irving said nothing.

'Okay?'

Irving slowly nodded, his lips pressed tight together, all his willpower employed to refrain from stating his actual viewpoint about this charade.

'So go find out,' Farraday said. 'Speak to *The Times*, see who took the picture. Get it nailed down, get this thing contained.' He turned to Langdon. 'You're coming to see the Chief with me. We go on the offensive, take it to him before he has a chance to bring it to us, okay?'

Langdon nodded reservedly.

'You're the public relations wizard, right? You have to come help me bail Irving out the crap.'

Farraday rose from his chair, opened the door for Irving.

'Call me as soon as you have a lid on this picture,' he said.

Irving hesitated.

'Go!' Farraday said. 'Get the fuck outta here and sort out this mess for God's sake.'

Irving, tempted to kick back with every frustration he felt, held his tongue.

He made his way down the hallway to the stairwell, took the risers two at a time, and slammed his office door shut.

The Times had not received the picture on syndicate, neither did it come from a staff photographer, and nor was it a still cut from the video footage taken by the numerous TV crews that had been present. The image of Detective Ray Irving and John Costello had arrived in a plain manila envelope, left by hand at the news desk at eleven-eight p.m. the night before. Irving spoke with the picture editor, a man called Earl Rhodes, and from all appearances it had been taken on a digital camera, printed hard copy on a good quality color printer, and delivered by motorcycle courier. The envelope had five words written across it – *News Desk, New York Times* – and no, he had not kept the envelope. Yes, there was CCTV in the foyer of the building, and within moments the courier company was identified and located. Asked why he had not kept the envelope, the picture editor said, 'This is *The New*

York Times, Detective. You have any idea at all how many pictures we receive on a daily basis?'

'And was there anything with the picture that told you who it was?'

'Piece of paper. Message on it read something like "NYPD detective employs help of crime researcher". Something like that.'

'And this didn't surprise you? You didn't wonder where it had come from?'

'Like I said, you have no idea how many pictures I get on a daily basis. I have staff photographers, freelancers, photo-journalists, syndicate traffic, stuff coming in from AP, Reuters . . . it's fucking endless. I don't know whether it's something that comes in because it's been ordered, whether it's a gift from the archangel fucking Gabriel or what. You have dozens of reporters, and they have their contacts and sources. The pictures come in, I send them on their way.'

'And this one?'

'Went to the crime desk,' Rhodes replied.

'And the slip of paper that came with it?'

'Went up with the picture.'

'To?'

'Hell, I don't know. You'd have to go on up there and find out which staff reporter they gave it to.'

Irving thanked Rhodes, took the name of the courier company, asked for directions to the crime desk.

Fourth floor, a maze of offices, a wall of noise from telephone conversations, printers, fax machines, doors opening and closing, the hubbub of activity that was 'all the news that's fit to print' on a Thursday morning.

The staff reporter responsible for the piece came out from his desk to meet Irving.

He smiled as if he knew Irving was pissed with him, but he held out his hand, introduced himself as Gerry Eckhart, directed Irving to a bank of chairs against the wall to the right of the elevator.

'The piece of paper that came with the picture?' Irving asked.

Eckhart frowned for a moment, and then he shook his

278

head. 'Hell, I just chucked it,' he said. 'Hang on a minute though . . .' He got up suddenly, walked away.

No more that thirty or forty seconds and Eckhart returned, in his hand a small slip of paper no bigger than a credit card. Typed neatly across it, a standard and unremarkable font, were the words *NYPD detective and crime researcher working together*.

'And from this you worked out that the picture was of me and John Costello?'

'Wasn't difficult,' Eckhart said. 'There were three guys who knew your face right away. One of them said you were from the Sixth, but the others said you were from the Fourth. You know Danny Hunter, right?'

Irving nodded. Danny Hunter had covered a lengthy murder trial in which Irving had been the arresting officer a year or so before.

'Well, Danny knew who you were, and then it was simply a matter of working out who the other guy was. So we called every paper in the city, asked them if they had a crime researcher who was working on something with the PD, and we came up trumps at the *Herald*. With the guy's name we had a different story, of course.'

'Hammer of God killings,' Irving said.

'Right,' Eckhart replied. 'Hammer of God killings.'

'This hasn't done me any favors,' Irving said unnecessarily.

'Whaddya want me to say, man? We do what we do the way we do it.'

'I'm gonna keep this piece of paper,' Irving said.

'No problem.'

Irving took out his notebook. 'Can you give me the names of all the people who might have touched the picture?'

'Just me, I think,' Eckhart said. 'I scanned it into my computer, sent it down to the desk. The picture is in a file over there.'

'You wanna get it for me?'

'Sure.'

'Hold it by the edges and put it an envelope or something.'

Eckhart nodded, went to collect the picture.

Irving's pager beeped. He looked it and felt the weight of responsibility. It was Karen Langley's number. He checked the earlier page. Also Karen Langley. He knew what this was about, and he didn't want to face her.

Eckhart returned with the original image of Irving and Costello in a clear-fronted envelope. Irving put the small note inside with it, thanked Eckhart and started toward the elevator.

'You figure your man took that?' Eckhart asked.

'I have no idea. And can I ask you—'

'Not to write anything more on this?' Eckhart pre-empted. Irving nodded.

'You can ask, Detective,' Eckhart replied. 'Don't mean I'm gonna pay any attention.'

'Anything you're gonna run, would you call me and let me know before it hits the newsstands so I can do whatever damage control I need to?'

'That I can do.'

'Appreciated,' Irving said, and hit the elevator button for ground.

The courier company he found without difficulty. He drove down there, through the diminishing gridlock to an address across from Grand Central.

The duty manager, a man called Bob Hyams, came out to speak with Irving. 'I was on last night. He brought it in by hand about ten-thirty or so.' Hyams was in his late forties, efficient in manner, but there was a limit to how much he could help. The offices of City Express Delivery did not have CCTV, and there was no signature from the individual who delivered the envelope.

'They come in, they give us the item, they pay the fee, we give them a receipt slip. End of story. The traffic we have through here, there's no way . . .' He left the statement unfinished.

Irving's pager beeped for the third time.

'So this guy comes in and just hands you the envelope?' Irving said.

'He sure does. He hands me the envelope, pays the fee, I give him a slip, he goes home.'

'And how does he look?'

'He looks good. Like he's lost some weight maybe, doing

280

good on quitting smoking.' Hyams shakes his head and rolls his eyes. 'How the fuck do I know what he looks like? He's a regular guy. He looks like every other guy who comes in here. Dark hair, clean shaven, shirt, sport jacket. Whaddya want me to tell you? I don't know what he looks like.'

'And it was taken directly to *The Times*?'

''S what he paid for. Immediate delivery. Cost him eighty bucks, didn't bat an eyelid. Paid his money, told me thanks very much, went away.'

'Paid in cash?'

'Yes . . . and before you ask for all the cash in the place, we bank first thing. We don't keep cash on the premises for obvious reasons.'

'Do you do a bag drop at the bank or pay over the counter?'

'We pay over the counter. We don't do that much cash work these days. Mainly account clients. Maybe five hundred dollars a day in cash.' Hyams smiled sardonically. 'Not your day is it?'

'Not my year,' Irving said.

'You after this guy then?' Hyams asked.

'Very much so, yes.'

'Well, I don't know that I can be any help to you, but if you get someone and you want me to come down and take a look at him, you know? Like if you do a line-up or something?'

'Thank you,' Irving said. 'I just might take you up on that.'

'Okay,' Hyams said. 'Good luck to you.'

Irving didn't reply, merely acknowledged him and left the building.

Back at the Fourth he turned the picture and the small typed note over to a uniform, told him to get them to Jeff Turner for prints, isolation of printer-make, any idiosyncratic element that might assist in identifying the source of the photograph or the message. He gave Eckhart's name, said that his prints would be on the system under *New York Times* staff so as to eliminate them. He also asked him to prompt Turner on the forensic report from the Lynette Berry murder scene. 'Tell him to page me soon as he has it,' Irving said. He hesitated for a moment in the hallway as the uniform hurried toward the stairs, and then turned back toward his office. Once inside he sat quietly for a minute or two, steeled himself, and then lifted the receiver to call Karen Langley.

FORTY-THREE

'He's not come in this morning.'

Irving said nothing for a moment.

'You've seen this story? The one in *The Times*?'

'Yes,' Irving said, 'I've seen it.'

'You have any fucking idea what this is going to do to him? Jesus, Ray . . . for God's sake . . .'

'I had no idea it was going to wind up in the paper. Come on, Karen, this is a major fucking story—'

'A major fucking story that your people pulled from under me—'

'I didn't pull that—'

'Whatever, Ray . . . truth is that we put a lot of work into that thing and we didn't get to run it. I forgave you that, but this?'

'I didn't mean—'

'You took him over there, Ray, a murder scene in Central Park. Didn't you even think about the TV crews? It wasn't back of some derelict tenement somewhere, it was Central fucking Park—'

'So where is he?' Irving asked.

'Home, no doubt. I imagine he's hiding in his apartment with the curtains shut and the doors locked and wondering whether serial killer number two is gonna come and hammer his fucking head in.'

Irving inhaled slowly, his eyes closed, massaging his forehead with his right hand. 'Jesus . . . fuck . . .' he exhaled.

'There's nothing that can be done about it now,' Karen said. 'The damage is done.'

'And you've had no word from him?'

'Nothing.'

'He's done this before?'

'John doesn't get sick, Ray. He doesn't miss work. He

doesn't take holidays or days off. In all the years I've known him—'

'I get the picture . . . and you don't think there's any possibility he hasn't seen it?'

'Well hell, unless this whacko got to him first and he's lying dead somewhere, then I can imagine John Costello was one of the very first people in the city to see this. That's what he does, Ray, or didn't you know that yet? He listens to police scanners, he reads newspapers, he trawls the internet for this stuff. Right now isn't he finding the connections for you guys? You remember that, right?'

'Karen . . . seriously, I am so fucking tired, and I am so on the edge with this whole thing, the last thing in the world I can use is a whole shitload of sarcasm from you.'

'Whatever, Ray . . . I'm gonna try and reach him, and when I reach him I'll find out what the fuck is going on, and then I will do whatever I can to help him deal with this. I might call you later.'

'If you do,' Irving said, 'can you try and convince yourself that I'm a half way decent human being beforehand?'

'Now who's the sarcastic asshole?' Karen Langley said, and hung up.

By ten-fifteen Irving had identified the four TV stations that had crews on-site for the Lynette Berry murder scene. NBC, NET, ABC and CBS. He called Langdon in Public Relations, told him he needed copies of all the footage from all four stations, not only the footage they planned to air, but the unedited takes. Langdon said he'd be back to him within the hour.

Irving didn't vacillate for long about visiting Costello. Waiting around would only make the situation worse. He thought about going over to see Karen Langley, but what would he say? He had enough to deal with without Costello's paranoia. He believed he should feel sympathetic – after all, the man was doing what he could to help them, and for this Irving should have felt grateful – but at this stage of the game sympathy seemed an irrelevant and unaffordable emotion. No-one had the time to be anything other than efficient and effective. Damage control on Karen Langley was a thing all its own. It would resolve or it would not. He liked the woman, but hell, she wasn't his wife. If she never spoke to him again would it be the end of the world?

The phone rang. Irving snatched the receiver and nearly brought the thing off the desk.

'Yes.'

'Ray, it's Karen. John has seen the paper. He doesn't want to leave the apartment. He says he's not being paranoid, he's being practical.'

Irving started to smile. It was a reaction, nothing more. It was the exhaustion, the stress, the utter disbelief attendant on such scenarios.

'So he says he's going to lay low for a little while—'

'Lay low? What the fuck does that mean?'

'Hey, don't speak to me like that, Ray. I'm not the one who created this fucking nightmare, you are. Treat me with some respect or go fuck yourself—'

'I'm sorry, Karen—'

'Enough already. I don't need apologies, I need you to shut the hell up and let me finish what I was saying. So, he's laying low for a little while. He says he needs to focus. He wants to try and understand some more about what's going on with this guy. He feels he's got too close to it and needs some distance.'

'What is going on here, Karen? What kind of person am I actually dealing with here?'

'Kind of person? Jesus, Ray, sometimes you really are the working part of an asshole.'

Irving couldn't help it then. He started laughing.

'God, you really have lost it, haven't you? I really am starting to worry a little about you.'

'You know something, Karen? You wanna hear something?'

'Go for it, Ray, give it your best shot.'

About to come back at her with some acidic one-liner, Irving stopped. He looked at himself. For a moment he really believed he was seeing himself from a distance – what he was thinking, what he was feeling, what he had planned to say to this woman at the other end of a phone line . . . a woman he barely knew, a woman he actually cared for in some strange and awkward way. And he held himself in check. He didn't say the thing. He just said, 'I'm sorry, Karen. I'm actually really sorry that this has happened. I do understand . . . hell, fuck no, I don't have a fucking clue what he must be going through, but tell him from me that I appreciate his situation. Tell him that I'm sorry it happened this way, and that if there was some way to turn it backwards then I would. Tell him to take whatever time he needs, that he knows where I am, and if he has any thoughts about this thing then he should give me a call . . .'

Karen Langley didn't speak.

'And as far as you're concerned,' Irving went on. 'I'm sorry that we started our friendship because of a serial killer. Maybe if we'd met some other way we'd be getting along just fine right now—'

'We are getting along just fine, Ray,' Karen interjected. 'This is the way things happen sometimes. I'll give your message to John, he'll appreciate it. Stay in touch, eh?'

The line went dead.

Irving was left with a profound feeling of solitude, as if he was now the only one in the world who could make this thing stop.

FORTY-FOUR

Seated in a small sound-proofed booth at the New York City crime lab, headphones clamped to his ears, sweat running down the middle of his back, Ray Irving worked with Jeff Turner from just before noon to nearly four o'clock. From the digital footage taken in Central Park they at first isolated the angle from which the image might have been taken. It was finally a choice between NBC and CBS. Then they looked closely at the faces of bystanders, TV crew members, newspaper photographers and journalists, all in an attempt to find the one face that didn't fit, the single individual with a camera who took a picture of Irving and Costello as they visited with Lynette Berry.

At four-ten, just as Irving believed that he would never feel anything other than desperation and futility, a CSA came to the booth with a message for him. He was to call Karen Langley. It was urgent.

'John needs to speak to you,' she told Irving. 'Where are you?'

Irving told her, gave her the number, and within minutes Costello was on the line.

'John . . . what's up?'

'It's a cop,' he said.

'What?' It was as if Irving had suddenly dropped off the edge of something and was plummeting toward the ground.

'No, shit . . . I didn't mean to say that,' Costello replied. 'I guess you've been looking at the footage from the park, right?'

'Yes, I have . . . but the cop thing, John. What the—'

'Someone posing as a cop,' Costello said. 'There were lots of cops down there. He was in amongst them. It's the Bianchi killing, right? Apparently the Hillside Stranglers posed as cops. Remember what I told you? About the fact that people

287

got so scared they wouldn't even stop for the police? They posed as cops. That's how they did it. I think he was there in the park. I think he was there and he was dressed as a cop. That's how he got close, and that's how he had the opportunity to take the picture.'

Turner was beside Irving, frowning.

'Jesus . . . Jesus . . .' Irving was saying.

'I think that he was there, Ray, I really do.'

'Okay, okay . . . right . . . I'm back on it. I'll call you. Hell, no . . . I can't—'

'You got a pen?'

'A pen? Sure—'

'This is my number, Ray. It's not in the book. I'm trusting you with it, okay?'

'Okay, yes . . . sure.'

Costello gave him the number. Irving wrote it down. Irving thanked him, hung up, looked at Turner.

'We have to find a cop with a camera,' he said matter-of-factly, and started back toward the booth.

NBC were the ones who caught him. A motorcycle cop. The only one present. He never removed his helmet, and despite the lack of sunshine he didn't remove his shades. He was in the frame for literally a handful of seconds, crossing the grass ten or fifteen yards from where Lynette Berry lay naked and cold. He held something in his hand which, at first, Irving assumed was his radio, but thanks to the quality of the digital system that NBC employed as standard they were able to enlarge the sequence frame by frame. A cellphone. Presumably a camera phone. And it was this with which he'd taken the picture of Irving and Costello. The clarity of image gave them the ID number on his jacket, they traced the number and found it was invalid.

Irving's frustration was epic.

'Jesus Christ, Ray, how in fuck's name were you ever supposed to know?' Turner asked him.

'He was there, Jeff. He was right there. Twenty yards from where we were standing. The guy was right fucking there and—'

'And you didn't know, and could never have known, and

there is absolutely nothing you can do about it now. You have a guy in shades and a motorcycle helmet. All we can judge from this is his approximate height and weight—'

Irving rose from his chair. He paced the room, thumped the wall a couple of times near the door, and then stood with his eyes closed. He was trying to center himself, trying to find some way he could feel something other than futility and desperation.

'Maybe he stole the bike, Ray. Check on whether there have been any police bikes stolen—'

'I know, I know.' Irving raised his hands and clenched his fists. 'I know where to go from here . . . it's just we were within fucking shouting distance of the guy and—' He gritted his teeth, stood there shaking his fists, his eyes closed, the muscles and veins visible in his neck.

After a while he lowered his arms, stood silently with his head bowed. 'Print me some hard copies of what we've got,' he said quietly. 'Close-ups of the side of his head, the jacket, the ID number . . . whatever you can make out, okay? Can you send them over to the Fourth soon as you're done?'

'I'll do them now. You can wait—'

'I gotta get out of here, Jeff. I gotta go get some air or something. I'm gonna . . . Jesus, I don't what the fuck—'

'Go,' Turner said. 'I'll get this stuff over to you within the hour.'

Irving thanked him, opened the door and let it slam shut behind him. He walked out through the crime lab and up the stairs to the street. He went around the block twice and then made his way to the car.

It was close to six, the traffic was really bad; it took him nearly an hour to reach the Fourth.

Turner came back with the autopsy results and the crime scene report simultaneously. Forensics had cigarette butts, a size eleven Nike sneaker print, a discarded can of Coke with three unidentified partials, a single blond hair caught in Lynette Berry's pubis. There was no sign of rape, no sub-cutaneous bruising, no tape residue from the wrists or ankles. She had been sedated with a strong barbiturate at some point within the twenty-four hours preceding her death. COD was asphyxiation; strangled with a piece of fabric, fibers from that fabric nowhere at the scene or on the body. Autopsy gave Irving nothing further. Central Park was the secondary, and from a series of small scratches on Lynette Berry's right shoulder, those scratches carrying a residue of motor oil, she had more than likely struggled involuntarily, despite the sedative, in an area where a vehicle had been parked. A garage, an auto shop, there was no way to tell. Once again, as with Mia Grant and Carol-Anne Stowell, the primary was unknown.

At twenty past eight Ray Irving called Karen Langley's desk and got her voicemail. He left no message; he wasn't even sure what he would have said had she answered. He sat in the incident room staring at the boards on the wall. Lynette Berry's face had been added to the group, and she looked back at him from a picture that had been taken very recently. She was a pretty girl, and from what he knew she had been a better-than-average student, no drug habit, nothing in the tox report but the barbiturates. Mother was alive, father was dead, three sisters, one brother, and she was the youngest of them all. Why she'd turned to hooking, all of nineteen years old and the world there ahead of her, Irving would never know. Casualties of war – that's how they all seemed to him now. Which war and who was fighting it, he didn't have a clue. An internal war, something that existed solely within the mind of one man, or a war against something, or someone, from the past – a hated sister, a cheating girlfriend, a sadistic mother. There was always a reason, however irrational, and knowing that reason served only one purpose: to prevent further loss of life. For Irving, the reason was just as unknown now as it had been when he walked toward the plastic-wrapped body of a teenager back at the beginning of June.

He typed his daily report for Farraday, the details of the photograph, the courier company, the information from *The New York Times*, and before completing it he called Jeff Turner.

'Nothing,' Turner said. 'Only prints on the picture are those from your guy at *The Times*. The note that came with it . . . best I can do is that it was printed on a Hewlett Packard laser printer, an older model, maybe a 4M or a 4M Plus. Picture was printed on a generic brand of paper, available in a million different places. That's as good as it gets I'm afraid.'

Irving thanked him, ended the call, added the frustrating last paragraph to his report. He instigated an action on any stolen police motorcycles, forwarded it to every police precinct in the city, marked *URGENT*, and then signed off.

He took his coat from the back of the door and left.

It was nine-eighteen, the sky was clear. He drove to Carnegie's simply for the warmth, for the familiar sounds, for the presence of people who knew nothing of the Anniversary Man.

FORTY-FIVE

Morning of Friday 20th a report came in regarding a stolen police motorcycle, taken from an NYPD-approved auto shop in Bedford-Stuyvesant, not far from Tompkins Square Park. The bike had been logged in on Saturday 14th, had remained uninspected until the afternoon of Tuesday 17th. According to the logbook, an initial inspection of the bike had occurred at three thirty-five on that Tuesday afternoon. It had been given a clean bill of health aside from the routine oil/brake-fluid/tire-pressure maintenance procedure, and nothing further had been done until the request came through from the Twelfth Precinct.

It was the desk sergeant who called Irving, relayed the report, and gave him the address of the shop. Irving went down there, arrived a little before noon, and spoke with the owner.

'I don't know what to tell you,' he told Irving. His name was Jack Brookes, seemed eager to assist in any way he could. 'We've been handling this business for years, never had a problem. Can't believe this has happened. Gonna make it very difficult to keep the contract.' He shook his head res-ignedly. 'It was logged in, inspected, a service was put on the schedule, and we would have gotten to it tomorrow. If the inventory request hadn't come in we wouldn't have known it was missing for another twenty-four hours.'

Irving had Brookes show him where the bikes were kept. They had a small secure warehouse facility, perhaps thirty or thirty-five bikes on site, and no CCTV.

'CCTV isn't a requisite for the contract,' Brookes said. 'Usually they're in and out of here within a day or so, certainly those that just need a service, but we've had some damaged bikes come in and they've been priority. Couple of them should have been scrapped, but I think someone is tightening up the budget, you know?'

Irving thanked Brookes, let him go. He spent an hour walking around the compound. He asked questions of the crew, the mechanics, the admin staff. Ordinarily the motorcycle officers just came in to collect their own machines. Irving's photographer could have walked right in, his uniform being the only identification needed, and just wheeled a bike right out of the warehouse. The auto-shop had a good working relationship with the police, they'd never had trouble, and operated on the basis that there was none on its way.

Irving left close to two with a heavy heart and a headache.

From the Fourth he called Costello at home.

'You were right,' he said. 'Motorcycle cop. Took a bike from an auto shop anytime since last Tuesday. No-one remembers anything, no CCTV, nothing.'

'He knows what he's doing,' Costello said. 'Perfectionist.'

'But why . . .' Irving was voicing a thought rather than intending a question.

''Cause he's fucking nuts,' Costello replied matter-of-factly. 'I don't think you need to get any more complicated than that.'

Irving was silent for a moment, and then he said, 'So how are you doing?'

'I'm okay, you know? It shook me up, seeing my picture in the paper. It really shook me up. But today? Today I'm actually okay. I'm going to go in after lunch, go see Karen, see what needs doing.'

'And the weekend?'

'Whatever. I don't make plans. I stay home usually, watch some movies, but you have my number now . . . if you need me.'

'Appreciated, John. I'll call if this goes anyplace.'

'Best of luck, eh?'

'Overrated commodity,' Irving said. 'Very fucking overrrated.'

Irving hung up the phone. He leaned forward and rested his forehead against the edge of his desk.

He was so tired, so unbearably exhausted that if the phone had not rung he might have fallen asleep.

FORTY-SIX

The letter had arrived with the regular mail. It was addressed *URGENT RUSH PLEASE HURRY* to Karen Langley. Karen opened it, read it, dropped it on her desk and called Ray Irving.

She had been out all morning, had arrived back minutes before to start through her mail, and there it was.

Irving put the light on his car and floored it to West 31st. He told her to stay put, do nothing, call no-one, not to touch the letter. His heart pounded in his chest all the way. His mouth was dry and bitter, though his hands sweated.

By the time Irving arrived John Costello was there, had already seen the letter.

'Plain white bond,' he told Irving. 'I haven't touched it. I know what it means.'

Written in a childlike print on a single sheet, the message was clear and disturbing:

> one killed in new
> york
> light Brown hair
> Blue eyes
> New York
> Buffalo
> would Have Been strangled
> with white cord
> gold ear
> pins
> had dress
> inside apartment
> white pretty teeth

with gap in front
Top Teeth
Blue eyes small pin
Ear
Hair below shoulders
through over
Bridge
with head and fingers
missing

Irving read it twice, standing ahead of Karen Langley's desk, Langley to his right, Costello to his left.

'Henry Lee Lucas,' Costello said. 'This is one of his confession letters from October 1982.'

'And the victim?'

'God, any one of dozens. He had a partner, a guy called Ottis Toole, and they went on a rampage along the I-35 in Texas.'

'MOs?'

'No one particular thing. They shot some people, beat them to death, strangled, set others on fire, crucified them. Usually they were sex killings. They raped and sodomised people. They had a couple of kids with them, a thirteen-year-old girl who they used as bait to get truck drivers to stop on the highway, and then they dragged them out and killed them.'

Irving took a deep breath. 'And the dates?'

'There's a number of them throughout October and November if that's what you're asking.'

Irving nodded. 'That's what I'm asking.'

'So what do you do with this?' Karen asked, indicating the letter.

'You got a plastic bag, a folder or something, anything to put it in? It'll go to forensics. I'll take it down there, see if there's anything on it. If earlier letters are anything to go by there won't be.'

Irving looked up at Karen Langley. Her face was pale, drained of color, and her eyes were wide. 'He knows who we are,' she said, her voice almost a whisper. 'He photographed John, and now he sent this to me—'

'It's not a threat against you—' Irving started.

'How do you know that, Ray? How do you know that it's not a threat against me?'

He started to respond, and then realized he had nothing to say.

'You don't know, do you?' she said. 'We don't know anything about him. We don't know what he's trying to do. We don't know—' She stopped mid-sentence, tears welling in her eyes. She backed up and sat down on a chair by the window.

Irving walked toward her, kneeled before her, took her hands in his.

'I'll have someone at your house,' he said reassuringly. 'I'll have a black-and-white in the vicinity of your house. I'll have someone come and see you at home. I'll make sure that if he has any such idea—'

Karen shook her head. 'Jesus, Ray, what the fuck did we do to deserve this? What the hell does this have to do with us?'

'We're just the opponents,' John Costello said. 'This is a game and we're the opponents, nothing more nor less than that. He has to have someone to play against, and we're right there in the frame.'

'But this is different,' Karen said. 'This is very fucking different now. I mean, Jesus, I've seen some things in my time, we all have. But it's out there isn't it? I mean . . . I mean it's out there in the world, and we look at it, and we write about it, and sometimes we see pictures, but this . . .'

She started hyperventilating.

Irving glanced at Costello. He felt awkward. He wanted to hold this woman, to pull her tight, tell her that it was going to be fine, that everything was going to be okay, but he didn't believe that, and Costello's presence made him feel awkward.

Karen tried to fingertip the tears from her lower lids and merely smeared her mascara. She looked beaten down, overwhelmed.

'I don't want to feel like this,' she said, 'so frightened . . . he knows who we are, Ray . . . he sent this letter to me, for God's sake.'

She took a deep breath. She closed her eyes and exhaled. When she opened her eyes she looked at Costello.

'I agree with Ray,' Costello said. 'He's not going to come after us. Why would he? This isn't about us, this is about him. This is about him doing whatever the hell he likes and getting away with it. This is about him performing his little theater and watching as the NYPD and the newspaper and the TV stations all start to sit up and take notice. If he comes after us then who's going to be left to play the game with him?'

Karen gathered herself together. She fetched a Kleenex from her purse and tried to fix her mascara. 'I need some coffee,' she said. 'I'm gonna go get some coffee from the canteen.' She rose from the chair and straightened her skirt. 'You want some?'

Irving said he would, Costello declined, and once she'd left the room Irving sat in her chair and looked over the letter.

'You actually believe what you just told her?' he asked.

Costello shook his head. 'No,' he replied.

'Me neither.'

'And there's not going to be anything on that letter that will get us any closer toward his identity.'

'I'd put money on it.'

'Was there anything from the scene in the park?'

'Nothing useful.'

'So all we know is that he has done, or is going to do, a Henry Lee Lucas killing.'

'Can you put together a calendar of the killings that were attributed to him?' Irving asked.

'I sure can . . . you wanna wait while I do it now?'

'Please, yes. That'd be good.'

Costello left the room.

Irving walked to the window and looked down into the street, was still there when Karen Langley returned with coffee and her false hope that this wasn't personal.

'Okay?' Irving asked.

'As can be.'

'I'm just waiting for some info from John, and then I'm going to take the letter to the forensics people.'

'Can you really get someone to check out my house?'

'Sure I can . . . in fact, you let me know what time you're done and I'll come check it out myself.'

'Who knows?' she replied. 'Six, seven, something like that.'

'So call me when you're through and I'll follow you home, okay?'

'Thank you, Ray.' She sat down, held the coffee cup between her hands and closed her eyes. 'Hell, I feel bad,' she said. 'This has really shaken me up.'

Irving stepped beside her, put his hand on her shoulder. 'I know,' he said quietly. 'I know.'

FORTY-SEVEN

Irving left the offices of the *City Herald* with the letter and Henry Lee Lucas's schedule of killings. They spanned the calendar, and there seemed no sequence to them, but between him and his partner, Ottis Toole, they had been busy. October 22nd, 1977, the gun killing of Lily Pearl Darty. In Waco, Texas on November 1st of the same year, they hogtied Glen D. Parks and then shot him with a .38. On October 31st, 1978 in Kennewick, Nevada, the duo raped and killed a girl called Lisa Martini in her own apartment. November 5th, 1978 they were driving along the I-35 in Texas when they spotted a young couple, Kevin Kay and Rita Salazar. Salazar they raped, and then shot six times; Kay they shot also, dumped both bodies unceremoniously at the side of the highway. A year later, 3rd October 1979, Lucas and Toole robbed, raped and murdered Sandra Mae Stubbs. Ten days later they shot and killed the mom-and-pop owners of a liquor store in Austin, Texas. October 31st, another woman was found dead on the I-35, unidentified. Twenty-first of November, while robbing a motel in Jacksonville, Cherokee County, Lucas raped, then shot to death, a thirty-one-year-old woman called Elizabeth Knotts. Eighteen days later a teenager was raped and stabbed in her own home, her remains found in nearby woods.

And so it went on – killings through Christmas, through January, February and March of 1980.

Their spree continued unabated until Henry Lee Lucas's arrest in October 1982. Ultimately Lucas confessed to one hundred and fifty-six homicides, and among his weapons of choice he claimed to have used pistols, shotguns, table legs, telephone cords, knives, tire irons, axes, vacuum cleaner cables, even a car. In retrospect, it was considered that many of the murders attributed to him were down to over-eager homicide detectives wishing to close as many outstanding cases as they could. Nevertheless, the schedule of killings gave Irving a small glimpse of the nightmare he was facing. The Lucas–Toole replica could already have happened, or it could only have been planned. There was no way to know which murder would be replicated, or when.

It was this scenario that he explained to Jeff Turner when he arrived at the crime lab a little before six that evening.

Turner took the letter, the schedule that Costello had typed out. He sat in silence for some time.

'You could commit the original sin,' he said to Irving.

'Which would be?'

'Leak something to the press, get the thing on the news. Stir up enough trouble to get some more people assigned to this.'

Irving smiled sardonically. 'I'm gonna make believe you didn't say that.'

'Make believe all you wish, Ray. The girl in Central Park consumed about twenty-five minutes all told. I saw the news on three different channels. People don't want to know. She was a hooker, for God's sake. People don't think of hookers as real people. Best kind of reaction you get is that they probably deserved it.'

'And this is something I don't already know?'

Turner leaned back in his chair. He looked as tired as Irving. 'So where do you go with this now?' he asked.

'I wait for your results on the letter,' he said, indicating the page on the desk before him.

'And when I come back and tell you that there's nothing on it, no prints, no distinguishing marks—'

'I hope that you don't, but if you do, which I'm sure you will, I'll jump off that bridge when I get there.'

Irving's pager beeped. Karen Langley again.

Irving got up. 'I have to make a call. I'll come back in a little while.'

'Karen.'

'You need to call John. He has something else for you.'

'Did he say what?'

'No. Just call him. I have to go into a meeting.'

Irving thanked her, dialed Costello's number, paced the corridor waiting for him to pick up.

'John, it's Ray.'

'He missed out a word.'

'What?'

'The letter he sent to Karen . . . he missed out a word.'

'What word?'

'Joanie.'

'Someone's name?'

'It's the Orange Socks Murder,' Costello said. 'That's what he's going to replicate.'

'The what murder?'

'October 31st, 1979, a motorist on the I-35 found a body in a culvert. She had nothing on but a pair of orange socks and a silver ring. No clothes, no purse, nothing. Just the orange socks. She had perfect teeth, no broken bones, no dental or medical records to help identify her, and as far as I know they still have no idea who she was. Only other thing was the contents of her stomach, and a pair of panties found nearby, inside of which was a makeshift sanitary napkin.'

'And this was definitely a Lucas killing?'

'Well, Lucas was arrested in Montague County, and one of the murders he confessed to was a hitchhiker he picked up out of Oklahoma City. He says that her name was either Joanie or Judy, and he took her down the I-35 to a truck stop where she had burger and fries and a Coke. The remains of such a meal was found in this girl's stomach. Then he said they had consensual sex, and when they were done he choked her to death and dropped her down a culvert. He also mentioned that she had some kind of sanitary napkin which he called a kotex.'

'And the word "joanie" was missing from the letter?'

'Yes, between "inside apartment" and "white pretty teeth" it should have said "joanie".'

'Jesus,' Irving exhaled. 'So if you're right—'

'Then we have a date.'

'Halloween. Eleven days.'

'And she'll be dropped off a highway somewhere into a culvert.'

'Okay . . . okay,' Irving replied, his mind already reeling at the number of highways and expressways that transected New York, and beyond that the number of storm drains and conduits that could be considered culverts.

'John . . . I have to get to work on this, okay? I'll come back to you.'

'Let me know what you find,' Costello replied, and then he hung up.

Irving left a message with the receptionist in the crime lab foyer. He drove back across town to the sanitation department, recruited the assistance of one of the engineers, and had him call up the grid systems and networks that spanned the city.

'So which ones do you want to include?' asked the engineer, a stocky, red-faced man called Victor Grantham.

'Can you just pull up a straightforward map of the city on this?'

'Sure can,' Grantham replied. He typed, he scrolled, he clicked, and an overview of the city presented itself on the screen.

'So let's take Hudson Parkway, the West Side Highway, South Street through to the elevated section. FDR Drive, Harlem River Drive, Bruckner, the bridges – Triborough, the Queensboro, Williamsburg –' Irving paused for a moment. 'Hang on,' he said. 'Which interstates do we have running through the city?'

Grantham scrolled down, opened a file, and said, 'Just the city, or do you want the county as well?'

'Just the city.'

'We have the I-87 which is the Major Deegan, the I-95 which runs across the Washington Bridge into New Jersey, Bruckner which is the I-298, and then the I-495 which connects up with 678 beyond the city limits. Oh, and beyond Lower Manhattan you have the Brooklyn Bridge Tunnel which is essentially the I-478.'

'Okay. So, sticking just to the interstate routes, how many drainage outlets and conduits are there?'

'You serious?'

Irving just looked at him.

'You're serious,' Grantham said quietly, and got to work.

It took less than a minute or two for Victor Grantham to tell Irving what he knew he did not want to hear.

'Just over eight hundred and fifty . . . and that's only so far as I can cover on this system. You follow those highways right to the edge of the city limits in all directions and there must be thousands.'

Irving closed his eyes. He sighed deeply and lowered his chin to his chest.

'Not what you wanted to hear, right?'

Irving shook his head without raising it.

'Can I ask why you want to know this?'

'Because we think someone might try and dump a body in one of those culverts on Halloween.'

'A body?'

Irving looked up. 'Yes, a body.'

'And you don't know which one?'

'No, I don't know which one. If I knew which one I could wait there and catch the guy.'

'So how many men do you have to cover these areas?'

Irving started to laugh, and then decided not to. It was simply not a laughing matter. 'Not enough,' he said quietly.

'Seems to me a body is going to block a culvert completely,' Grantham said. 'And if it blocks the thing completely it'll come up on the screen. That's the way the system is designed, so we can tell when there's a blockage that'll prevent run-off, and we send a crew out there.'

Irving sat up, eyes wide. 'How many crews do you have?' he asked.

'How many do we have here, or how many do we have for the entire municipal system?'

'The entire system,' Irving said.

'Well, at a stretch we could mobilize maybe three hundred crews, two men to a crew.'

'And how far apart are these culverts?'

'Different for different sections of the highway. Depends on inclines, whether the water comes down rapidly or slowly, the usual quantity of traffic—'

'Roughly,' Irving interjected. 'Roughly how far apart?'

'God, I don't know . . . maybe two, three hundred yards, something like that.'

304

'So if you had all three hundred crews mobilized they could cover three culverts each within the eight hundred and fifty range, and if they were stationed at the culvert in the middle of the three there would be a team of two men no more than two or three hundred yards from any one point in the entire system.'

Grantham nodded. 'Be a hell of an operation, organizing something like that, but yes, if you had every team out there you'd be within shooting distance of every single drain in the network.'

Irving didn't reply. There was a light in his eyes. His heart was going twice its pace.

'And from here,' Grantham added, 'someone at this desk could tell within ten or fifteen seconds whether something was blocking one of the conduits.'

'And we'd have someone there already,' Irving said. 'We'd close off the highway and question every single driver within half a mile of the drop site.'

'Seems so,' Grantham said. 'That seems like a plan to me. A plan that requires a dead body, however . . .'

'I know that,' Irving said quietly. 'But the way this is going . . .' He didn't complete the sentence.

'Go,' Victor said. 'Tell whoever you need to that it can be done.'

FORTY-EIGHT

'Not a prayer,' Farraday stated matter-of-factly.

Forty minutes later, Fourth Precinct, Irving standing by the window of Captain Farraday's office.

Farraday had cut short a telephone call to see Irving, thinking perhaps that Irving's urgency was due to some progress, not an insane scheme to bring the New York City Sanitation Department on board.

'They have a system,' Irving reiterated. 'Every single drain is on their screen. Someone puts a body down there—'

'And he's armed, and dangerous, and he's alert for the slightest sign that he might be being followed, and you have some poor schmuck of a sanitation engineer coming up behind him and getting his fucking head blown off. Jesus, Ray, are you even thinking straight?'

'Captain—'

'No,' Farraday said. He came from behind his desk and stood in the middle of the room. 'I understand what you have . . . this letter, the fact that there's every possibility that this is the next murder, but do you have any idea what it would take to instigate a collaborative action between the NYPD and the sanitation department, the amount of money it would cost, the lives you would put at risk? And that doesn't even take into consideration the cost of whatever resources would be required to close off the expressway and speak to every driver within a half mile radius . . .' Farraday stopped and caught his breath. 'I can't even begin to imagine what such a thing would take.'

'So what the fuck do you want me to do with this?' Irving said. 'What the hell am I supposed to do with this? I'm busting my balls trying to—'

'I know you are. I see the reports, Ray, I do actually see your reports and I read them beginning to end. I understand how hard you are working, but this goes back to the same discussion we had before. This is not the only case we're dealing with, and with the evidence we've got these could be viewed as unrelated cases. What we have as far as these anniversaries is concerned is essentially nothing more than circumstantial—'

'I can't believe that anyone would—'

'Consider them circumstantial,' Farraday finished for him. 'I know, but the people I have to deal with are not cops. They are not homicide detectives. They're bureaucrats, Ray, nothing more than bureaucrats, and they're looking at the big picture. They see the muggings, the rapes, the car-jacking, shoplifting up twenty-six percent since last quarter . . . these are the things they look at. Homicides . . . Jesus, Ray, homicides are down nineteen percent on this time last year, and the evaluation period against which stats are being published is over. Your victims . . . well they are next quarter's problem, and by next quarter the election will be over, and Chief Ellmann will either be the chief or he won't, and the Mayor will be the Mayor or he won't, and it doesn't get any more complicated than that.'

'So what can you give me?' Irving asked. 'A public warning?'

'A public warning? A warning about what? We tell every girl in the city that they have to be alert for someone trying to kill them? That if anyone stops them and tries to get them to put on some orange socks they should run for the fucking hills?'

Irving was silent. Farraday stood up, paced the floor, thinking. Finally he spoke.

'I'll tell you what I can give you. Maybe twenty motorcycle units, and maybe ten squads on call for the 31st. I see what you have, and what you have seems solid enough for me. First and foremost I'm a cop, and I couldn't give a rat's ass about the election except that if the election goes the wrong way it could mean a lot less policing gets done around here. You don't even want to know what the next administration has in store if they get in. The public overview and oversight committees, the reclassification of offences, the miles of fucking paperwork we'll get ourselves wrapped up in. I have to think about that, Ray, that it's not just one victim whose life is at stake, it's a thousand victims, and what might happen to them if we have a change in this system. Only problem is that the people in this city might just be short-sighted enough to get excited about something new, and not look at the long-term disaster they'd be voting themselves into.'

'Twenty motorcycle units, ten squads?'

'What day is the 31st?' Farraday reached for his desk calendar. 'Tuesday. Okay, Tuesday is a hell of a lot better than a Friday or Saturday. Yes, I can give you that, maybe more, depending on what's happening.'

Irving turned to leave.

'And between now and then?' Farraday asked after him.

Irving looked back, and the expression on his face said that such a question was precisely the kind that he didn't want to be asked.

Farraday didn't push it, he let Irving go. He'd been in homicide for enough years himself to know that it was perhaps the darkest place of all.

Quarter past six Ray Irving stood patiently in the foyer of the *City Herald* offices. He'd called up to let Karen Langley know he was there. A message had come back that she wouldn't be long.

He asked her if she wanted to go get some coffee before he escorted her home, and in the warm seclusion of a diner on West 28th he told her of Farraday's response to his suggestion.

'The difficult thing is knowing that someone is going to die,' he said. 'Knowing *how* they will die, and how their body will be disposed of, but not knowing who or where.'

'This is awful,' Karen said. 'This has to be the sickest thing I've ever heard of. I can't believe . . .' She shook her head. 'Who am I kidding? I can quite easily believe that someone is this crazy.'

'Seems to me he's enjoying himself,' Irving said. 'He knows who I am, he knows John, and just to insure that we're aware of his brilliance he sends the letter to you . . . just to make sure we realize how fucking smart he is.'

'So what are you going to do?'

'I've been back through everything. I've spoken to every relative, every witness, every person who has been directly or indirectly involved.'

'Did you ever get a chance to find out about that group that John belongs to?'

'The Winterbourne Hotel people. No, that's one thing I never followed up on. Not directly anyway. John told me there were four women and two men besides himself.'

'And the women?'

'Our guy is not a woman.'

Karen didn't challenge Irving's certainty. She sat silently. She drank her coffee. She felt she had nothing of importance to say.

They left at seven-ten. Langley led the way, Irving followed in his own car, and when they arrived at her apartment by the Joyce Theater in Chelsea, Irving had her wait in the front hallway while he searched the place.

There was nothing. He'd known it, as had she, but it felt as if he was doing something that made sense. He was there to protect and serve, and that's what he did.

At the doorway she kissed his cheek. She held his hand for a moment and thanked him.

'Maybe when this thing is over . . .' she said, and Ray Irving felt something stir briefly in his tired and broken heart.

He left without saying another word, but he smiled from the stairwell and she raised her hand.

He walked to the car, hurried the last few yards as it started to rain. He drove back to the Fourth, for no other reason than he did not wish to be alone.

It was the 20th of October. Ten victims to date. Eleven days to wait for someone else to die.

FORTY-NINE

And those eleven days proved to be among the worst of Ray Irving's life.

Deborah Wiltshire had died on him. After however many years of a real relationship – a relationship that included eating out, going to movies, a concert in Central Park, a time he got sick with flu and she came to his apartment with Nyquil and Formula 44 – there was nothing. Something good had gone, and he was perhaps more aware of its absence in those eleven days than in the entire year since her death.

Karen Langley was also a good person. Irving believed that. But neither of them lived in a world that was forgiving. Their worlds seemed to revolve in different orbits, and trying to make anything further of their friendship felt somehow inappropriate and unmanageable.

The Anniversary Man, for that was how Irving had resolved to call him, had interrupted his existence.

The Anniversary Man had made any possibility of a regular life impossible, and for this Irving resented him. An unknown person had collapsed Irving's world, and he looked out from beneath the rubble and waited in anticipation for the architect of this collapse to show his face.

The night before the 31st October Irving could not sleep.

Four minutes after midnight the phone rang.

'Ray?'

'John?'

'Yeah . . . figured I'd call and see how you were doing.'

'Not gonna sleep,' Irving said. 'Thanks for calling.'

'Sure.' Costello paused. 'Anything useful I can do?'

'God knows, John . . . I don't know what else there is to do. We just have to wait and see.'

'This is not a good position to be in.'

'Have to face facts . . . goes the way we think it's gonna go, then someone is gonna be dead by this time tomorrow.'

'That's a terrible thought.'

'But true.'

Costello didn't speak for a while, and then he cleared his throat and said, 'You have my number.'

'Think of anything smart I'll call you,' Irving said, and tried to make it sound like he was smiling, that he was positive, that he believed that something good would come of this. He couldn't think what that might be, but it didn't stop him hoping.

'Tomorrow then,' Costello said.

'Tomorrow,' Irving echoed.

Morning of the 31st it was raining heavily. Irving called Victor Grantham at seven-thirty. They had spoken twice during the previous week, and Grantham had clearance to work with Irving throughout the day.

'I'm sitting here in front of this thing,' Grantham said. 'I have a malfunctioning trap release on East 128th just before it crosses the Hudson to the I-87, but aside from that we're clear. If anything, the rain is gonna help us.'

'How so?'

'Whole network is designed to carry stuff away, you know? If it isn't carrying then we know about it soon enough.'

'So who do you have with us today?' Irving asked.

'I have about ninety crews theoretically. There's substations all over the city, different shifts, different duties, but there's no breakdowns in the network as far as I can see. We have the whole day ahead of us.'

'Not a day I've been looking forward to,' Irving said.

Grantham didn't reply.

'So you stay on the direct number, right?'

'I'll be here throughout,' Grantham said. 'My wife made sandwiches, I got a flask of coffee, got a couple of books to read. Gonna be right with you 'til the end, one way or the other.'

'Okay . . . this is very much appreciated, Victor.'

'Hell, man, what you gonna do eh? This is someone's life we're talking about, right?'

'It is, yes,' Irving replied. 'So you have this number. This is a dedicated line. No-one else on this line but you and me.'

'You got it, Detective . . . just you and me.'

Neither spoke for a moment, and then Victor Grantham asked the question that neither of them wanted to answer.

'You figure we got a prayer, Detective Irving?'

'You want the truth, Victor? No, I don't think we have a prayer, but like you say, what you gonna do.'

'Good luck.'

'Same to you.'

Irving hung up, sat back in his chair and looked at the cork boards that faced him on the opposite wall.

'This is it,' he said to himself, and he wished it wasn't.

There were three false alarms before it got dark. Two of them were simple mechanical faults, the third was a plastic bag full of beer cans that someone had thrown from a moving car. Irving had reached the 23rd Street subway station by the time Grantham came back to him on his cellphone and gave him the news. Lights flashing, siren wailing, Irving had hit the ground running and made it away from the precinct within minutes. His heart racing, his pulse running twice its rate, he'd pulled over to the side of the road and hammered the heels of his hands on the steering wheel. He'd sworn loudly, repeatedly, and then sat for some minutes, his eyes closed, his head back against the rest, until he felt his body return to normal. All that remained as he pulled away from the curb and started back toward the Fourth was the mess of nerves in the base of his gut. Only other time he'd felt such a thing, such intensity, such impotent desperation, was before the doctor walked out to tell him that Deborah Wiltshire was dead. That had been for minutes. This had gone on all day. Emotions were uncontrollable and unrelenting. Emotions nailed you, and there was no way to escape.

So darkness came, and by seven Irving was climbing the walls in frustration. He paced the incident room ceaselessly. Farraday came down to see him twice, told him that if any further units became available he would let him know. Irving barely heard him, standing there at the window, looking out into the kaleidoscope of streetlights, broken up and scattered through the rain on the glass. He was out there. Somewhere. Driving perhaps. Carrying some dead girl to a side-street, some predetermined drainage outlet where he would just tip her over the edge of the freeway and watch her stop in the channel. And then walk away, dust down his jacket and get in the car. Buckle up and drive carefully. Wouldn't want to get pulled over for speeding, for failure to wear a safety belt. Drive five miles an hour over the speed limit so cops didn't think you were trying to be inconspicuous. Make a clean getaway.

Irving had no idea whether it was possible to feel worse than he did. Didn't want to know. Four times he called Victor Grantham just to make sure that the line was clear, that it was still functioning, and four times Victor Grantham assured Irving that he had a cellphone, that he had Irving's own cell number, the number of the station house, and if he had a heart attack his supervisor would call Irving to let him know that he was taking over Grantham's position.

'This end we got covered,' he said.

Irving tried to read through some of the case files. He made a note regarding the Winterbourne group, that he should really check each member directly, despite Costello's reassurances that these people were victims not perpetrators. That had been unprofessional. That was something he would be called to account for if—

A uniform stopped in the door, asked Irving if there was anything he could do.

Irving shook his head. 'We're just on wait here,' he said.

'Know exactly what you mean,' the uniform replied.

In your dreams you do, Irving thought, but said nothing.

He stared at the phone on the desk. He willed it to ring, but nothing happened. He tried counting like John Costello, the carpet tiles on the floor, the repetitive pattern on the wall, the number of cars that passed the corner between the green light and the red . . .

When the telephone finally did ring, Irving damn near pulled the cord out of the wall as the phone tumbled to the floor leaving him with the receiver in his hand.

'Detective . . . I got one where the Queens Midtown

Tunnel comes in off the river. It's actually in the tunnel . . .
right beneath FDR . . .'

Irving dropped the receiver and started running.

Victor Grantham carried right on talking until he realized
there was no-one there.

By the time Irving reached the scene there were four motorcycle units, a black-and-white, and three of Grantham's
engineering teams already there. Seven blocks had taken
him twenty-two minutes despite the siren and the lights. He
had radioed back through to the Fourth from his car. Road-
blocks had been actioned on Borden Avenue at the Hunters
Point end of the tunnel, at East 36th and 37th, also Second
Avenue at the Tudor end. But they had been actioned too
late, and there were too many cars, and there was no way in
the world that such a step could ever have worked with the
volume of traffic, the dark, the rain, the limited resources.
The driver of the vehicle could have taken a straight right
onto 55th and been lost around the back of the Long Island
City station within five minutes of leaving the scene.

They found the girl at two minutes past eight. She was
naked but for a pair of orange socks and a silver ring inlaid
with abalone. Nearby a pair of panties, a bundle of tissue
inside them to serve as a makeshift napkin. There was no
purse, no handbag, no other clothes. There were no marks on
her body beside the strangulation bruises on her neck. Irving
called Turner from his cellphone. Turner was en route within
minutes. Irving then called the coroner, and once the coroner had been dispatched he walked up the tunnel a good
thirty yards and called John Costello.

'You got her, didn't you?' Costello stated matter-of-factly
before Irving had even spoken.

'Wha—'

'Your cellphone number came up,' Costello said. 'I figured
you weren't in the office.'

'Orange socks. Silver ring. It's her.'

Costello didn't speak.

'I thought you should know, John, that was all . . . I have
to go. I have work to do now.'

'Call me if there's anything I can do.'

314

'I will.'

Irving closed his phone, turned around, walked back to the flashing lights and confusion of the eighth murder scene, the eleventh body.

CHAPTER FIFTY

Turner stayed after the body had been taken away. He brought three other CSAs with him, and together they cordoned off the scene, photographed, collected, rigged arc-lights, and fingertip-searched the road for twenty feet in both directions until Turner was certain that nothing had been missed.

'I don't think there was anything *to* miss,' he told Irving. Already eleven p.m., and Irving stood cold and detached and emotionless, hands buried in his pockets, vaguely remembering that he'd eaten nothing since late morning.

'This was simply the dump site. He drove up, pulled over, took her out, dropped her down the culvert, and drove away.' He turned and looked back toward the Hunters Point end of the tunnel. 'Heading in that direction.'

Irving said nothing. He merely turned and looked where Turner indicated, perhaps believing there might be something to see. The Queens-Midtown Tunnel, uncharacteristically devoid of traffic, looked back at him. Vacant, soundless, it was almost taunting him.

'I'm done here,' Turner said. 'You want a ride somewhere?'

'No. I've got my car.'

'I'm at the crime lab until six,' Turner said. 'Call me if there's anything I can do.'

Irving didn't reply. He stood silently while Turner collected his staff, directed the loading of equipment back into the convoy of vehicles, watched as they disassembled the kriegs, wound up the black and yellow tapes, hefted the bollards and folded up the sawhorses. Within twenty minutes there was no-one left. Irving stepped back, close against the wall, and watched as the traffic started back through the tunnel.

Had you not known, it would have been hard to believe

that only a handful of hours earlier a dead body had been dumped no more than ten yards from where he stood. He bowed his head and started back along the service engineers' walkway that ran the length of the tunnel. He paused at the culvert for one last futile moment. He saw nothing, because there was nothing to see.

This was a game. Elaborate, complex, driven by something he couldn't even begin to comprehend, yet nothing more than a game.

And as of this moment Ray Irving knew he was losing.

Deputy Coroner Hal Gerrard met Irving in the corridor outside Theater Two.

'She was scrubbed,' he said. 'She was strangled, and then she was bathed and scrubbed with some kind of carbolic soap that's got phenol in it – a benzene derivative – and it cleans and disinfects pretty thoroughly. I'm not completely done, but right now all I can give you is that she was strangled by a right-hander, nothing under her fingernails, nothing in the pubis. No sign of assault, either physical or sexual, nothing from the rape kit.'

'Was she a hooker?'

Gerrard shrugged. 'Your guess is as good as mine. Her prints aren't on AFIS. We haven't checked DNA yet, haven't done tox so I don't know if she was a user. No tracks on her arms, nothing between her toes or behind her knees. She seems in pretty good shape, all things considered.'

'Time?'

'Late afternoon,' Gerrard said. 'Liver temp, lividity . . . I'd say about five.'

Irving tried to remember what he'd been doing at five. He couldn't.

'So how long before you're done?'

'Tox and everything, you're gonna have to leave her with us. I'll get the DNA checked, dental x-Rays, whatever we can do to ID her, and I'll call you.'

'You have my cell, right?'

'I have your cell.'

Irving walked back the way he'd come. He sat in his car in the lot. It was nearly midnight. He wanted to drive over to

317

Karen Langley's apartment in Chelsea. He wanted to knock on the door and tell her what had happened. He wanted her to tell him that it was okay, it was going to be fine, that he should come in, take off his shoes, relax for a little while. Have some wine, watch some TV, fall asleep beside her with the smell of her hair and her perfume all around him . . .

That's what he wanted, but it was not what he did.

He started the engine, turned the car one-eighty, and headed back to the Fourth.

Ray Irving didn't go home on Tuesday night. While half of New York slept with the memory of trick or treat and sacks of candy, while people arrived home, and left again as they prepared for work, for a day off, for a trip to see friends in the country, he sat at his desk in the incident room and imagined what he would do if he were a smarter man.

And there he was still, wearing the same clothes, unshaven and unslept, when a call came in from the *The New York Times* that another letter had arrived.

FIFTY-ONE

Perhaps it was the threat, perhaps the fact that the author of the letter alluded to earlier killings. To date, it seemed that nothing had created sufficient impact to unify the thoughts and minds of those directly or indirectly involved with the investigation.

Perhaps – as Irving had earlier suspected – the simple truth was that Farraday, Chief Ellmann, others who read the reports, had convinced themselves that there was such a thing as coincidence. Coincidence, they had decided to believe, had played a part in this. There was no serial killer; it just appeared that way.

The letter that arrived at the offices of *The New York Times* on the morning of Wednesday, November 1st, 2006, was compelling – and it was detailed enough to vanquish any doubt anyone might have possessed about the nature of this thing.

On a single sheet of cream-colored vellum, in the same generic typeface as the note that had arrived with the Irving–Costello Central Park photograph, the letter spoke of how Mia Grant had gone *oh so very quietly into that long goodnight;* of *two girls in halter-tops and jeans who begged like sorry-ass bitches, telling me how they weren't guilty of anything, that they were innocent, and I listened to what they had to say, and I made them beg a while longer, and then I shot them both dead right where they knelt and that was the end of that.* He spoke of John Wayne Gacy, called him *a faggot motherfucker piece-of-shit loser who couldn't get what he wanted without sticking a gun in someone's face.* And then he spoke of hookers, how they were *nothing better than animal filth, worse than animal filth, the base dregs of humanity, carrying their disease and absence of morals.* Finally he quoted Isaiah, Chapter 60, Verse 24, and he wrote, 'And they shall go forth and look on the dead bodies of the

319

men that have rebelled against me; for their worm shall not die, their fire shall not be quenched, and they shall be an abhorrence to all flesh.'

And he closed the letter by carefully explaining what he wished, and what would happen if his desire was not satisfied.

Print this on the front page of your New York Times, he wrote.

Print this in capital letters for all of New York and the world to see.

I AM THE CLEANSING LAMB OF CHRIST.

I AM EARTH AND AIR AND FIRE AND WATER.

SEEK FORGIVENESS, REPENT YOUR SINS, AND I WILL SET YOU FREE.

And then he gave instructions that the photographs of all his victims be printed beneath his words, with the final caution:

And if you do not do this I will send another family of sinners to Hell.

At least six.

Perhaps more.

And after that it will become personal.

The letter was not signed, there was no attention-getting alias.

And the collected gathering of men who stood in the boardroom of *The Times* and looked down at that letter – among them Ray Irving and Bill Farraday, the paper's editor, assistant editor, news-desk co-ordinator, two lawyers on contract to *The Times* who were permanently stationed on the premises – men who, between them, had seen and heard a great deal of life, were somehow diminished and incapacitated by the chilling simplicity and brutal frankness of the letter.

Irving wanted to know who had touched the letter, and he called the Fourth to have someone come over to take prints for elimination purposes.

Farraday spoke to the precinct desk sergeant, told him to call the assistant district attorney and Chief Ellmann, to find whatever homicide detectives might be within the city limits who were not actually busy at a crime scene, and bring them all together at the Fourth for eleven a.m.

The paper's lawyers took the situation under advisement, initially concurred with Farraday's instruction that no such headline be printed, said they would take orders from the DA's office on this one. This was not a situation with which they were familiar. They handled slander and libel litigation, they were experts in such matters, not in criminal law. Here, there were lives at risk. They backed out of the office and disappeared.

Irving and Farraday left the meeting close to ten. They'd arrived in separate cars and departed the same way, Farraday carrying the letter in a clear plastic envelope, and he drove it directly to Jeff Turner who would supervise the analysis and organize a copy of it for Farraday to take to the meeting at the Fourth.

Irving and Farraday met again in the incident room at quarter of eleven. Homicide Detectives Ron Hudson and Vernon Gifford were present, and within moments Irving heard Assistant DA Paul Sonnenburg making his way up the stairs, cellphone in hand, arguing with someone about 'the unalterable fact that they have nothing more than cir- cumstantial evidence, for God's sake.' He ended the call with a dismissive grunt as he stepped into the room, and after nodding an acknowledgement to those present he asked who else was due.

'Just the Chief,' Farraday said, and indicated where he should sit.

Ellmann arrived four minutes late. He made no excuses, took his chair and read the copy letter. He handed it back to Farraday, leaned back in his chair and steepled his fingers.

'How many have you got that can work on this?' he asked.

'Right now three,' Farraday replied. 'Irving here. You've read his reports. He's been at this since the beginning. Hudson and Gifford can be reassigned.'

'Who's on the original letter?'

'Jeff Turner.'

'Isn't he doing the tunnel girl?'

'Done already,' Irving interjected. 'Autopsy and crime scene reports are on their way.'

'Your take?' Ellmann asked Irving.

Irving shook his head. 'I don't doubt that he'll do what he says. It's simply a matter of how long before it happens.'

'And is there anything in this letter that you think can help us?'

'Maybe,' he replied. 'I think everything he does is done for a reason. I think every word of that has been chosen—'

Ellmann cut across him. 'What do we have to do to get it out of *think* and into *know*?'

'Give me a little time . . . ?' Irving said, a questioning tone in his voice.

Ellmann looked at his watch. 'I have meetings,' he said, and started to rise from his chair. 'Back here at two, and I need answers by then. Nothing goes in the papers, nothing at all.' He indicated that Farraday should follow him from the room. Words were exchanged at the top of the stairwell before Ellmann left.

Farraday stepped back into the room. 'So?' he asked Irving.

'Let me deal with the letter,' Irving said. 'I need a little time with this.'

'To do what?'

Irving rose from his chair. 'To figure out what it really means.'

'You think it means something other than what it says? Seems pretty damned simple to me. Print this bullshit or he kills another six.'

'That's what I'm going to find out.'

'Don't disappear, do not switch your phone off,' Farraday said. 'Back here by one. And I need some progress, okay?'

Irving was already dialing Karen Langley's number as he left the room; it was ringing before he reached the top of the stairs.

FIFTY-TWO

'The only question,' John Costello said, 'is whether he's in fact a religious nut, which I seriously doubt, or is all this simply a misdirector?'

'And the second thing,' Karen Langley said, 'is who does he mean when he says that after this it's going to get personal?'

The three of them – Irving, Costello and Karen Langley – were seated in Langley's office. By the time Irving had arrived it was already eleven-forty.

Costello reached for the letter again, read through it once more, closed his eyes for a moment.

'The Shawcross letter, the one in the Zodiac cipher, was simply a transcription of an already extant letter. The Henry Lee Lucas letter, the one with the word missing, was exactly as Lucas wrote it but with the girl's name removed. This one—'

'Is all his own work?' Irving asked.

'I'm certainly not familiar with anything that looks or sounds like this,' Costello said, 'but that doesn't mean that someone else who knows more about letters and written testimonials of serial killers wouldn't recognize it. Someone like Leonard Beck, maybe.'

'The letter collector, yes. Maybe he would know,' Irving said.

'And I tell you who else might be able to shed some light on this,' Costello went on. 'If only from the viewpoint that there could be any number of hidden meanings in it.'

'Who is that?'

'The people from the Winterbourne meetings,' Costello said.

'You think—?'

Costello got up from his chair and walked to the door. 'You call your guy,' he said. 'I'll call mine.'

Leonard Beck was pleased to assist, though he was on the far side of the city and had a meeting to attend. He remembered his discussion with Irving in September, was somewhat concerned to hear that Irving was still investigating the same case.

'They don't go away,' Irving said. 'Not until you actually find the truth.'

'So I don't know how I can help you,' Beck said.

'I have a letter,' Irving explained. 'It has Bible references and references to earlier murders, and there's a threat at the end of it that says if we don't do a certain thing that the author requires then there will be further killings.'

'Well, well, standard egotistical shit,' Beck said sarcastically. 'And what do you want from me?'

'I would like you to take a look at it, see if it reminds you of any earlier letter you might have come across.'

'Don't you guys have entire units that deal with this sort of thing? Doesn't the FBI have profilers and document analysts and—'

'They do,' Irving said, 'but this isn't a federal case. The only line they could come in on is the kidnapping angle, and right now we have nothing more than circumstantial evidence to suggest that any victims were kidnapped.'

'You have access to a computer and a scanner?'

'I can get one.'

'So scan it and e-mail it to me . . . I'll take a look.'

'You'd need to do it now, Doctor Beck . . . before your meeting.'

'So send it now. You got a pen?'

'Sure.'

Beck gave Irving his e-mail address. Irving hung up, gave the document to Karen who scanned it, attached it, sent it to Beck.

'And if your captain finds out that you did this?' she asked as she watched the e-mail go.

'Then I don't have a job,' Irving said, 'and you'll have to take me in.'

Moments later Costello appeared in the doorway. 'You've got five of them,' he said breathlessly. 'One of the women is out of town, but the others are willing to help . . . not here, though, and not at a police station. There's a hotel on 45th near the Stevens Tower. They'll meet us there at quarter of one.'

Irving was shaking his head. 'I'm supposed to be back at the Fourth by one.'

'So you'll be late,' Costello said.

Irving glanced at his watch. 'We need to leave in the next ten minutes,' he said, and then his cell rang.

'Detective Irving?'

'Doctor Beck. You got it?'

'Got it, looked at it . . . doesn't seem familiar to me. Truth is that there are thousands of letters with Bible references, but as far as it being the same as any letter I've seen . . .' He left the sentence incomplete. He didn't need to say anything further.

'Doctor Beck?'

'Yes.'

'I need you to do something for me.'

'You need me to delete the e-mail from the computer, and this conversation never happened, right?'

'Right,' Irving said.

'Consider it done, Detective, and good luck with this thing.'

'Appreciated, Doctor Beck, really appreciated.'

Irving ended the call and looked up at Costello. 'We're out of here then,' he said, to which Karen Langley responded by reaching for her jacket.

Irving raised his eyebrows.

'You don't think I'm gonna sit here and wait while you pair run around the city do you?'

'Karen—'

She raised her hand, a clear and emphatic gesture. 'Not another word, Ray. I'm coming.'

Irving looked at Costello, who smiled, shrugged his shoulders. 'Not my war,' he said. 'You fight your own battles.'

FIFTY-THREE

The five available members of the Winterbourne group arrived punctually, no more than a handful of minutes between the first and the last. Irving hadn't known what to expect – anxious and subdued individuals showing an abundance of nervous traits perhaps, but that was not what he got. The people who entered the room one after the other appeared no different from the thousands of professionals who travelled daily on the subway, or drove to work, who raised families all over the city. John Costello introduced them and each one shook hands with Irving, with Langley, and then took a seat around the semi-circular meeting table in the center of the room.

Three women – Alison Cotten, early thirties, an attractive brunette not dissimilar in appearance to Karen Langley; Barbara Floyd, half a dozen years older than Alison, short hair almost too severe for her face, but a relaxed and natural manner that gave her the appearance of one accustomed to listening; lastly, Rebecca Holzman, mid- to late twenties, blonde hair, green eyes, a little too much make-up disguising a rash of acne that covered the lower half of her face and much of her neck. Of the two men present, the first – George Curtis – was in his early to mid-fifties, with a shock of grey hair that gave him the look of a math professor or somesuch. Beside him sat Eugene Baumann, immaculately dressed in a midnight blue three-piece suit, white shirt and pale blue tie – the kind of man who would manage a bank, or make senior partner in a substantial city law firm. Nevertheless, Irving imagined that how they appeared and who they really were was more than likely worlds apart. If nothing else, John Costello was testament to the fact that appearances belied reality.

Costello sat to Irving's right, and it was he who spoke first.

'This is Detective Ray Irving of the Fourth Precinct Homicide Division. And this,' he added, indicating Karen Langley to Irving's left, 'is Karen Langley, the senior crime correspondent for the *City Herald* . . . and as I said when I called you all, we need your help with something.'

Baumann leaned forward, cleared his throat, and addressed Irving. 'I'm willing to do whatever I can, Detective, but I can only give you half an hour of my time at the moment.' He glanced at his watch. 'Obviously, if this is a longer term thing then I'm sure—'

Irving smiled. 'Frankly, Mr Baumann, I have less time than you today. This is something very straightforward, and you'll either be able to shed some light on it or not, but before I explain the situation, I want to make it very clear that there must be an understanding here. Whatever we discuss stays inside this room—'

'I don't think you should have any concern whatever about that,' Alison Cotten said. 'Because of our personal circumstances, we're precisely the kind of people who do not, and would not, want to draw attention to ourselves.' She smiled patiently, as if she knew things that Irving could never begin to comprehend.

'I didn't mean to imply that—'

'Let's cut to the chase, eh, Detective?' Curtis said. 'How do you think we might be able to help you?'

Irving started talking. He went back to Mia Grant, right back to the beginning as he knew it, and summarized the nature of the case. He spoke of the replica killings, the Shawcross letter, the use of the Zodiac code, and then he produced the latest letter that had been mailed to *The Times* and held it up for them to see. After a moment or two he passed it to Costello, who gave it to Barbara Floyd. Each of them studied the letter in turn, read back through it, consulted with one another. Irving let them be, watched as they asked and answered questions of each other, as suggestions were made, and it was only when Eugene Baumann slid the letter back toward him that he realized they had come to some sort of conclusive viewpoint.

'It means nothing,' Baumann said. 'It makes no real sense. The only hookers were the Carol-Anne girl you spoke of, and the other girl in Central Park. The teenage girls weren't prostitutes, right?'

'Right,' Irving replied.

'Seems that the only significant element here is the threat itself, that he will kill six more people if you don't get this printed in the newspaper, and in my opinion . . .' Baumann paused and looked at the other members of the Winterbourne group.

'It makes sense,' Rebecca Holzman said. 'As far as the date is concerned, you know?' She smiled. 'Richard Segretti could be a help to us right now. He knew everything there was to know about this.'

Irving frowned.

'He was a member of the group some while ago,' Baumann said, 'but as far as I know he moved out of New York.'

'It's DeFeo, isn't it?' Costello suddenly interjected.

Baumann smiled. 'You didn't need us here, did you?' he said. 'You have Costello.' He started to rise from his chair.

'What?' Irving said, the sense of agitation evident in his voice. 'What do you mean, DeFeo?'

'Tell him,' Costello said to Curtis.

'The DeFeo killings,' Curtis said. 'November 13th, 1974, the anniversary of which is just over a week from now.'

Costello turned and looked at Irving. 'You ever hear of a movie called *The Amityville Horror*?'

'Sure,' Irving said. 'I've seen it.'

'That was based on a book written in the seventies,' George Curtis said. 'Supposed to be about paranormal phenomena witnessed by the family who moved into one-twelve Ocean Drive after the DeFeo killings. The parents were murdered, Ronald and Louise DeFeo, and four of their kids. Dawn, Allison, Marc and John. Ronald junior was the eldest, and he was . . . well, he was convicted of their murders.'

'You sound uncertain,' Irving said.

'There were inconsistencies,' Curtis said. 'The eldest girl, Dawn, was eighteen years old. Firearm discharge residue was found on her nightgown, which indicated she might have held and fired a gun herself, and there were other things too . . . but Ronald DeFeo was convicted of six counts of second-degree. He was given six consecutive twenty-five-to-life terms. He's up in Green Haven, right, John?'

Costello nodded. 'Yes, Green Haven Correctional in Beekman.'

'Family was all killed with a 35-caliber Marlin rifle,' Baumann said. 'Speed with which it was done, the fact that the weapon wasn't silenced, and the way the bodies were found . . . all face down, none of them tied up, none of them sedated, and right to the last one it looked like the sound of the gun going off didn't wake any of them . . . all these things were inconsistencies in the original case.'

'Yet DeFeo was convicted,' Costello said. 'He's made numerous pleas for parole but all of them have been declined.'

'So is that what we're dealing with here?' Irving asked.

'Only thing that rings true,' Curtis said. 'He rants about hookers, but his victims have primarily been teenagers, boys and girls. Only two of the ten have actually been prostitutes.'

Irving looked at the letter once again, unable to ignore a sense of impending horror at what was happening. And it was his case, ultimately his responsibility alone, to direct, decide, delegate and act.

The Anniversary Man had promised another six killings and, if past experience was anything to go by, he seemed to have no great difficulty in keeping his word.

Fifteen minutes later the meeting disbanded.

Irving and Langley, Costello beside them, thanked each of the five as they left.

The last one to leave was Eugene Baumann, who paused for a moment and leaned close to Irving.

'I was attacked in 1989,' he said. 'I spent four months in a coma, and while I was getting ready to die my wife had an affair with a much younger man. Last week I had a medical check. Doctor said I was healthier than I've ever been. My wife, however, has a very serious heart condition and might not make Christmas. What I went through taught me something very valuable. Taught me that the only real failure was to give up fighting. Cliched sure, but what the hell eh?' He smiled warmly, gripped Irving's hand. 'You call me if there's anything I can do. John knows how to reach me. I might be a little crazy, but what the hell, if there's something I can do I'll do it.'

Irving thanked him, saw him to the door and closed it firmly behind him.

'I've got to get back to the office,' he said. 'I'll drop you off at the *Herald*.'

'Go,' Karen said. 'We'll get a cab.'

Irving reached out, held her hand for a moment, squeezed it reassuringly.

He nodded an acknowledgement to Costello, and then he too left the hotel room and hurried out to his car.

FIFTY-FOUR

Farraday shook his head slowly and dropped into his chair. 'Jesus,' he exhaled. 'Jesus God almighty . . .'

'It's the only line to follow,' Irving said. 'Seriously, I don't see any other way to do this—'

'You have even the slightest idea of the kind of manpower something like this would take?'

'No,' Irving said, 'and I don't think there's any way of determining that until we know how many families we're dealing with.'

'So where was this place?'

'Amityville? It was – *is* – on Long Island.'

'And you think this will happen somewhere within the New York City limits?'

'Every killing we know of has occurred within the city limits. He's not sticking to the original locations, just replicating the killings themselves, and I think this won't be any different. He'll kill a family of six, precisely the same way, and it will be somewhere relatively close.'

'Okay,' Farraday said, suddenly cognizant of the fact that in the absence of anything else this was at least action as opposed to inaction. 'Speak to city records, the electoral registry . . . I'll get the Chief briefed and see if we can't get some help from the FBI on collating some sort of database . . . go for having some kind of complete list within twenty-four hours. Agreed?'

'Agreed.'

It didn't take twenty-four hours. It took closer to ninety-six. The better part of four days, and still Ray Irving believed that there was no way to compile a concise and definitive list of all six-member families with teenage children, or younger, within the New York city limits. People moved, people got divorced; sometimes where there were two adults and four kids, they would suddenly find that one of the kids had moved to another state. One family had lost three members in a car crash only the previous month. The records office was involved, and the staff at the New York State Electoral Registry, and Ellmann secured the services of four federal agents in a supervisory capacity. They couldn't employ their own database because the Anniversary killings were not a federal matter. Federal could only investigate espionage, sabotage, kidnapping, bank robbery, drug-trafficking, terrorism, civil rights violations and governmental fraud. However, the agents were good men, hardworking, and they instigated a cross-checking system that reconciled one database with another, eliminated duplicate names and addresses, narrowed the thing down, narrowed it down again, and put some sense of order into the operation. Without them Irving would have been lost.

Still, by early evening of Saturday the 4th of November, despite the fact that they had managed to compile a list of five hundred and forty-two extant six-member families within the city limits, everyone engaged in the project knew that there was no way to determine whether they had covered all bases. The list was as complete as it ever would be. It spanned the entirety of New York City, and Irving and Farraday, back of them the Chief of Police and the Mayor's office, carried the responsibility of alerting these people to the risk that now appeared to face them. Or not. They couldn't be one hundred percent sure. But, as Irving kept repeating to himself, any course of action, no matter how poorly executed, was better than passively waiting. Ellmann held firm to his decision regarding the newspapers. Nothing would be printed.

'Eleven years ago there was something similar,' he told Farraday. 'Before my time as chief, but something my predecessor will all too willingly talk about. Guy had lost his wife and child in some hospital fuck-up. She died in labor, the baby with her, and he was up for taking it out on the medical profession. The same kind of deal as this one, a threat that if something wasn't printed in the newspapers he would go on some sort of revenge thing against doctors.

So they printed the warning in some newspaper, and doctors started carrying handguns. In the subsequent couple of weeks there were eleven unlawful shootings by doctors. Doctors were playing vigilante, you know? And at least half a dozen innocent people got seriously hurt. That is not something I intend to have happen again.'

Farraday relayed this to Irving, and Irving – sitting at his desk in the incident room, exhausted beyond anything he'd experienced before – understood and appreciated Ellmann's point of view, his concern also, but he was still faced with the prospect of co-ordinating the task of alerting five hundred and forty-two families to the potential risk they could face in nine days' time.

'We do everything we possibly can,' Farraday said. 'We have authorization to divide these families up between all relevant precincts. We're gonna use the black-and-whites to go out and see these people on their routine circuits. Some-how, someway, we're gonna reach every one of them, talk to the head of the household, brief them on what we have so that they'll be alert to the fact that if something untoward occurs on the night of the thirteenth, the matter will be treated as a priority.'

'This is some operation,' Irving said.

'It's massive,' Farraday said. 'Biggest single action I've ever seen for one case, but we're doing everything we can. I know how hard you've been working on this, and—'

'And we could still have missed one family, or six, or twelve . . . seriously, Captain, I don't know that there is any way to isolate every single family that could fall within this demographic. What if he's got a four-member family in sight, but he knows that on the night of the thirteenth grandma and grandpa are gonna come over and stay for a few days—'

'Ray . . . enough already. Hold up there. You've done everything you can. This thing is gonna roll out exactly as we've planned. These people will be contacted. They may decide to leave the city for a while—'

'And what if we've got it wrong completely? What if it's nothing whatsoever to do with the killings that occurred back in '74?'

'Ray, I need you to do something for me.'

Irving looked up.

'I really need you to go home and get some sleep. I'm not talking about two or three hours with your head on your desk. I need you in better shape than this. I need you to go back home and actually go to bed. Lie down, you know? Actually lie down in a damned bed and get seven, eight hours sleep. I need you to do that, okay?'

'But—'

'Go,' Farraday said emphatically. 'I'm ordering you to go and you will go.' He stood up. 'We'll meet tomorrow morning.'

Farraday crossed the room to the door. 'I'm sending someone back here in fifteen minutes to make sure that you've left the building.'

Irving smiled. 'I'm going,' he said. 'I'm already on my way.'

En route home Irving stopped at Carnegie's. It seemed an age since he'd sat in his corner booth, drinking coffee and making small talk with the waitress. He ate as much of an omelette as he could, but his appetite was poor, had been slipping for days, and he knew that Farraday was right. Sleep was required. And he needed to speak with Costello, also with Karen Langley. Of all people, they perhaps better understood the situation he was in, the days that lay ahead. He didn't want sympathy, that least of all; it was simply the need to be around those who understood what was happening. These people had become his friends. That was the truth of it. In their own way they were doing all they could to make a difference, and that was a rare and extraordinary commodity among people. Most people were oblivious, or didn't care, or did all they could to convince themselves that the hard angles of the world would never reach them—

Irving stopped, smiled to himself.

Hardangle.

The name Costello had invented for him.

He could hear Deborah Wiltshire's voice then, something she had said too many times for him to forget. *You have to let people in a little bit, Ray . . . have to give them a little of yourself before you'll get something back . . .*

He wondered in that moment if he would be the same man when this thing was over.

Somehow he doubted it, and in some strange way he hoped that he would not.

FIFTY-FIVE

Throughout the next seven days, despite the bitter cold that suddenly seemed to grip New York, despite the forthcoming Thanksgiving celebrations and the approach of Christmas, Ray Irving worked eighteen and twenty hours a day. He never stopped, he didn't slow down. He spoke to Karen, to John Costello; he held meetings with Farraday, with Chief Ellmann, with the FBI agents, with officers assigned to assist in the division of labor; he ran Detectives Hudson and Gifford ragged at the edges – checking, cross-checking, visiting people themselves. Then the inevitable occurred.

Mr David Trent, mid-forties, married, an unemployed father of four, kind of guy who believed implicitly that the world owed him a living, took it upon himself to tell the world. Despite Detective Vernon Gifford explaining the situation and stressing the necessity of keeping some sense of balance about the nature of what they were dealing with; despite impressing upon Mr Trent that confidentiality was of the utmost importance, that everything should be done to prevent any panic regarding a potential serial killer . . . regardless of whatever efforts had been made to make Mr Trent understand what was happening, Mr Trent called *The New York Times*, he visited with them, and he told them that there was something going on.

Later, the article in his hand as he sat before Captain Farraday and Chief Ellmann, Irving realized that such a situation would have been impossible to avoid entirely. Evidently, Trent had spoken to *The Times* on Thursday, November 9th, and on Friday the 10th, three days before the anniversary of the Amityville killings, a decidedly attention-grabbing headline appeared on page two of the largest circulation newspaper in the State:

IS NEW YORK IN THE GRIP OF A SERIAL KILLER?

Somewhat inconclusively, the article covered the Mia Grant killing, the deaths of Luke Bradford, Stephen Vogel and Caroline Parselle from the 6th of August, an unrelated murder from the same month, and then went on to 'alert the people of New York, as was the duty of the press' to the fact that the police had undertaken a huge program to caution several hundred families. The article gave no specifics as to the caution, aside from the fact that these families 'could be in danger from a person, or persons, unknown.' The report didn't isolate solely those families with six members, and it created sufficient noise for Chief Ellmann to call a press conference in the early afternoon of Friday the 10th in an effort to allay fears and minimize panic.

'We are in possession of no conclusive evidence at this time that New York is under threat from a serial killer. In fact, it is possibly incorrect to employ this term at all.' He spoke with authority. Had Irving been uninformed he might even have believed this. After all, Ellman was New York's Chief of Police.

'An operation has been ongoing for some days,' Ellmann went on, 'to contact a number of families within the New York City limits – families that could be classified as occupying a particular demographic. The purpose of this operation is to prevent harm, not to cause concern or instigate panic among New York's inhabitants. Let me assure you that if you, or a member of your family, has not been contacted by someone from the New York police department or a federal representative, then you fall outside the relevant demographic and have no cause for concern.'

When asked by an NBC journalist what had prompted this action, Ellmann responded without hesitation.

'Through one of the many lines of investigation we have been pursuing, we have unearthed some information – at this time unsubstantiated – that an individual may make an attempt to commit further murders. As I have said, and will say again, there is no cause for alarm. Through actions currently being undertaken by the New York Police Department, very ably assisted by representatives from the Federal Bureau of Investigation, we have this situation well in hand. I can assure you that the likelihood of any untoward occurrence is very slight, and that all measures to prevent any harm coming to any citizen of New York are being taken with the greatest speed and efficiency possible. I wish to make it clear once again that there is no significant cause for concern. I would urge all New Yorkers to go on about their business as usual. We have one of the finest police departments in the country, and they are committed to making the streets and homes of this great city completely safe.'

Amidst a hubbub of questions and flashguns Chief Ellmann concluded the press conference.

Ray Irving and Bill Farraday, watching the TV in Farraday's office, looked at one another for a moment as Ellmann walked from the podium. Farraday switched off the TV and sat down at his desk.

'Very smooth,' Irving said.

'That's why he's the Chief,' Farraday replied.

'Seems that despite everything our guy has got a little of what he's looking for.'

'You think that's all that this is about . . . some press coverage?'

'God almighty knows. It has to be part of it, doesn't it? Isn't that the cliché? Someone didn't listen, someone didn't pay attention, so now the whole fucking world has to see what he can do?'

'Well,' Farraday said, nodding toward the TV, 'all I can say is with that statement now public we better not get it wrong. Family of six winds up dead on Monday and . . . well, I don't even wanna go there.'

'Neither do I,' Irving replied.

'So how much progress has been made?'

'Eighty, eighty-five percent,' Irving replied. 'There's limits of course. Families away, families with the head of the household out of state, all the things we predicted we'd run into . . . but as far as the five hundred-odd families are concerned, we've got in touch with about eighty-something percent of them.'

'Keep on going,' Farraday said. 'There's nothing else to do.'

'My sentiment exactly,' Irving said as he backed up toward the door.

'And Ray . . .'

'What?'

'If this all goes to shit on Monday . . . I mean, if we do wind up with another six dead, the press will descend on us like vultures.'

'Way I feel right now, by the time they get here I don't think there'll be anything left to scavenge.' He closed Farraday's office door behind him, and made his way quickly down the stairs.

FIFTY-SIX

Her name was Marcie, at least this was what she wished herself to be called. Christened Margaret, she believed – even at eight years old – that Margaret was clumsy and old, an old woman's name, and that Marcie was pretty and simple, and two syllables. Two syllables was perfect. One was too few. Three was too many. Marcie. Marcie Allen. Eight years old. One younger brother, Brandon, whom they all called 'Buddy', and he was seven, and then there was Leanne who was nine and Frances who was thirteen. That made four, and with Mom and Dad there were six, and on the evening of Sunday the 12th of November they watched a goofy movie together, the whole family, and they had pizza and popcorn because it was the last night before school, and they always did things together on Sunday nights, because that was the kind of family they were.

Jean and Howard Allen were good people. They worked hard. They didn't believe in luck or good fortune, except where such luck and fortune had been created by themselves. Howard was a hopeful golfer, and constantly reminded himself of the old Arnold Palmer saw: *Seems the harder I practice the luckier I get.* Howard figured that such a philosophy applied to pretty much everything, and thus they made their way forward in life through diligence and their commitment to certain values. Though they were not a religious family and didn't attend church, the Allens had nevertheless raised their children on the sound principles that what you gave was what you got in return. *Bullshit out, bullshit in* was a phrase Howard tended to use, though Jean disapproved of such language around the children.

Bedtime was staggered in the Allen household. Buddy went up at seven-thirty, Marcie and Leanne at quarter past eight. Teenager Frances got to stay up 'til nine, though she always protested nine was too early and her friends went to bed at ten, and there was always some kind of performance on the landing until Howard did his *loud whisper* and stern face, and commanded her to go to bed or she'd be grounded. She was not a bad girl, not by any stretch of the imagination, but her parents considered her *willful* and *strong-minded*, and secretly believed that such qualities would stand her in good stead for the future. They didn't, of course, tell her this, but they believed that, of all of them, Frances was going to carve her way through life and make a difference.

Howard Allen was a proud man, and he had every right to be. He ran his own business, a commercial electrical components supply facility, and the three-story townhouse they owned on East 17th near the Beth-Israel was paid off but for thirty thousand dollars. There was a college fund for at least two of the kids, and the Allens had discussed the possibility of putting a down-payment on a condo in the Kips Bay Plaza area, a place to rent to students at NYU Medical. There was a lot of future, there were things to plan, and things to take into consideration, and never once did they consider the possibility that it could all so suddenly end.

At eight-ten, evening of Sunday 12th, Ray Irving called Karen Langley at the *City Herald*. What it was that prompted the need to talk he could only guess, and beyond that the possibility that she might not be there didn't enter his mind, so he called, got her voicemail, and left a simple message: *Just wanted to talk, nothing important. Call me when you can.*

Somewhere he had her home number, and could anyway have easily located it from any number of sources, but he did not. Perhaps he didn't really wish to speak with her. Perhaps he only wished it to be seen that he'd had the thought, that he'd made the effort, for if she'd answered he wouldn't have known what to say.

Tonight. After midnight tonight. If we're even close to right he's gonna go out there tonight and kill six people . . .

And what would she have said in return?

Ray Irving paced the office. He'd had a bank of telephones installed the previous day, a separate receiver for every two precincts within the city limits. Detectives Gifford and

Hudson would man the desk, and there were four uniforms available for any additional assistance required. Black-and-whites city-wide were on alert, and an individual frequency had been allocated to the Fourth Precinct as control center. There were so many variables, so many unknowns. There were too many possibilities, too many potential errors human and otherwise, that Irving couldn't bear even to consider all that could go wrong. Right now, even as he paced back and forth between the window and the door, cursing Gifford and Hudson, who were already twelve minutes late, six people might be dead somewhere. The killings, if they were going to happen at all, could already have occurred. He had studied the Amityville case endlessly: The appearance of the eldest son, Ronald 'Butch' DeFeo, in Henry's Bar around six-thirty, evening of November 13th, 1974, shouting, 'You've got to help me! I think my mother and father are shot', all the way to his final confession the following day with the words 'Once I started, I just couldn't stop. It went so fast.' Aside from obtaining copies of the original case notes, Irving had read everything he could find about the murders themselves. Trying to understand perhaps, trying to isolate something that would give him some indication of how, or why, or where. He had found nothing, nothing that made his task any easier or less complex.

And so he paced the room, and he waited for Hudson and Gifford, and the bank of telephones sat silently, anticipatorily, and Ray Irving carried such heaviness in his heart.

Eight minutes after Frances finally resigned herself to the confines of her bedroom, Jean and Howard Allen sat in their kitchen and looked at one another expectantly. There was a matter of significance to discuss, and neither wished to broach the subject. Jean's mother, a difficult woman at the very best of times, a widow for eleven years, fiercely independent and even now somewhat disapproving of her daughter's choice in husbands, was awaiting the results of a biopsy. Current indications did not bode well. She had lost weight, a considerable amount in the last three months alone, and twice she had experienced *a funny turn*, once in the shopping mall, a second time at Sunday dinner in the Allens' house.

Now, finally, that Sunday evening, Jean said, 'If it turns out to be positive, you know we'll have to take her in.'

Howard said nothing.

'That house is way too big, Howard. She should have sold it after Dad died—'

'I don't think she'll want to come,' Howard said, all too aware of the fact that such a comment meant nothing.

'I know that she won't *want* to come. That's never been a question. She'll *have* to come. We'll have to make her see that she doesn't have a choice.'

'There's always the other possibility—'

'No way am I having her put in a home, Howard. Besides, there's no way in the world that we could afford it—'

'The house?' Howard ventured, knowing that he was walking on thin ice, running to be more accurate, and running with heavy steps, as if he was trying to break through to the dark and icy water and drown himself in shame and ignominy for suggesting such a thing.

'I am not selling the house where I grew up to pay for my mother to go into a nursing home, and you know she'd never agree to such a thing. Jesus, Howard, sometimes I wonder whether you actually care for her at all.'

Howard, skillful at tempering the frayed edges that appeared every once in a while in their relationship, reached out his hand and closed it over Jean's. He smiled warmly, the kind of smile that reminded Jean that here was a good man, a real man, a man with a heart and a head and a strong sense of what was right. A man she was right to have married. Fifteen years they'd been together, and through that decade and a half Howard had weathered the sniping comments, the little digs, the sly criticisms couched as *constructive ideas*, volleyed by Jean's mother, Kathleen Chantry. For Kathleen had standards, standards higher than any man might reach and, unaware that such an individual could ever walk the face of the earth, she believed that Jean had short-changed herself by marrying Howard Allen. Howard, with his commitment to his work, his extraordinary patience with his children, and his tireless devotion and unfailing fidelity to his wife who,

343

from the light in his eyes when he looked at her, knew that she would always be loved unconditionally . . .

Jean and Howard had been born good people, and they would die that way.

By ten Irving was convincing himself that they had interpreted the letter incorrectly. He questioned the validity of his assumption, and tried to forget how Farraday had finally nailed him down long enough to explain why he'd come to such a conclusion.

'You can't be serious. Jesus, Ray, a bunch of whacko murder victims . . . and you showed them the letter?'

And whatever Irving had said, however he tried to explain why he'd done it, there was no forgiveness from Farraday. But by then it was too late. The project had already been three days forward. Farraday had made Irving swear that such information would never reach Ellmann. He could only begin to imagine what Ellmann would have to say about the quality of Fourth Precinct leadership if it was known that the most time-consuming and expensive police operation in the last three years was based on a supposition made in a hotel room by five serial-killer survivors. Farraday, much to Irving's relief, didn't mention it again, and when Farraday himself appeared in the incident room that Sunday night, when he stood beside Irving for a good ten or fifteen minutes, saying nothing, perhaps willing one of the telephones to ring just to end the terrible sense of apprehension, Irving was somehow reassured. Farraday, above and beneath all else, was a policeman. Always had been, always would be, and his sense of duty lay with the people of New York far more than it did with the politicians.

'Nothing?' Farraday said.

Irving shook his head.

'Let's hope it stays that way.'

And then there was silence once again.

Which, as silences went, was not entirely dissimilar to the one in the Allen house. A respite from discussion of matters capable of generating tension, a brief hiatus within which Jean and Howard faced one another across the kitchen table, comfortable in one another's presence, appreciating each other's viewpoints sufficiently well to understand that such an issue as Kathleen Chantry would never resolve in one evening.

'Let's wait for the results,' Howard said, and once again smiled that smile and held Jean's hand reassuringly.

She nodded, feeling that if she spoke further she might end up crying, and tonight she didn't want to cry, tonight she wanted to get to bed early and get a good night's sleep, for tomorrow she would visit her mother and start the long and slow process of dealing with the woman's resistance to any sort of change. For change was coming – it was inevitable.

She glanced at the wall clock above the stove. 'It's ten already,' she said. 'I want some tea . . . you want some?'

'Earl Grey,' Howard said. 'I've got to type up a quote for tomorrow.'

'How long?'

'Fifteen minutes?'

Jean held out her hand and touched Howard's cheek. 'And then,' she said, 'you can take me to bed and read me a story.'

'Oh, I'll read you a story all right,' Howard replied suggestively, and rose from his chair and stepped behind her. For a moment he gripped her shoulders, and then he leaned forward and kissed the top of her head.

'So get going,' she said. 'Any more than fifteen minutes and I won't play.'

FIFTY-SEVEN

The feeling that assaulted Ray Irving's nerves when the telephone rang was indescribable.

He had foreseen the moment, had imagined so many things – his reaction, what would be reported at the other end of the line, the way his heart would jump suddenly, kickstarted as if wired to a car battery – but nothing could have prepared him for the sheer rush of adrenalin that assaulted his body.

Vernon Gifford snatched the receiver up, barked into the mouthpiece, was already standing as he listened, and Irving was almost running across the ten or so feet to the desk.

'East 35th and Third, East 35th and Third,' Gifford was saying over and over again, and Hudson was already on the other line, a single-number speed dial that connected him to the central switchboard, and the details went through, and even as Gifford dropped the receiver and started toward the door, even as Irving went after him, shouting behind him that Hudson should stay on the desk, field any other calls, insure that black-and-whites were on the way, Irving could feel the punch of the thing . . .

Three risers from the bottom of the well he almost lost his footing, felt something twist in his ankle, but there was no pain at all, nothing that even registered beyond the urgency, the panic, the *need* to be outside, in a car, speeding toward East 35th and Third from where the report had come.

It was one of the families. One of the families they had spoken to. Two parents, four kids, and a call had been made, a 911 call . . . someone had been seen in the back yard of the property.

Irving had his keys in his hand, was jerking the car door open as Gifford slammed the passenger door behind him. Leaving a scorched arc of rubber on the asphalt they pulled away from the curb, siren wailing, roof-light flashing, Irving weaving his way into and through the traffic that seemed to fold away before him as if it understood.

Twenty or so blocks south east, heart out of control, images flashing through his mind, palms sweating, pulse in his temple, in his neck, guts all churned up, feeling that this had to be it, this had to be it . . .

Even the lights stayed green – not that it would have mattered with three black-and-whites matching his speed from Herald Square, a blaze of cherry-blues following him, people pulling over to the side to let them pass.

Irving floored the car, peaked at eighty-five, had to slow as they reached the Park Avenue corner, and then they were away again.

Gifford said something, had the handset, was keeping a dialogue going with central, but Irving didn't even hear him.

Ray Irving could think of nothing but those words from Ronald DeFeo: *Once I started, I just couldn't stop. It went so fast.*

Howard wrestled with his quote for ten minutes and then gave up. He wanted to go with the Philly supplier, but the Japanese were so much cheaper. If he went with Philly he'd get a shorter delivery lead, but he'd pay an extra two and a half cents per unit. Two and a half cents across a one hundred and seventy thousand-unit order made a difference of more than four thousand dollars. That was enough of a difference to hurt either his own profit margin, or the customer's confidence if they checked manufacturer prices. It was one of those situations where you just decided on a hunch and went with it.

Howard shut down his computer just as Jean called from the top of the stairs.

He went through the ground floor, checked the windows and doors, switched off all the lights and left the place in complete darkness aside from the green glow from the digital clock on the stove. He paused for a moment at the base of the stairs. *Things could be one hell of a lot worse than this*, he thought to himself. *We're okay.* He put his hand on the banister just as the faint wail of sirens echoed from somewhere in the distance, and made his way up to bed.

A total of seventeen uniformed officers descended on an address at the corner of East 35th and Third at precisely ten forty-eight p.m. Taking the lead were Detectives Ray Irving and Vernon Gifford. Central Dispatch had maintained a constant telephone dialogue with the family inside – Mom and Dad, the four kids – all of them locked in the master bedroom. They had been instructed not to leave the room under any circumstances, not until they received word from Dispatch that the police were in the house, that the entire property had been searched and given the all-clear by the detective in charge of the operation, Ray Irving. The father, Gregory Hill, assured the operator that leaving the bedroom was the very last thing in the world they would do. His wife, Laura, the children, Peter, Mark, Justin and Tiffany – the youngest four, the oldest eleven – stayed still and silent and scared while Gregory whispered to the operator, was constantly reassured by her that everything was under control, that the police officers knew precisely what they were doing, that all would be well.

The operator, a seventeen-year police dispatch veteran called Harriet Miller, could not have been more right. Her measured voice, her calm and supremely confident delivery of instructions, saw the Hill family through the very worst hour of their collective lives. And Desmond Roarke – a twenty-seven-year-old opportunist thief, housebreaker and small-time fence, already on parole for three counts of attempted credit card fraud and wanted for questioning in relation to an outstanding grand theft auto investigation – perhaps believed that God truly had it in for him. As he came down from the roof of the Hill's garage, in his hand a small black carry-all containing a box-cutter, a flashlight, a tire iron wrapped in a hand-towel, two pairs of surgical gloves, a roll of duct tape and a thirty-foot length of nylon cord, the combined brilliance of a dozen police arc lights illuminated him starkly against the night sky. Desmond Roarke lost his footing, dropped his carry-all, and came skidding down the tiles, saved from dropping a good fifteen feet to the concrete patio beneath by sheer good luck. Somehow he managed to anchor himself flat on his back, his heels on the edge of the guttering, both hands clawing desperately for purchase. And that was where he stayed until three officers stood beneath him, guns trained unerringly, Irving commanding him to lie still, not to move a muscle, to remain exactly and precisely where he was until ladders were fetched. The ladders came within minutes, and Desmond Roarke, having already urinated through his jeans, was brought down from the garage roof to the most anticipatory reception he was ever likely to experience.

By eleven-thirty they had Roarke's name and had run it through the police computer. They knew who he was, had a very certain idea of why he was there, though this in itself would provide a far more significant revelation in the coming hours. The Hill family had been rescued from the confines of the master bedroom. Gregory Hill had spoken with the police, had seen Vernon Gifford, had been reassured that all was well and life could return to how it had been before this nightmare had unfolded. There would always be a shadow, of course, but at the same time an awareness that what might have happened that night could have been a lot worse.

Ray Irving knew with certainty that Desmond Roarke was not their man, and he also knew why. It was not yet midnight. It was not yet the 13th of November. In the confusion and panic of the moment, the belief that perhaps their many hundreds of hours of work might finally be paying off, that there was a family here that had been saved from a terrible catastrophe, they had overlooked the simple fact that the Anniversary Man was just that. The *Anniversary* Man.

The Amityville killings had taken place on the 13th, not the 12th.

And Ray Irving, who had forgotten that he had been waiting on midnight, stood looking out from the back lot of the house, insensible to the bitter cold, unaware that his eyes were watering involuntarily from the icy breeze that had wound its way through the city, and knew that they did not possess a prayer.

Howard Allen lay awake beside his sleeping wife. He loved the feeling of her naked body beside him. Four children, fifteen years of marriage, grey hairs, laughter lines, and still

349

there was no-one who came close to Jean. They shared a quiet passion borne not out of intense sexual attraction, but out of familiarity. They were familiar to one another. Each knew what the other liked. She knew what made him crawl the walls. He knew what made her claw holes in the bedsheets. It was good that way, and he didn't wish for any other.

Howard Allen glanced at the bedside clock. Eleven fifty-six. He was tired, overtired perhaps, and though making love usually led him into deep sleep within fifteen minutes, he was still wired about the business. He smiled at the pun, tried to focus on the difficulty, but his mind wandered, and tomorrow was Monday, it was a new week, and perhaps he would call the client and have a heart-to-heart about lead times versus shaving two and a half cents off a unit. Maybe the guy would be patriotic enough to screw the two and a half-cent saving and keep the work in the States. Howard smiled at the thought, and closed his eyes.

He heard a sound, something like a greenstick twig snapping beneath the pressure of a boot, but he was already on his way, floating into sleep, for the bed was warm, and Jean was beside him, and the kids were out for the count.

'Says he wasn't trying to steal anything,' Gifford told Irving. 'Says he was paid by someone to break into the house and look for evidence.'

Irving frowned. 'You what?'

They were seated in Irving's car, doors open, still there on East 35th, no more than twenty yards from the house. 'Paid by someone to look for evidence?'

Gifford nodded. 'That's what he said.'

'Paid by whom? Evidence of what?'

'He won't say.'

Irving shook his head. 'This is bullshit. Jesus . . .' He sighed, looked out at the house once more, and then pulled the car door to.

'We're going back to the Fourth,' he said. 'He's not our guy, we know that much at least. You take him back and book him, get some more specifics on this story if you can, and let me know what the deal is. I have to stay on this thing.'

Seeming to grow out of the shadows in the upper hallway, it was as if he had somehow managed to materialize out of the air itself. There was nothing, and then there was something. There was no-one, and then there was someone, and that someone stood for a long time – ten, perhaps fifteen minutes – and he was utterly motionless, nothing but the rising and falling of his chest as he breathed, and beside him, resting there against the carpet, was the butt of a rifle.

The figure eventually moved, took two steps forward, and before he reached Frances Allen's bedroom he propped the rifle against the edge of the jamb. With one hand against the upper frame, the other on the handle, he eased it open, pushed it wide, and stood there – again for some considerable time – perhaps listening to her breathing. He did the same with each door until he found the main bedroom, the sleeping parents – Howard and Jean Allen – and then he walked around to Jean's side of the bed and leaned down to look at her face. After a moment or two he reached forward, closed his hand firmly over her nose and mouth, and waited for her eyes to open in surprise.

Which they did – wide and frightened – and when she saw the eyes looking back at her, eyes looking out of the single slit in a ski-mask, she felt as if her heart was exploding out of her chest in sheer terror.

And when she saw the rifle, and the way the figure calmly leaned across her and nudged Howard until he woke, she knew with a sense of utter certainty that something terrible was happening – and that it was not a dream.

At twelve forty-five Gifford came through to Irving's incident room and stood in the doorway until Irving had finished his telephone conversation with Captain Farraday.

'I have a name for you,' Gifford said.

'What name?'

'Name of the person that supposedly employed our friend Desmond to break into the Hill house.'

'He's still holding onto that?'

'He's still holding onto it yes, and I think you need to come and hear what he has to say.'

351

'Why? What's he telling you?'

'That it was Anthony Grant.'

Irving stopped dead. He shook his head for a moment, and then looked back at Gifford with disbelief. 'Anthony Grant?'

Gifford nodded. 'He said the guy was a lawyer, his name was Anthony Grant, and he paid Desmond Roarke two thousand dollars to break into Gregory Hill's house and find evidence that Hill had murdered Grant's daughter—'

Irving rose to his feet slowly, felt as if he might lose his balance. 'You can't be serious . . . you cannot be fucking serious . . .'

'Even gave the girl's name . . . Mia Grant. Clear as fucking daylight.'

'And?' Irving asked, his tone incredulous.

'He says that Grant thought Gregory Hill had killed her and there was evidence in the house.'

Naked, paralyzed with utter horror, barely able to stand as the man with the rifle held her hair, as he pushed the muzzle beneath her chin, Jean Allen looked back at her husband as he stood there, unable to speak, unable to think, unable to even look at what was taking place.

The rifleman marched Jean through to the hallway, told Howard to walk ahead of her, to make his way down to the end of the landing and step into the second bedroom.

It was fast. Breathlessly, unbelievably fast. The way he pushed them both into the room – Marcie and Leanne still sleeping, the house in darkness – and then he was standing there, no hesitation at all, and the sudden roar and flash of the gun as he shot both girls, one after the other, and Howard started screaming, and Jean was screaming too, and when Howard lunged forward to wrest the gun away the man just turned, and with the butt of the rifle he floored Howard with a single blow to the head. Jean looked down at her husband, the wide gash across his face already running with blood, and she went down like a stone. Fainted cold. The rifleman left them there on the floor. He took off at a run, one room to the next, shooting as he went, killing each of the remaining two children in turn before returning to the parents. He set his gun down on the floor, and one by one he carried Jean and

Howard back to their bedroom and lay them face down. Jean began to stir as he re-entered the room with the rifle. He shouldered the gun, took aim from a distance of two or three feet, and he executed her. Unmitigated, unequivocal, decisive.

He did the same to Howard. Wide symmetrical arcs of blood and brain matter were sprayed across the wall over the headboard.

From the moment he leaned over Jean Allen and pressed his hand over her mouth, to the moment he started back down the stairs to the front hallway, was less than two minutes.

He left behind him six dead. Two parents, four children.

It was sixteen minutes past midnight, early hours of November 13th.

FIFTY-EIGHT

At twelve fifty-five Ray Irving sat facing Desmond Roarke in an interview room at the Fourth Precinct. Roarke had pleaded for cigarettes, but had been given none. Twice he had used the bathroom, both times handcuffed, two officers with him, and aside from that he'd done nothing but argue back and forth with Detective Vernon Gifford about his rights, his access to legal counsel, about the fact that being found on someone's roof was – in and of itself – nothing more than a trespass charge. Away from the Hills' house he seemed to have regained some composure, even self-confidence, and whatever explanation he had given earlier about Anthony Grant, about being paid to break into the house to look for evidence, seemed to have been forgotten.

'You're going back,' Irving told Roarke emphatically. 'Whatever the hell charge we bring against you, you're still on parole, and any arrest means you go back.'

Roarke didn't respond.

'How much time is that? Another nine months?'

Once again, Roarke said nothing. He looked back at Irving contemptuously.

'And aside from the grand theft auto thing that we're gonna need to talk about, there's also the girl's murder—'

'What the fuck?' Roarke snapped, and stood up suddenly.

Gifford, behind him, grasped Roarke's shoulders and returned him forcibly to the chair.

'Hey, you were the one who used her name,' Irving said. 'Until her name came out of your mouth we had nothing to tie you to Mia Grant. Now we have at least sufficient to hold you while forensics takes a look at the stuff in your bag.' Irving looked up at Gifford. 'Wasn't the girl bound with duct tape . . . same tape as in Desmond's bag, right?'

'Exactly the same,' Gifford replied, and once again held Roarke down as he tried to get up from the chair.

'You're full of shit!' he snapped. 'You guys are so full of shit. You're just fishing on this. You have nothing, absolutely fucking nothing to tie me to some girl's murder.'

'Not what Grant says.'

'What?' Roarke said. 'What are you talking about?'

'Grant. Anthony Grant, right? We already spoke to him. Says he never heard of you—'

'That's bullshit, man, and you fucking know it. He was my defense lawyer—'

Irving looked up at Gifford. Gifford smiled.

'Whatever, Desmond . . . fact of the matter is that Anthony Grant has been very adamant in denying any knowledge of you. Says he never heard of Gregory Hill. Never spoke to you, never paid you any money. You don't think we didn't check this thing out soon as you mentioned it?'

'That fucking asshole . . . Jesus, man, what the fuck *is* this? This is some fucking railroad bullshit. He was the one who called me, said he needed me to do this thing, said he'd pay me . . .' Roarke tried to wrestle free from Gifford's grip on his shoulders, but Gifford held him still. 'I even have half the fucking money . . . half the fucking money up front, half the money when it was done.'

'And what exactly was it that he wanted you to do, Desmond?' Irving said.

'Check out the house,' Roarke replied. 'Go in there and check out the house. Said his daughter was killed by this freak, this Gregory Hill character. Said that his teenage daughter was killed by this whacko and I should go in the house and find something that belonged to the girl . . . prove it, you know? Prove that this guy was the one who did her.'

'And when was the last time you saw Anthony Grant?' Irving asked.

'See him? I never saw him. All done by phone. He called me last week, said he had a job for me, something simple. Said he needed me to go in some place and get something for

355

him. Said he'd stay in touch, call me when he knew exactly where it was, and that I should just make myself available.'

'And then he called you when?'

'This evening. Like eight o'clock or something. Gave me this guy's name and address, said I should go down there and get in the place. Said there'd be something like some clothes, maybe a piece of jewelry. He said there'd be no-one in the house, that the people were away. It wasn't a robbery or anything. It was just – well, like he was trying to get something that would nail this motherfucker for doing his teenage kid, you know? I figured it was a good thing, that I should do the guy a favor. He was a good lawyer. He looked after me, got me a community order for something that I shoulda done some time for.'

'So you didn't actually see him?' Irving asked. 'You didn't actually have a face-to-face with him?'

'Hell no, I ain't seen him since he was on my case four years ago.'

'So how did he get you the money, the half up front?'

'Put it in my mailbox, that was all. Brown paper envelope, bills inside, clean and new, and that was that. A thousand up front, a thousand when it was done.'

'And you never saw him?'

Roarke shook his head. 'No, I said that already. It was all on the phone. He calls me up, he tells me what he wants, we agree a price, he pays the half, I wait for the instructions. It ain't fuckin' rocket science.'

'So you have no way of knowing that it was definitely Grant that contacted you?'

'Sure it was Grant. Jesus, who the fuck else would it be? Some stranger calls me up, says he's gonna pay me two grand to break into someone's house just for the hell of it?'

Irving understood exactly what had happened. He rose from his chair. 'You're staying for a while,' he told Roarke. 'Keep your mouth shut and behave yourself.' He looked at Gifford. 'Get Grant in here now,' he said as he reached for the door.

'What the fuck?' Roarke said. 'You said you'd already spoken to Grant.'

Irving ignored Roarke, ignored his hollerings about his

rights, about legal representation, about violation of civil liberties.

Irving and Gifford hurried from the interview room and started up the stairs.

FIFTY-NINE

One-twenty a.m., and Anthony Grant sat across from Ray Irving in the detective's office. Irving could have taken him to the incident room, but there were photographs of his daughter on the cork board. He could have taken him to an interrogation cell, but he believed that Grant had nothing to do with Roarke's appearance at the Gregory Hill house. He also believed, though it was yet to be established, that Gregory Hill had never heard of Mia Grant, let alone had anything to do with her disappearance and ultimate murder.

'Desmond Roarke? Sure I know him. Defended him on some two-bit thing a few years ago. Why?'

Irving leaned back and felt the weight of the thing, the pressure, the fact that he was digging a hole that he knew would lead nowhere. Meanwhile, midnight had been and gone. It was the 13th of November.

'Because, Mr Grant, he has made a very serious accusation against you that we have to determine the validity of.'

'Accusation? Accusation about what?' Grant said.

Irving watched the man. Despite the defense lawyer presence, the skill he evidently possessed in hiding his hand until the final moment in cross-examinations and rebuttals, it appeared that Grant was genuinely surprised. Gifford had fetched him from his house, and Grant – despite the hour – had come willingly. Perhaps he had believed that it was something to do with his daughter, and it was, though not in the way Grant might have expected.

'That you paid him, or at least offered to pay him, two thousand dollars to break into someone's house and look for evidence relating to the death of your daughter.'

Grant frowned. And then he shook his head, and then he kind of did a double-take, and hesitated a few moments before asking, 'He said what?'

'I assume you didn't,' Irving said.

'God, man, I haven't spoken to Roarke since I defended him, and that was – when? Four years ago? He said I paid him to break into someone's house? Whose house?'

'I'm sorry, I can't tell you that, but nevertheless I'm going to need your co-operation, Mr Grant. I need to verify that no calls were made from your phone to Desmond Roarke.'

'What? From my landline? My cellphone? That won't prove a goddamned thing. I could have called him from a phone booth, or a single-use cellphone . . . any number of places.'

'Sure you could,' Irving said, 'but I have to start somewhere. I have a case to build against someone, and I need as much evidence to exclude people as I do to include them. I know you understand the situation.'

'So how does this relate to Mia?' Grant said. 'Does this bring you any closer to finding out what happened to her?'

Irving hesitated for a moment.

'It doesn't, does it?' Grant said. He sighed deeply, lowered his head, and when he looked up Irving could see the depth of shadows beneath the man's eyes, the fact that he was carrying a burden comparable to his own, but with Grant it was so much closer to home.

'I employed a PI,' Grant said.

Irving's eyes widened in surprise. 'You did what?'

'What the fuck did you expect me to do?' Grant said. 'My daughter is dead. My wife is a mess, Detective, an absolute mess. Five months and we have nothing. Mia died back in June. It's now November. You have any idea—' Grant shook his head and looked down. 'No, you don't, do you? You have absolutely no idea what it's like to lose a child.'

Irving didn't speak.

'So I hired someone, and he made some inquiries, and no, they've come to nothing, so at least I know that you didn't miss anything obvious—'

'Mr Grant, I assure you that we're doing—'

'Everything you possibly can. Sure, Detective, I've heard it so many times, how you're doing everything you can. I don't want to hear that any more.' Grant rose from his chair and buttoned his overcoat. He was unshaven, his hair was

359

tousled. He wore odd socks – one brown, one black – and the kind of moccasins that you slipped on to empty the trash, not to visit a precinct house.

'I need to ask you not to leave the city,' Irving said.

Grant buried his hands in his pockets. He shrugged his shoulders. 'Where the hell would I go, Detective? I've got nowhere *to* go. I want to see the end of this thing more than anyone. I want to know who killed my daughter, and why.'

'I have to tell you, Mr Grant, that it's sometimes the case—'

'That you never actually find out who did it? Is that what you're going to tell me?'

'It's unfortunately the truth, Mr Grant.'

'I know,' Grant replied. 'I'm a lawyer. I spend my life defending people like Desmond Roarke. I see both sides of it, and sometimes I wonder which is worse, you know? No offense intended, but I read through case files where the investigative work is just bullshit amateur—' He stopped mid-sentence. 'I'm going to leave now, Detective Irving, before I say something that both of us are going to regret.'

Grant held out his hand. Irving took it and they shook.

'Have to go home and tell my wife that there's no news.'

'I'm sorry, Mr Grant, I really am.'

Grant nodded, but said nothing.

'Oh, Mr Grant? The name of the PI you hired.'

'Roberts. Karl Roberts.'

'And he's based here in New York.'

'Yes,' Grant replied. 'I'm sure you'll find him in the Yellow Pages.'

Irving showed Grant out, and moments later tracked down Gifford in the incident room.

'Get me Gregory Hill,' Irving said. 'Wherever he is, whatever they're doing with him, I need him now.'

SIXTY

'We're being played . . . we're being played like a fucking orchestra,' Irving said.

He dropped into the chair facing Gifford. A squad had been sent out to the address at East 35th and Third to get Gregory Hill. Forensics were all over the place down there, trying to find anything at all that might connect Hill to Grant or vice versa.

'There's no connection between Greg Hill and Anthony Grant. I'm sure of it,' Irving said. 'Our anniversary guy called up Desmond Roarke and said he was Grant. He set Roarke do this thing tonight. Picked a family of six—'

'You think that's all there is to it?' Gifford asked. 'He wanted us to know he could get to a family of six?'

Irving didn't reply. He could never have been so optimistic. The man they were dealing with had murdered eleven – all the way from the Grant girl to the unidentified 'orange socks' girl.

Irving glanced at his watch. It was approaching two a.m. It would be November the 13th for another twenty-two hours. He walked to the board on the wall, looked at each of the victims' faces in turn, and wondered for the thousandth time at the insanity of someone who believed that such destruction and horror was their true calling. This would be their legacy, just like Shawcross and Bundy and Henry Lee Lucas and the others. Too many others . . .

'You get the ID on the last one yet?' Gifford asked.

Irving shook his head. 'No, we still don't know who the fuck she was . . . two weeks now.'

The internal line rang. Gifford picked it up. He listened, thanked whoever was on the line, and then hung up.

'He's here,' he said. 'Gregory Hill.'

*

Hill was still visibly shaken. He was one of the several hundred people who'd been reached by Irving's operation. He'd been contacted four days earlier regarding the potential danger to himself and his family, and had been particularly alert to any untoward occurrences in the vicinity of his property. It was this alertness that had been Desmond Roarke's undoing, for the moment that Hill had heard something from the direction of the garage he'd called 911.

'We appreciate your coming down here,' Irving told him. 'I understand that this has been a very traumatic experience for you and your family.'

'Un-fucking-real,' Hill said. 'Was he the guy you were looking for? The one that the police warned me about last week?'

'We don't know yet,' Irving said. 'But your vigilance at least resulted in his arrest. We are obviously very grateful for your co-operation—'

'Hey, no problem. Whoever the fuck he was he was trying to break into my house. If you guys hadn't come to see me last week and told me about this I doubt I'd have even been awake. We're just really appreciative, you know? A little shook up, but thankful that it wasn't one hell of a lot worse.'

'If it's okay with you, Mr Hill, I wanted to check a few things with you. I could wait until tomorrow, but I always figure it's best to get these formalities out of the way as early as possible so you can get back to your life.'

Hill nodded.

'Anthony Grant,' Irving said matter-of-factly.

Hill frowned. 'What about him?'

Irving's expression visibly changed. 'You know a Mr Anthony Grant?'

'The lawyer? *That* Anthony Grant?'

Irving looked at Gifford. Gifford looked like a hare in headlights.

'The lawyer, yes. You're telling me you know him, Mr Hill?'

'What the fuck is this? Has that asshole got something to do with this? Did he have something to do with this guy trying to break into my house?'

'Well . . . well we thought not, Mr Hill, but now you're saying you know him?'

Hill started to get out of his chair, and then he sat down again. 'Jesus, man, what *is* this? Tell me what the fuck is going on here? How the fuck is he connected to this?'

'Calm down a minute, Mr Hill,' Irving said, finding it very difficulty to remain calm himself. 'Tell me how you know Anthony Grant.'

Hill crossed his arms on the table, and then leaned forward and rested his forehead against them. 'Fucking asshole,' he said under his breath. 'Fucking asshole—'

'Mr Hill?' Irving prompted.

Hill looked up suddenly. There were tears in his eyes. 'Five years ago,' he said, his voice an angry whisper. 'Five years ago he . . . my wife . . . shit, fuck! Asshole motherfucker!'

'He what, Mr Hill?'

'He had an affair with my wife, okay? Anthony fucking Grant had an affair with my wife. That's what he did. Damned near ruined my fucking life!'

Irving nodded at Gifford. Gifford nodded back, already on his way to the door.

Irving waited until he was alone with Gregory Hill, and then he leaned forward, put his hand on Hill's arm, and said, 'Tell me, Mr Hill. Tell me exactly what happened.'

SIXTY-ONE

It was the better part of an hour before Irving, Gifford and Anthony Grant were reunited at the Fourth Precinct. Grant was agitated, having been fetched from his home for the second time, and though he'd been told only that there were other questions that needed to be answered, that no, they could not wait until morning, he had been relatively compliant. The usual bluff and bravado that spouted from the mouths of lawyers was evident by its absence.

At ten past three in the morning, Ray Irving sat down across from Anthony Grant and asked him a simple question that changed the man's color and broke a sweat on his forehead.

'Tell me, Mr Grant . . . tell me about Laura Hill.'

Grant, visibly anxious, opened his mouth to speak, and then closed it once more. He looked at Irving, turned and looked at Vernon Gifford, and then asked if he needed a lawyer.

Irving shook his head. 'We're not charging you with anything, Mr Grant, because right now we have nothing to charge you with. However, if you don't tell me the truth right now then we're looking at obstruction at the very least—'

Grant raised his hand. 'Tell me something,' he said. 'Did Greg Hill have anything to do with what happened to my daughter?'

'Why on earth would you think such a thing, Mr Grant?'

'Because of what happened with Laura. Because I had an affair with Hill's wife.'

'Why didn't you mention this earlier, Mr Grant?'

'Is this the house that was broken into? What I'm supposed to have paid Desmond Roarke for?'

'Time to answer some questions, Mr Grant, not ask them. What happened between you and Laura Hill?'

'We had an affair.'

'How long ago?'

'Five years, a little more than five years ago.'

'And how long did this affair last?'

'Seven, eight months . . . it ended noisily.'

'Meaning?'

'Her husband found out and beat the shit out of her.'

'Your wife didn't know?'

'No, she didn't know.' Grant closed his eyes, and for a moment looked utterly overwhelmed. 'Evelyn didn't know, I'm sure of that. But I think Mia might have known.'

'Why do you think that?'

'Just my perception. She was a bright girl, very bright indeed, and one time I picked her up from school after I'd been with Laura Hill and Mia said I smelled of perfume. I said it must have been a client. She laughed, said that I was getting too close to my clients. It was just the way she said it, that was all.'

'Hence your failure to mention it earlier.'

'Mention what earlier? That I had an affair with someone? You didn't ask me about that, and you didn't mention Greg Hill. You didn't tell me that that was the house where you caught Roarke—'

'I haven't told you now, Mr Grant.'

Grant smiled knowingly, and shook his head. 'You can't pull this shit on me, Detective Irving. The mere fact that you have asked me about Laura Hill tells me that it was the Hills' house that Roarke was trying to break into . . . otherwise where the fuck would her name have come from?'

Irving nodded patiently. 'Okay,' he said. 'Cards on the table for once. Desmond Roarke was arrested trying to break into the home of Gregory and Laura Hill. Are you going to tell me that you know nothing about this?'

'Yes, Detective, I am. I know *nothing* about this. You think I set Roarke up to break into that house?'

'It's a possibility, yes.'

'What on earth for?'

'Because you believed that Hill might have had something

to do with the death of your daughter . . . because you thought there might be some evidence in the house.'

'Jesus Christ, that's stretching it a bit. You think Greg Hill killed Mia? For revenge you mean, to get back at me for sleeping with his wife? Well, if that's the case then why the hell did he wait five years?'

'Maybe he didn't mean to kill her? Maybe he intended to assault her sexually and he killed her by mistake—'

Irving watched as Grant clenched and unclenched his fists, as he breathed deeply – in and out, in and out, trying to do all he could to center himself, to keep himself in check, to withhold his rage and hatred.

'If Greg Hill . . .' Grant paused, opened his eyes, looked back at Irving.

'You said that Greg Hill beat his wife.'

'Yes, he beat the shit out of her repeatedly, Detective. He beat her so many times she could barely speak for a fortnight.'

'And she reported this?'

Grant laughed. 'Report it? Report it to whom?'

'To us. To the police.'

'Did she, hell! No, she did not report it. What the fuck do you think that would have done, eh? You think that would have solved the problem? The guy was insane with rage. He was always a jealous bastard, but when he found out that she was having an affair he threatened to kill her, threatened to kill me—'

'You're serious?'

'Of course I'm serious. You don't think I'm making this up?'

'So if he beat her, and he threatened to kill her, and he threatened to kill you as well . . . does it not then seem possible that he was capable of killing your daughter, even if it was unintentional?'

Grant didn't reply. He looked away toward the door, and when he turned back to Irving there were tears in his eyes. 'Possible?' Grant shook his head. 'I don't know anymore what is and isn't possible, Detective. I've lost my only child. My wife is devastated, my marriage is coming apart at the seams. Now, as if this wasn't enough, the fact that I had an affair with someone five years ago is going to be dredged up again—'

'And you're concerned that your wife will find out about it?'

Grant used the cuff of his shirt to wipe his eyes. 'I think she has more than enough to deal with already, don't you?'

By four Irving was coming apart himself. He sat at his desk in the incident room, Hill and Anthony Grant having returned to their respective homes, both of them cautioned that they were to remain within the city, that there would be further questions.

'In essence,' he told Vernon Gifford, 'we have cir-cumstantial evidence and hearsay. There's nothing to prove that Grant did or didn't contact Roarke. Roarke never spoke to him directly, and voices . . . well, what someone said on the telephone is about as inadmissible as it comes as far as evidence is concerned. The fact that Hill beat his wife is simply hearsay from Grant. We can speak to Laura Hill tomorrow, but . . .' Irving shook his head. 'Who the fuck knows, eh? Old wounds have been opened up. She might talk, she might not. If her husband *is* the crazy fuck that Grant says he is then she might be too scared to say a thing.'

'You figure him for the Grant girl's killing?'

'I don't,' Irving said. 'I figure him for being an asshole, but from what I've seen of him he seems . . .' Irving paused. 'I've got Jeff Turner over there. If there's something to find he'll find it. If Hill did the Grant girl then he did all of them, right? We're holding onto the certainty that this is the work of one man. All of them, right from Mia Grant to the one we don't even have a name for.' Irving indicated the cork boards ahead of him. 'You think someone like Gregory Hill would be capable of all of this?'

Gifford was shaking his head. 'I don't see it,' he said. 'I mean, shit, I've been wrong before but I don't see it on this one.'

'Which means that the whole thing is a set-up. The whole thing has been rigged by our anniversary killer . . . but for what purpose?'

'Our guy calls Roarke. He pretends he's Anthony Grant.

367

Roarke hasn't spoken to the guy for four years, he's not going to remember his voice. He's gonna take the guy's word for it, especially when there's money involved. So the killer tells Roarke to break into Hill's house.' Gifford paused for a moment. 'If that's what happened, then the killer must have known that we had the patrols out alerting these families . . .'

'That wasn't difficult to figure after Ellmann's statement on the TV.'

'Hell, Vernon, he warned us didn't he? He sent us a letter saying he was gonna do six—'

'And you think he's gone out and killed another six people? You think this was just a diversion?'

'I fucking hope not, Vernon, but like I said before, he seems to have no difficulty keeping his word.'

'Gonna be the thirteenth for a good while yet,' Gifford said, glancing at the clock above the door.

'You should go,' Irving said. 'Get a few hours if you can.'

'And leave you with this? No, I'm not bailing out until we've seen the day through to the end.'

'Doesn't mean anything,' Irving said. 'He killed one girl in an apartment on Montgomery Street and we didn't find her for twelve days.'

'Don't matter,' Gifford said. 'You're staying then I'm staying.'

Irving got up and walked to the window. Early mornings, late nights, all of them blurring seamlessly one into another, and all because of one man. Was that man Gregory Hill? Irving doubted it, but nevertheless he had the Hill family securely ensconced in two upstairs rooms while Turner and his people went through the house with a fine-toothed comb, ostensibly to determine whether there was any further evidence to incriminate Desmond Roarke on his B&E, but in truth to find out whether there was more they needed to know about Gregory Hill.

And that anonymous caller? The one who pretended to be Anthony Grant and who paid Roarke to find something in the Hill house? That could very well have been Grant's PI, this Karl Roberts character. Acting a little beyond the parameters of the law, a little further than the limits of his brief. It had been known. But as of that moment Irving possessed neither the mental energy nor the resources to pursue the man. He would deal with it once the night was over, once they knew if the attempted break-in at the Hill house was all they'd have to deal with tonight . . . or if there was something else far worse awaiting them.

SIXTY-TWO

Had Vernon Gifford acquiesced to Ray Irving's suggestion that he go home, he would have been called back before he'd even reached his apartment.

At four fifty-eight a.m., early morning of Monday, November 13th, a call came in to the Second Precinct. At first the operator had difficulty understanding the caller, for he said the same hurried sequence of words over and over again, and after asking the caller to repeat the message slowly, she finally determined that he was saying 'Fourteen forty-eight, East 17th. Tell Ray Irving once I started, I just couldn't stop. It went so fast . . .'

Once the caller had established that his message had been understood, he hung up. The call would ultimately be traced back to a phone booth on East 17th, but by the time Irving received word, by the time black-and-whites had been dispatched, by the time he and Vernon Gifford had established that there was no response from the house at fourteen forty-eight, East 17th Street, whoever might have made that call had long since gone. The phone booth would be cordoned, photographed, even the coinbox carefully emptied, and each of the thirty-one coins within would be printed. It would give up nothing.

'Allen,' Gifford told Irving, as they stood outside that house. 'Howard and Jean Allen.'

There was nothing but silence. The flashing light-bars reflected in the windows of the property lent the scene an eerie carnival atmosphere.

Nothing so scary as a clown after dark, Irving thought, remembering how James Wolfe's painted face had looked up at him from a hole in the ground.

It was five thirty-six. Farraday had been alerted, had been

apprized of the Anthony Grant/Gregory Hill situation, had authorized any action that Irving felt necessary.

'Get the fuck into that house,' he'd said. 'If it turns out there's no-one there we'll repair whatever damage is done . . . just get in there and tell me we don't have another six dead people.'

Irving was still for a moment, and then he looked back at Gifford. He knew there was something else, something he really didn't want to hear.

Gifford looked away, didn't want to face Irving. 'Four kids,' he said, his voice restrained.

Irving lowered his head, his heart a tight knot in his chest. 'No,' he said, solely to himself, but Gifford was nodding. Irving had received the message from dispatch, and he knew exactly what it meant. *Once I started, I just couldn't stop. It went so fast.*

'Four kids,' Gifford repeated, and then waved over the two patrol officers who had just emerged from the rear of the lot.

'All locked up,' the first one said. 'Looks like the back door is alarmed, but it's a hell of a lot less work to get through there than the front.'

'No response on the phone?' Irving asked.

'Nothing sir,' the officer replied. 'We've had the phone ringing for a good five or ten minutes.'

'We'll go in through the back,' Irving said.

The patrol officers led the way, the detectives following, and two further officers called to assist from a second squad car.

Irving took a leather glove from his overcoat pocket, slipped it on, and then selected a fist-sized stone from the yard at the rear of the house. Before he punched a hole through the small pane of glass nearest the lock he looked up at Gifford.

'Do it,' Gifford said. 'Let's get it over with.'

The pane went through with the first strike, and even as Irving opened the door, the alarm strangely silent, the house cold and dark within, he had a premonition and a sense of foreboding that he all too easily recognized.

371

He turned to Gifford before he'd even crossed the threshold.

'Call Jeff Turner,' he said quietly. 'Call him and tell him I'm gonna need him.'

Gifford went back to the nearest squad car and put a call through to dispatch. While he waited he looked up at the rear of the property, noticed the severed alarm wiring beneath the shadow of the gutter. Whatever sense of optimism he might have felt – that it was a hoax call, that they were going to find nothing but an empty building – rapidly evaporated.

Irving, meanwhile, stood in the cool silence of the Allens' kitchen. It was a kitchen not unlike so many others in a thousand homes across the city. The refrigerator door was peppered with magnets, one of them a crude smiley-face in black and yellow. A child had made it, no doubt, more than likely one of the Allen kids. A crude splotch of color with legs and a barely recognizable plumed head adorned another sheet of yellow construction paper that had been pinned to the wall. Beneath the picture was the word *turkey*, a mixture of lower and upper case letters, the final *y* sliding off the corner of the page. A Thanksgiving painting from pre-school activities.

The tight knot that was Irving's heart now felt like a cold fist.

He turned to the two officers behind him, read their names from the tags above the breast pocket – Anderson and Maurizio.

'You stay here,' he said to Maurizio. 'Wait for Gifford and search this floor and the basement. Look for any sign of forced entry. And you,' he said to Anderson. 'You come to the upper floor with me.'

At the head of the stairs Irving knew. Almost without hesitation he isolated the single smear of blood on the doorjamb to his right. He turned and raised his hand. Anderson came to a halt on the last tread but one.

'Let me see what we've got,' Irving said quietly. 'At this point the fewer people up here the better.'

Anderson nodded but didn't speak. There was something

in his expression that belied his considerable size. Irving recognized it. Anderson was young, still retained some small belief in the balance of things, pretended to himself that things turned out right more often than wrong. He didn't want to see what was waiting for them on the upper floor of fourteen forty-eight East 17th Street. He would have bad dreams. The cynicism would start its work – slowly, inexorably – and within a decade, if he stayed with it, he would look and sound like Irving.

The relief in Anderson's expression quickly dissolved as he watched Irving push open the first door with his gloved hand.

'Oh my God . . .' Anderson heard him say, and the feeling that suddenly radiated outward from his lower gut, a feeling that seemed to render every muscle in his body utterly useless, was one he would never forget.

Later he would get to see the bodies, and he knew there would be nightmares.

Jeff Turner arrived at six-eleven a.m. He met Irving in the back yard.

'Nothing in the Hill house,' he said. 'But I s'pose Gregory Hill can't be your man now, can he?'

Irving looked up at the windows of the Allens' house. 'This happened recently,' he said. 'Sometime in the last few hours. Certainly during the time Hill was home with his family. Greg Hill couldn't have a better alibi.'

'I heard word Grant was connected, the father of the first girl?'

'It was all a set-up,' Irving replied. 'Or not. Jesus, who the fuck knows? There's a possibility Grant's PI—'

'His PI?'

'He hired a PI,' Irving explained. 'Wanted to make sure we hadn't missed anything obvious. Anyway, that's not the issue right now.'

'And the fact that Hill has a wife and four kids, and Roarke tries to break in tonight of all nights . . . we're saying that this is a coincidence?'

'We're not saying anything right now, Jeff. Right now—'

'Right now we're just delaying the inevitable.'
'We are.'
'You coming in with me?' Turner asked.
'Yes,' Irving said. 'It's bad . . . real bad.'

SIXTY-THREE

Jeff Turner was not a native New Yorker. He hailed originally
from California, graduated from U.C. Berkeley with a degree
in Criminalistics and Criminal Science, transferred to New
York after serving two years' apprenticeship at CSA Level I in
the San Francisco Sheriff's Department, made CSA Level II at
thirty-three. Turner was now close to forty-four, back of him
a decade of further studies, a three-year term in the Scientific
Investigation Division under the aegis of Support Services,
further qualifications and certificates in Photographic, Latent
Print, Electronics, Questioned Document, Toxicology, Peer
Review and Supervision. He was single, childless, collected
baseball cards, and watched Marx Brothers movies. He had
seen everything there was to see in San Francisco and in New
York, and if he'd not seen it in actuality he'd seen it in stills,
on video, on 16mm, in digital.

Turner's life was populated with the dead. He understood
the dead far better than he'd ever understood the living. The
dead spoke to him without words. They told him things they
never would have communicated in life. And though he was
not a religious man, he nevertheless believed in the fundamental spirituality of Man. He credited some higher power
with the foresight and imagination to make Man something
more than a hundred and sixty pounds of hamburger with
a chemical street value of nineteen dollars. And throughout
his career there had been moments. That was all he could
say. *Moments.* The feeling that somewhere in the vicinity of
the body, the person themself was still there. Looking down
at him. Perhaps hoping that he, in his infinite wisdom, might
give them some understanding of why this terrible thing had
happened to them. The spirit of the individual? The soul? Jeff
Turner didn't know. He didn't try to know. He just sensed
what he sensed, perceived what he perceived. And on the

upper floor of the Allen house, in the hour or so between his arrival and when he completed his initial examination of the six bodies present, he believed he'd experienced more *moments* in that one period than all the others combined.

When Deputy Coroner Hal Gerrard arrived, his presence required by law before the bodies could be moved or examined further, he found Jeff Turner standing in the kitchen, his face pale, his eyes glassy, a thin film of sweat across his forehead.

'How many you got?' Gerrard asked.

'Six in all,' Turner replied. 'Mom, Dad, four kids. Youngest seven, oldest thirteen. Fatal GSW, headshots, all of them . . . looks like a .38, but Irving says it's gonna be a .35 rifle.'

Gerrard frowned.

'He was expecting this,' Turner explained.

'I'm not gonna ask,' Gerrard replied. He looked around the kitchen, out through the window into the back yard. 'And he is where?'

'Talking to Farraday from the car.'

'You need anything other than the usual from me?'

Turner shook his head. 'Just pronounce dead, authorize a full examination. I'm gonna need to move them to get my team through every room. Find what we can, you know? Take pictures of everything.'

Gerrard paused for a moment before making his way to the stairs. 'You okay?'

Turner shrugged. 'Kids. It's the kids that get to me. Even after all these years . . .'

'I know, Jeff, I know exactly what you mean.'

Irving came in through the back kitchen door. He greeted Gerrard, told Turner that Farraday and Chief Ellmann wanted the crime scene processed as rapidly as possible. 'Said he would authorize however many people you need.'

'More people than I've got is not gonna help me,' Turner said. 'I have two CSAs, that's enough.'

'I'll do what I need to and get out of your way,' Gerrard said.

Irving looked at his watch; it was seven forty-two.

'How long since you slept?' Turner asked him.

Irving smiled – sort of. 'I don't remember,' he said.

'Who's on this with you?'

'Vernon Gifford, Ken Hudson if I need him.'

'From what I've seen so far there isn't a great deal I can give you—'

'Anything is good,' Irving said. 'Anything at all, Jeff . . . because right now we have nothing.'

Irving and Gifford waited in the kitchen.

Hal Gerrard was done and gone within twenty minutes. He shared a few words with Irving before he signed the necessary forms and left.

'I called Ken Hudson,' Gifford said. 'I've got him tracking down this PI that Grant hired. Told him we might need to follow up on this Greg Hill thing as well, whether or not there's an abuse situation.'

'The PI, yes,' Irving replied. 'Don't go near the Hill situation until we know what's happening here. Right now it looks like they're not connected, and I don't want to stir anything else up.'

'We have a TOD yet?'

'Somewhere between midnight and one,' Irving said.

'And Hill called us at what time?'

'We had squad cars on East 35th at ten-fifty, give or take.'

'So Hill is out of the frame for this.'

'He is,' Irving said, and then looked up toward the ceiling as the sound of footsteps echoed through from the landing, the bathroom, the master bedroom. Turner and his two CSAs were up there, would be up there as long as it took, and then they would have something. Or they would have nothing.

'Gotta make a call,' Irving said. 'Stay here, I'll be back in a moment.'

Gifford sat down at the kitchen table. Irving left by the rear door, walked around the side of the house and got in the car.

He sat there for a minute, and then reached for his cellphone and dialed a number.

It rang four or five times before it was answered.

'John? It's Ray Irving . . .'

Costello didn't speak.

A moment's further silence, and then Irving said, 'He did it . . . Mom and Dad and four kids. Killed all of them.'

SIXTY-FOUR

Turner came down to the kitchen a few minutes before seven-thirty. He sat at the table across from Irving and Gifford, and spread out a sheet of paper on which he'd drawn a plan of the upper floor, the position of each room, an outline where each body had been found.

'You were right on the .35 caliber,' he said. 'Looks like he woke up the parents, made them walk ahead of him from one room to the next. As far as I can tell he shot the two youngest girls, then the boy, finally the eldest girl. Mom and Dad were last—'

'He made them watch their own kids being executed?' Gifford said, his tone incredulous.

'Looks that way. The dad has a wide gash on his head, looks like the butt of the rifle. Maybe he tried to get the gun away from the killer and he hit him down. Either that, or he shot the kids, the sound woke the parents, and he came into their room as they were getting up. Made them lie down again, and then shot them. It's not possible to determine the precise sequence of events from the physical evidence, but as far as I can figure it happened one of those two ways. My guess, for what it's worth, is the former not the latter.'

'Far as we can tell he came in through the back door,' Irving said. 'He disabled the alarm outside, cut the wiring just beneath the eaves, and then picked the lock. He knew what he was doing. There's barely a mark on the cover or the striker plate.'

'I cannot believe that the guy just walked in here and executed an entire family,' Gifford said, still stunned, still in disbelief.

Turner seemed not to hear him; he didn't comment or reply. He looked back over his shoulder toward the stairs as if

379

he'd heard something, and then he gave Irving a brief summary of what he had been able to determine.

'As you can imagine there are partials everywhere. We've printed the entire family for elimination, but the bulk are transfers, smudges, overlays, the usual traffic you'd get in a residential property. Every room is carpeted except the bathroom. That's floored in linoleum, but it's heavily embossed, too ridged for footprints to be determined. There are no shell casings, but entry wounds tell me he used a .35 rifle. It's different from a .38 even though the caliber is so close. They were all hit at close range, less than four feet in each instance. Death would have been instant, no question. Blood spatter tells me that all of them were recumbent. Rifle could have been silenced, so no-one got out of bed or sat up as a result of the noise. No indication that any of the bodies were touched post mortem. We'll autopsy of course, but I don't think that'll give you anything we haven't already got as far as COD is concerned.'

'And the house?' Irving asked.

'We'll do the whole thing,' Turner said. 'Back door, rear of the building, under the eaves, everywhere there's indications of physical contact, but you know how this goes, right?'

'Right,' he echoed, fatigue and desperation coloring his voice. 'Won't make any difference now, but I'd like to know if these people were visited, if they were on the list of families that were warned.' He rose to his feet, feeling the immense weight of his burden. 'We're going to do the street,' he said.

'Best of luck,' Turner said.

They went out together, Irving and Gifford, and began the long and laborious process of canvassing the street. They took the first dozen houses on either side of fourteen forty-eight, Irving to the left, Gifford to the right, and then the houses opposite. They made notes of the empty properties for later visits, but they were fortunate in that the majority of residents had not yet left for work. Not so fortunate in the number of people who had seen or heard anything out of the ordinary. By nine-thirty they still had nothing of significance. Farraday had paged Irving three times, but Irving hadn't yet called him.

Nine-forty and Turner called Irving to let him know that

380

the bodies were coming out. By this time there was sufficient police activity to have attracted a gathering of onlookers on the sidewalk. Irving asked them to step back to make way for the gurneys, to let the coroner's staff and the forensics crew do their jobs uninterrupted. They complied, somewhat resentfully it seemed, as if it was their right to see what had happened. Fortunate they didn't see, Irving thought. Fortunate indeed.

Turner sent his own CSAs with the bodies, stayed behind to walk Irving and Gifford through the upper rooms, show them the precise position of where each body had been found, the route he thought the gunman had taken.

While Turner and Gifford talked in the master bedroom, Irving stood alone in the little boy's room for quite some time. Kid's name was Brandon. All of seven years old. A stack of X-Men DVDs were scattered beneath the player. Action figures sat on bookshelves and spilled from a nest of brightly colored storage boxes. A white snowman night-light still burned ever so faintly, and Irving stepped forward to flick off the switch with the toe of his shoe. November 13th, a handful of days to Thanksgiving, less than six weeks to Christmas. He imagined the boy had already made his list.

He looked around as Turner and Gifford appeared in the doorway.

'Anything?' Gifford asked.

Irving shook his head. 'Nothing.'

'Feeling I get,' Gifford said, 'is that if there's anything here it'll have been left intentionally.'

'Agreed,' Irving replied. He took one more look around the boy's room and walked back to the top of the stairs. 'We're heading to the Fourth,' he told Turner. 'Keep me posted on the autopsies. Gonna need the reports as soon as they're done.'

'I'll do my preliminaries as well,' Turner replied. 'I'll e-mail them to you direct.'

They parted company, Irving and Gifford to the car, Turner through the house once again to insure it was securely contained. A squad car would remain out front for the rest of the day, perhaps longer. They would prevent entry to the property, both by the press and that small and elite collective of individuals who violated crime scenes in order to steal artifacts and take pictures. Thinking of such people, Irving was reminded of the Hammer of God article, the complaint made by the owner of the auto-shop where Robert Clare had worked.

Gifford drove. Irving sat in silence. He saw action figures and blood spatter. That was all he saw. Couldn't get the image out of his head.

Action figures and blood spatter.

Irving spoke with Hudson as soon as he reached the incident room. Hudson had not yet located Anthony Grant's PI. He had a name, a cellphone number. Karl Roberts. That was all. Operated out of a one-room office on East 25th near the Manhattan Appellate Court. Hudson had gone down there, beat on the door until the tenant in the adjacent office came out to ask him what in God's name was going on. Grant had been contacted, was unaware of Roberts's whereabouts. Irving was not overly concerned at this stage. Roberts may or may not have given Desmond Roarke instructions to break into Greg Hill's home. It didn't matter how it had come about. Greg Hill was off their radar as far as the Allen killings were concerned. Irving had even considered that Mia Grant might have been murdered by Hill, and his MO had merely been coincidental with the original Kathy Sue Miller killing from 1973, but he'd immediately dismissed the possibility. Hadn't *The New York Times* 'Isaiah' letter that promised another six deaths made specific reference to Mia Grant, how she had gone *oh so very quietly into that long goodnight*? They were the same person – this was the only thing of which Irving was sure – and if Hill wasn't the Allens' killer, then he was out of the picture for all the others.

Irving's thoughts were more for his meeting with Bill Farraday than whatever else Ken Hudson might have had to say. He told Hudson to keep working on finding Grant's PI, and headed on up to the captain's office.

SIXTY-FIVE

'Karl Roberts,' Irving said. 'We have no way of knowing if he was involved until we track him down. Right now all we have is Desmond Roarke saying that it was Grant who called him. Grant says he hasn't spoken to the guy for four years and I'm inclined to believe him. We're having the phone records checked at Grant's house, but if it was Grant who set Roarke up I don't think he would have been so stupid as to have called Roarke from his own home.'

Farraday stood by the window, back to the room, hands in his pockets. 'So what do you make of it?'

'I think our killer did some digging on Grant, not only on his personal life but also on his client history. Grant said that Mia might have suspected him of having an affair. Maybe she knew more, maybe she knew that it was Laura Hill. There's always the possibility that Mia's killer made her tell him everything she knew about her father. And then from Grant's client history he tracked down Desmond Roarke and set him up to break into Greg Hill's house. Several things result. We get a false alarm on the six killings he spoke about in the Isaiah letter, Evelyn Grant more than likely finds out about the affair with Laura Hill, we have resources tied up investigating Hill and Roarke, and he reminds us how many steps ahead of us he is. He knows who we are. He knows I'm heading up this investigation. All it would take was seeing Chief Ellmann's statement, a little surveillance over the last week or so, check some of the addresses I've visited, look on the voters' register, put two and two together. He's not stupid. He clued us in on the six victims in his letter, and worked out what we would do.'

'And then there's the other matter,' Farraday said. He turned and faced Irving, walked to his desk and sat down.

'The bit about it becoming personal?'

Farraday nodded somberly. 'He said that it would be at least six, perhaps more, and after that it would get personal.'

'Far as I know we've had no other homicides reported in last night.'

'We haven't,' Farraday said, 'but that doesn't mean that they didn't take place. The Montgomery Street girl we didn't find for twelve days.'

'And the personal thing?' Irving said. 'That could mean me, or it could mean something else entirely.'

Farraday leaned forward. 'We now have a total of seventeen victims, almost conclusively attributable to one man. This is not going to stay off the radar any more. We cannot hold this thing down any longer. The police presence at the Hill address, again at the Allen crime scene . . . we had press down there, both locations, and they only need to speak to Desmond Roarke, maybe to Greg Hill, a few of the neighbors that you canvassed, and they'll start putting things together.'

'So – how long?'

Farraday turned his mouth down at the corners. 'A day? Two at best.'

'So I'm following up on the crime scene reports, the autopsies as well. I've got Ken Hudson tracking down Karl Roberts, see if he had anything to do with the Roarke break-in—'

'When I said a day or two, what I meant was that I'm going to have to make a statement in the next day or two. Once we make a statement we're in the headlines. That means we have to get something solid—'

Irving got up. He straightened his jacket. 'The only eyewitnesses I have are dead. The evidence I've got, certainly from the crime scenes, is not only circumstantial, it's inconclusive. I have a picture of someone dressed as a cop who may or may not be our guy, could even be someone who was paid to turn up in Central Park and photograph me and Costello—'

'Which brings me to the next point,' Farraday interjected. 'And sit the fuck down, will you?'

Irving did as he was told.

'So has this guy been of any use to you at all?'

'Sure he has.'

'So it's worth keeping him around?'

'If you need someone to justify why we did this—'

'Don't worry about justifying anything. The public don't give a fuck what we do as long as we get results. We hire the New England fucking Patriots to run this investigation and no-one will actually give a damn if we nail the guy.'

'I know that,' Irving replied. 'But you're asking me for something substantial, something probative, and you want it in the next twenty-four hours. The real truth of this entire situation is that it's been more than five months since Mia Grant was murdered and we have nothing—'

'*That* kind of statement stays inside this room,' Farraday said.

'I know it stays inside this room. Jesus, Bill, what the hell do you think is going on here?'

'So what do you need? Seriously. Your friends down at the *City Herald*, the vultures at *The Times* . . . they're going to be onto the Allen murders already. I mean, for God's sake, four kids have been killed in their beds. This is going to go down like . . . Jesus, I can't even imagine what the reaction's going to be, but with the political climate as it is now, with all these questions being raised in the Mayor's debates about police funding and God only knows what . . .'

'I know all about that,' Irving said. 'I just need people and time. That's all I need.'

'Time I can't give you. You've got Hudson and Gifford. Who else do you need?'

'I need at least six uniforms. I have a lot of houses, a lot of questions. I have missing people who might have been there last night. I have to follow up on the Greg Hill wife-beating thing. I have no shortage of fucking work, and true, some of it might be bullshit. This PI could have nothing at all, and the situation with Hill and his wife might be so far from relevant it's not even funny, but all of these things have to be followed up, and if I'm following them up then I'm not pursuing the direct line of inquiry with Jeff Turner. Our best hope is that we find something about the victims, something in the house that tells us a little more about who we're dealing with. It's a jigsaw puzzle, Bill . . . I mean, for God's sake, I don't need to tell you how this goes. This isn't TV show stuff. This doesn't start and finish within the hour with all the clues just lying there for Briscoe and Green to find—'

'Six gonna be enough?'

'For now, yes. I just need all these lines pursued, and I sure as shit don't have the time to do it. If I need more I'll let you know.'

'Who was at the Allen house with you?'

'Anderson and Maurizio.'

'Keep them. I'll give you Goldman, Vogel . . .' Farraday leaned forward and tugged a shift schedule from beneath a heap of papers on his desk. He scanned through the names. 'Anderson, Maurizio, Goldman, Vogel . . . and Saxon and O'Reilly. That's six. I need detailed reports. Everything you find. Then we'll review where we're going and reassign as needed. And if you need more detectives just holler. Where the fuck I'm going to get them from I don't know, but I will.'

Irving didn't speak.

'Now you can get up,' Farraday said. He looked at his watch. 'It's ten-fifty. Let me know where you're at by noon. Get the desk sergeant to round up these uniforms and you and Gifford can brief them in the incident room.'

SIXTY-SIX

Before the assigned crew arrived, Irving checked his inbox for any mail from Turner. There was nothing as yet.

Eight minutes past eleven he stood before the gathered detectives and officers in the incident room and began by outlining the case as it currently stood.

'I'm taking you off the Grant PI thing,' he told Ken Hudson. 'I need you to go see Gregory Hill. Anderson, you're with Ken. Talk to Hill, find out what, if anything, he really knows about Anthony Grant. Find out what the deal was with the affair. Apparently Hill beat his wife when he found out about it, but she didn't press charges against him so we have nothing on file. Find out what really happened. Speak to Laura Hill on that point if you need to, but right now I'm more interested in what Hill thinks about Grant. Was he holding on to a grudge? Is there anything that suggests he might have had sufficient hatred for Grant that he would harm his daughter? Once you're done with him I need you to get Laura Hill to tell us everything she can about Grant. How did she meet him, how long their affair went on for. Everything you can find, okay?'

Hudson and Anderson got up and left the room.

Irving turned to Detective Gifford. 'Vernon, take Maurizio with you . . . go see Anthony Grant. Get *his* take on the affair with Laura Hill. I want to know everything from his point of view. Remember that right now Evelyn Grant doesn't know about the affair, unless he's told her in the last few hours. Tread careful. The guy's a lawyer. I don't want any harassment suits.'

Gifford got up. 'What time do you need a progress report?'

'Most important thing is information. If you get these people talking don't worry about the time. When you get a chance, send me a text or something, give me some idea of what the deal is, okay?'

Maurizio followed Gifford from the room, and Irving waited until he could no longer hear their voices before turning back to the remaining four uniformed officers.

'Saxon, O'Reilly, I need you to pursue this Karl Roberts guy. You've got the address for his office there. Go chase him up. Speak to him, question him about Desmond Roarke. Does he know the guy? Ever heard of him? Have a look round without being too obvious. Get a feel for who he is, whether or not you think he might be involved in this. Find out what Grant told him about his daughter's murder when he was first hired. Ask a lot of questions. One of you talk, one of you write things down. He's a PI. He'll be used to questions. Experience tells me that these guys love the sound of their own voices.'

Saxon and O'Reilly got up.

Irving was left with Vogel and Goldman. 'You guys,' he said. 'I need you to follow up Desmond Roarke. He's still in the tank, but we're gonna arraign him in the next hour or so. Only reason we're hanging on to him is to get a warrant signed. We're gonna put a line on his phone, see who he calls, who calls him. You guys need to go get jeans and sweatshirts on and follow him. We're treating him as an indirect suspect in the murder case. A bit thin, but right now everyone's sufficiently wound up about this thing to let us get away with it. What we want to know is whether or not he receives any further calls from Anthony Grant, or someone pretending to be Grant. That's why the tap on his phone. Surveillance will deal with that from the Second – that's where the anonymous call about the Allen murders came in – and if Roarke gets anything incoming or outgoing that sends him out to visit someone, then that information will come to us directly so we can tail him.'

Irving looked back over his shoulder at the cork board, the faces of the victims, a space to the far right where a mother and father and four children would soon look back at him. 'My opinion, I don't think Desmond Roarke is directly involved in this, but he received calls from someone, and that someone could very well have been our man pretending to be Anthony Grant. Either that, or the PI that Grant hired went a little beyond his brief. Either which way, it doesn't matter. We need every base covered.'

Vogel and Goldman got up. Goldman thanked Irving for the assignment, the expression in his eyes all-too-obvious. He was after making detective – Vice, Homicide, Narco, it didn't matter. The vast majority of these guys figured that anything less than that was nothing. Irving watched them go, and believed that as of that moment speeding tickets and domestic disturbances were an infinitely more attractive proposition.

Irving called Jeff Turner's office, left a message that he would now be away from the office, that he could be reached on his cell. He then called Farraday's assistant, told her that he would be back before one, that Farraday had expected a report at noon but he needed an extra hour.

He gathered what notes he had on the Allen killings and drove away from the Fourth toward the offices of the *City Herald*. The traffic on 34th was not too bad, and he reached 31st and Ninth by ten of noon. He wanted to see Karen Langley. He wanted to see her simply because she made him feel more human. John Costello was a different matter however. In all truth, he did not want to see Costello. He *needed* to see him.

SIXTY-SEVEN

'Your guess is as good as mine,' Karen Langley said. 'I can't remember how many times I've called, but no answer.'

'I spoke to him this morning,' Irving said. 'Must have been about eight. I told him about the Allen killings—'

'He never failed to show up for work before. In the time that you have known him he has done it twice.'

Irving assumed a somewhat sardonic expression, and sat down. 'I don't think you can hold me responsible for that, Karen—'

'You don't think that this stuff affects him? He's been through this sort of thing himself. Personally, you know? Not like us. It can't be the same for him, can it?'

'Appears to me that he made his own choices a long time ago. You've got to remember, he was the one who did the research on the original article that brought you and me together.'

'But that's the point, Ray. He does this stuff at arm's length. That's how he deals with what happened to him. He's a spectator, not a participant, and you've put him in a situation where he has to be involved—'

'You're talking about Central Park? He *wanted* to go out there, Karen. You make it sound like I forced him.'

'You obligated him, Ray. You made him feel like he could do something to help, and that was all it took. He's a child, Ray, that's the truth. This thing happened to him, and everything since then has been carefully constructed to make sure it never happens again . . .'

Karen Langley looked away toward the window, pensive for a moment, almost sad, and when she turned back to Irving it appeared that her defenses had come down a little.

'I don't even know what I'm talking about,' she said. 'I've worked with him all these years and I don't even know who he is. I say these things because I don't have any other explanation for his behavior. He doesn't go out, except to this meeting with these other victims at the hotel. He doesn't have a girlfriend, has never had one as far as I know . . . not since her. Not since he was with—'

'Nadia McGowan,' Irving interjected.

'Right. Nadia. He told me once that it was Russian for hope.'

'Ironic.'

'No, Ray, not ironic. Just very fucking sad, that's all. His whole life has actually been really fucking sad, and I often wonder why he isn't totally insane. Sometimes I wonder what it would have been like to go through that, to be in that situation, the things that would go through your mind after the fact. The explanations you would try and find for yourself to help deal with it.' She sighed audibly. 'It's a mess, and that's the truth, and the only thing that I figured was keeping him sane was working here, you know? Doing something that he could do in an environment where people just let him be who he was . . . and right now it looks like even that is under threat as a result of what's happening.'

'So how do we best reach him?' Irving asked.

'Well, I can't help you,' Karen said. 'I'd go over there, but right now I don't have time to breathe. He'll show up sooner or later, and I'm sure he'll have a perfectly acceptable explanation for his disappearance—'

She stopped mid-flight when she saw Irving's sudden change of expression.

'What?' she said.

'You remember the letter?' Irving said. He was standing up then, standing slowly.

'The letter to *The Times*? Sure I do,' she said. 'What about it?'

'He said he was going to kill six people, maybe more, and then he was going to get personal.'

'You think—'

'He was there in Central Park wasn't he? Either he was, or he sent someone to take pictures of me and John.'

'You think he's after John? You think that's what he meant?'

391

Irving didn't reply. He was already at the door.

'Jesus, Ray . . . no, for God's sake . . .'

Irving didn't hear her because he was already running, the sound of his feet on the stairwell, his cellphone in his hand, already speed-dialing the Fourth to get a squad car out to 39th and Ninth, the third floor apartment near St Raphael's Church in the Garment District.

Like John Costello had told him, every single day was an anniversary for someone's death.

Howard and Jean Allen could have vouched for that.

SIXTY-EIGHT

Vogel was recalled from the Roarke stake out, O'Reilly from the interview with Anthony Grant. Irving called Farraday from the car and requested he expedite an At Risk warrant on John Costello's apartment.

'Jesus, Ray, that shit is for abused kids, not newspaper researchers who didn't show up for work—'

Irving cut him short, explained his fear, that the threat to get personal may already have become more than just a threat.

Farraday said to move ahead with the operation, that he would handle the paperwork.

Irving arrived at Costello's apartment building at five of one. He went up the stairs with his gun drawn, his senses attuned to every sound in the place, and had already knocked several times without any response by the time Vogel and O'Reilly arrived.

'There's another black-and-white out back,' Vogel told Irving. 'If you need them on the back stairway—'

'Tell them which apartment,' Irving said. 'Tell them to stay silent, that we may not need them to access, but be alert for anyone trying to leave.'

Irving banged on the door again, called Costello's name, identified himself, waited patiently for any sound from within.

Five minutes later, he nodded to O'Reilly. The officer had brought the hydraulic punch from the car, came forward to position it over the lock. He switched it on, and there was a whining sound for a few seconds before it lit up green on top.

Irving stepped back, hollered Costello's name one more time, waited for a handful of seconds and then gave the go-ahead to O'Reilly.

O'Reilly fired the punch, and with a sound like a gunshot a

hole was driven through the door. O'Reilly stepped back, and the section of door containing the lock fell through into the interior of the apartment. The door, however, remained rigidly in place.

'Deadbolts above and below,' O'Reilly said, and Irving stepped back as he reached through the hole and felt along the doorframe.

Within a moment Ray Irving stood on the threshold of John Costello's world, looking down the clean and undecorated hallway, the walls bare of pictures, a strip of featureless linoleum on the floor. The place was cold, and for a moment Irving wondered whether a window had been left wide somewhere within the place. Thankfully, the smell of the dead, that cloying and unmistakable odor that filled the nostrils, the mouth, the throat, the chest, was absent. Neither could he smell the precursor – the rich, coppery haunt of blood, pooled and drying somewhere close.

Irving turned and looked back at the uniforms. Guns drawn, all three of them made their way down the hallway toward the doors at the end, one to the left, one straight ahead. Irving indicated that he would go through the door directly facing them, that Vogel should take the left, O'Reilly acting as cover for both of them in the event that defensive action was required.

But Irving sensed that the apartment was empty, and so it was with something less than his usual caution that he opened the door and stepped through into John Costello's living room.

At first it was difficult to appreciate what he was seeing, and even after some moments – turning back to look at O'Reilly, O'Reilly frowning, looking puzzled, almost bemused – Irving still wondered whether there was some trick being played, some *trompe l'oeil*, for ahead of him was a series of metal bookshelves, erected so close together there was barely space to stand between them, and upon those shelves were the spines of some sort of journal, literally hundreds of them, side by side, spanning the room from one wall to the next. In each corner of the room was a small device rather like a computer modem, a series of lights on its top, a number of holes in its fascia, and these devices hummed, and somehow served to emphasize the restful, almost timeless atmosphere in the room.

'I think they're ionizers,' O'Reilly said. 'My wife has one of them . . . something to do with purifying the air or something. I don't really get it . . .'

Irving backed up to where Vogel stood in the small and pristine kitchen. The work surfaces were spotless, uncluttered with any of the usual accoutrements and utensils one would find in such a room, and when he opened one of the eye-level cabinets on the wall Irving was somehow not surprised to see every can sitting beside its neighbor, label faced forward, stacked one on top of the other by content, and then he noticed something else. Apricots, borlotti beans, cannellini beans, chicken soup, clam chowder . . . The cans were alphabetized.

A further door led through to Costello's bedroom, and an en suite bathroom where the character of the man was further exemplified. The bathroom cabinet contained eight bars of boxed soap, all the same, stacked end to end, beside them four tubes of the same toothpaste. Behind the toothpaste, carefully arranged, were Bufferin, Chloraseptic, Dristan, Myadec Multiples, Nyquil and Sucrets, again in alphabetical order. This time there was a further detail in that each container carried a small label that had been carefully stuck to the front in such a way that all the labels were not only of the same size, but they were positioned at precisely the same height. The labels gave the expiration date of the product.

'What the hell . . .' Vogel started, but didn't finish. There was nothing to say.

Irving headed back to the front room, but before he started looking through the binders on the bookshelves he noticed a small alcove at the rear of the room. Here a desk had been placed in front of a window and the edge of the window frame sealed with some kind of heavy-duty white tape. The desk surface was clear, and each of the drawers was locked.

Irving turned back and lifted a journal from the shelf behind him.

Newspaper clippings. Pictures from magazines and pamphlets. Diagrams. A seemingly unrelated series of random mathematical shapes. A full page where the word *simplicity* had been cut from fifty or sixty different publications, different sizes, different fonts, different colors, and glued side by side from one edge of the page to the other and right to the bottom. The next page was nothing but a single word printed very carefully right in the middle, centered with unquestionable accuracy:

deadface

Irving returned the journal to its place and selected another. Here he found a similar thing – images, diagrams, symbols, apparently random shapes drawn around letters and words in the middle of newspaper cuttings, but all of it executed with the greatest precision. A third journal was full of the neatest handwriting Irving had ever seen, penmanship so accurate it could have been printed on a computer. Some passages read like diary entries, connected and rational; others were continuous variations on some subject or word:

Easier said than done easier than breathing easy come easy go easy for you to say easy is as easy does easy on the eye easier than falling off a log easy like Sunday morning . . .

'What the hell is this?' Vogel asked, looking over Irving's shoulder.

'I think it's someone's mind,' Irving replied. He closed the book and returned it to its rightful place, wondering if he hadn't made the most serious misjudgement of his entire life.

Within fifteen minutes Irving had determined that there were in excess of three hundred and fifty journals in the room, each of them unique, each of them following its own vague sequence or subject matter. From what he could surmise they contained the thoughts and conclusions of John Costello from his late teens to the current day. The journal nearest Costello's desk, placed within arm's reach of his chair, was incomplete, though the last entry, dated November 11th, was very clear:

There is no doubt in my mind. I think I under-
stand the necessity to carry through with this. Six
will be killed, and they will be killed in exactly
the same way. It is almost unavoidable, and I do
not see that Hardangle can stop it from happening.
With the six, the total will come to seventeen, but
it will never stop, not until it is stopped by some
external force. The thing is driven. It is com-
pulsion. It is not a matter of choice. It is not a
subject for discussion or negotiation. There is
simply the need to do this thing, and in doing this
thing be recognized for at least something. Perhaps
there are more meaningful and significant
motivations, but at this stage I do not know what
they are. I would be guessing, and I hate to guess.

Irving's heart seemed to slow in his chest. He felt nauseous and disoriented.

'We got anything on where he might be?' O'Reilly asked.

'No idea . . . he could be anywhere.'

O'Reilly indicated the rear of the apartment. 'Vogel's going through some stuff back there, see if there's any clue where he might have gone to. What's the deal with this guy? Flight risk, or what?'

'I thought he might have been a victim,' Irving replied. 'He's been working with me on this case.'

'Working *with* you on the case? Jesus, the look of this place, it seems like he's the one that should be investigated.'

'You'd think so, wouldn't you?' Irving replied, and he smiled tiredly, and didn't know what to think, or how to express what he felt.

He didn't want to consider that he'd made a mistake. He didn't want to consider the consequences of his most recent decisions if Costello proved to be who he was now imagining he might be.

This was not the apartment of a normal person, not by any stretch of the imagination. The things he was seeing defied reason and explanation, except in some strange and frac-tured reality occupied by John Costello, serial-killer survivor, apparent savant, possibly unhinged and blowing in the breeze . . .

Was this man capable of these monstrous killings that had been happening? Was he that good? That smart? Had Costello broken into the Allen house with a rifle and killed six people?

What now? Where did he go from here?

Irving had no time to consider what he would do next, for someone was coming through the front door of the apartment and before he had a chance to employ standard protocol, O'Reilly was out ahead of him, gun drawn once again, and Irving reached the front hallway only to find O'Reilly had wrestled someone to the ground, was demanding a name, an explanation of their presence . . .

And Irving heard the breathless response, the awkward sound as John Costello struggled beneath O'Reilly's weight.

'I live here,' he gasped. 'This is my apartment . . . I live here for God's sake . . .'

SIXTY-NINE

At three-eighteen Ray Irving was called from the interview room by Bill Farraday. Apparently Karen Langley had been in the lobby for over an hour, had told several officers to *go fuck themselves* when they requested her to leave. She was waiting for Irving. She would not go anywhere until Ray Irving came to speak with her. And if they ejected her forcibly she would *write up such a fucking shitstorm about you assholes that you won't know which fucking day it is, you understand me?*

Whatever friendship might have been burgeoning between Ray Irving and Karen Langley seemed already to have died a swift and definitive death – more than likely within the first five minutes of her being informed of what Irving had done.

The fact that he had John Costello in an interview room, the fact that he was actually *questioning* Costello, with the implication – direct or not – that Costello was in some way involved in these killings, was as far from acceptable as could be imagined.

'You, Ray Irving,' she hissed as he walked toward her, 'are an asshole of the most extra-fucking-ordinary dimensions.' Red-faced, fists clenched, her eyes narrowed, she was all but ready to roundhouse him. Visions in her mind of Ray Irving, his face bloodied, kneeling on the floor, pleading for her to stop hitting him. 'I cannot believe . . . I just cannot fucking believe that you could be so insane, so fucking ignorant—'

Irving raised his hands, conciliatory, placatory. 'Karen. Listen to me—'

'Karen listen to me?' she echoed. 'Who in God's name do you think you are? You have any fucking idea what something like this is going to do to him? God, you have done nothing but cause chaos in my fucking life ever since I met you—'

'Hey, that's not fair . . . and could you please get the fuck out of the lobby and have a proper conversation with me?'

'A proper conversation? What the fuck are you talking about?' she snapped. 'And did it even cross your mind for one fucking second that I might appreciate some kind of forewarning of what the hell you were going to do, eh?'

'Karen, this is a murder investigation, for God's sake!'

Her eyes widened. 'Don't you dare raise your voice at me, and no, I will not have a proper conversation with you. I'm giving you the same consideration that you gave me. You went and broke into his apartment . . .' Karen Langley, her fists still clenched, stepped back a couple of yards, turned on her heels and walked toward the desk as if trying to prevent herself from physically laying Irving out. When she headed back, it was with that cool and distant look of disdain and contempt that she could so effortlessly muster when required.

'Are you going to charge him with something?'

'I'm not going to answer that question, Karen, and you know it.'

'Is he a murder suspect?'

'I'm not answering these questions.'

'You understand that I'm planning on never fucking speak to you again—'

Irving was beginning to get angry. He didn't believe that she had the right to make him feel so small and apologetic. 'What the fuck do you think is going on here, Karen?' He reached out, took her elbow, led her away from the middle of the lobby to the right-hand wall. 'You think I went in there guns blazing for my own health, eh? You think I *wanted* to do this? I went to find him because he was *missing*. I went to find him because I actually give a fuck about where he is and what he's doing, you know? I actually give a damn about the guy. He helped us, did what we asked him to do, and then he vanishes. To all intents and purposes the guy has just walked off the face of the earth. So we go down there. We knock on the door and there's no answer. Now I'm beginning to worry. Now I'm thinking that the last little paragraph in that letter, the thing about getting personal . . . I'm thinking that maybe, just maybe, it might have been directed at John, you know? That this fucking madman got it into his head that it might be a good idea to finish up where Robert Clare left off. To go over to John Costello's apartment, and, just to prove that he's the best of the best, he's gonna finish up what some other sick psycho fuck left incomplete, and hammer the guy's head to bits. You following me so far?'

Karen Langley looked right back at him, defiant and aggressive, and Irving launched right in again.

'So I don't turn around and go home. I don't think "Oh what the fuck, he's probably out somewhere having a pizza, or maybe he's gone dancing", you know? No, I don't think that. I go for the worst-case scenario. I go the pessimistic route, and I figure that maybe I've let this guy get a little too close to what's going on. Maybe I shouldn't have let him go down to Central Park, even though he insisted, even though he pretty much made it a condition of his willingness to help us . . . maybe I shouldn't have let this sick fuck find out that John Costello is on the case, that maybe I've set the poor bastard up to get killed. So I go in there. I make the decision, Karen, for John's sake, not for my own fucking excitement. And what do I find?'

Irving turned away, faced the front door for a few moments, and when he turned back to Karen Langley there was something in his expression that unnerved her.

'I'll tell you what we found, Karen. We found things that seem really strange to me. Even after all these years of seeing some of the weirdest shit that the world can offer, what I saw in there seemed really fucking strange. Okay, granted, there was no direct evidence and maybe I did fuck up, okay . . . Maybe I should have looked a little harder for him before I went breaking into his apartment, but I made a decision, a decision only I can be responsible for, and if he wants to level a formal complaint then there is a means and a method for him to do that. He is perfectly within his rights to file a complaint against me and drag me into court with a charge of harassment. As far as I'm concerned he can go hire Anthony fucking Grant to sue me in this and five other states. This is what this fucking job is about, Karen. This is about making a fucking decision, rightly or wrongly, and sticking by it, because most of the time there isn't the luxury of review or

401

consideration, and there certainly isn't any opportunity to go back and do it right. Hindsight is a wonderful thing, but by the time you've got it, it's too fucking late—'

'What did you find?'

Ray Irving stopped. He was on a roll, he had more things to say. He had more he *wanted* to say. For the first time since the case had started he was taking advantage of this opportunity to vent his spleen, to empty everything out. The fact that Karen Langley considered she had a right to be pissed with him didn't matter. She was there. She had opened her mouth to complain, and that was that. She got it coming right back at her with both barrels.

'I can't tell you what we found, Karen,' Irving said.

'You have something that implicates him in—'

'Karen, seriously . . . you understand this as well as I do—'

'No, Ray, I don't, and that's the whole point here. I *don't* understand. I really don't have the faintest fucking idea what it is you are *doing*—'

'Karen, I have to go,' Irving said. 'I've told you everything that I can right now, and to be completely frank with you, the only reason I came out here is that my captain called me to let me know that you were at the front desk telling people to go fuck themselves. You need to knock this shit off right now, and you need to let me do my job, okay?'

'So how long are you planning on keeping him?'

'Only so long as he's willing to stay. Right now, you are the only one who seems to be upset about this thing.'

Karen sneered. 'What the fuck would you know about it? You don't know the guy at all. You have absolutely no idea what might be going on inside his head at this moment—'

'And that's why he's here, Karen, because what's going on inside John Costello's head might actually help us understand what the fuck we are dealing with.' Irving leaned a little closer, lowered his voice. 'I have seventeen dead. I am not playing games. This is not a time when I am particularly concerned about whether or not someone's feelings might get hurt.'

'That's pretty obvious, Ray—'

'And you can skip the sarcasm, Karen. You are a newspaper reporter. I am a police detective, and you're in my precinct.

402

We are not in your apartment, your office, or any-fucking-place else where I have to be on my best behavior.'

'Fuck you,' Karen Langley said.

'I think you should leave now, Karen.'

'You dare hurt him, Ray, and I'm the one who'll go hire the fucking lawyers, you understand me?'

'Do your worst, Karen . . . right now you are not helping me one bit.'

The cold and hateful expression was there in a heartbeat. It was all Karen Langley could do to restrain herself from slapping Ray Irving as hard as possible.

'You,' she said, 'are a fucking asshole of the first order.'

'Well hell, at least I made the grade at something, eh?'

Karen Langley turned away. She walked to the door, and as she reached out to open it she glanced back at Irving.

'If you need me,' she said, 'forget it. You can go fuck yourself as well.'

The door opened, she walked through, slammed it shut behind her.

Irving turned, saw the desk sergeant watching him.

'First date didn't go so good then?' he asked.

Ray Irving smiled and shook his head. 'They never do.'

SEVENTY

Vernon Gifford was outside the door of the interview room, waiting for Irving's return. 'He says you've betrayed him,' was the first thing he said.

'Betrayed him?'

'That's what he said. Says that you had no right to go into his place, and worst of all you had no right to look at his private possessions.'

'You don't think I know this?' Irving buried his hands in his pockets. He walked half a dozen yards down the corridor, then turned and walked back.

'You gonna keep him?' Gifford asked.

'For what? On what basis? There's no charge, there's no evidence of anything—'

'Except being seriously fucking crazy. No shortage of evidence there, wouldn't you say?'

Irving didn't reply. He took two steps forward, opened the door, and walked in, followed by Gifford. Irving sat down, facing John Costello, Gifford took a chair against the wall.

'John—'

'Was that Karen?'

'Yes, it was.'

'She okay?'

'No,' Irving replied. 'She told several of us to go fuck ourselves, and as far as I'm concerned she's pretty much convinced herself that she'll never talk to me again.'

Costello didn't reply.

'So, John . . . we need to talk about this stuff.'

Costello looked up, eyes wide, expectant almost. 'Stuff?' he asked, in his voice an undertone of surprised innocence.

'Your books. Your writing. The things in your apartment.'

'*My* books. *My* writing. The things in *my* apartment?'

'I know, John, I know, but you have to agree that there's something strange about—'

'About me? About who I am? About the way I live my life?' Costello smiled sardonically. 'I don't think it would take a lot of work for someone to consider that there's something strange about *you*, Detective Irving. You live alone, you eat in the same restaurant every day, you have no friends, no social life. You can't start a relationship, let alone make it work—'

'This isn't about me, John—'

'Isn't it? I think perhaps you should take another look. I think that *you* is exactly and precisely what this is about. This is who you are, Detective Irving. What you are doing right now, what you have been doing over the last few weeks, seems to be the only thing that defines you—'

'John . . . seriously. I need to understand who I'm dealing with here—'

'What *you* are dealing with? Why do you think you are dealing with something?'

'The books in your apartment . . . a room full of books. Ionizers or whatever—'

'Dehumidifiers,' Costello said matter-of-factly. 'They're there to make sure the room doesn't get damp.'

'But what does it all mean? What does—'

'What does it mean? It doesn't mean anything, Detective. Or maybe it does. Fact of the matter is I don't care if who I am and what I do means anything to you or not.'

'John . . . goddammit, John, I have to justify my decisions here, and one of them was having you work with us—'

'You don't have to justify anything any more, Detective. Don't concern yourself with that. I quit.'

'You what?'

'I just quit,' Costello said. 'Real simple. No problem at all. You don't have to explain yourself or justify anything to anyone.'

Out of the corner of his eye Irving caught a flash of movement through the small window in the door.

Gifford evidently saw it too, for he got up and stepped out into the corridor. He returned moments later, tapped Irving on the shoulder, indicated that he was needed outside.

The expression on Bill Farraday's face said everything. 'The news has it,' he said under his breath. 'I've had Ellmann on the phone ten times already. What the fuck is it with this guy?'

'Who the hell knows,' Irving said. 'A fucking weird apartment. A lot of material that I'd like to take a close look at, but right now I have no reason to. I can explain breaking into his apartment, but I have nothing to hold him on, nothing to charge him with except suspicion of being fucking nuts—'

'Let him go,' Farraday said.

Irving looked down at the floor. It had been inevitable.

'Get him out of here,' Farraday said. 'Tell him to get his door fixed. Tell him to have it billed to us. Get him out of the building, off the payroll . . . Jesus, I knew this was a fucking mistake—'

'He already quit,' Irving said.

Farraday sneered. 'Oh that's really rich, isn't it. God, this has become a fucking circus. I need you to finish with him, Ray, I need him out of here – and I need him muzzled on this. His story in the fucking papers is the last thing in the world I want to deal with right now.'

Irving knew there was nothing on which they could hold Costello, no justification for searching the apartment, no reason to pore over the several hundred journals that were book-shelved and dehumidified and extraordinarily suspicious.

'Six dead, and four of them were kids . . .' Farraday left the statement incomplete.

Irving returned to the interview room, told Costello that he could go, that there was no reason to hold him. He also asked him to maintain confidentiality regarding what had happened.

John Costello smiled, standing there at the door, the look in his eyes one of unspoken patience.

'Tell me something,' Irving said.

Costello raised his eyebrows.

'Tell me that I didn't make a mistake about you. Tell me you're not involved in this thing.'

And Costello smiled again, but this time there was something that appeared almost superior – not disdainful, not

406

critical or censorious, but knowing – as if Costello knew he was so far beyond the banality of Irving's thought processes.

'Involved in this thing?' he said. 'Of course I'm involved, Detective, and you're the one who got me involved.'

And with that he opened the door and left the room.

Irving looked at Gifford. Gifford looked right back.

Neither of them spoke, because neither of them had anything to say.

SEVENTY-ONE

By five that afternoon, Ray Irving was certain that Anthony Grant and Desmond Roarke had not spoken to one another since the conclusion of their professional relationship some years before. Detective Ken Hudson, pursuing whatever lines he could regarding the whereabouts of Karl Roberts, Grant's PI, also found time to meet with Gregory Hill. Ostensibly to elicit any further information regarding the Roarke break-in, Hill was brought to the interview room and questioned without his wife. For this he was grateful. She had been through enough. Her affair with Grant was in the past. They had managed to get over it. She had recognized it as a huge mistake, something that she had convinced her husband was a once and once only thing, and he had forgiven her.

'And were there physical confrontations?' Hudson had asked Hill, a question that had prompted Hill to avert his gaze, to look ashamed, to respond in a whisper.

'I was drinking,' he told Hudson. 'I said some things . . . did some things . . .'

'Did you physically harm her, Mr Hill?'

'I was a different man back then,' Hill said. 'I hit her. I cannot tell you how ashamed I am of my behavior. Regardless of what someone might have done, violence is never justified.'

Hudson believed the man to be genuinely contrite. The Hills had weathered the worst that could happen to a marriage, and they had somehow survived. The way the attempted break-in now appeared confirmed that the focus of the investigation was not to be Anthony Grant, nor Greg Hill, nor Desmond Roarke. The subject of their concentration and focus was the man who had called Roarke and pretended to be Grant. The man who had hired Roarke to break into the Hill house, suggesting there was evidence that implicated

Hill in the murder of Mia Grant. CSAs at the Hill house had found nothing. Roarke had made no calls to any number registered to Grant. Access to Roarke's phone records gave them three phone booths, all within a ten-block perimeter of the Fourth, from which calls had been made coincident with the times he believed Grant was calling him. There was nothing probative to tie these men together. Their stories held.

Desmond Roarke would carry through on the attempted B&E. He'd invalidated his parole and would return to complete his sentence. Laura Hill would not be dragged through an interview regarding her infidelity. Evelyn Grant would not be told of her husband's affair with Laura Hill five years earlier. Grant was a lawyer. He knew how far the police could walk, and where they had to stop. There were lines, and some were not crossed.

Each way Irving and his men turned there were walls, and the walls were wide, and they were high, and there appeared to be no way around them.

At quarter of seven a meeting was held in the incident room. Present were Farraday, Irving, Gifford, Hudson, Jeff Turner, and the assistant CSA from the Allen house.

'Before we go through all the crime scene and autopsy reports we need to consolidate what we have,' Farraday said.

'What we don't have,' Irving said.

Farraday ignored the comment, read through some notes on a sheet of paper, and then said, 'Roarke is being processed on the B&E attempt, right?'

'He'll be done tonight,' Hudson said. 'We'll turn him over to County in the morning.'

'Where's he going?'

'We don't know yet. All of them are overcrowded. We'll get a decision tomorrow.'

'Make sure they tell us before he vanishes. We may need to speak to him again.' Farraday found another sheet of paper, read over several points, and then set it aside. 'So where are we? Greg Hill is not our man. We're sure of that?'

'There's nothing in the house. He has alibis for pretty much every date of the recent murders. Out-of-state, three days extended weekend holiday through Sunday, August sixth. The weekend when the three kids were killed. I don't get him for this.'

'And the wife situation?'

'Laura Hill?' Hudson shook his head. 'She was banging Grant for a while. Grant's wife didn't know then, doesn't know now. Hill admitted to hitting his wife, said he was drinking too much. A domestic situation that stayed indoors. No report filed, no complaint from the wife. We've not solicited any request for investigation or charge. They seem to have dealt with it.'

'Which leaves us with two assumptions,' Farraday said. 'First, that our man knew we were talking to families with six members. Secondly, that he was the one who set Roarke up to do the Greg Hill break-in.'

'And if Roarke had actually broken in?' Hudson asked. 'How did that fit into anything?'

'I have no idea,' Farraday replied. 'I think that sending Roarke to the Hill house was not a diversion for us, but another *fuck you* from our guy. He's ahead of us. He wants us to know that. He does whatever he has to do in order to remind us that we're way behind on this one.'

'Roarke, Grant, Hill,' Irving said. 'They're all out of the frame as far as I'm concerned. Chase those and we're up a blind alley.'

'Which gives us the crime scene and autopsy reports from the Allen house,' Farraday said, and looked at Turner.

Turner shook his head before he even started talking. 'I am not the bearer of revelations,' he said. He tapped his finger on a stack of manila folders on the desk. 'Six autopsies, a full crime scene report. Tox, firearms, fingerprinting, the wire to the alarm outside, lock-pick marks on the back door . . . we've been through everything. We found one print in the soft earth of the verge outside a window. Size eleven sneaker, generic brand, same size as the print found at the Central Park site, but that confirms nothing. No prints inside but those of the family, a couple of smudges, a couple of unknown partials on the mailbox outside. There was a mess of them around the external fuse box, but we contacted the electric company and the Allens had a registered electrician service the box less than two weeks ago. The perp left nothing behind to make your job any easier.'

'Did you get anything more on the .35 rifle?' Irving asked.

'Firearms said that Remington Marlin produce a model called a 336. They have them chambered for a .35.'

'Jesus,' Irving said. 'He even used the same brand of gun.'

'Well, it's not a rare gun. So far we've got three hundred and forty registered in the city, and if we go county-wide we're into the thousands.'

'Excluding the illegals, the pawn shops, the unreported thefts,' Irving said.

'Trouble this guy goes to he's not going to use a gun that's registered to himself,' Farraday said. 'I think that's a dead-end . . . wouldn't waste any time on the rifle.'

'Truth of the matter is that every line we've followed has gone dead,' Hudson said. 'Certainly that's been the case so far.'

'Well,' Farraday said, 'we're gonna have to do whatever the fuck it takes to bring them back to life.' He glanced at his watch. 'It's ten past seven now . . . I need you guys to get your heads together and write a proposal that I can take to Chief Ellmann at nine. We've had headliners on three news stations on the Allen killings. It'll die down, but the more attention it gets the more phone calls come through from the Mayor's office—'

Irving opened his mouth to speak but Farraday stopped him with a gesture. 'I have enough to deal with without your viewpoint on the Mayor's office,' he said, and rose from his chair. He straightened the stack of papers on the table and then made his way to the door. 'Nine o'clock,' he reiterated. 'A sensible fucking proposal, not some bullshit whitewash job that we all know won't work, okay?'

Turner looked at Irving, Irving looked at Hudson and Gifford. All of them watched Farraday as he left the room and headed for the stairs.

'Right then,' Turner said, 'I'll leave you ladies to it.'

'The fuck you will,' Irving said. 'Sit the fuck down. You're in this as deep as we are, and we're gonna go through it all again until we have something for the Show 'n' Tell.'

411

SEVENTY-TWO

It was gone eleven p.m. by the time Irving arrived home. In his pocket he had a small slip of paper upon which he'd scribbled Karen Langley's home phone number.

He made some coffee, he sat in the front room looking out through the window into darkness, and he wrestled with himself.

At eleven-twenty Ray Irving picked up the receiver and dialed her number.

'You're an asshole,' she said.

'Karen—'

'Don't *Karen* me, Ray. Fuck you. Fuck off out of my life okay? Let me get on with what I was doing. Things were fine until you came barreling into this like some—'

'Listen to me now—'

'Ray, seriously, I haven't got time for this. It's late and I'm tired. I've had John to deal with all evening, and right now I'm going to bed, because thanks to you I've got more of the same situation tomorrow—'

'Everything that happens is a fucking situation, Karen. This is what I do. I deal with all the situations that no-one else wants to deal with—'

'But Ray, Jesus Christ, Ray . . . he comes home and before he even gets inside the door there's some asshole sitting on him trying to handcuff him—'

'You have any idea—'

'Enough already,' Karen interjected. 'This is not a conversation I want to be having right now.'

'So when? When *do* you want to have this conversation?'

'Never, that's when. That's really how I feel right now, Ray . . . that I don't ever want to have this conversation with you.'

'You're just running away—'

'Screw you—'

'Screw you right back, Karen—'

'I'll tell you something, Ray . . . I might have no idea what it's like to stand on the stairs outside someone's apartment and wonder whether or not there's a dead body inside, but that's not the only thing I'm talking about. Truth is, I don't have room in my life for someone who doesn't talk to me—'

'Talk to you? Talk to you about what, for God's sake?'

'About what's going on. About what's happening.'

'Like what? Like what I do? You want me to call you up in the middle of the night and tell you what I'm doing? Like, hey Karen, you should see this guy here. Someone came over and beat his head in. His eyes are all eight-ball hemorrhaging, all bugged out and black you know? Or how about telling you how we went over to some junkie's place and we found mom and her three little kids all carved up by junkie dad, who's so strung out on crack and fuck knows what else he doesn't even realize what he's done—'

'Ray. Shut up! Just shut the fuck up, okay? I'm putting the phone down now—'

'Don't you hang up on me, Karen, don't you fucking hang up on—'

'Goodbye Ray.'

'Kar—'

The line went dead in his ear.

He sat there with the receiver in his hand for quite some time, and then he hung up and sat back in the chair.

It hadn't gone as well as he'd planned.

Like most things.

SEVENTY-THREE

Early Tuesday morning, the 14th of November. Irving's sleep had been restless and fitful. Several times he had woken with a start, images playing in his mind, disturbed and fractured. Mia Grant's black plastic-wrapped body. James Wolfe's hollow-eyed clown face staring back at him from a hole in the ground . . .

Everything taunted him, challenged him, made him feel impotent and weak. The Anniversary Man had defined his own proving ground, and had demonstrated his superiority without exception.

I am better, smarter, faster . . .

I am so many fucking steps ahead of you . . .

You people . . . you people make me laugh . . .

Beyond that, the stress and pressure of the investigation was beginning to show itself. Whatever relationship, professional or otherwise, Irving might have established with Karen Langley was now in pieces, and as far as John Costello was concerned . . . well, he tried hard not to think of John Costello.

He made coffee. He sat at the kitchen table. He wanted a bottle of Jack Daniels and a carton of Luckies. He wanted a break. He wanted some peace.

His pager went off at eight-ten. He called back, was informed that Farraday wanted him in his office at eight forty-five.

'You're late,' was Faraday's greeting. His face was a blank. No sympathy, no empathy, no compassion, no understanding, no humor.

'I have more calls to deal with,' he said. 'I have newspapers, the press people in the Mayor's office, Chief Ellmann, the DA. I have TV stations, radio stations, even internet fucking

414

chat-rooms posting cut-and-paste sections from newspaper articles about these killings . . .' He leaned back until he looked at the ceiling and closed his eyes. 'I have people putting two and two together, just like we said they would, and this time they're coming back with four. This thing is now in the public domain, Ray, and I need it gone—'

'I am doing everything—'

'I know, I know, but everything you can do is evidently not enough. I need more. I need you to collaborate with FBI profiling, with forensics, with the coroner's office. I need you and Hudson and Gifford to burn the midnight oil. I need files reconstructed and tabulations done. I need reviews of all crime scene reports.' Farraday lowered his head and looked directly at Irving. 'What I need more than anything in the world is results.'

Irving didn't reply. He'd heard this before, would hear it time and again until the case was closed. He didn't dare consider the possibility that the case might remain open.

'So go,' Farraday said. 'Work out what you're going to do, then tell me what you need. I'll see if I can give it to you.'

Irving smiled sarcastically. 'TV coverage on all stations. Three hundred homicide detectives. Throw in the National Guard for good measure.'

'We are never anything other than on top of these things, Ray. You know the routine. The questions come at you, you don't answer them. It's a *no comment* scenario all the way down the line. You never give them the impression of anything but complete control—'

'I know, I know,' Irving said, his tone betraying his exhaustion.

Farraday leaned forward, elbows on the edge of the desk, hands together as if in prayer. 'Tell me,' he said. 'Tell me for real if you have the slightest fucking clue who this guy is.'

'I don't have the slightest fucking clue who this guy is.'

'Nothing.'

'Nothing,' Irving echoed.

'You don't see anything in the group that Costello met with in the hotel?'

'We've checked them all out – four of them are women, for God's sake – no records, no priors, only common denominator is the fact that they were all intended victims of some whacko way back when. The two men are clean as you get . . . nothing there at all.'

'I read the report for Ellmann. This shit sounds great on paper but you know as well as me that half this shit doesn't work in the real world.'

'The only lead I have left is the PI that Grant hired. He's vanished, and I have a horrible feeling that he might have been onto something and he'll wind up in a dumpster somewhere with his eyes missing.'

'You think he was onto our boy?'

'I don't know, Captain, I just don't fucking know. You think about how you'd explain this kind of thing to someone who isn't a cop. You imagine trying to explain that it's possible to kill so many people and leave absolutely nothing conclusive or probative behind. After the fact yes, when all the circumstantial evidence corroborates a confession, but before you get the guy this shit is worth nothing.'

'You don't need to tell me,' Farraday said.

'So I think we should go public.'

Farraday didn't reply. He didn't refute. He didn't immediately reject the idea out of hand. This told Irving that he'd considered the same route himself.

'And do what?' Farraday asked.

'Tell the truth, or as much of the truth we need to get the point across.'

'We don't even have a picture, not even an artist's impression. What the fuck are we going to ask them to look for?'

'We're not going to ask them to look for anything. We're going to ask them to look *out* for each other.'

'You want to put a whole city on alert.'

'I want to put a whole city on alert . . . we field the calls, the false alarms, we get as many people assigned to this as we can, and we get this thing broken before Christmas—'

'I need it done a long way before Christmas.'

'So you need to co-ordinate with whoever you have to co-ordinate with, get the resources we need assigned to us, and we put this thing in the papers and on the tube.'

'You wanna know my view? I don't think it'll go.'

'So we don't even try?'

'We try yes, but I don't want you to come in here fists flying when it gets kicked out on its ass.'

'Fuck 'em. They don't give us what we need they can find someone else to head up this thing.'

Farraday smiled wryly. 'There is no-one else to head up this thing.'

'Well then, they're gonna have a fucking problem on their hands, aren't they?'

Farraday was silent for some time. Eventually he said, 'So there's no other route? This is what you want to do?'

'That's what I want to do . . . that's what I *believe* we should do.'

'Because it's the best course of action, or because it's the only course of action?'

'The latter,' Irving said.

'So put something together for me, but when you write it I need it to read like this is the *best* course, okay?'

'I can do that.'

Farraday looked at his watch again. 'Nine twenty-five. Get it back to me by eleven. You need the precinct shrink?'

'You think I need to see a shrink?'

'For the article. For the wording of the article, you dumb motherfucker. I'm thinking we put a hook in the statement to get the guy interested.'

'What? Like we tell the world he's a faggot or he's got a two and a half inch dick, that sort of thing?' Irving shook his head. 'God, no. I don't want this guy any more pissed at the world than he already is. And anyhow, what shrinks actually know about human behavior I could write on a postage stamp.'

Farraday said nothing, but he smiled knowingly. 'So go,' he said. 'Give me something I can use today.'

SEVENTY-FOUR

The ability to wait was a skill, perhaps even an art. Either way, it was not something Irving had mastered.

He wrote the statement. He put together the body of a newspaper article. He didn't do these things out of familiarity or previous experience, but out of sheer necessity. Because, in all truth, it seemed that no-one else but himself and the men he directed were truly determined to see this thing to its close. Those who haunted the edges of this thing – representatives from the Mayor's office, those in press relations, even the federal agencies – wanted the killer, but they didn't want the work. The police were there. Taxes paid for the police. The police always knew precisely what to do, and got it done.

Like hell they did.

Hudson and Gifford went after the PI, Karl Roberts. They found his offices and his apartment empty. They secured photographs of him and put out an APB. What they did not do was put his face on TV in case he was still alive, the opinion being that such an action could only serve to make him a potential victim.

Irving believed, however, that the man had perhaps unearthed some information regarding Mia Grant's killer. If that was the case, there was a strong possibility that Karl Roberts was already dead.

Irving spoke to Anthony Grant again, questioned him extensively about anything that Roberts might have said about the death of Mia, what leads he was following, the lines he was pursuing. Grant knew nothing of any great significance. He said that Roberts was a serious man, almost humorless, but evidently focused, committed, professional in his approach. Grant said that Roberts appeared to be sufficiently familiar with police procedure to suggest that he might have been ex-PD. Such a thing was not uncommon. Irving had Hudson and Gifford trawl the PD databases – past, present, other nearby states. There was a Carl Roberts on the Upper West Side, a Karl Robertson in New Jersey. That was all they got.

Five days elapsed. It was Monday the 20th by the time the NYPD's press office came back with an approved statement and article. It went to *The Times*, the *City Herald*, the *Daily News*, in hard copy, on websites. It was picked up by NBC, ABC and CBS and WNET. Chief Ellmann delegated the public statements to his deputy. He had no wish to be remembered as the face who delivered bad news.

New Yorkers learned that they had been plagued by a killer for five months. To date, all of seventeen killings had been attributed to this individual. The victims' faces were printed, displayed on websites. A hotline was established to receive calls from anyone who recognized the victims, anyone who had seen them in the hours or days before their deaths, anyone who was in possession of information they believed the police should know.

Ellmann and Farraday drafted in fifteen additional staff to man the phones. By four-thirty on Monday afternoon they were already overwhelmed. There was an underlying sense of panic, both inside and outside the department. Gifford, Hudson, Saxon, O'Reilly, Goldman and Vogel were reined in again. Farraday briefed them in Irving's presence. Three detectives were loaned from the Seventh to deal with the routine traffic at the Fourth while the homicide detectives were deployed to address the follow-up on every call that wasn't obviously and blatantly a crank. Ellmann concurred with Farraday's view that men already familiar with the case should continue working on it, thereby circumventing the necessity to start from scratch with those temporarily delegated.

By seven that evening there were three hundred and fourteen further leads that had not even been considered. By nine o'clock the figure exceeded five hundred. The newspapers ran with assumptions and misleading reports. The sense of panic increased. Irving couldn't decide if it was imagination or reality, but every time he left the precinct house the city's atmosphere felt charged.

At ten Irving called Karen Langley and left her a message.

'Karen, it's Ray. I have over five hundred leads backing up on this thing. Get John to call me, tell him I need his help. This is now beyond anything personal, you understand? This has to do with other peoples' lives. Tell him that from me. Tell him if he doesn't come and help me—'

The line clicked suddenly and he heard Karen Langley's voice.

'Ray?'

'Karen . . . I was just leaving you a message.'

'I heard the message, Ray. He's disappeared.'

'What?'

'John. He's disappeared—'

Irving felt the hairs rise on the nape of his neck. 'What d'you mean, disappeared?'

'What I fucking said. It's not hard to understand. He's disappeared.'

'Since when?'

'Last saw him Friday afternoon. He asked if he could leave early, and then he didn't show up this morning and there's no answer on his phone. Nothing. I even sent someone round there to see if there were any lights on at his place, but there's nothing.'

Irving felt sick. He felt disturbed.

'Ray?'

'Yes?'

'I'm worried about him . . . like he might go and do something.'

'You think he's that unstable?' Irving asked.

'Jesus, Ray, I don't know what to think, except my absolute certainty that he has nothing to do with these killings. I know that you're still suspicious.'

'I wasn't, Karen . . . I'd got over that, and then I saw his apartment. That made me think . . . God, I don't know what it made me think.'

'I just see it as his way of dealing with what happened to him, like everything else that doesn't make sense about him.'

'Says a great deal for how different we are,' Irving said.

'We're not that different, Ray. You're just more ignorant and self-centered, and not quite as bright as me.'

Irving smiled. It was difficult under such circumstances to retain any humor, but here she was – Karen Langley – reminding him once again that there was something to life outside of the Fourth Precinct.

'So what are you going to do?' she asked.

'I'm gonna find him, Karen. I have to now. It's gone a little beyond curiosity about where he's at into a necessity for us to really determine if he's involved.'

'I really—'

'I know, Karen, I know, and I hope to hell that he has absolutely nothing to do with this, but I have to be completely certain. There are too many things at stake to let it rest.'

'I understand.'

'Thank you for picking up the phone.'

'You take care, Ray Irving.'

'Same back to you.'

The line went dead. Irving hung up, hesitated for a moment, and then he lifted the phone and called for Hudson and Gifford.

'APB on John Costello,' he told them. 'Whatever it takes, he has to be found, understand?'

SEVENTY-FIVE

The world seemed to stop for three days. Within the walls of the Fourth Precinct there was pandemonium and chaos. A constantly changing army of telephone operators monitored and routed all the irrelevances, suppositions, assumptions and inconsistencies of a publicized investigation. For every fifty calls there were a half dozen leads to follow down. The uniforms, Vogel, O'Reilly, Goldman and Saxon, were out in cars; the detectives, Hudson and Gifford, worked on locating Karl Roberts and Costello.

The newspapers and news stations started turning on the department. Why was this still going on? Where were the taxpayers' dollars being spent? Despite citywide coverage and seemingly endless resources were they still no closer to catching the man who was terrorizing New York?

The world and all it possessed gave them nothing until the morning of Thursday the 23rd of November, and when it did it was the very last thing that Irving had expected.

Seven a.m., minutes after, Irving was seated at his desk in the incident room. He'd been at the precinct house for two hours already, having left a little after one that same morning. Barely three hours' sleep, and he was walking the edge of the abyss once more.

Three days since the story had broken. Twenty-four hours for New York to absorb it, twenty-four hours for the instinctive backlash against the police and the current civil administration. The next twenty-four saw the onset of public paranoia. People were either tough, cynical, or terrified.

That morning Irving almost didn't answer the phone. He was reading through the previous four hours of reports that had accumulated in his absence. There had been two messages from the same person, a woman who sounded frightened, who had communicated something to two different operators that implied an eyewitness possibility for the Allen killings. She lived two streets east, had a friend who lived opposite the Allens. She had visited there until late that night, had walked to the end of the street just as a dark pick-up came around the corner and slowed. She had hurried on, self-conscious, aware of the lateness of the hour in a dark and now deserted street, and the fact that despite the short distance to her own house, it would only take a moment for someone to exit a vehicle . . .

She had remembered three of the digits on the license plate. Why? Because they were three of the digits of her sister's birthday: *116*. January 16th. A dark pick-up – black, perhaps midnight blue, more than likely a Ford – with 116 on the plate.

And then the phone rang, and Irving reached for it, but paused halfway. The additional lines brought in for the incident room had overloaded the system and thrown so many curves into it, and too many times incorrect routing had given him a call for an entirely different department.

But after the phone rang a third and fourth time there was something about its seeming insistence that compelled him, and so he reached again, lifted the receiver, and raised it to his ear to hear the duty desk sergeant say, 'Ray . . . there's a call from someone who says you've been looking for him,' and that was all it took.

Irving knew it was John Costello, and when he said, 'Yes, hello . . .' he expected Costello's voice, and was preparing for the raft of apologies he would now have to give the man, to say whatever was needed to corral the guy back into the field and bring him to the precinct.

But the voice that responded, the single word that was uttered, was so clearly *not* John Costello, that Irving felt a chill throughout the entirety of his body.

'Detective.'

'Yes . . . hello there . . . who is this?'

'I think you've been looking for me.'

'Looking for you?' Irving felt his nostrils clear as if he'd smelled ammonia. Every single hair on the nape of his neck stood to attention. He shuddered, imperceptibly to anyone who might have seen him there at the desk, but it was there, and he felt it so strongly, and he didn't know whether or not he was capable of speaking again.

'I'm scared, Detective . . . truly scared . . . I have been in hiding for a while . . .'

'Scared? Who is this?' Irving said.

'I'm the person you've been looking for. I've heard things from people I know—'

'What people? What have you heard?'

'I'm the investigator,' the voice. 'Karl Roberts.'

The rush of relief flooded through Irving.

He believed he had never felt such a conflict of emotions in his life.

The sense of overwhelming fear that he could have been on the phone to the anniversary killer . . . the all-too-real possibility that the egotistical son-of-a-bitch could have actually called him up to taunt him, to challenge him . . . Against that the sense of disappointment – no, something far deeper than disappointment – that it *was not* the killer, that whatever Roberts may have found would lead them nowhere . . .

Irving sat for some time, almost as if he had forgotten to breathe, and then he said, 'Yes, Mr Roberts, we have been looking for you,' to which Roberts responded, and what he said brought everything rushing back once again for Irving.

'I think . . . God almighty, man, I think I know who it is.'

Irving didn't speak.

'And I think he knows who I am . . . and I think if I do anything that makes him aware of where I am—'

'Where are you now, Mr Roberts?' Irving asked. His heart rate had doubled. He felt sweat on his scalp, that crawling, itching sensation.

'I'm not going to say,' Roberts replied. 'Not on the phone.'

'I need you to come in, Mr Roberts. We can protect you—'

Roberts laughed nervously. 'I'm sorry, Detective. I've been a private investigator for far too long to actually believe that. You have to remember that before I started this I was one of you.'

'You were a cop?'

'I was a detective. Vice, Narco, did a good few years on the sharp edge of things.'

'We looked for you . . . we didn't find anyone with your name in our records.'

'You looked where? New York? New Jersey?'

'Sure, yes, we looked for you—'

'Seattle,' Roberts said. 'That's where I'm from originally, but anyway, that's beside the point right now.'

'You say you know who this person might be?'

'Yes.'

'You're willing to tell us what you've found?'

'Hell yes, what the fuck d'you think I called you for? Jesus, man, you think this is some kind of game?'

'So we meet somewhere. I'll come get you personally. I can guarantee—'

'Nothing,' Roberts said. 'You can guarantee me nothing, Detective. You have secure lines there, at least within your department, your own precinct right?'

'Of course we do.'

'Bullshit. Not when we're talking about what I know.'

Irving paused. 'Someone inside—'

'Enough already. Like I said. We're not dealing with this right now, and no, I am not coming in to your precinct. We need to meet somewhere.'

'Yes, definitely . . . we need to meet.'

'And I want a public place. Somewhere where there's other people . . .'

'Okay,' Irving said. 'Where?'

'Jesus, how would I know? A department store, a restaurant . . .'

'A diner? We could meet in a diner.'

'Sure. A diner's okay, and . . . and bring someone with you.'

'Bring someone?'

'Yes, bring someone. Not a police officer . . . someone neutral.'

'Like who?'

'Anyone. I don't fucking care. Just not a police officer.'

'What about Karen Langley?'

'Who's that?'

'She's a reporter from the *City Herald*.'

'Yes, that'll do. Bring her.'

'You know Carnegie's on Seventh Avenue, at 55th Street?'

'No, but I can find it. This evening, okay? And give me your cell number.'

Irving did so.

'I'm gonna call you later. I'll give you a phone box number. You go out of the precinct to another phone box and you call me back. I'll be waiting. I'll tell you what time we're gonna meet. You come with the reporter woman, but please, no-one else. I see anyone else I'm gone, you understand?'

'Yes, I understand . . . understand completely.'

'Okay, so we're done. Wait for me to call you, don't do anything else to try and find me. Nothing to create attention, you know? What I gotta tell you . . . fuck, man, you don't want the NYPD helping this guy to track me down.'

'Someone inside the department . . . that's what you're saying, isn't it? You're telling me it's someone within the department—'

'Later,' Roberts said, and the line went dead.

SEVENTY-SIX

Irving found records relating to Karl Roberts in the Seattle PD database. Made Detective in '87, Vice for three years, Narcotics for eight, wound up taking early retirement in early '99, moved to New York in 2001, registered as a licensed PI in July 2003. No question about it. The face on his police file matched the face on the ID card he'd been issued. The man was real. He was not a ghost. He had trained as a detective, had served with a good record, and now had worked on the Mia Grant killing as a private investigator. And Karl Roberts said he knew who the perpetrator was. He had implied that the perpetrator was within the New York Police Department. This of all things was the hardest for both Irving and Farraday to swallow, but such a thing was not unknown. Farraday authorized that the Roberts APB be pulled, but agreed with Irving that they keep the Costello one live.

'And you're going to take Langley with you?'

'I don't have a choice,' Irving replied. 'I'll go over there and see her. I want as much of this off the phone lines as possible.'

Farraday shook his head resignedly. 'You really think that this could be someone within the department?' And then he added, 'That was rhetorical, you don't need to answer.'

Irving drove across to the *City Herald* offices, spoke briefly with Emma Scott at the front desk, and she put a call through to Karen Langley.

Langley – believing perhaps that Irving had news of John Costello – told Emma to let Irving come on up right away.

He found her standing at the window in her office. She looked agitated, distraught, and he knew that what he had to tell her would not make things any easier.

'Why me?' was her first question, and before Irving had a chance to answer she threw a further barrage of questions at

427

him. Did Irving think that John was dead, that he'd committed suicide, that he might have been murdered? Could John Costello actually be the insider within the police department that this Karl Roberts was speaking of? Wasn't Costello now 'inside' the police department as a result of his work with Irving? That would make sense, that would explain why Roberts had demanded that Irving come with someone who was not directly connected to the police. But then, if that was indeed the case, surely Roberts would have realized where Costello worked, and who he worked for? But if that were so, then he surely wouldn't have wanted her to be at the meeting. Didn't that prove that John couldn't be involved . . . ?

'Karen, Karen, Karen.' Irving went to her and gripped her shoulders firmly. He directed her back to her chair and sat her down. He stood there for a moment looking at her. She seemed utterly lost. Terrified. As if the slightest thing might now send her spinning over the edge into such a depth of emotional devastation that she might never return complete.

'The answer to everything is that I don't know, Karen. Not for sure. The answer to every single question you have is going to be one hell of a lot easier once we've met with Karl Roberts and learned what he knows.'

'But why me?' she asked once more. 'Why does he want me to go with you?'

'He didn't ask for you. He asked for someone who isn't in the department. He's a frightened guy, Karen. He may have been a police detective, but he's still a human being, and he thinks his life is in danger. He knows something, and he feels he needs someone neutral there . . . maybe he thinks I might be involved . . . God knows. Or he might think that we already know it's someone in the department and I've just been assigned to clean it all up and keep it out of the papers. I think if I was in his shoes I'd do the same thing . . .'

'Jesus, Ray, I can't say no, can I? This thing scares the crap out of me . . . and I tell you something, if I only knew where John was I'd feel one hell of a lot better.'

'We're doing everything we can,' Irving said. 'I've got everyone I can looking for him, and now we've pulled the APB off of Roberts it'll improve our chances.'

Karen was silent for a time, and then she leaned forward and said, 'Tell me the truth, Ray. Tell me honestly, deep in your heart, do you really think that John might have done these things?'

Irving shook his head. 'I don't think so,' he replied. 'And I really don't *want* to think so, but it's a possibility . . . hell, Karen, however slim it might be, it's a possibility that I can't rule out completely.'

'And if he did . . . and we've been living with that all this time, and you had him inside the precinct, working alongside you, telling you where to look—'

'Then I'm out of a job, Karen, and I'm gonna come ask for a job here.'

Karen Langley smiled weakly. Irving was trying to inject some light into the moment, but there was no room for it. It was dark, claustrophobically so, and it would remain that way until they knew the truth.

'So?' Irving prompted.

'So?' Karen echoed. 'So nothing, Ray . . . of course I'll come. It's not a choice, is it?'

Irving sat down facing her, and the exhaustion, the bone-deep fatigue that wracked his body showed in every line and crease and shadow on his face. 'No,' he said quietly. 'It's not a choice.'

The hours crawled, as Ray Irving knew they would. He returned to the Fourth, spoke with Farraday, and Farraday – understanding the huge pressure brought to bear upon Irving by the intensity of the investigation, perhaps sensing he needed to show some compassion for the position Irving was now in – let him be. He asked nothing further from him at that time, and Irving sat in the incident room, even spent the better part of an hour in the station canteen, considering all that had happened, trying so hard not to raise his own expectations of what Roberts could tell them. Ex-police detective or not, Roberts could still be wrong, and even if he was right, would there be anything but circumstantial evidence? Would there be a case? Or would this be another step forward toward further irresolution?

At five Irving called Karen Langley but got her voicemail.

At five-eleven his cell rang and Roberts was there.

'Six o' clock,' he said. 'Where you said . . . the diner. Okay?'

Irving was on his feet. 'Yes, we'll be there.'

'And you're bringing the woman, right?'

'Yes, she'll be there.'

Roberts hung up.

Irving called Karen Langley.

Karen left the *Herald* offices at five twenty-two, crossed the street and walked half a block to her car. She was unaware that the driver of a dark grey rental sedan was watching her closely from the corner of West 33rd opposite the General Post Office.

At five twenty-eight she pulled out onto Ninth Avenue and headed toward Central Park. The sedan went after her, hanging back like a shadow, the driver tracking her all the way to the car park back of the 57th Street subway station, watching her as she made the short walk to the Carnegie Delicatessen & Restaurant at 854 Seventh Avenue. He parked the sedan near the corner of 58th, kept the front entrance to Carnegie's in his clear line of sight, and was pleased to see Ray Irving arrive. He knew Ray Irving's face as well as anyone's. Ray Irving was as much a part of this as anyone, as much a part as Mia Grant, James Wolfe, the Allen family or any of the other victims. Ray Irving was the hub about which this small universe now turned. It had begun with him, and with him it would end.

'Ray,' she said as he approached the table. She was seated in a corner booth, almost as if seclusion from the main hubbub of the restaurant, the distance from the street, would somehow divorce her from the reality of what was happening.

'You okay?' Irving asked as he sat down across from her. Instinctively he reached out and closed his hand over hers.

'God, you're cold,' she said, and then she smiled, trying perhaps to make this rendezvous seem something other than what it was. They were friends, good friends, perhaps even lovers; they were meeting for dinner; the world they faced was nothing more nor less than the world which they themselves had created. There were no dead people, there was no serial killer; there was no meeting with a retired Seattle detective who possessed information that could give them the truth of what had happened to seventeen innocent people in the space of five months. There were regular days, kids to collect from drama class, a discussion about whose parents were coming for Thanksgiving . . .

The kind of conversation Jean and Howard Allen might once have had.

But no. This was neither of their lives. And however innocent and ordinary Ray Irving and Karen Langley might have appeared, the reality of who they were and why they were there could have been understood and appreciated by so very few people.

They were there because people had been brutally and sadistically murdered. They were there because someone had taken it upon himself to carry forward a mission to rid the world of those he considered unworthy. There was insanity, inhumanity, a complete lack of mercy, compassion or compunction. And these things had now crawled beneath the skin of Ray Irving and Karen Langley and darkened their perspective of the world even further. This was not TV. This was no R-rated movie on limited release. This was the worst the world had to give, and they were walking rapidly toward it in the hope that it could be stopped.

They held hands for a moment more, and then Irving sat back. He smiled – that all-too-familiar expression of philosophical resignation – and Karen smiled back.

'I don't know if sorry is appropriate,' he said, 'for everything that has happened with John.'

'I'm too tired,' she said. 'I pray that he's okay. I don't know what to think, and I'm past the point of trying to figure it all out.'

'We need to know what this Roberts guy has learned.'

'So we wait,' she said.

'We wait.'

'You hungry?'

'No,' Irving replied. 'You?'

'Could use some coffee.'

Irving got up, walked to the counter to speak with a waitress. He returned to the booth and moments later the waitress appeared, filled their cups, asked them to call for her if they decided to eat.

They sat in silence, the tension written on their faces, reflected in their body language, their eyes.

The driver of the sedan sat in silence too, and though he couldn't actually see Irving and Langley, he knew they were there, somewhere back of the glass, somewhere within the light and warmth and safety of the diner.

Such light and warmth and safety were transient, as were all things. What you believed you possessed could be lost in a heartbeat. Taken away forever. Such was the way of the world.

SEVENTY-SEVEN

Time seemed to collapse in upon itself, for when Irving's cellphone rang, when he snatched it from the table and saw the unidentified caller ID, it seemed as if they had been talking for no more than a handful of minutes. It was already three minutes to six.

'Yes?'

Karen raised her eyebrows.

Irving snatched a napkin from the dispenser, took a pen from his jacket pocket and wrote down a number. 'Okay,' he said, and he hung up.

'Let's go,' Irving said, little more than a whisper, but compelling in its urgency.

They hurried across the street to a phone booth on the facing side.

They angled their way through the folding door, pressed one against the other, Irving clutching a handful of change, pushing the first of three or four coins into the box. His heart racing, his pulse doubling up, feeling it in his throat, in his temples, eyes wide, breath like smoke, the two of them cramped together as if they were sharing the same skin, and emotions running high . . .

The sound of the coins dropping through the slot and rolling down. The metallic click as Irving lifted the receiver. The sound of the tones as he punched the buttons, and knowing that this was the break, the thing he'd been looking for, praying for, hoping against all intuition and experience that told him something like this could not happen.

In minutes, no more than minutes, he would be face-to-face with someone who understood what had happened to Mia Grant, someone who had exposed a single layer of deceit that surrounded this nightmare, and had come back with an idea, a thought, a belief, a supposition, anything . . .

Perhaps even a name.

And in that moment Irving was aware of how deeply he had submerged his own doubt, his own fear that this could be something else entirely. He had convinced himself that he didn't care who the Anniversary Man was, didn't care whether or not they were crazy. He did not want to understand the reasons for their actions. He didn't care whether it was someone he knew, someone he'd met, even if it was someone with the police department . . .

He just wanted to know, and he wanted them stopped.

'Irving?'

'Yes, it's me, I'm here,' Irving gasped.

'She's with you? The reporter?'

'Yes, she's here, she's right beside me.'

'You know Madison Square Park?'

'Yes, I know it.'

'Meet me there. Fifteen minutes—'

'I don't understand,' Irving interjected. 'We're here now, where we agreed to meet, at the diner—'

'We're not meeting there. I've changed my mind. You come to Madison Square Park, or we don't meet at all.'

Irving looked at Langley. She could see the anxiety in his expression.

What's happening? she mouthed.

'Where exactly?' Irving asked.

'There's some benches in the north east corner. Same corner as the New York Life Building.'

'Yes, I know where that is.'

'Fifteen minutes. Just the two of you. I see anyone else I'm gone. Don't be late.'

'I got it—'

The line went dead.

Irving stood there for some seconds, his heart threatening to hammer its way right out of his chest, and then he hung up the receiver, started maneuvering his way back out of the booth, Karen Langley beside him, talking as he went, telling her where they were going, that the location had been changed.

'You believe this guy?' she asked, as Irving grabbed her hand and started across the street toward his car.

434

'Believe him?' Irving said. 'Jesus, Karen, I stopped asking myself what I believed a good while back. Right now there isn't anyone else. Right now I just have to find out what he knows.'

They took Irving's car, pulled out of the car park and headed south toward Madison Square.

A minute later the dark grey sedan pulled away from the sidewalk and entered the stream of slow-moving traffic right behind them.

They didn't see a thing.

From the car Irving called Farraday. He told him where he was going, that Langley was with him, that they were meeting Roberts in the park, not at the diner as originally planned. Perhaps something had spooked him. Perhaps he just figured an open space was better. Irving asked for unmarked cars on each corner of the park – West 26th and Fifth, West 23rd by the station, south east at the corner of Madison and East 23rd, and then half a block over from where they would meet Roberts, parked against the curb beneath the shadow of the New York Life Building.

'Roberts was a cop,' Irving said. 'He knows this shit as well as we do. Put one guy in the driver's seat, another on the floor back of him. Two guys in a sedan is just too fucking obvious.'

Farraday gave Irving a cleared frequency for his radio. 'Take it with you,' he said. 'Leave it switched on inside your coat.'

'This has to be airtight,' Irving said. 'Anyone makes their presence known we're fucked.'

Farraday understood. He said that no-one would be seen. He gave his word, and Irving believed him.

Eight minutes to go and they were still caught in the gridlock between the 34th Street subway and Penn Station. It cleared suddenly, a line of traffic taking the 32nd Street exit. Irving floored the car and they made it to 26th where he turned left and took Broadway down to the edge of the park.

They left the car and walked half a block. Irving held Karen Langley's hand, a message of reassurance that neither of them were doing this thing alone. They didn't speak. Seemed that everything needing words had already been said.

Ray Irving ignored a sudden and unnerving premonition, the feeling that he might walk away from this meeting understanding even less of the truth.

Stationed at the four corners of the park were unmarked sedans, each carrying two officers and waiting on radio silence. Through the cleared frequency each of them could hear Langley and Irving talking to one another. A row of wooden benches stood empty in the north eastern corner of the park, and it was here that they sat.

'This scares the living crap out of me,' Karen Langley said at one point, and Ken Hudson, looking at them through binoculars from his vantage point at West 26th, understood precisely what she meant. The emotion she felt was something with which he was very familiar. People literally lost their minds. It was something he would never wish on anyone, especially a civilian, especially someone dragged into this thing through no real choice of their own. He watched them, Irving and Langley, two narrow silhouettes on a park bench between the trees, and he knew that Irving, despite his training and experience, would be caught between the necessity to meet this Karl Roberts and the drive to protect Karen Langley. Rock and a hard place. Couldn't do one without the other.

No more than three or four minutes after they were seated, Irving saw someone cross the grass to his left and make their way toward the trees. He had on a long overcoat, tan-colored from what he could make out, and he seemed purposeful but cautious.

Irving's stomach turned over.

From another police car, Vernon Gifford saw a second man exit a cab at the corner of East 25th and Madison and make his way toward the park railings. He had on a black jacket, hands buried in the pockets, shoulders hunched and head down, his face obscured by a baseball cap. The uniformed officer back of the driver's seat, crouched down in the rear foot-well, felt the pressure of Gifford's back as he pressed against the seat. He was sweating profusely, could feel the corner of his radio digging painfully into his thigh, but he couldn't move.

Words were exchanged between the four stationed teams. They were now watching four people – Irving and Langley, the tan overcoat, the baseball cap.

Seventy twenty-nine Irving rose slightly as the man in the overcoat crossed his line of vision, turned left, and then started to walk slowly toward them. His heart ran ahead of itself.

Vernon Gifford watched as Baseball Cap followed the railings and entered the park through the north eastern gate. Gifford sensed something was awry. He shifted awkwardly, reached for the door lever, told the officer behind him to move slowly into the front seat once Gifford had cleared the car.

'Moving in,' Gifford said across the radio. 'Everyone stay back for the moment.'

Gifford eased the door open and slipped out soundlessly. He closed the door behind him and hurried down the sidewalk to the corner. His breathing was heavy – white ghosts ahead of him as he exhaled. He felt the extraordinary tension of the situation.

Screw this up and they were all fucked.

Screw this up and God only knew how many more might die.

He withdrew his .38 and slowed down. He reached the railings just as Tan Overcoat appeared behind a tree to the left of the path. He was the better part of fifty yards away, but he had Irving and Langley in his sights on the bench, saw Baseball Cap approaching them from the rear, and Tan Overcoat now walking toward them from the trees. He felt the sweat along his hairline break free and run down the side of his nose.

'Baseball Cap from the rear,' he said into his mouthpiece. 'Tan Overcoat from ahead. Unit Three: send your lead man out to the far right of the park and come in slowly. Unit Four on hold. Irving? You have an unidentified man in a baseball cap approaching you from the rear, and the man in the tan-colored overcoat ahead of you. Raise your left hand and touch your ear if you read me.'

437

Gifford watched as Irving slowly raised his hand and touched his ear.

Irving lowered his hand and sat forward. He gripped Karen's hand firmly as he saw a shadow emerge from back of the trees and walk toward them. Overcoat was now directly ahead of them. He approached slowly, his hands in his pockets, his head bowed. He wore a scarf, wound around the lower half of his face. Even at five yards Irving couldn't make out his features, but there was something about the certainty with which he approached that told him this was Karl Roberts, that something might at last break on the case, something to resolve the deadlock within which he had found himself for the last endless number of days . . .

Karl Roberts was no more than ten feet from where Irving was now rising from the bench.

Irving did not dare look over his shoulder, but perceived the presence of whoever might have been behind them. The man in the baseball cap. Had Roberts brought along his own security?

From Gifford's vantage point it appeared that Baseball Cap had not been seen by Overcoat. Gifford went down to the ground, aware that any movement would alert Overcoat to his presence. He lay on the cold, wet grass, the .38 in his hand, his heart pounding, his breathing labored as he tried to make no sound at all.

'Mr Roberts,' Irving said.

'Detective Irving,' the voice came back, and Karl Roberts crossed the last few feet between himself and Irving, unaware of Vernon Gifford spread-eagled on the grass no more than fifteen feet from where he paused.

'Please,' Roberts said. 'Sit down.'

Irving backed up and sat beside Karen.

'You are afraid for your life,' Irving said.

Roberts, standing ahead of them, coat to his knees, scarf wrapped around the lower half of his face against the cold – and against being identified by whoever he believed might be the anniversary killer – seemed to sigh audibly. Irving knew this could not have been the case – not with the sound of traffic in the street behind them, not with the sound of his own breathing, the thundering of his own heart – but he sensed it nevertheless.

Perhaps, Irving believed, there was resolution for both of them here. In hiding, unable to speak to anyone, Karl Roberts would perhaps find his own escape as he communicated what he knew to someone who had been involved in this thing even longer than himself.

'Afraid?' Roberts said. 'Yes. Afraid of everything. Afraid of my own shadow these past few days.'

'So what is it that you know?' Irving asked. Again the disturbing feeling, the dark edge of premonition around everything.

'This is Karen Langley?' Roberts asked.

'Yes, this is Karen Langley.'

Roberts nodded. 'Thank you for coming . . . I know this must be terrible for you—'

'It's okay,' Karen said. 'Really. I wanted to come. I wanted to help in any way I could.'

'It's appreciated,' Roberts said, 'but unfortunately this is a hell of a lot worse than I think either of you could have imagined.'

Irving felt a chill of disquiet. 'Worse?' he echoed. 'In what way? How could it be worse than it already is?'

Roberts lowered his head. When he looked up he seemed distracted by something in the trees. 'Is there someone with you?' he asked. 'You told me there'd be no-one with you . . . if there's someone with you—' He backed up, turned and glanced over his shoulder toward the path. He was checking that his route away was clear.

Irving half-rose from the bench. He raised his hands in a placatory manner. 'There's no-one else,' he said. 'I assure you we're here alone, just the two of us. No police . . . nothing.'

Roberts paused, perhaps reassured by Irving's insistence.

'Please,' Irving said, sitting down again. 'Please tell us what you know. Tell us what you know and then we can take whatever action we need and remove this threat—'

Roberts took a step toward them. 'I know who it is,' he said. It was a simple statement, and delivered with such certainty that Irving could not speak for a moment.

'You know who it is?' Irving said. He felt his heart racing. His hands were literally running with sweat. He glanced at Karen Langley. Her eyes wide, her skin pale, she looked like a terrified child.

'Yes,' Roberts said calmly. 'I know precisely and exactly who it is.'

He took another step forward, and in that moment Irving knew the source of his disquiet. The man in front of him was too tall. More than six feet. He'd seen the records of Karl Roberts' police service, his PI application forms, documents that detailed his height and weight, the color of his eyes, his race, religion, gender . . . his prints . . .

Irving rose and took a step to the left. The backs of his knees were against Karen Langley's legs, and he instinctively held out his arms wide, put them out beside him at waist height. Trying to shield her, to protect her . . . because even as he was questioning his own recollection of Roberts' details, telling himself that something was wrong, the man drew an object from his overcoat pocket, something immediately identifiable, and the words that issued from the man's mouth were as clear and uncomplicated as anything Irving had heard:

'I am the Hammer of God,' he said, and his voice was level and insistent and certain, and betrayed nothing whatever of the depth of anger and hatred that might lie behind it.

'I am the relentless fucking Hammer of God . . .'

Irving, trying desperately to reach his gun, went down with the first blow. Even as he collapsed to the ground, even as he heard Karen Langley screaming, he realized they had made a terrible, terrible mistake.

The sound of the hammer connecting with Karen Langley's head was indescribable, but immediately after – almost as if from a dream – there was the sound of gunshots, and in the madness of what was happening, looking back through the space beneath the bench, Irving saw someone standing no more than twenty feet away, someone in a baseball cap, his hand raised, the barrel of a gun erupting, and suddenly the assailant was staggering back, and before Irving could try and turn his head to see the gunman, he heard the familiar voice of Vernon Gifford.

Gifford was shouting, then screaming at the top of his voice for the man in the baseball cap to drop his weapon, and there seemed to be some confusion, because the man in the cap hesitated, turned back toward Gifford, then suddenly started running toward Irving and Langley.

And he did not drop the gun. He raised it as the attacker lifted the hammer once again, and it was in that moment that Gifford fired. Confused, disorientated, stunned with pain and trying to shield Karen Langley from the mayhem erupting around them, Irving was unable to reach his gun with his shattered forearm, and Gifford took the shot for him. He made a decision and went with it. It was a clean shot. A good shot. A single .38 caliber bullet found its mark in the upper right thigh of the man in the baseball cap. It was a through-and-through. The front of the man's leg exploded outwards and he fell to his knees, his gun gone, his hands clawing at the wound in his leg. Perhaps he didn't see the assailant towering over him, but Gifford saw him, saw him clearly, recognized the shape of the hammer as it came crashing down. Baseball Cap turned awkwardly and the hammer glanced off his shoulder. The scream of agony was indescribable

Baseball Cap collapsed sideways, his hand on the far edge of the bench, and for a moment he seemed to be caught in an indecision of self-preservation versus the apparent need to protect Karen Langley from further attack.

Unable to move his right arm, Irving tried to maneuver his handgun from its holster with his left hand. Consciousness was evading him. He felt the gun slip from his fingers and land on the grass.

Baseball Cap tried to pull himself forward, put his hand on the front edge of the bench to lever himself up, but the man in the overcoat was there. Standing right over him. The hammer came down and glanced off his ear, down the side of his neck, and Irving heard something break and the man in the baseball cap dropped to the ground like a deadweight.

Irving fought against waves of pain and blackness. He found his gun, felt the sweat on his hands, struggled to gain purchase, somehow turning over while still shielding Karen Langley. He tried to lift the weapon, but the gun slipped again and fell to the grass. And then his assailant was there again, looking down at him, and it seemed for a moment that the man possessed no face at all, just the impression of features somewhere within the shadows, as if he had simply grown out of darkness . . .

Irving screamed. And then there were voices, so many voices in his ear, and he wondered for a split second where those voices were coming from until he heard *Clean shot! Clean shot!*

The sound of a single gunshot, and the man staggered back, the hammer falling from his hand and landing on the grass. Irving could not see where he had been hit, only saw him take another handful of awkward steps backwards and then fall to the grass.

And then Gifford was there, and within moments there was someone else, and someone else, and the voices were too loud, and there was a bright light in his eyes . . .

Ray Irving turned his head sideways to look back between the feet of the bench, and he saw the man in the baseball cap lying there, and he knew who it was. And he knew the date, and he understood how this could have concluded no other way.

And then he remembered Karen, and Vernon Gifford was kicking the hammer away, and someone was kneeling beside Roberts, and then Irving felt himself being lifted from the ground, and the pain was indescribable . . . and people were struggling to get him onto the bench, all the while shouting into radios.

He could hear people running along the path, the sound of people screaming, and somewhere there was a siren . . .

Gifford was beside him then, and Irving tried to say whatever he needed to say without words, for the darkness that swallowed him was deep and endless and full of the blackest shadows, and there was neither a sound nor any element of familiarity within it. He went silently, because there was nothing left with which to fight.

SEVENTY-EIGHT

November 23rd, 1984 – the Hammer of God killing of Nadia McGowan.

November 23rd, 2006 – twenty-two years after the fact, the final Hammer of God killing had been replicated, this time with Karen Langley and Ray Irving the intended victims. They had survived, but this time – the casualty of some terrible, bitter irony – John Costello was the one who did not walk away. He was murdered by a killer posing as Karl Roberts; murdered by the Anniversary Man. And that man – a man whose real name was as yet unknown – had undergone surgery to arrest the potentially fatal consequence of a clean shot to the chest. Word had come down that he would survive, that he would make it, and even now the DA's office, the relevant precincts, everyone who had been touched by this thing was preparing themselves to confront this horror of a human being.

Vernon Gifford, an experienced homicide detective who had seen nothing but an unidentified man in a baseball cap aiming a gun in the direction of Ray Irving and Karen Langley, had taken the only rational action in such a situation. Had he not fired at Costello, had he not put a bullet through Costello's thigh, the outcome might have been different.

Irving, sitting beside Karen Langley's hospital bed while he waited for her to regain consciousness, considered every angle of the event. Somehow he convinced himself that the manner of Costello's death would have been the same regardless of what Vernon Gifford had done. It seemed to Ray Irving that John Costello had been waiting for this to happen since November of 1984.

At nine-eighteen, morning of Saturday, November 25th, 2006, Karen Langley surfaced into consciousness in the postop recovery room of St Clare's Hospital on East 51st and Ninth. The surgical team had operated on a skull fracture that extended from the upper edge of her right ear and around the back of her head for four and a half inches. She had also suffered a fractured right clavicle and two broken ribs.

Ray Irving was there when she woke, his right arm and shoulder bandaged tightly, beneath the bandages a wound that had taken thirty-eight stitches to close.

And it was Ray Irving who told her that John Costello was dead, killed by a single hammer-blow to the head. It was Costello who had followed them, his baseball cap pulled down over his face, his collar turned up; Costello who had understood the message from the Anniversary Man that the next killing would be personal . . . and it was Costello who had been prepared to do whatever was necessary to protect Karen Langley.

'Who is he?' she whispered to Irving through dry and swollen lips.

'He isn't Karl Roberts,' Irving replied. 'We haven't found Roberts yet. We can only presume he's dead somewhere. Anthony Grant identified the man in the park as the Karl Roberts he had spoken to.' Irving shook his head. 'Hard to believe, but Grant hired his own daughter's killer to investigate her murder.'

'You know his name?'

'Not yet. His fingerprints aren't on record and he's certainly not on our files in New York, but that doesn't mean he's not on file someplace else. We have the FBI working on it with us . . . they're going to help us identify him.'

There were tears in Karen's eyes then, as if she knew she could no longer escape the reality of John Costello's fate.

'John is dead,' she whispered.

'Yes,' Irving said. He leaned forward, reached out his hand and closed it over hers.

'He was a good man, Ray . . . he really was a good man.'

'I know,' Irving replied.

'He was killed on the same day . . . all these years later . . .'

'Ssshhh,' Irving whispered.

'He saved our lives . . . and . . .'

'Enough now,' Irving said. He took a tissue from the box on the shelf beside the bed and gently wiped the tears from Karen Langley's cheeks. 'Rest,' he whispered. 'Get some sleep, okay? Close your eyes and get some sleep.'

The painkillers, the aftermath of anesthetic, the overwhelm and emotional devastation of all that had happened closed in on her and she succumbed, let herself go, for it was greater than her, and in that moment she too – just like Ray Irving – possessed nothing with which to fight.

SEVENTY-NINE

New York did mornings like no other place on earth. Different mornings for different seasons, but each unique. Perhaps those who lived there took no notice, became inured to their surroundings through familiarity and habit, but it was there, right before them, if only they'd stop to look.

Every once in a while, but less frequently with the years, Ray Irving saw something in the city that was at once surprising and familiar, as if he were being reminded of an old friend, a forgotten lover, a house he'd lived in when life was a different thing. And it was in such brief moments that he saw beyond his work – past the faces of the dead, past those unfortunates left to bleed out alone as if life meant nothing much of anything at all – and recognized that, despite everything, he was still a human being, and his responsibility was to make it through the other side. The other side of what, he was sometimes unsure. But he had to make it through.

Morning of Tuesday, December 19th, the clean light reached Irving as he stood on the little balcony of his apartment, looking at the silhouette of St Raphael's against the bright sky, and considered all that had taken place since November 23rd. *Perhaps there is a God*, he thought, *but he saw the way things were going and went into hiding*.

On Monday, November 27th, they identified the Anniversary Man. His name was Richard Franklin Segretti. Forty-one years old, hailed out of Malone, upstate New York. Head south along the I-30 out of Lake Placid, just a handful of miles before the St Lawrence separates you from Canada, and there you'd find a small town with small-town views and small-town people – good, hardworking people, and straight-minded, and it was from this unlikely setting that Segretti had come. People there knew the Segrettis – Richard and his younger sister, Pamela – and though the parents were now dead, though Pamela had moved south to Saratoga Springs where work was better paid and people weren't so set in their views, the townsfolk of Malone still responded the way that all people respond when they learn of a killer in their midst: with disbelief and dismay; a feeling that if they had been so long unaware of something so important and profoundly disturbing, then what else might there be that they did not know.

Suspicion became a shadow that would haunt them for weeks, even months, and then it would pass, and they would do their utmost to forget.

And Segretti had visited with the Winterbourne group so many years before. Visited, but hadn't stayed. Extensive research on Irving's part couldn't determine whether Segretti had ever survived an attack from some unknown serial killer. But then, as Karen Langley had reminded him, weren't those the real unfortunates? The intended victims, those who survived but would never know the truth? The ones who stayed frightened for the rest of their lives for something they hadn't done. She spoke of the articles that she and John Costello had planned to write. The forgotten victims. Perhaps Segretti was one of them, perhaps not. In the cold, hard light of day it hardly seemed to matter.

Irving caught a squib in the New York *Daily News*:

Town Residents Picket Killer House Tours

'It's ghoulish,' said Mr Jack Glenning, resident of Malone for twenty-three years. 'Folks coming up here all the way from New York to look at that house where Segretti lived. Heard some kids tore up part of the fence and stole it. Mementoes they wanted. Makes you wonder what the hell is going on with the world when teenage kids idolize someone like that.'

Back of Richard Segretti there was no jacket, no list of priors, no childhood incidents of animal torture or arson, no six

447

months in juvy. Segretti's father was a logger, his mother a seamstress. Churchgoing people, committed to family values, dying within three years of one another, Segretti Senior from a stroke in the fall of '99, his wife already dead from a heart attack in '96. Richard Segretti had maintained the house precisely as it had been when his parents were alive, right down to his father's reading glasses balanced on an opened copy of *Serenade* by James M.Cain on the nightstand beside his bed.

Irving went to the house after the FBI, crime scene analysis and forensics had done their work. He took Jeff Turner with him. The place was pristine, immaculate, spotless. Books were arranged alphabetically on the shelves, as were CDs and video cassettes. In the kitchen the canned goods were stacked by contents, by use-by date, all of them lined up with the labels facing outward. A cupboard in the bathroom contained eleven bars of unopened soap, eleven tubes of toothpaste, eleven packets of dental floss, eleven new toothbrushes. They were all the same brand, the brushes all the same color. Along the halls and in the front room pictures were hung so the upper edge of the frame was precisely six foot, one and a half inches from the floor.

Segretti's height.

In one room they found photograph albums, boxes of keepsakes from each killing he had carried out, all of them bagged and labeled and ready to transport to the DA's office in preparation for Segretti's trial. They found Carol-Anne Stowell's clothes, a box of theatrical make-up, a number of hairs that matched James Wolfe caught in a stick of white greasepaint. Other such things.

Irving and Turner drove back to New York in silence.

Turner had also seen Costello's apartment in the days since Costello's death. The racks of journals, the CDs, the video cassettes, the DVDs – all the same, alphabetically arranged, dust-free and pristine. The kitchen, the bathroom, the way the towels were folded, the way the shower curtain was hung, each plastic hoop the same distance apart along the rail above the bath.

The two homes could have been occupied by the same man.

448

The similarity between Costello and Segretti set Irving to thinking – thinking too long and too hard until it gave him a headache. One man went one way, another took a different route. Irving remembered a quote from a film he'd seen about Truman Capote, how Capote had spoken of the similarities between himself and the killer, Perry Smith: *It was as if we grew up in the same house, and then one day I went out the front door and Perry went out the back*. Something like that.

Irving caught himself counting things. Phone boxes. Girls with red hair.

Like there was some kind of safety in numbers.

After a while he stopped trying to make sense of it.

There was no sense to make.

The death of John Costello was investigated by an internal enquiry review. The NYPD Shooting Board questioned both Vernon Gifford and Ray Irving. Had Karen Langley been sufficiently well to appear she would have been called as an independent witness. The Board convened, interrogated, and adjudicated in her absence. The shooting of John Costello, though unfortunate, was deemed *in policy*. Gifford was neither suspended, reprimanded, nor given a one-eighty-one for excessive use of force.

John Costello's funeral was held at the church of St Mary of the Divine Cross on Sunday, December 3rd. Irving attended, but Karen Langley was not permitted release from the hospital. Alongside Irving were Bryan Benedict, Leland Winter and Emma Scott from the *City Herald*. Irving took only Gifford, Hudson and Turner along, for he knew that John Costello had not been a man for friends and wide social circles. Such life as John Costello had lived beyond the *Herald* and his brief involvement with the Fourth Precinct, was represented by George Curtis and Rebecca Holzman from the Winterbourne Hotel group, both clearly shattered by John's death. There were no family members to say words of remembrance, so Irving rose and spoke for them. Later he couldn't remember what he'd said, but Gifford said it had been appropriate and meaningful, and Costello would have approved.

Segretti was bound over for trial by the state. His sister

chose not to drive down from Saratoga Springs to visit with him, and she refused to give statements to the press.

Within a week it was as if neither John Costello nor Richard Segretti had ever lived. Each was relegated to the collective memory of New York, a memory that seemed caught somewhere in limbo, a memory filled with things that no-one hoped to recall, that everyone wished had never taken place. The Segretti trial would not begin for six months, perhaps a year, and by then everyone would have forgotten who he was.

It was while talking with Irving that Vernon Gifford said, 'He'll spend the rest of his life knowing he didn't win after all, that he wasn't smarter than everyone else in the end.'

'Yes,' Irving replied. 'And now he'll have to face the McDuffs and Gacys and Arthur Shawcrosses of this world in the prison yard. They deserve each other, don't you think?'

It was so true, so fitting. A beautiful irony.

As of the third week of December the body of Karl Roberts, ex-Seattle PD, one-time private investigator, had still not been found. There was insufficient manpower available to continue the search, but it was presumed that he must be dead, that Segretti had killed him, had assumed his identity for the purposes of getting close to Grant, and from there to Irving and Langley.

How had Grant come to hire him? How had Segretti passed himself off as Roberts and secured employment from a grieving parent? Grant told Irving how they'd met, and it had been too simple for words. Segretti had staked out a bar where Grant was known to drink every once in a while. He had waited until Grant was inside, had gone in with a photograph of a missing girl, asked the bartender some questions, acted insistent, aggressive almost, and Grant had swallowed the bait.

'Said he specialized in missing kids,' Grant told Irving. 'Said he was ex-PD, had contacts across New York, New Jersey, Atlantic City, the entire eastern seaboard. Said he knew people who knew people. He came across as a very genuine guy, told me he had two daughters, grown-up now, away at college, and he empathized. I really felt he was a sincere and dedicated man. He said he would be happy to help, if only to use his contacts to get me some inside information on the case, you know? I can't believe it . . . I just cannot believe that I sat in a bar buying drinks for the guy that murdered my daughter . . .'

Irving believed it; believed it without hesitation. He understood now, if he hadn't already, that human beings were capable of pretty much anything.

That morning, December 19th, 2006, Ray Irving turned away from the clean light, away from the silhouette of St Raphael's, and picked up his jacket from the back of the chair. He paused for a moment at the door, then closed it securely behind him and left the building. The gridlock had eased, and it was not too many minutes before he pulled up in the car park back of St Clare's Hospital.

Karen Langley was in the lobby waiting for him, a weekend case at her feet. Her head was still bandaged and, although the swelling had diminished, the ghost of her injuries was visible around her eye, the line of her jaw. It had been the better part of a month, yet for both of them it felt as if no time had passed at all.

Irving had seen Karen Langley only the day before, but each time he visited he realized how differently he felt, how important her survival was to him, how devastated he would have been had she not made it through.

Such events defined mortality.

'Ray,' she said.

He smiled, helped her up, took her case and walked her out to the car.

They reached his apartment before either of them had a chance to really say anything of significance, but once inside, standing in the small kitchen, he put his arms around her, held her close, and stayed silent while she cried.

Eventually she sat down. Irving made coffee, listened as she talked, her words falling over one another as if a month of disconnection from the world needed to be remedied in minutes.

And at last, after she'd said whatever she needed to say, she asked the big question: Why.

And Irving turned and went to her, sat beside her and took her hand.

He held it tight, shook his head slowly, and smiled a sad and gentle smile. 'I don't know,' he said quietly. 'And I don't know that we'll ever find out.'

Karen looked away for a moment, out through the small window into a New York morning, and then she turned back. 'I have to convince myself that I don't need to know,' she said.

For a while they were silent, and then Irving reached out and touched the side of her face.

'Stay,' he whispered. 'Here. With me. Stay here, Karen.'

And Karen Langley closed her eyes, and she breathed deeply, and when she looked at Ray Irving there were tears in her eyes.

'We're not supposed to be alone, are we?' she asked, and there was something in the question that told him it was not meant to be answered.

And so he did not try.

AUTHOR'S NOTE

Undoubtedly it would be comforting if the many serial killers who played a major role in the drama that unfolded in these pages were a product of my fevered imagination but, sadly for humanity, they were not.

Extensive research was undertaken to ensure that names, dates, times and locations were as accurate as possible. I also used a number of documented reports, choosing those that I believed to be the most reliable and trustworthy. But murderers are liars, and sometimes conflicting statements left precise details open to an element of doubt.

On the matter of my chosen location, New York, I must ask for the readers' indulgence. I took a few liberties with minor geographical details purely for the purposes of the story. New Yorkers are understandably proud of their great city, truly one of the most remarkable in the Western world, and I hope that my dramatic license hasn't offended.

RJE